Praise for

THE REQUIEM ROSE

"Waverly Hills Sanatorium is the location of the dramatic un-folding of this page turner. *The Requiem Rose* is a touching and inspirational story set in a frightening time in our history . . . the tuberculosis epidemic of the early 1900s. James Markert's skill-fully woven novel is a testament to the human spirit."

—*Madeline Abramson*

"*The Requiem Rose* is a must-read for any fan of Louisville history and a true pleasure for lovers of classical music. Through a wealth of fascinating historical detail and a wonderful portrayal of the power of music, Markert spins a richly melodic tale of redemption in the unlikeliest of places and times."

—*Jason Weinberger, resident conductor, Louisville Orchestra*

"*The Requiem Rose* is a story that touches on many human univer-sals ranging from disease, death, loss, and racism to music, love, self-sacrifice and faith. The themes are heartfelt, powerful and cin-ematic, and the story has the potential to resonate with people on many different levels. It recreates a dark time in American history but it is ultimately a tale of triumph and redemption."

—*Peter Gelfan, writer and editor*

"It's not every day you read a novel that you actually find inspiring. It's definitely not every day that you read an inspirational novel set in a tuberculosis sanatorium. However, it's not every day novelists like James Markert are bor[n] . . . . nt, we make an effort to appreciat. . . . . story he wanted to tell, and so di. . . . .

—*The . . . . izona*

Butler Books
Louisville, Kentucky

THE REQUIEM ROSE

A WAVERLY HILLS STORY

James Markert

Original illustration on title page by Robert Markert, inspired by photograph copyright © Diane Deaton-Street

FIRST EDITION

Designed by Eric Butler
Cover Design by Scott Stortz

ISBN: 978-1-935497-19-6

For information, contact the publisher:
Butler Books
P.O. Box 7311
Louisville, KY 40207
(502) 897-9393
fax (502) 897-9797
www.butlerbooks.com

In memory of Bill Butler
A talented publisher of books . . .
and an even better person

Requiem aeternam dona eis, Domine,
et lux perpetua luceat eis.

Grant them eternal rest, O Lord,
and may everlasting light shine upon them.

Cantate Domino

A person who gives this some thought and yet does not regard music as a marvelous creation of God, must be a clodhopper indeed and does not deserve to be called a human being; He should be permitted to hear nothing but the braying of asses and the grunting of hogs.

—MARTIN LUTHER

Prologue

Waverly Hills Tuberculosis Sanatorium
November 1928

FATHER WOLFGANG PIKE first felt the stiffness in the morning, soon after the roosters had begun to wake the hillside, and by afternoon it had become a constant ache in the bottom of his right calf. The ankle joints had all but locked up, and no amount of massaging could loosen the atrophied muscles, tendons and warped bones of his withered right foot—a foot that could not be maneuvered or bent in such a way as to even place his right heel on the floor. That heel would always be raised in a permanent tiptoe. Polio at age eight had rendered the foot nearly useless, a constant crutch used for dragging the rest of his leg along, but also a part-time weathervane. Wolfgang Pike could always tell when the rain was near. His leg would first feel the tingling signs of wind change, and the ache would soon follow. The current ache was nearly crippling.

Not a drop of rain had fallen on the sanatorium for twenty days. The woods were full of color and the dry air carried with it a crispness that led to watery eyes, bloody noses and a tickling in the back of the throat that could only be squelched with bouts of phlegm-throttled coughing. But the blue skies would not endure. The cumulus clouds skittered above the rise of the bell tower as the front moved in, a clear dividing line of light and dark in the sky. Low-lying smudges of gray and purple clouds blotted out the sun, coasting in with a vengeance, with a purpose. And when the first drop plopped against the tiles of the rooftop, it came as a sign that the onslaught was coming. Scattered fat drops with two-inch splatters hit like hail all over the ground, pinging off the gutters and walkways like machine-gun fire for about two minutes. And then it all stopped. A few seconds of silence followed—the calm before the real storm—and then the dark sky opened up all at once, letting loose as if the clouds had been saving up the water from those twenty dry days and dropping it all at once. Torrential rain pelted the trees, the rooftop and the grassy knoll that led down to the woods.

Nothing was safe from the heavy water. The leaf-clogged gutters were quickly overwhelmed, the overflow spilling like a waterfall down the five stories, coming down in sheets past the windows of the solarium porches and hitting the grass that was quickly becoming over-saturated. Leaves ripped from the trees. Dirt near the entrance turned to mud within minutes. The sheer force of sound drew reactions of awe from the nearly five hundred patients that witnessed it from their beds on the porches. The children wanted to play in it. The pigs snorted and rolled in the deepening mud. The cows mooed, and the chickens fluttered their wet wings. The entire sanatorium was in an uproar.

Had he the foresight to know what was to come with the rain, Wolfgang could have called it a warning. But like all mortals, even priests couldn't tell the future. So all he knew now was the present—that he'd just witnessed the tenth death of the morning. The stench of urine and vomit still lingered in his nose, his skeletal umbrella provided little, if any, protection and it was raining harder than he'd ever seen before. But he had multiple jobs to do, and he couldn't allow a thorough soaking to impede his progress.

Wolfgang Pike stepped back out into the hard rain and peered down upon the muddy grounds from the rooftop of the five-story tuberculosis sanatorium, where on a clear day he could see the city for miles above the treetops. Today his visibility was a mere fifty yards, at best. He hurried away from the mental ward and turned into the wind-slanted deluge, no longer protected by the length of the looming bell tower, fighting the pull and tug on his crumpling umbrella, his footfalls barely steady on the tiles. Careful to avoid the slick wet leaves that had blown to the floor, he braced his left hand on the ornately capped brick-and-stone wall that bordered the rooftop and squinted into the downpour.

An ambulance was coming up the wooded hillside. The cones from the two electric lights propped in front of the black Buick flickered between the tree trunks as the car noisily climbed the serpentine road. The yellow, orange and red leaves that fully shrouded the hospital like an impressionist painting an hour ago were now hanging heavy, limp and dull from dark, gnarled tree limbs. Many fell prematurely from the weight of the water, piling up on the dense undergrowth, starting to get that wet foul stench as the layers began to build. The fall season gone in a flash. Soon the limbs would be naked. The morale would decline. Four hundred fifty patients in their beds out on the solarium porches, staring at sunless skies and trees with nothing to offer but the hope of another season. If the disease didn't get them first.

The cold temperatures would not deter the treatment. Rest and fresh air, regardless of the cold. Only the rain would keep the heliotherapy patients and children off the rooftop. It was vacant now as Wolfgang plowed into the wind, limping and dragging his right foot. The seesaw across the way moved as if ridden by unseen tubercular children, not to be outdone by the three rocking swings behind it. It saddened him to see them being unused. It seemed too much of an omen.

A door slammed behind him. Wolfgang looked back over his shoulder toward the small rooftop building he'd just exited that housed the nurses' station and four rooms for the mentally ill tuberculosis patients. The wind had blown the door open, sending it crashing into the brick wall. Nurse Rita appeared in the doorway. She fought the elements, holding on to her white cap as she reeled the door back in. Above her the bell tower touched the low-lying clouds and a rumble of thunder enveloped the property.

One of the mental patients screamed, and Wolfgang moved away from the shrill sound. His pace quickened as he neared the stairs to the fourth floor. He could tell by the piercing voice that the screamer was Maverly Simms, the fifty-year-old woman with schizophrenia and TB in every part of her body except her tortured brain. She'd most assuredly just noticed that her roommate, Jill, had died. Jill was a mute, prone to violence against others and to herself, but for whatever reason Maverly's bouts of hysteria and rants of senseless drivel calmed Jill. So they'd been placed together, and the situation had worked well for three weeks. But, Jill had passed away during the night. Nurse Rita had called Wolfgang up to the rooftop first thing in the morning to help prepare Jill's body.

Maverly had been awake, but far from lucid when Wolfgang arrived less than thirty minutes ago with his black bag. She'd been in her rocking chair, staring out at the rain and approaching storm clouds. "Maverly." Wolfgang's calming voice had drawn no reaction from her.

Nurse Rita was young and, in Wolfgang's opinion, not seasoned enough for her current duty. She had a pretty face and innocent dark eyes. Wolfgang questioned Doctor Barker's decision to put her on the rooftop, but Doctor Barker was one to throw his staff right into things. He was known to baptize them by fire. When Wolfgang had arrived she appeared distraught. She'd been crying. Her jaw trembled. Her hands were clinched into tight balls, her fingernails pressing hard into the meat of her palms. Wolfgang approached her but kept his eyes on Maverly.

"Has she noticed yet?"

"No." Rita stared out Maverly's window. "She's just been sitting there. In one of her trances."

"Come on then. Lincoln's on his way to remove the body."

Wolfgang had opened his bag and got to work cleaning Jill's blood-spotted face. After a moment, Rita wet a rag and dabbed it on the congealed blood that stained Jill's wrinkled left cheek and hallowed eye sockets. It was important to get the dead in the best possible condition before another patient saw them. Especially Maverly. After Jill's face was free of blood, Wolfgang had propped her head up on pillows, closed her eyes and put in her false teeth. Rita had cleaned beneath Jill's fingernails and combed her silver hair.

That's when they'd heard the first drop of urine fall from Maverly's left calf. And the smell immediately followed. The urine had taken a noticeable path down Maverly's leg, meandering around and over the fine brown hairs that dotted her leg, not a trickle but a stream. The puddle on the floor had grown quickly. Maverly had remained focused on the window and the rain, despite her freshly stained white shift. She didn't even turn to acknowledge their presence when Rita turned away from Jill's bed and vomited in the corner of the darkening room. Such was life in the mental ward.

Wolfgang had his own aversion to vomit, deeply rooted in his childhood memories, the kind of vivid memories that still had a stench to go with it. He had to leave the room. Wolfgang had placed a hand on Rita's shoulder on his way out. Baptism by fire. She'd managed to tell him she was okay. Wolfgang trusted that she would be.

As Wolfgang's hand found the rain-soaked stairwell railing, he futilely exhaled from his nostrils in an attempt to rid his senses of the lingering smells of Maverly's urine and Rita's vomit. At the bottom of the stairwell Wolfgang lowered his tangled umbrella

and smoothed his hands over his short black beard and dark wavy
hair. A few seconds in the rain had soaked him to the bone. His
white lab coat clung heavily against his narrow shoulders. By the
time he reached the fourth floor solarium porch, where nearly a
hundred beds faced the long screened windows and falling rainfall, he couldn't hear Maverly's screams anymore. Either she'd
stopped or her voice was drowned out by all the other noises that
frequented the sanatorium—noises that chased him down the solarium as he quickly passed the beds; choking, groaning, moaning
patients with pale haunted TB faces, coughing and spitting blood-
tainted sputum to the concrete floors as mist from the heavy
rainfall found its way through the tiny holes of the screened porch
and wet their bed covers. Some patients smiled and talked, read,
played checkers or chess, some shaved and listened to music, some
cried out in pain, some still slept, others drank glasses of milk and
watched the weather with emotionless faces. Piss and vomit still
followed him. Wolfgang's eyes caught glimpses of the patients to
his left and the lights from the approaching ambulance outside and
down the hillside to his right. The choking throttle of the ambulance engine drew closer.

Another patient was coming.

WOLFGANG WAITED IN the Grand Lobby on the first floor,
staring out the glass doors as the ambulance came to a stop on
the rutted road before the sanatorium's main entrance. He popped
his umbrella open and the skeletal spokes jutted out at odd tangents, the cloth ripped and hanging like dead skin from three of
the metal arms. Water from earlier spilled down the handle and
onto his shoulder as he stepped outside again in a meager attempt
to keep himself dry. With his free hand he grabbed a wheelchair
next to the doorway and navigated it downhill. The concrete walk-
way soon gave way to sodden grass and then mud as the grounds
slanted down toward the road. Pushing the wheelchair, even with

no one in it, proved difficult with his aching foot, especially while holding onto an umbrella that was being torn apart by the wind.

The large, thin wheels and running board of the ambulance were coated with mud and grass. The dirt-smeared windshield and the top of the black ambulance were covered with wet leaves and twigs from where it had brushed the low-hanging boughs that canopied the roadway all the way up the hillside.

The driver was a short, fleshy man who appeared none too pleased to be out in the rain. Instead of getting out, he rolled down his window and beckoned Wolfgang closer with a wave of his chubby hand. He produced a clipboard that Wolfgang quickly signed while he read the patient's name.

"Just one?"

The driver nodded and stared up at the massive sanatorium with fear in his eyes. No sooner than Wolfgang let go of the pen, the window was on its way up again, squeaking and clouding up with the man's breath while Wolfgang stood ankle deep in the muck. He grabbed the wheelchair and half walked it and half kicked it toward the back of the ambulance, where the double doors burst open. A young male ambulance attendant stood with one hand propping the closest door open and the other holding a cloth over his nose and mouth.

Inside, sitting on a suspended cot in the shadows of the Buick, was a stern looking middle-aged man with red hair sprouting out beneath a brown bowler hat. He was dressed as if he'd come from an opera or concert. Brown trousers and a brown frock coat, both with beige pinstripes. A white, cotton shirt with a club collar. A gold pocket watch tucked inside the pocket of his green and blue paisley vest. He had a paisley cravat to match. His mid-calf brown boots were shiny and clean. The man coughed into his right hand. The attendant flinched. There was a twinkle in the man's mischievous green eyes, as if he'd summoned up the cough on purpose to put a scare into the young attendant.

Wolfgang stepped closer to the rear of the ambulance and shouted over the rain that pelted the roof. "Mr. McVain. Welcome to Waverly Hills. I've got a wheelchair. We'll try and keep your clothes clean from the mud." Just then the wind lifted the umbrella, snapping another portion of it, rendering it useless in the tumult. Wolfgang smiled but Mr. McVain wasn't amused. He stared out past Wolfgang to the trees in the background. He stood on his own, lowered himself down from the back of the ambulance and sat in the wheelchair. The ambulance attendant quickly closed the doors. A few seconds later the vehicle kicked into gear with a metallic grunt and pulled away.

Wolfgang held what was left of the umbrella over McVain's head and put all his weight behind the wheelchair, leaning on it to get it rolling through the mud.

"I'm sorry for the weather, Mr. McVain. Is it Tad? Is that right?"

No response from Tad McVain. He sat with his hands on his thighs, his fingers visible. Five fingers on his right hand. Two on his left. Wolfgang stared at McVain's mangled left hand as he maneuvered the incline. The wind finally took the umbrella from Wolfgang's grip and sailed it about ten yards away where the tip of it stuck in the mud. The rain tapped against McVain's hard felt hat and dripped from the rounded crown. Still, he said nothing. He didn't even hunker down in fear of becoming soaked as Wolfgang now did as he pushed, the three missing fingers on McVain's left hand still capturing Wolfgang's full attention. The pinkie and thumb remained. The middle three ended in nubs just above the knuckles of the hand. Wolfgang could tell by the upward tilt of McVain's cap that he was staring up into the rain to get a glimpse of the massive Gothic sanatorium before them.

"Don't worry. You'll receive top-notch care here, Mr. McVain. I assure you." Wolfgang tilted the chair back slightly to get it over a root, and as he did so he lowered his face toward McVain's right shoulder. "By the way, my name is Wolfgang Pike. I'm a doctor here. I'm also a Catholic priest. You can call me father, or doctor, or—"

McVain reached his right hand up in a flash, gripped the lapels of Wolfgang's lab coat and pushed him away from the wheelchair. Wolfgang lost his balance and fell into the mud.

Maverly must have been watching from her rooftop window because she began screaming again. "Maverly at Waverly," she shouted from above. "Maverly at Waverly. Maverly says welcome to Waverly."

Wolfgang sat in the mud, rain pounding his head and shoulders, watching as McVain rolled *himself* into the sanatorium.

1

WIND PRESSED AGAINST the thin clapboard walls of Wolfgang's hillside cottage, the January air stubborn in its refusal to stay outside. He doubted there was any insulation, just empty space between the drywall and outside wall, enough room for a family of birds to build a nest every spring and keep him up all hours of the night. A cold draft hovered around his ankles. He could feel it even through his wool socks as his feet touched down on the piano's pedals. He felt as if he had to play faster to keep warm, but faster always turned into sloppy work. By the number of crumpled pages on the floor beside his bed, it could be concluded that he'd been playing too fast for some time now.

He blew hot air into his hands, rubbed them together for warmth, shifted his weight on the rickety wooden bench and then touched his fingertips to the keys again. He continued warming up with Mozart's piano sonata in C minor. After a few minutes he stopped. The candle flame atop his piano flickered with unseen shifts of air and then settled. A fresh red rose stood inside a white vase next to the candle. He looked to it for inspiration.

"Give me strength."

He closed his eyes and imagined the low humming of a trio of violins. The harmony brought a smile to his face. And then, ever so softly, the clarinet eased in, rising above . . .

His doubt was replaced by an inkling of hope.

Muffled laughter from outside ripped him from the creative moment. Footsteps on dead leaves. Someone coughed. His fingers eased from the piano keys as a male voice called out.

"Hey nigger lover. The devil pisses on your popery!"

Wolfgang looked to the four frosted panes of glass that protected him from the voice outside. A brick crashed through the lower right pane, sending shards of glass to the wood-planked floor. The suddenness of the attack sent him reeling back from the bench, landing on the floor with a thud. Cold air whistled through the broken window, and right behind it a second voice.

"Catholic heathen!"

Wolfgang curled up into a fetal position and covered his head with his hands, expecting another brick to come flying through the broken window, or something worse. He waited thirty long seconds before mustering the courage to get up. He brushed glass from the worn knees of his tweed trousers, straightened, and then tip-toed closer to the window, where he was able to see two dark silhouettes disappear into the woods, their footsteps fading with their laughter.

"Fools."

He leaned with both hands on the windowsill for a moment, staring out, daring them to come back. Mouse droppings and glass covered the sill. He looked down and noticed that his right hand was bleeding, right in the middle of the palm. He wiped his hand on the sleeve of his shirt, staining it red, and approached the brick. A slip of paper protruded from one of the three holes. His fingers shook as he unfolded it.

GO TO HELL, PRIEST, it read in dark, blocked letters. He crumpled it and tossed it toward the wicker wastebasket that was already overflowing with wadded pages of work that was far from sufficient.

He knew about the Ku Klux Klan, and it was not the first time he'd witnessed the hatred up close. The KKK had made a terrible, fascist-like resurgence in the 1920s behind their Imperial Wizard, the dentist, Hiram Wesley Evans. Only WASPs could belong. White Anglo-Saxon Protestants. They hated blacks, Jews, liberals, foreign-born and Catholics. The KKK was seen as an organization that shared traditional values and moral righteousness. They burned churches, murdered, raped and castrated all in the name of keeping America safe. And to the new Klan there was nothing more un-American than the foreign influence of the Roman Catholics, and the belief that Catholics held allegiance to the Pope and Rome over and above the United States and the President.

It was nonsense, and nothing roiled Wolfgang more than intolerance. It was the Natives, the Know-Nothing Party, who had caused the riots in Louisville decades ago. His grandfather, his father's father, had been a member of the Know-Nothings. Wolfgang had spent his lifetime distancing himself from that hatred. And now the KKK was on the rise, trying to force its grimy hands into politics across the south.

Wolfgang lifted the brick and threw it back through the broken window. How dare they enter his home. He spun in a slow circle, surveying the four walls of his cottage. Next to the stone fireplace was a baseball bat, a Louisville Slugger with Babe Ruth's signature burned into the barrel. He often held it while composing in his mind, swinging it slowly as he paced his creaking, slanted floor, relieving tension so his mind could create. He hurried across the room—which contained a bed, a couch, a piano and little else— grabbed the baseball bat, and opened the front door.

Freezing air filtered into the openings of his baggy white and now bloodstained shirt. His sleeves were rolled up to his elbows, exposing his hairy forearms, but he was too moved by adrenaline to feel the cold on his skin. His breath was visible in front of him, crystallized and steaming from his flared nostrils in long plumes. Like a dragon. That's what he felt like. He dared them to come back. He beckoned them closer by beating the barrel of the bat against the meat of his bloody palm. Babe Ruth's signature became smeared with his blood. He stepped down the three steps of his porch to the frozen ground of pine needles and leaves and stared out toward the darkness between the trees. He touched the index and middle fingers of his right hand to his forehead, chest, left shoulder and then right, motioning the sign of the cross.

"Come on, you cowards!" he shouted. "Show yourselves."

Wind shook the treetops. Fifty yards in the distance, above and through the boughs and limbs, portions of the sanatorium's rooftop were visible, the bell tower highlighted by the glow of a crescent moon. Up the hill and to his right he heard leaves crunching. He approached the sound, gripping the bat taut now in both hands, ready to give a swing that would make Babe Ruth proud if the situation called for it.

Snorting followed the rustling of the leaves, and then a pig came running out of the shadows. Wolfgang lowered his bat and kicked the ground. The pig wiggled its snout, snorted a few times and then continued down the hill. Wolfgang waited a few more minutes before returning inside.

He locked the door behind him, stood for a few seconds with his back to the door and listened to the wind push through the broken window next to his bed. Last night's fire was now gray ash, but a distinct, charred smell still lingered inside the stone fireplace. The smell sparked his mood to write and compose again. Atop the piano his quill pen awaited. He exhaled slowly, releasing the tension in his shoulders. He wiped his blood from the bat's grip and then returned it to its resting spot next to the fireplace.

Beside the bed on a dresser was an empty glass, stained red from the remnants of the evening's wine—his stash untouched by Prohibition. The walls were utterly absent of any decoration except for a clock and the cross hanging on the wall opposite his bed. The left side of his bed was in disarray. The other side was kept neat as always, the sheets pulled tight, the covers tucked around the outline of a pillow he was still accustomed to smelling before he went to bed every night. He eyed the closet next to the piano. There was a portrait inside that he badly wanted to take out, but he remained strong to temptation. Instead he lifted the necklace from his shirt and kissed the cross that hung from it.

And then everything went dark. Wolfgang spun toward the door and then the window. The breeze whistled through the opening. He grinned at his uneasiness and took a few cleansing breaths to slow his heart rate. The wind had blown the candle flame out. He moved the candle toward the dresser, away from the cold rush of air, and lit it again. His home had electricity but he preferred candlelight to the monotonous droning of current. Automobiles and electric appliances had made people's lives easier at the beginning of the twentieth century, yet Wolfgang feared he would always remain tethered to the past.

A small kitchen and a bathroom extended out from the main room with a window above the kitchen sink that overlooked the porch. He grabbed the bottle of red wine from beside the sink and took a heavy swig. The rest he poured into a clean glass and took with him to the piano. He sat down on the bench again and glanced at the clock on the wall. It was quarter past two in the morning. Plenty of time to lose himself in his work. The ink on the yellow pages had long dried from the evening's scribbles. He read what he'd composed just before midnight, then crumpled the page into a ball and tossed it into the wastebasket. There were simply not enough notes, not for something so special.

"You'll never finish."

He dipped the tip of the quill into the inkwell above the piano keys and stared at the blank page. His father had been a hard, strict man but also an accomplished composer. He used to watch him write at night, always by candlelight and always with a quill pen. He'd claimed the fountain pen dampened his creativity. Wolfgang feared he was becoming too much like him. He grew up having nightmares that he would die the same way his father had, which was why he was such a light sleeper.

Wolfgang shook the memories of his father from his mind. To-night, he would focus on the music. He glanced out the broken window toward the dark woods, finally feeling the cold air. He sipped wine to keep warm and dared them to step foot inside his home. Maybe the crisp breeze would inspire him even more. His piano music would carry farther now. To hell with them, he thought. He dipped his quill and found the page . . . his train of thought . . . oh yes . . . violins, and the clarinet . . .

2

WOLFGANG SHIVERED ON the couch, arms crossed, his hands gripping his biceps. He couldn't breathe. Something covered his face, pressing down. Patches of light and dark flashed across his vision. Muffled screams sounded from deep inside his head. He pulled his knees up to his chest, and finally, the whistling of a chorus of birds woke him. He opened his eyes, panting, forcing out heavy pushes of air. It was only a dream. Another nightmare.

His home was freezing cold now that the air had been coming in all through the night, his breath visible. He sat up straight and yawned, staring out the broken window, spotting three of the noisy birds perched on a low branch of an oak tree. He rubbed his arms and stood, accidentally knocking over the empty wineglass he'd left on the floor in front of the couch. It rolled unevenly toward the bed and stopped without breaking against one of the wooden legs.

The muscles below his right knee ached with stiffness. He massaged the muscles and stretched the leg. He feared the polio would come back as he got older, so he always tried to keep his hands clean. He washed them dozens of times a day. He shook his right leg, which felt partly asleep, and then stretched it out the best he could. He rubbed his temples in an attempt to massage away his headache. Dozens of his papers had been blown from the piano and were now scattered all over the floor. His head throbbed as he bent over to collect them, so he tried to stay as level as he could. But his cold fingers were clumsy against the hardwood. He duck-walked from page to page, contemplating tossing them immediately. A rectangle of sunlight lit the floor. The warmth of the light felt good on his chilled skin. He decided to keep what he'd written. He gathered the papers into a stack, put them into a black lacquered box atop the piano, flipped the tiny latch to lock it and slid it under the bed.

It was six-thirty. The patients would be waiting. He hurried into the kitchen and started his morning cup of coffee. While it percolated he changed into black pants and a black shirt with the white clerical collar. He covered both with a white lab coat that ended just below his knees and then he stepped into his cramped bathroom. In it was a small tub on four wooden legs, a toilet crammed beside it, and a sink that was positioned in such a way that the door could never be fully opened. He looked in the mirror and winced. He needed sleep. That much was evident in his blood-shot eyes—that and too much wine. He shaved his neck below his dark, trimmed beard. He wetted his short dark hair with a comb and parted it on the left side. Splashes of cold water on his face rejuvenated him, and by that time his coffee was ready.

He sidestepped from the bathroom back into the kitchen where the pleasant smell of coffee beans dominated the small space. He poured a cup from the stovetop and inhaled the steam, clearing his airways. He sipped and swallowed. It tasted bitter and bland, not nearly as good as it smelled, and not as rich as the coffee made at the sanatorium.

He heard a gentle tapping on his front door. And then a female voice.

"Wolfgang."

The knocking again.

"I'm coming." Wolfgang knelt down to see his distorted reflection in the glass percolator and stood back up somewhat satisfied. There was little room for vanity in his life.

"Wolfgang."

He smiled. He truly believed she harassed him on purpose. So went the morning ritual. Susannah was here. He grabbed his black bag of musical instruments, straightened his lab coat and opened the door to a cool but now sun-drenched winter morning. The temperature was predicted to reach an unseasonably warm sixty-five degrees by afternoon.

Susannah waited at the bottom of the concrete steps, standing on a patch of dead grass with both hands folded in front, one of them gripping a small black purse. Her dress was standard white and hung below her knees, matching her white shoes and the white cap atop her wavy blonde hair. Her skin was pale, a stark contrast to her pretty brown eyes and rosebud lips.

She smiled. "Morning, Wolf."

"Morning, Susannah." Wolfgang made his way down the steps and together they walked up toward the trees. "You sleep well?"

"I did. You?"

"I don't sleep."

They walked silently through the woods for a few minutes as the wind rustled the dead leaves and naked tree limbs. The sunlight penetrated the tree branches above, highlighting the forest floor in a pattern of striped shadows. Mostly Wolfgang kept his eyes ahead but he could feel her occasional stare. Susannah lived in the nurses' dormitory near the back of the Waverly property. His home was roughly fifty yards away. They walked to work every morning. Silence was sometimes their best communication.

"Do you have enemies I should know about?" Susannah glanced at him. "Your broken window."

"A brick came flying through about two in the morning."

"Were you hurt?"

He showed her the cut on his right palm but then quickly dropped his hand back to his side. "It's nothing. Just misguided intolerance. Probably a few hoodlums from the KKK."

"Why would they bother us here on the hillside?"

"I fear they live here now."

"What do you mean?"

"They were patients. They must have sneaked out."

"You saw them?"

"No."

"Then how do you know they were our patients?"

"One of them coughed. I know a tuberculosis cough when I hear one."

THE SPOTTING OF a deer or two was a daily occurrence in the woods at Waverly. The wooded area was full of squirrels and rabbits, raccoons and chipmunks, stray cats and dogs, and at night the occasional possum would appear. But the pig that darted across their path just before they reached the top of the hill was a new wrinkle to the morning ritual. It seemed that the pigs were getting loose a lot lately. This one was extremely fat, crusted with mud and searching the woods for acorns. It waddled and snorted, then faced them. Susannah squatted down and gave it a quick snort of her own. The pig turned and scuttled back into the trees.

Susannah stood straight again and ironed out her dress with her hands. "Jakes needs to learn how to keep those beasts locked up proper."

Wolfgang began walking again. "Suppose they don't want to be cooked."

"Ah, they keep us fed, Wolf. The cows, the chickens, the pigs . . ."

"Yes, we *are* a village of sorts."

"Better off than some, I guess."

Just then a chubby balding man in a gray uniform came running and huffing from the trees to their right. The letters WHS were stenciled in white above his left shirt pocket. He leaned over, hands against his thighs, breathing heavily.

Susannah patted him on the back. "Keep'm penned, Jakes. Can't have our dinner running the hillside. The patients need that good meat."

Jakes scratched his wispy gray hair. "Which way'd it go, Miss?" They both pointed toward the left side of the footpath. Jakes followed their extended fingers and disappeared into the trees.

They were nearly to the clearing where a grassy field rolled downward from the facade of the sanatorium. A tall black man with thick dark hair and bulging muscles walked away from the building pushing a loose-wheeled wooden cart stacked high with food and supplies. Apples, oranges and bananas. Wheat bread and cucumbers and tomatoes. Beneath the cart rested a dozen glass jars of white milk. Steam rose from beneath a beige towel at the front of the cart. It smelled like fresh breakfast. The bacon was noticeable and enticing.

"Morning, Big 15." Wolfgang lifted the towel and snatched a piece of bacon.

"Morning, Boss." Big 15 rested on the cart for a moment, wiped sweat from his forehead with his index finger and nodded toward Susannah. "Miss."

Susannah nodded without smiling and walked on a few steps into the sunshine.

Wolfgang patted Big 15 on his thick shoulder. "First trip of the morning?"

Big 15 nodded. "Gots to feed my people, Boss." He stared across the lawn toward Susannah, who stood facing a cluster of crows eating breadcrumbs around the base of a pine tree. "Why don't she talk to me, Boss?"

"I little shy, I guess." Wolfgang inhaled the pleasant aroma wafting up from the cart. "What else they cook up this morning?"

"Bacon . . . and some eggs and sausage."

Susannah folded her arms across her chest and spoke over her shoulder. "We'd have more of the bacon if Jakes would keep the pigs bottled up."

Big 15 lifted the cart. "Reckon so, Miss." He smiled. His muscles flexed beneath his long-sleeved gray shirt and he continued down the hillside.

"Good day." Wolfgang watched him descend the uneven terrain, hardly straining on the downhill. Big 15 stood at least six-foot-six and his hands were enormous, big enough to palm the largest of pumpkins from the patch on the north side of the hillside. They called him Big 15 because of the size of his fifteen-inch boots, and it just so happened that it was also Big 15's fifteenth year at Waverly. He'd spent two years as a patient, the rest as a worker after he'd been healed. Three times a day Big 15 trekked the hillside with a cart full of supplies for the colored hospital and never a complaint. He was cured of TB in 1916 when the hospital was a mere flicker of the size it was now. He'd insisted on staying on to help the colored folks down the hill. He'd never say it, but Wolfgang could tell by the looks Big 15 would give Doctor Barker that he wasn't satisfied with the conditions at the colored hospital. It was cramped, dark and over-crowded. And if it was the fresh air that helped cure the disease, the white folks got the best of it, perched as they were at the highest point in the county. The colored hospital caught everything downwind—the smell of the pigs and the cows, the smell of the freshly-baked food before it was transported, the flooding from the heavy rains.

"Wolf, why does he call you boss?" asked Susannah.

"Not sure." Wolfgang continued up the knoll, the sanatorium now catching his eyes. Its beauty never ceased to amaze. It was the grandest building of its kind in the entire country. It was completed in 1926 with a capacity of 435 beds and a waiting list to boot. Each bed was equipped with a radio, phone, bell signal and an electric light socket. It was limited to local residents and maintained by taxpayers.

"Mrs. Potts seems to be doing better," said Susannah.

"Avulsion can be a tedious procedure." Wolfgang glanced at her. "And she has you to take care of her."

The comment drew a smile from Susannah. "Miss Schultz spoke of you before I left last night. She hopes you'll play for her today."

"Doctor Barker says my music therapy is a waste of time."

Susannah waved her hands. "Doctor Barker is a bore who's mad at the world because his wife won't sleep with him anymore."

"She's afraid of catching TB," Wolfgang said. "I'd be careful too."

"Would you?"

"You know what I mean."

She watched him curiously. "Barker doesn't see how your music draws them in. He doesn't see how you connect with them."

"Don't worry, I'll play for her."

They were twenty yards away from the entrance portico on the south side of the sanatorium. The portico had archways with alternating sections of brick and stone that gave it a mosque-like appearance, although the building itself looked more like it was stolen from an Ivy League college campus. It was a five-story monster made of brick and stone, ornately fashioned by Gothic architecture from the first floor all the way up to the rooftop and bell tower. Solarium porches stretched the length of the building on each floor, six hundred feet long. Every room on the south side opened to the sleeping porches, where the patients who still had a chance at survival stayed. The terminal cases were on the other side of the hallway. The building was designed in the shape of a boomerang with the idea that it could catch the breeze and keep fresh air on the patients at all times.

Rest and fresh air supposedly healed tuberculosis. The building was built high upon the hillside so that the patients could breathe it in. So why were they always dying? One death per hour now, and it showed no signs of slowing. Wolfgang spent much of his day now hearing confessions, regardless of faith or denomination.

Father, bless me for I have sinned . . .

"Wolfgang?"

"Yes?"

Susannah grinned. "Where were you just now?"

"Contemplating whether or not to open the door for you." He stepped forward and opened it. They stood in the center of a hallway that stretched three hundred feet on either side of them. Shiny black and red tiles formed a checkered pathway down the center of the hallway. The walls were gray, the woodwork a dark brown. Globe lights hung down from the white ceiling. Everything was clean.

Retching and coughing echoed down the hallway, reminding Wolfgang that it was still a home for the dying. Their medical treatment was primitive at best. They performed lobectomies in which they surgically removed parts of the lung, and in some cases the entire lung. They performed phrenicotomies, cutting the nerve supply to one of the diaphragms in hopes of allowing the disabled lung to heal. They used heliotherapy, or sun treatment, because they believed that sunbathing killed the bacteria that caused tuberculosis. With a surgery called thoracoplasty they removed several rib bones from the chest wall to collapse the lung. But they were all treatments, not cures, and the procedures, bloody and dangerous as they were, only delayed the ultimate outcome.

So the doctors, nurses and volunteers made it as much like home as possible. Waverly was a completely self-sufficient community. Cattle, hogs and chickens were raised to provide meat, fresh eggs and dairy products. They had a nondenominational chapel on the second floor that was run by Wolfgang. They had a school for the children in the pavilion building, with a playground—seesaws, swings, and slides. They had a theater for movies and plays and an extensive occupational therapy program to help patients get their minds off worrying about recovering. The activities, which ranged from rug weaving and making toys to copper hammering and manufacturing furniture, gave them a sense of worth and enjoyment, and the goods made were displayed and sold each year at the State Fair.

Wolfgang brought them music.

"Doctor Pike!" The stern voice came from down the hallway. Wolfgang was to report to Doctor Barker's office first thing every morning, but half the time he didn't have the chance. "Doctor Pike!"

Susannah and Wolfgang turned to face the chief doctor, who wore a stethoscope around his thin neck. Doctor Evan Barker was dressed in his white lab coat buttoned all the way up, covering what appeared to be his usual three-piece suit. Under the hanging hall light his gray hair showed hints of the blond it had once been. His blue eyes moved behind the wire-framed glasses that rode high upon his blade-like nose, positioned in such a way that he was always looking down on the unfortunate soul that had to listen to him. His thin, upturned nostrils flared.

"Morning, Doctor Barker," Wolfgang eventually managed to say, although he badly wanted to turn and ignore the marching orders.

Doctor Barker glanced at Wolfgang's bag of instruments. "I see you have your *healing* supplies."

"I don't go anywhere without them."

He handed Wolfgang a clipboard full of charts—forced them into his chest was more accurate. The impact made him step back a few feet to balance himself. "After rounds I need you to tend to those patients. They came in very early this morning."

"Yes, sir."

"Treat them. Run sputum tests on them. Medical tests, Wolfgang. Not theories on music." He glanced at Wolfgang's black bag again and then stared at Susannah, who was not so smoothly disguising a smile with her right hand. He faced Wolfgang again. "Last night, there were patients who didn't get checked on because of your playing music for others."

"Name them."

Doctor Barker started to but then stopped to exhale a breath he must have been holding onto all morning. He pursed his bloodless lips. "Just see to the new patients, Wolfgang. We're being overrun by them now."

"I have Mass at nine." Wolfgang took pride in that—not so much the Mass itself, but the fact that Doctor Barker had little to no control over how he performed his priestly duties. And they both knew it. An incident two weeks ago had nearly elevated to blows, when Doctor Barker had looked into the chapel to find Wolfgang performing a Mass in Latin to a crowd of no more than twenty people. Doctor Barker was a strict Methodist who was quick to jump into any religious argument, and on that particular day Wolfgang was his target, accusing him of trying to spread Catholicism to sick patients who were desperate for any kind of hope. Wolfgang had quickly, and quite authoritatively, backed him against the wall. How dare you accuse me of such a thing? Every patient in that chapel for that Mass was Catholic. Doctor Barker hadn't apologized, but he had been rendered speechless by Wolfgang's defensive reaction to the accusation. He'd slithered away and had said nothing about it since.

So all Doctor Barker said when Wolfgang told him of his Mass at nine was, "Fine." And then he'd spun on his heels like a soldier and hurried away to the sound of his echoing footsteps.

Wolfgang and Susannah watched him go before she followed in the same direction. She looked over her shoulder. "Lunch?"

"Sure."

She'd caught him staring. "Think McVain will talk today?"

Wolfgang smiled. It was a daily joke between them. McVain was a patient on the fourth floor who had yet to utter a word to anyone in nearly two months since his arrival during the great rainfall. Wolfgang had been fascinated by McVain ever since he'd been pushed into the mud and watched him wheel his own wheel-chair inside the sanatorium. The staff knew to get out of his way that day. He picked his floor. He picked his room. The fellow patients looked at him as they would a walking virus. The repellent looks he'd give were enough to dampen the hopes of an entire floor. There was something about the man. Wolfgang could see it in his eyes. He was a man of many stories and secrets, a man of many opinions. He was probably the most intriguing man Wolfgang had ever known, simply because he knew absolutely nothing about him other than what he could see on the surface—his watchful, para-noid eyes, hard-lined face and blocked jaw, his unruly red hair . . . and the three missing fingers on his left hand.

3

Every room in the sanatorium had the capacity for two beds but the patients spent most of their time on the porches. Mr. Weaver was forty years old but his gray hair made him look twenty years older—that and the sickly pale color that masked his gaunt face. He had the unfortunate and uncomfortable job of being Tad McVain's roommate, so when they were in the room together the only conversations he was getting were those he'd have with himself. So Weaver smiled every time Wolfgang entered the room to check on him and he cherished their conversations about music.

"Guess what today is, doc?" Weaver said, his throat raspy.

Wolfgang hovered over Weaver's torso. "Your birthday?"

"Nope. I've been here twelve months today."

Truthfully, Wolfgang feared Weaver didn't have that much longer. He put on a fake smile that he hoped appeared genuine. "Maybe we'll get you out of here soon." Wolfgang added four more ounces of shot to the bag that rested on Weaver's right collarbone. It was called the shot-bag method of treatment, and it was typically used on patients with infections in both lungs. Several weeks ago Wolfgang had begun the procedure by placing a one-pound bag of shot on both collarbones. He increased the weight by about five ounces a week. The weight restricted the excursions of the lungs, made them quiescent, and it taught correct breathing.

Weaver was a good patient, and he was always careful not to move around a lot with the bags on him. Only his beady eyes roamed. "What are we up to?"

Wolfgang squinted as he dropped the last ball of shot on the bag atop the right collarbone. "Four-and-a-half pounds."

"That good?"

"It's better."

Wolfgang glanced over his shoulder at McVain, who lay in bed only a few feet away, eyes staring blankly toward the gray wall or maybe at the sunlight out on the solarium porch. Other than his coughing spells he was quiet as usual, his lips formed in a scowl that Wolfgang feared might become permanent if not rectified soon. McVain's nose was flat and bent slightly to the left side up near the bridge, as if it had been broken several times and not set correctly. Wolfgang wondered if he was once a boxer. Probably not. His hands seemed too delicate. His hair was uncombed, perpetually tousled by the constant breeze, and fiery red. His eyes were green. He looked Irish, possibly Catholic, not that it mattered to Wolfgang. Either way he would welcome him to Masses. The chapel was never full except for an occasional Sunday or Christmas or Easter Mass.

Wolfgang stared at McVain's hands, his left one in particular. His fingers were long, the ones still there. The three middle fingers were mere nubs, blocked off at the knuckles. Was that the reason for his foul mood? But who was Wolfgang to judge? He wasn't in that uncomfortable bed with the hard mattress and loud box springs. He wasn't dying of a disease for which they had no cure, a disease thought best treated by rest and fresh air.

"Doctor?" It was Weaver again. Wolfgang carefully placed the last few ounces of shot on his far shoulder. Weaver stared up at him with kind, trusting eyes. "Or should I call you Father, like some of the others? I'm Baptist, you see."

Wolfgang smiled. "Call me whatever you like, Mr. Weaver. My parents were strict Protestants."

"How'd you become Catholic?"

"The ultimate rebellion, I guess." Wolfgang patted his arm. "Perhaps another time."

Weaver stared, perplexed, and Wolfgang was careful to avoid his gaze until Weaver moved on to the next subject, which he did almost immediately. Weaver wasn't one to pry. "Do you like jazz?"

"I don't dislike it." Wolfgang straightened the supplies on his cart. "I'm sure it would grow on me."

McVain coughed painfully loud and then spat a honker of bloody phlegm onto the floor. He ratcheted up another clump of something and expectorated it next to the first.

Wolfgang looked over his shoulder again. "You okay, McVain?"

McVain looked away and grunted.

Wolfgang faced Weaver again but nodded toward McVain, speaking loud enough for both men to hear him. "Does he ever talk to you?"

Weaver tilted his head. "Never the first word. Hey, McVain, you like jazz?" They waited for an answer but none came. McVain lifted up his right hand and produced his middle finger for them both to see and he held it ramrod straight for at least ten seconds before lowering his arm back down to the wrinkled sheets that enclosed his body like a cocoon. Weaver looked up at Wolfgang. "Sign language?"

"An enigma," Wolfgang whispered to Weaver. "But we'll crack him." He pulled Weaver's bed sheet up to his chest and patted his arm again. "Classical music is what drives me, Mr. Weaver. Mozart, especially. His music put me to sleep every night as a child. I would hear it and put everything else in the background."

"Can you plug me in?" Weaver lifted his headphones from beside the bed. "I like Mozart."

Wolfgang plugged the wire into a receptacle between the solarium doors. "My parents named me after Mozart. My mother wanted me to become a preacher. My father demanded that I become a composer."

"So what'd he say when you became a doctor? And a Catholic priest?"

"He died long before I ever made the decision." Wolfgang chuckled. "But he would have been furious. He detested science. He was no fan of any talk about evolution, especially in schools. He was a strict man of God, a Bible reader."

"And your mother?"

"We haven't spoken for almost ten years."

Weaver paused to see if Wolfgang would offer up anything else but he didn't. Weaver started to put on his headphones but stopped. He motioned for Wolfgang to lean down. "McVain's fingers," he whispered. "They move at night."

Wolfgang shot McVain a glance and then whispered to Weaver. "Move? How so?"

Weaver lifted his hands and forearms from his sides, careful not to dislodge the bags of shot, and wiggled his own fingers. "Goes on for hours." Wolfgang helped Weaver put on his earphones. "I hear you playing for the patients," Weaver said. "I like that. How many instruments do you play?"

"A dozen or so. But that's always been my curse. I'm an expert at none of them."

"Nurse Susannah says you play the piano like Mozart."

Wolfgang couldn't contain his smile. "She's kind."

Weaver turned the volume up on his headset, closed his eyes and smiled as jazz tunes poured into his ears. "Ahhh . . . like Heaven."

Wolfgang turned toward McVain again. "Anything I can get you, Mr. McVain?"

McVain didn't even shake or nod his head. Wolfgang stood at the head of McVain's bed and used his right foot to unlatch the lock at the wheels. He rolled McVain from the room, through the double solarium doors and toward the sunshine, where dozens of other patients lay in their beds up and down the long fourth floor solarium porch. He wheeled him through the shade, past an old woman knitting in a rocking chair with a plaid afghan draped over her shoulder, and into the sunlight, which was where, Wolfgang assumed, McVain liked it best. There were more than a hundred beds on each floor and most of them were out now, facing the trees and tranquil landscape that surrounded the building. A swift breeze vented through the screens that stretched the massive solarium windows. It was becoming a warm day for January—a treat for the patients because they would have wheeled them out regardless of the temperature. The theories were graven in stone. Whether it was raining, snowing or blustery cold, fresh air was of the utmost importance. To Hell with comfort. But with the current temperature the rooftop was probably full of children playing on the swing sets and seesaws, men and women playing cards and chatting, trying to absorb as much sunlight as they could. At lunch and dinnertime it was easy to spot the rooftop dwellers, especially on the sunny days. Their skin was often red from the burn caused by both the wind and sun.

Wolfgang patted McVain on the shoulder. "Good day, McVain." McVain shifted in his bed but said nothing. Wolfgang stared at his hands briefly and then walked away.

4

TUBERCULOSIS DIDN'T DISCRIMINATE. It invaded the bodies of the young and elderly, black and white, men and women. From a sneeze, or a cough, by speaking or a kiss, airborne particles containing tubercle bacilli float unseen in search of another host to infect. They become established in the alveoli of the lungs and spread throughout the body. Waverly had men and women of all ages and a pavilion just for the children. They had a separate hospital down the hill for the colored folks. Wolfgang didn't think it was right, but he didn't make the rules and, at the moment, lacked the passion and time to change it. Yet daily he felt the guilt of treating and playing for only the white patients.

It wasn't that he felt his music was so special. Often times it was merely adequate to the ears, but he could see the look in the patients' eyes when he played for them. He empathized with what they felt. Music took them away from the present. Music took them to better places, to times in their past when their bodies were free of disease and they had the strength to walk to the bathroom on their own or throw a ball with their son or work in the garden. Music was the ultimate distraction.

Miss Schultz was probably Wolfgang's biggest fan. He played his harmonica for her, one of the hundreds of short tunes he'd come up with over the years. It had no title and, like many of the others, it changed depending on the day or the instrument chosen, the notes existing only in his mind and therefore never right or wrong. He pulled the harmonica from his lips and leaned back in his metal folding chair. Miss Schultz was lying back on her fluffy white pillow, staring at him with two rheumy eyes glazed by cataracts. Her charts said she was sixty, but her skin looked younger. Only her eyes dated her, but when she smiled her youthful side always won out.

"Thank you, Father." She gazed out toward the woods from her third floor spot on the solarium porch. Wolfgang put the harmonica inside his black bag, placing it right next to a piccolo his father had given him when he was five years old. "You had a nice homily this morning," she said. "It made me appreciate what I have."

Wolfgang's hair blew in the light breeze. He could have sat out here all day in the Indian summer. He felt as if God was rewarding them for enduring the rains of last month and the frigid temperatures of the weeks that followed, during which a few of the patients had died of exposure.

Miss Schultz tugged on the sleeve of his lab coat. "You think I need a haircut, Father?"

"It looks fine to me." It was brown with hints of red and gray, pulled back from her pale forehead with a black clip.

"Oh, applesauce!" She waved her arthritic hand at him. "You're just being kind."

"The color in your cheeks is better," he said. "You look stronger."

She touched her hair, checking for bounce. "Is the barber here very good? The same woman has cut my hair now for thirty years. I'm very particular."

Wolfgang stood. "I think you'll be pleased with the work Dolores does, Miss Schultz." He touched his own hair. "She cuts mine, you know."

"With those bangs you could be a Roman Caesar, you know that?"

A slight chuckle. "Get some rest."

Miss Schultz touched her hair again. "I've been considering getting it bobbed."

The harmless comment tugged an emotional chord somewhere deep within Wolfgang. He blinked to dampen the reverberation. "I think a bob would look nice." He thought she was too old for a bob but he wasn't one to critique any woman on fashion.

"Father?" She nodded toward an old man in a bed a few rooms down the porchway. "Will you play again today? Your music helps Mr. Jenkins relax at night. He misses his wife."

Wolfgang sighed. "I'm sure that I can."

"See if it doesn't make him smile. His cough is sounding dreadful."

"We can only pray for him now."

"Father? Where do we go when we die?"

"I'm asked that question quite often," he said. "Where do we go when we die—"

"That's not what I'm asking, Father. What do you do with our bodies when we die?"

"Don't worry yourself with such details, Miss Schultz. By the looks of your improvement, you aren't likely to be among them. But I assure you they're properly taken care of."

"Do you believe there really is a Heaven?"

"Why . . . yes, of course I do."

She shook a finger at him and gave him a wry smile. "A priest shouldn't hesitate when asked that question."

Nurse Cleary, a perpetually slow-moving nurse with wide hips and a pleasant demeanor hurried with flushed cheeks toward Wolfgang. It was uncommon to see her moving so quickly and the sight of it started Wolfgang's heart racing.

"Doctor . . . Doctor . . . "

"What is it, Nurse Cleary?"

"Doctor Barker needs you," she said. "Quickly. Room two-oh-seven."

MR. HOAGLAND WAS dying. Wolfgang wasn't summoned as a doctor but as a priest. As soon as he entered Room 207, three pairs of eyes centered on him. Lincoln—his trusted and oftentimes confrontational, sandy-haired assistant—appeared confused. Doctor Barker stared with anger in his narrow eyes. And in poor Mr. Hoagland's eyes he saw nothing but pain and misery, a look he'd seen all too often of late.

"There you are," Doctor Barker shouted. The room's bright light glistened off his high forehead, making the red in his face more prominent, the strained veins in his neck more visible. "Hurry!"

Mr. Hoagland's chest rose from the bed. Blood spewed from his mouth and rolled down his convulsing neck. There was nothing they could do. Mr. Hoagland's thirty-year-old lungs were probably on fire, his chest feeling like it was about to explode, his throat closing up. His lungs had already begun to disintegrate. His roommate, a new patient whose name Wolfgang had failed to memorize, watched in horror from his bed across the room. It was in his eyes. *Is that going to be me? Am I next? How long before the disease rips me apart?*

Wolfgang looked at Lincoln and pointed to the roommate. "Roll him outside. Lincoln—now." Lincoln snapped out of his funk and quickly rolled the roommate's bed out to the solarium porch.

Wolfgang gripped Mr. Hoagland's hand. He showed no signs of feeling Wolfgang's touch. Some have said they heard a buzzing in their ears before they died—a dizziness caused by constant fever and lack of oxygen to the brain. He choked on more blood, some of it landing on Wolfgang's hand. Doctor Barker felt for the man's pulse. Mr. Hoagland's eyes were red. His face was pale, ashen. His body had stopped producing enough red blood cells to keep the pigment in his skin. His eyes opened wide.

"I see . . ."

"You see what?" Wolfgang asked.

He stopped moving. His hands fell limp on his chest. He stared unblinking at the bright ceiling. The pain was gone, but the disease still ate away at the inside of his body.

Doctor Barker threw his bloody towel to the floor. "Damn it!"

Wolfgang drew the sign of the cross over the man's body and closed his eyes. "Requiem aeternam dona eis, Domine, et lux perpetua eis." Wolfgang looked upward. "Grant them eternal rest, O Lord." He touched Mr. Hoagland's forehead. "And may everlasting light shine upon them."

Doctor Barker walked toward the porchway and stopped at the threshold. He was tall, probably six-three or six-four, and the top of his head nearly reached the frame over the doors. "These patients need medicine, Wolfgang." His eyes were cold and piercing. "They need rest, not music."

"I got down here as fast as I could."

"Not soon enough." His anger toward the music was personal, something deeply rooted, but Wolfgang had no idea what lay behind it. Doctor Barker pointed his long, talon-like finger toward the bed. "He said he had sins that needed to be cleansed."

"I played for him last night. He mentioned nothing."

"Perhaps you couldn't hear him."

"He died with music in his soul."

"Be their doctor," Barker said. "Be their priest. Hear their confessions and stop wasting time on tunes." He left with a swift turn that spun his white coat in a dove-like swirl. Lincoln stepped back in the room.

"Help me clean him," said Wolfgang.

Lincoln's face was still frozen in shock. He was a jokester, but here there was often no time for it. He usually saw the bodies after they were dead. He had no connection. His job of late was mostly in the morgue. "The morgue is full, Wolf. Three trays aren't enough. I need more help in the chute."

"I'll see that you get it."

"I'm calling it the Death Tunnel now," he said. "I spend all day in there. It never stops. The smell is getting to me, Father."

Wolfgang nodded as if he understood, but he didn't. He wasn't stuck in the chute all day long, accompanying the dead as they descended the hillside, unseen, all hours of the day. Wolfgang handed Lincoln a clean towel and together they began to wipe blood from Mr. Hoagland's neck.

WOLFGANG SPENT THE rest of the sunny day in a somber mood
while the morgue continued to fill. He had an afternoon gathering
in the chapel, where he gave a sermon on hope and togetherness to
seven patients—three Catholics, two Protestants, a Jewish woman
and an atheist searching for answers. While he spoke, he eyed a patient in the back row, a hulking farm boy with a crew cut named
Jesse Jacobs. The baby-faced young man, who appeared barely over
twenty, had been with them at Waverly for almost four weeks with
not one appearance in the chapel. Every morning during rounds
he'd ask Wolfgang to pray for him and his fourth floor roommate,
Ray—a dark-haired young man who was as thin as Jesse was large,
a man whose name never failed to escape Wolfgang's overtaxed
brain.

Jesse's skin was naturally pale, his cheeks pink and scattered
with freckles. He had a toothy grin that filled out his box-like jaw.
His arms were thick and strong but relatively free of muscle tone.
He was one of those brute strength kids, the type that could lift
a Buick over his head but still look fat doing it. Jesse approached
Wolfgang after Mass and shyly thanked him for his uplifting
words. Jesse then asked if Wolfgang needed any help in the chapel.
Jesse had thought about becoming a priest and wanted to know if
Wolfgang needed help. He could be somewhat of an altar boy and

learn from him. Wolfgang had been slightly stunned that someone of Jesse's stature would covet the clerics, and because of it he'd been reluctant to give Jesse an immediate answer. Of course he said yes, but inside he doubted that he was the best role model for a budding priest. If nothing else he could use his size to intimidate Doctor Barker. He'd dare him to interrupt another Catholic Mass, not with Jesse Jacobs standing beside the altar. Nevertheless, the introduction and resulting conversation had brightened Wolfgang's mood for the rest of the day. He would finally have help in the chapel.

Three times throughout the day he'd attempted to coax McVain into speaking but he only closed his eyes, grunted and faked sleep. Whatever he was, acting was not his strength. Over the weeks that McVain had been a patient, he'd gradually conformed to the crowd. For the first several days he'd dressed in his suits and frock coat, vests and cravats, as if in denial, as if he dressed the part he would remain healthy. The days passed, then weeks. In the mornings he'd dress before anyone saw him. He'd change in the dark when everyone else was asleep. Now as Wolfgang stared at him, McVain wore a simple pair of tweed trousers and a heavy white shirt with no collar and wrinkled sleeves. Wolfgang left him to his thoughts and promised to return.

In the evening Wolfgang granted Miss Schultz's request and stopped on the third floor solarium for a visit with Mr. Jenkins. He played tunes on the harmonica for him for nearly thirty minutes while Mr. Jenkins listened silently with a smile on his face, his liver-spotted hands clutching and releasing his bed sheets, clutching and releasing as if trying to restart some clogged blood flow. His fever was high. His skin was chalky, his eyes sunken in and darkened by the shadowed pockets of his skull. He was tired of fighting. He was an old man who seemed ready to go.

"Thank you." Mr. Jenkins craned his head toward Wolfgang's chair. He coughed and gagged. Blood trickled from the left corner of his mouth. He wiped it on his shirtsleeve and settled his bald, spotted head on his flat pillow. Behind them the woods were silent. The night was dark, the moon concealed by layers of cloud cover. It was much cooler now. Dozens of patients remained out on the porchway, some sleeping, some talking. Plumes of steam escaped from their noses and open mouths.

"The night has a chill to it." Wolfgang was lost for words. They looked to him for conversation, comfort, even wisdom, but often he felt empty and fake.

Mr. Jenkins looked up at the ceiling. "When I was a boy my father used to take us to the lake. We'd sit around the campfire. I'd fall asleep to him playing the harmonica." Wolfgang thought of his own father and how he'd play the violin and piano at night and how their living room was full of musical instruments. And how his father, despite all his faults and eccentricities, had been taken from him at too early an age.

Mr. Jenkins' hands shook noticeably. That was why he was clutching and releasing the bed sheets. To give his hands a job. To keep them from shaking. Wolfgang opened Mr. Jenkins' left hand, pushed the harmonica into his palm and gently closed his fingers around the small instrument. His hands stopped shaking. All the lines in his face seemed to soften. Wolfgang started to get up slowly, for this was when many confessed. They could feel their death coming. They often waited until the last moment and Mr. Jenkins was no different.

"Father? I'm not a Catholic. Can you hear my sins?"

Wolfgang sat back down. "Of course."

"I've never been to any kind of confession."

"Contrition is the beginning of forgiveness. I can see the sorrow in your eyes." Many of his confessions came from non-Catholics who had no one else to turn to. In years past, Waverly had preachers from other denominations. There were options. But not now. If they couldn't spill their guts to Father Pike, they took them with them to their graves. Wolfgang often set the procedures aside and simply gave them his ears and heart. "You must regret your sins, resolve not to repeat them, and then turn back to God."

"Yes, Father." He looked Wolfgang in the eyes. "I used to drink a lot." He moved the harmonica inside his grip. "I hit my wife one night when I was drunk." A tear formed inside his right eye. "She has forgiven me but my daughter never will. We don't speak. She won't see me." He sighed, still watching Wolfgang. "I can't go to my grave without the forgiveness of my little girl."

Wolfgang extended his right hand toward his head. "I absolve you from your sin in the name of the Father, and of the Son, and of the Holy Spirit." Wolfgang lowered his hand. "The absolution may take away the sin, Mr. Jenkins, but it does not fix all that the sin has caused. You must—"

"There's a box in my room," he said. "On a shelf above the bed. I write to her every day. Her name is Amy."

"You don't send them?"

He shook his head. "Can you see that she gets them?"

"Of course." Wolfgang placed his hand on Mr. Jenkins' frail shoulder.

"Will I be forgiven . . . you know . . . when I'm gone? I don't want to go to Hell."

"The Lord has freed you from your sins. Go now in peace."

"Am I supposed to say something here?"

"Most would now say, thanks be to God."

"Thanks be to God, then." He wrinkled his brow. "What about some kind of penance?"

"Those letters you've written to your daughter are penance enough, Mr. Jenkins. I'll see that she gets them. Your heart is pure."

Mr. Jenkins made the sign of the cross, more than likely because he'd seen Wolfgang do it at the beginning of the confession. His eyes were wet with tears. He closed them. Without another word

Wolfgang stood and walked away, trying to ignore the feeling of guilt he felt every time he answered their questions.

Susannah stepped out of the shadows. "You ready?"

Wolfgang jumped back.

"Sorry. Didn't mean to startle you."

A little boy stood by Susannah's side, a brown-haired ten-year-old patient with dimples named Abel Jones. Wolfgang gave him a wink. "How's it going, Abel?"

"Swell." He licked on a lollipop Susannah had most assuredly given him. His special treatment was deserved. He'd arrived at Waverly in 1927 as an orphan. Because he had no family he received no visitors, no pictures from loved ones and no letters from anyone. Susannah was like a mother to him, and at times Wolfgang felt like the only father figure in the boy's life. Abel didn't seem too bothered by his apparent loneliness. He claimed to love it at Waverly. Never had he enjoyed the company of so many children—albeit sick children, but playmates nevertheless. The entire staff adored him, and Susannah was especially torn by his plight. She prayed for his health but at the same time knew of Abel's intentions of never wanting to leave the hillside. The hillside was the best home he'd ever had. Deep down she believed that Abel wanted to remain slightly sick for the rest of his life.

The three of them walked along the third floor solarium. With each bed Wolfgang passed he wondered who the possible brick-thrower could have been. Eventually he would find out, but until the incident repeated itself he wouldn't lose sleep over it.

Abel walked near the edge of the porchway, looking over and down toward the front lawn below and the woods beyond. He was a resilient young boy who'd arrived with stage two tuberculosis. Like many of the children he'd shown improvement since his arrival at Waverly. Wolfgang attributed his recovery to Susannah's presence. They'd become instant friends. Wolfgang feared the day if he were to pass away.

"Wolf," Susannah whispered as they passed a male patient who was snoring loudly, and the noise coming from his clogged nostrils sounded like a whistle. Susannah covered Abel's mouth to keep the boy from laughing. "Wolf, you gave Mr. Jenkins your harmonica."

"I've got several." He walked on. "I need to make a stop before we go."

"Where?"

"McVain."

"He talk yet?"

"No."

"Who's McVain?" Abel asked.

"A mute," Wolfgang said.

Abel chuckled. "What's a mute?"

"Same thing as a McVain."

"What's a McVain?"

"You'll see," said Susannah, enjoying the give-and-take from her two male companions.

They took the nearest stairwell to the fourth floor solarium and quietly passed the beds lining the porch. Some patients slept. An old woman with very little hair waved and smiled. A middle-aged man simply stared out the windows, oblivious to the runs of snot dripping from his mustache. Wolfgang found Mr. Weaver asleep on the porch, snoring in a much deeper octave than the man on the floor below. Even so, Abel thought it funny and stifled his laughter with his own hands this time. Susannah gently placed her hands on his shoulders and he continued to lick his lollipop. Wolfgang looked inside the room and found McVain on his bed in the far corner. He inched closer. It was dark, but Wolfgang could still make out McVain's hands. Mr. Weaver was right—his hands *did* move at night.

Abel and Susannah stepped closer. "Where'd his fingers go?" Abel whispered.

Susannah put her finger to Abel's sticky lips.

Wolfgang watched McVain. "I'll be damned." McVain's eyes were closed. His hands were raised above the covers, slightly bent at the wrists. His fingers, long and arched, moved as if hitting unseen piano keys, side to side, up and down—precisely, gracefully, with authority. Even the nubs from his three missing fingers moved ever so slightly from muscle memory.

Wolfgang backed away with his mouth open.

"What is it?" asked Susannah.

Wolfgang tiptoed from the room and they followed.

Abel looked over his shoulder toward McVain's room. "Is he a monster?"

"No," Susannah said in a hushed voice, although it had a twinge of humor in it. "He's not a monster."

Wolfgang gripped her shoulder. "My Lord, did you see that? He was playing the piano."

"Yes, I saw it."

"Now we should have something to talk about."

"Unless he is a mute."

"I'll find out tomorrow." Susannah had taken off her nurse's cap. Her hair had lost some of the morning's curl, but it was still enough to get Wolfgang's attention. "Look," he said. "I have a plan for tomorrow night." He leaned closer and whispered in her ear.

Susannah came to a sudden halt and stared at him. "Wolf, have you gone nuts?" Wolfgang said nothing in reply. He stared at her with a boyish grin that could have been mistaken for being nuts. After a pause, she started walking again. "Okay . . . Fine . . . I'll go along with it."

"Atta girl. Tomorrow night it is."

Abel looked up. "Can I come?"

"It'll be past your bedtime," said Susannah.

"It's past my bedtime now."

"That's different."

"How?"

"You have school in the morning."

"It's okay if we miss."

"And what would the other kids say then?" Susannah said. "They already think you get special treatment."

Wolfgang touched Susannah's left arm. "Wait. Listen."

"What?"

"You hear that?"

They all stopped. Directly below them on the third floor solarium, Mr. Jenkins had begun to play his new harmonica.

6

WALKING SUSANNAH BACK through the woods to her dormitory at night had always been something Wolfgang looked forward to. It was a time when they could both let go of the tensions of the day, breathe the fresh untainted air of the wilderness, listen to the crickets and the wind, and the deadfall crunching beneath their tired feet. They'd discuss different stories of the day: new patients, funny patients, and usually their conversation leaned to the positive aspects of the hospital. Death talk on the way home was taboo. But tonight Wolfgang walked with a quicker pace, staying closer to Susannah than was the norm. His eyes were on alert. If there was someone prowling about who was willing to throw bricks through windows, they were probably capable of more. They'd dropped Abel off at the children's pavilion, where several of the kids were already asleep on their little screened porch. Susannah had walked him inside and returned with sadness in her eyes. She was always sad to part ways with Abel, even knowing that she'd see him in the morning. Of course that was her greatest fear, that one morning he wouldn't wake up, that he'd become one of the growing, unstoppable statistics that were quickly making the sanatorium the talk of the city. Tuberculosis was hitting every household in some way. If a family had been spared from the disease, chances are they knew someone who had it. As the saying went, everybody knows someone at Waverly.

Tonight, little was said after they'd dropped off Abel. Susannah seemed too preoccupied with her thoughts and Wolfgang was too focused on the increasingly spooky surroundings for conversation. He'd never looked at the woods as spooky before, but now he couldn't help it. Someone was out there who didn't like what he represented.

Come after me if you must, he thought, but leave my friends in peace.

"Wolf, what's eating you?"

Wolfgang hesitated and spoke half the truth. "McVain. He was a pianist."

"You said so earlier."

"I don't just mean he plays the piano. Didn't you see him?"

She folded her arms against the cold wind. "I saw him the same as you did."

"His arm movements, how his fingers moved. Even the nubs. Piano wasn't just a hobby for him."

She smirked. "The real McCoy, huh?"

They stopped outside the nurses' dormitory, a two-story rectangular brick building that housed thirteen women who split two daily shifts, seven days a week. Susannah was a veteran of the crew and was fortunate enough to have her own room on the second floor. She was one of three with such a luxury. The rest slept two to a room, grouped by the closest ages and, according to Susannah, when they weren't in the sanatorium they didn't skimp on the fun. Pillow fights, drinking after hours, smoking and playing cards, laughing and talking about men half the night. But who could blame them? They needed their release. The fun was necessary to their sanity, and occasionally Susannah, admittedly and with only the slightest bit of shame, joined in.

Wolfgang shoved his hands into his pockets and stared at the dormitory. Four of the dozen windows were lit. The shadow of a nurse passed by a drawn shade in one of the second floor rooms. "I need to get to McVain."

"And do what with him?"

"I don't know yet." Wolfgang stared at the ground, thinking of his plan for tomorrow night. He hoped Susannah wouldn't back out. He was sure he could get Lincoln if she were to get cold feet, but he couldn't trust Lincoln to keep quiet.

"There's . . . something I'd like to show you," said Susannah.

Wolfgang looked up into her blue eyes and then dropped his chin slightly. "Show me? Where?"

"Inside," she said. "In my room."

"Susannah . . . I can't—"

"It's something I've been working on for a long time. Two years, in fact. I'd like you to see it."

"What is it?"

"It's kind of a surprise. Not a gift, but . . . it's something I'm proud of. You'll see. It's no big deal, really . . . " She grabbed his right forearm and urged him closer to the dormitory.

"I'm not supposed to be in there," he said. "I'm a man. It's late. Can't you bring it out here?"

"No." She let go of his arm, but he continued to follow her to the small three-stepped concrete porch that sat crooked in front of a wooden door. "Come on."

He'd never dealt with peer pressure very well. His instincts told him to run. He checked the woods to see if anyone was watching, now for different reasons than before.

"This is how rumors get started, Susannah."

"Come on," she said, amused by his comment. Or was it something else? "It'll only take a minute. And then you can get back home to your work."

She opened the door to a dimly lit lobby area that was just smaller than the rooms in the sanatorium. A couch and an end table covered the main wall to their right. The rest was just a passageway to the main hallway. A bookish nurse named Josephine looked up from whatever it was she was writing and nodded toward Wolfgang, who sheepishly nodded back and then kept his eyes on the nape of Susannah's neck.

What happened next was so sudden he didn't have time to cover his eyes. A door down the short hallway burst open and a cloud of steam misted out. An auburn-haired nurse stepped out into the hallway, giggling with a white towel over the mounds of her breasts. The flesh of her exposed shoulders was pink from the heat and steam, and still slightly wet by the glistening look of it. The bottom of the towel barely covered the opening between her thighs. A hand reached out of the steamy room, which Wolfgang would later realize was the shower room Lincoln had so often talked about, and playfully tugged the end of the nurse's towel. The nurse in the hallway giggled louder, slipped slightly on the wet tiled floor and in regaining her balance she braced her right hand against the hallway wall. The towel slipped, exposing her right breast. Wolfgang saw the bouncing weight of the breast and he felt like the dark nipple was staring right at him.

"Oh, God," he whispered, turning away in a hurry and heading back toward the front door. Nurse Josephine grinned but, otherwise, kept her eyes glued on her work.

"Wolf." Susannah hurried after him, catching him on the porch, struggling to contain her amusement.

"Did you set that up?" Wolfgang asked.

"No, of course not." She folded her arms. "Don't be silly."

Wolfgang managed a smile. He felt his face blushing. "I'd better be going. Another night maybe."

She smiled. "Okay."

"Good night, Susannah."

Susannah laughed as she closed the door, and then the laughter inside intensified. Weren't they having fun now? Wolfgang felt like a fool. They laughed because he was a priest, and priests shouldn't see such things. Which was silly in itself. He'd seen breasts before. The art world was full of naked women and bare breasts—paintings, murals, statues. It wasn't anything he hadn't seen before.

After all, he was once married for four years.

WOLFGANG MOVED AS briskly as his limp would allow down the rest of the hillside to his cottage and locked the front door behind him. His heart raced, partly from the walk but mostly from the peep show and the lingering images of Marlene's right breast. That was her name. It had come to him halfway down the hillside, not that it mattered. But it did matter. He couldn't get the lone nipple from his head, and the way the breast bounced from the confines of her towel. Lincoln had told him on several occasions about the shower room in the nurses' dormitory. He'd told him about the hole in the wall on the back of the building. It stood about seven feet off the ground and Lincoln needed to stand on a log to get eye level with it. But it was a half-inch in diameter, apparently made by some kind of sharp hand auger and big enough to get a good look at one of the shower stalls.

"Just make sure Nurse Beverly ain't the one naked," Lincoln had told Wolfgang, as if Wolfgang had any intention of sneaking over to the nurses' dormitory in the middle of the night to check and see if the hole was even there. "Marlene's the one you want to catch," Lincoln had said. Little did Lincoln know, Wolfgang had plenty of experience looking through peepholes. He'd spent his childhood looking through such a hole—spying, curious, frightened—and what he'd seen through that hole one night had changed the course of his adolescence. What he'd seen had tormented him for the rest of his confused childhood, the disturbing vision clinging to every waking nightmare he would have for the rest of his life. No, he was done with looking through peepholes. He didn't want to hear of any more peeping holes and naked women in showers.

Marlene's the one you want to catch . . .

Wolfgang moved from candle to sconce and back to candle, lighting the wicks until his cottage was aglow with flickering light. He lit the candle atop the piano, and then the one beside his bed. More light. That's what he needed. More light. He unbuttoned his lab coat and loosened his collar. He was physically spent, emotionally wired and hormonally confused, so he refused to go directly to bed, not without working for a while. That's where he would channel his thoughts—to Rose, as he did most every night until his job was complete. He pulled the black box from under the bed, removed the pages and put them atop the piano. He poured a glass of wine, swirled it repeatedly, the meniscus sloshing expertly to the rim of the glass but no more. He never spilled a drop. He let it breathe for a few minutes, swirling it, smelling it, and then he took a sip. He savored the warmth as it barreled down his throat and spread out through his stomach.

The window next to the piano had been repaired during the day. The new panes were still smudged with remnants of fresh putty but they appeared to be tightly in place and they fit well enough to keep the cold air out. They had the best handyman at Waverly, a man named Biven who'd retired from his hardware business of thirty years to become a volunteer in his free time. Like everyone, he took a chance by working at the sanatorium. The staff wasn't immune to the disease. The risks were high. They all knew it, and some became infected.

Wolfgang sipped his wine again and placed it on the piano bench. His right foot throbbed as it did near the end of every day, so he more or less dragged it across the room to the fireplace. There was no shame in dragging it while he was alone. A few more glasses of wine would help numb the pain, and then he would hardly care about anything. Next to the fireplace was his father's Edison phonograph. It was the Gem, the smallest of the Thomas Edison models. Beside it and stacked ten rows wide and six high was Wolfgang's canned music collection, some of which he'd taken from his father's collection when he'd left home and the rest he'd acquired over the years. The music ranged from Mozart to ragtime, from Beethoven and Bach to Gregorian chants his father had recorded at a monastery in the late 1890s. The cylinders were all protected and labeled in cardboard tubes. Wolfgang chose the Gregorian chants, popped the lid and removed the cylindrical record. He was careful not to touch the outside surface as he fit it inside the phonograph. He touched the stylus down on the grooves of the rotating cylinder and, moments later and fighting through the crackle of static, a burst of male baritone voices came forth from the arched amplifying horn.

At the piano he decided to warm his fingers with Beethoven, and within twenty minutes his creative juices began to flow. The wine had begun to enter his brain cells. Marlene's right breast and staring nipple were slowly fading into the folds of his memory. He dipped his quill into the inkwell and scribbled a few notes, tested the sound with a few keys and then scribbled some more.

Thirty minutes later, Wolfgang sat with his elbows propped on the keyboard, his hands spread out, fingers interlocked and holding his drooping head. Between his spread fingers he could see the half dozen pages he'd crumpled into balls and tossed on the floor minutes ago. It just wasn't right. He feared he would never finish. Four years and he'd yet to complete a simple requiem Mass. Except it wasn't so simple. The requiem had to be perfect. Rose's memory demanded that it be just right, and he wouldn't stop until he could make it so. If nothing else in life, he was driven. His mother told him at age eight that he'd never walk again and he did. His father was convinced that he'd never learn the piano and he did. His mother said he'd never become a doctor. He'd never amount to anything without knowing and following *The King James Bible*, memorizing and writing its every word.

Wolfgang let his fingers roam over a few keys and then stopped.

He couldn't concentrate. The rose atop his piano was wilting, the petals no longer bright red and flowering. Instead they'd become darkened to rust, hardened and crisp and a few of the petals had fallen to the piano top. He blew the loose petals to the floor, stood from the bench and limped across to the front door. He grabbed a candlestick, lit the candle inside of it and stepped outside where the cool temperatures made his arm hair stand on end. On the edge of the porch was a pair of scissors. He grabbed them and navigated with his candlestick around the corner of his cottage, where the hard ground undulated down to soft deadfall. Behind the cottage was a concrete birdbath full of dirty, leaf-filled water. Wolfgang balanced the candlestick in the grass and knelt beside the birdbath, where he immediately felt the warmth of the heat lamps. Spread out before him on the ground in the embrace of the candlelight was a ten-by-six-foot rose garden. Dozens of red roses stood before him, protected from the cold by heat lamps and metal mirrors that reflected the sun's rays. Lincoln had put the contraption together, borrowing everything from the sanatorium without Doctor Barker's knowing. Wolfgang had not believed it would work. Roses would not continue to grow in the winter. But Lincoln had been adamant about trying and Wolfgang was glad that he had. Turned out Lincoln had a green thumb. More than that, Wolfgang was convinced that the roses were growing on will power alone. Or were they possibly little miracles? He had blessed the garden the day it had been planted. He had scattered some of her ashes behind the cottage.

Wolfgang perused the choices and found the one he wanted in the middle of the leafy patch. The sturdy stem was upright and scattered with thorns and tiny green leaves. He clipped it, lifted the candlestick from the grass and returned back inside. He removed the wilted rose from the vase, replaced the old water with fresh new water from the kitchen sink and then sank the new rose's stem into it. He swirled it, as was his habit, and then placed it back on top of the piano. He felt better now.

He worked for another hour before his eyelids grew heavy. He turned off the phonograph, finished his third glass of wine and blew out all the candles. A pleasant tipsiness made his walk to his bed unsteady. He found his side of the bed and rested his head on the pillow. He said a prayer for the patients. He prayed for McVain. He was eager to face him tomorrow. He nestled into the covers, pulled them up above his chest and closed his eyes.

THIRTY MINUTES PASSED and Wolfgang found himself staring at the ceiling, listening to the night, his eyes way too adjusted to the dark. He reverted to what he always did when he couldn't sleep. In his mind he talked to Rose. He asked her questions. He laughed about their memories. He opened all his thoughts to her. He wondered where she was and if she could even hear him.

Rose never answered back.

7

THE INDIAN SUMMER returned the next day. The empty feeling Wolfgang had during the night vanished with the rising of the sun in the morning. His mood improved even more with his walk up the hillside, where Wolfgang and Susannah were again confronted by an escaped pig. The muddy animal tagged along with them, snorting its porcine commentary on the state of the world, until Susannah cocked her arm as if to hit it with her purse and it scurried back into the woods. Nothing was said about the incident last night with Marlene. Susannah had arrived at Wolfgang's cottage with a grin on her face, which he returned with a glance and smirk as he locked his door, and the awkwardness lasted no longer than that. Wolfgang hoped he didn't run into Marlene during the day. If he did, he promised himself he would keep his eye contact well above her neck and he'd act as if nothing had happened.

The warmth followed them inside to the Grand Lobby where swaths of sunlight hit the shiny floor. Motes of dust particles swam in the light. The Grand Lobby was located at the corner of the sanatorium where the east and west wings joined on the first floor. Roman-style columns stood like centurions throughout the space, crowned with carved swirls and geometric shapes that matched the deep, reddish-brown woodwork, warming its grandeur with a feeling of home.

Susannah veered off toward the east wing while Wolfgang headed toward the north wing looking for Lincoln, who, no doubt, was buried in the body chute or the morgue tagging bodies. Wolfgang pushed through a set of doors into the north wing and ducked his head into the morgue, which reeked of metal, blood and an overdose of some cleansing solution. The floors had recently been washed. Dead bodies lay under blue sheets on all six tables. The three trays on the far side of the room were occupied as well. The corpse on the middle tray had long red hair that reminded Wolfgang of his mother. Curls of it fell from the end of the tray, the tips scraping the wet surface of the floor. No Lincoln. Wolfgang checked the freezer room next. It was a cold storage for their dairy, meat, vegetables and fruits—and it probably wasn't too far away from being used as cadaver storage if the death rate didn't slow.

Wolfgang continued down the hallway and through a pair of metal doors. The large roll-up gate that led directly to the body chute was open. Amidst the darkness and cobwebs he heard footsteps and then a clanking noise. He stepped into the tunnel and spotted Lincoln kneeling down beside a coffin.

"There you are."

Lincoln, his face half concealed by shadows, looked up from his kneeling position on the floor. "Peeping Tom." His voice echoed in the cool, dank air. "You sly devil. Marlene, huh?"

Wolfgang ignored him. He shuffled fully into the tunnel and squatted down to help Lincoln position the wooden coffin on the pulley system to the right side of the chute. "Did Mr. Jenkins make it through the night?"

Lincoln stood, knees popping, and tapped the top of the coffin.

On the left side of the tunnel, a set of elongated platform stairs ran alongside the winch system that gradually lowered the coffins downward. Wolfgang took a step down and stood beside the coffin, careful not to look Lincoln in the eyes and invite a deeper discussion of the Marlene incident. The tunnel was initially used to carry supplies in and out of the sanatorium and it came in especially handy during the winter. Wolfgang peered downward but could only see so far before complete darkness filled the chute. There was no electricity. The only light came from the airshafts that had been spaced in the ceiling every hundred feet or so.

Lincoln gave him a hand with the top of the coffin. It creaked, then snapped when they opened it. Splinters of wood dropped to the concrete floor. Mr. Jenkins rested peacefully inside, his blood drained from his body. His eyes were closed, his face drooped and waxy, his hair neatly combed for the trip downward. Wolfgang gave Lincoln a quick look of admiration. Under the kid's rambunctious nature was a huge heart. Only Wolfgang knew that Lincoln combed the hair of the victims before their descent down the chute. What they did to the dead in the rooms was a quick and hasty once-over to keep the living from seeing the recently deceased. Lincoln went beyond that. He took his time, male or female.

Wolfgang had seen him in the morgue a few months ago. It was the beginning of October. The sun was shining and the summer temperatures still lingered. Wolfgang stopped at the doorway when he sensed that Lincoln was crying. Maybe not crying, but sniffling. He was working on a male patient he'd befriended at the beginning of the summer. Wolfgang saw the black comb in Lincoln's hand, and how carefully his young assistant was dividing the part on the left side of the dead man's hair. Wolfgang left him alone, saving his question for the afternoon. He knew Lincoln well enough to know that any interruption would have embarrassed him. Any word to the others about him combing their hair would have probably stopped him from doing it in the future. Lincoln was the type that didn't want anyone else to know that he had a heart. He wanted to be known as tough and unflappable. So Wolfgang kept the secret to himself.

Wolfgang stared down at Mr. Jenkins and the harmonica that

still rested inside the clawed grip of his left hand. "He died with a smile on his face."

"I found him this morning," said Lincoln. "Couldn't pry it from his grip."

Wolfgang let out a small breath and touched the side of the coffin. "Play for the rest of 'em, Mr. Jenkins." They closed the lid and stood silent for a moment. Wolfgang traced the sign of the cross over the top and whispered a quick prayer. "Did you find a bundle of letters in his room?" Wolfgang asked. "I promised I'd get them to his daughter."

"His stuff's in a locker. Barker wanted his room cleaned out right away. Someone else is already moving in."

Would the death ever end?

AFTER HIS MORNING rounds, Wolfgang met the farm boy Jesse Jacobs in the chapel to go over how to make communion bread. Jesse seemed eager to learn, although all Wolfgang would let him do was watch. He couldn't allow a TB patient to handle bread that would at some point make it into the mouths of other TB patients. So Jesse watched from a safe distance with a goofy smile on his face. Wolfgang worked quickly because he was preoccupied by his thoughts of McVain. He was determined to get the man to explain why he played an imaginary piano at night. So when Wolfgang showed Jesse each step of the process he did so with haste. How to warm the honey and mix it into the dry ingredients. He explained how long to bake it, how to cut a cross into it, how many pieces to break it into and how to refrigerate some and store the rest in the freezer. How to take his time and not rush. And how to do it all with a pleasant smile because the Lord would be watching him prepare the very bread that was going to be consecrated into the Body of Christ. Once they were done, Wolfgang left Jesse to clean up the mess, which he began to do with the same goofy smile he'd had before they'd started. God love 'em, Wolfgang had thought, as he'd hurried up to the fourth floor solarium to find McVain resting with his eyes open.

Wolfgang would not leave without something. Maybe poke and prod until he was forced to respond and prove he wasn't a vegetable. So far he hadn't taken the bait. His head hadn't moved from the pillow in the twenty minutes Wolfgang had been there. He simply stared toward the woods from his isolated spot on the fourth floor solarium.

Wolfgang sat by his side, gazing out at those same trees, as if having the same focal point would help him tap into McVain's thoughts. Ten minutes of meaningless questions, which turned out to be a droning monologue about his Edison records and the new blue cylinders that held four minutes instead of two, had left McVain on the verge of sleep. Or maybe it was nausea.

Wolfgang waited until McVain's eyes were nearly closed.

"You used to play the piano, didn't you?"

McVain flinched slightly. He attempted to hide his mangled left hand beneath the sheets. He closed his eyes.

"My father played the piano." Wolfgang watched him for a reaction. "He loved Mozart. Maybe we should start over." Wolfgang laughed. "No mud to push me into this time." When he saw no amusement on McVain's face he plowed on. "My name is Wolfgang Pike. I'm a doctor and priest here at Waverly."

McVain opened his eyes. He coughed and then spat phlegm into a bucket beside his bed. Wolfgang could tell by the flat sound of the plop that the bucket needed to be changed. McVain resumed his gaze out toward the trees.

"I saw your fingers last night." Wolfgang shifted on his seat and leaned forward with his elbows on his knees. "They moved as if you were playing the piano."

McVain clenched his jaw.

"I know I shouldn't have been prying, but . . . look, I consider myself a composer. I'm working on a requiem." Wolfgang folded his hands. "It started out as a simple Catholic funeral Mass, but I've begun to expand it and make it grander. It'll be a concert requiem. I have a full orchestra with piano in mind. And wonderful singers." He leaned back and straightened his lab coat. McVain's eyes never wavered from the woods. "I could use your opinion, Mr. McVain. I've come into a bit of trouble, you see, and I can't seem to finish it with an ending it deserves. It all ends up in my garbage can. Would you like to see it?"

McVain caught him totally off guard. Wolfgang had never been in a physical altercation in his life and was slow to react. McVain's fist struck Wolfgang across the right side of his jaw. Wolfgang rocked back and his chair toppled. He landed on his side and rolled to his knees, feeling for missing teeth. They all seemed to be in place but his jaw felt numb. Several patients leaned up from their beds but were apparently too shocked to say anything. They stared and gawked. McVain grinned and looked out toward the trees again.

Wolfgang wiped his mouth with the top of his hand and it came back with a smear of blood on it. "So you *can* smile." McVain said nothing. "TB hasn't ruined that, you stubborn mule." Wolfgang backed away. "Stay angry at the world, but not at me. I didn't cut your fingers off."

A possum-eatin' grin spread across McVain's face. He was proud of what he'd done. Wolfgang waited, turned and left McVain alone, touching his sore jaw as he hobbled away.

Wolfgang waited until most of the patients were asleep and Doctor Barker had walked the trail to his cottage. His jaw was slightly swollen and bruised on the right side. The cut on his lower lip had formed a healthy scab that felt twice as big as Susannah said it really was. He would not be deterred tonight.

Susannah followed him into McVain's dark room, where the

cantankerous man snored like a hibernating bear. "I don't know about this, Wolf."

Wolfgang put a finger to his lips and then winced upon the touch. He stopped a few feet from McVain's parked bed. Luckily, Mr. Weaver was sleeping out on the porch, so they'd have plenty of room to maneuver. He still wasn't sure if Susannah was a willing partner or not, but she remained by his side.

"Barker will fire us," she whispered.

"He'll fire me." Wolfgang winked. "I made you help me, okay?"

Susannah rolled her eyes and mumbled under her breath. "You don't *make* me do anything, Wolfgang Pike."

"Why don't you ever call me Father?" He said it without looking at her.

She brushed past him and headed toward the foot of McVain's bed. "Let's get this over with."

Wolfgang rolled a wheelchair next to McVain's bed. Weaver had told him that McVain was a solid sleeper. Several times, Weaver had told them, he'd made noises during the night, like coughing, clapping his hands and even yodeling to try to wake McVain but nothing had worked. Wolfgang snaked his left arm under McVain's neck and locked his hand beneath McVain's left armpit. McVain grunted but didn't awaken. Wolfgang did a silent count to three and nodded. He lifted McVain's torso while Susannah lifted his feet, and McVain continued snoring as they lowered him, as gently as they could, into the leather seat of the wheelchair. Suddenly McVain snorted awake, but a few seconds of disorientation gave them plenty of time to tie his arms to the chair and then strap his legs. Before he was alert enough to tell it wasn't a nightmare and his doctor and nurse were indeed tying him to a wheelchair with rather coarse pieces of rope, it was too late.

"What . . . what the shit is this?"

"He speaks," said Susannah, seemingly upbeat now that they'd gotten him locked in the chair.

"Quiet," Wolfgang said.

McVain wrestled against the makeshift restraints, grimaced, and then allowed his body to settle. He was too weak and tired to fight and the ropes burned his arms.

Wolfgang rolled McVain from the room and out onto the crowded solarium porch, where Mr. Weaver lay asleep with one arm dangling off the side of the bed. Susannah draped a shawl over McVain's shoulders, covering the restraints, so that if anyone were to see them they'd think nothing of it.

"Where in the hell are you taking me?"

"I can gag you if you like." Wolfgang plodded along, his foot hurting more the faster he moved, weaving behind and around the scattered beds, hoping that no one called out for him. No confessions tonight. They made it to the elevators and down to the first floor without anyone seeing them. It wasn't as if Waverly was a prison, but Doctor Barker had made it clear that they weren't supposed to leave the hillside, and that went double for the patients. Tuberculosis was a highly contagious monster that had plagued humanity for centuries. There was no cure. He wouldn't take McVain off the hillside. It was just a little trip. Wolfgang's heart pounded as the wheels of the chair sped over the checkered tiles in the center of the hallway. He hadn't done anything this mischievous in years. The adrenaline brought a smile to his face. He dared Doctor Barker to show up now and open the doors to the portico just as they were leaving. He imagined the confrontation. He imagined knocking him aside and continuing on.

Susannah held the doors open and the coast was clear outside. Wolfgang didn't break stride outside as the wheels went from tile, down a level to concrete and then finally to grass. Moonlight lit the clearing. An owl hooted from a nearby tree. Bats circled the bell tower, flying in a frenzy equaled only by the madness inside Wolfgang's head. Crossing the grassy knoll that rolled down toward the woods was a bumpy ride for McVain. His neck lolled. He grunted every time the wheelchair plummeted down from an exposed root. He moaned when the wheels slammed into and up every incline, and it only got bumpier in the woods, with the uneven ground of brambles, twigs, leaves, acorns and deadfall. Susannah jumped ahead to kick away a few branches that had fallen across the trail. Wolfgang pushed as quickly as he could, using the momentum of the downhill, knowing that if he slowed his pace he might not be able to muster enough strength to get the wheelchair moving again. McVain was heavy, probably 220 pounds or more.

Susannah caught up to them and straightened the shawl around McVain's shoulders. "I can't believe I'm doing this."

"Where the shit are you taking me?"

"It was her idea," said Wolfgang.

Susannah slapped Wolfgang's shoulder. "Don't believe him."

McVain surveyed the trees and the darkness beyond. "You should be fired for this."

McVain was stronger than Wolfgang had thought. From the lingering pain in Wolfgang's jaw and the spasms that shot up his cheek every time the wheelchair caused a jarring movement, he didn't know why he'd doubted McVain's strength. McVain had managed to wiggle his left arm free from the chair. He flung the shawl from his shoulders. "Wherever the hell I'm going, I can walk there. Untie me, God damn it."

After a short hesitation, Wolfgang untied McVain's right arm. McVain nudged him away before he had a chance to untie his ankles. McVain bent strenuously at the waist and worked on the ankle ropes. His fingers moved effortlessly, as if he'd escaped from restraints many times before. "So what happened to your leg?"

Wolfgang watched the top of McVain's head move. He finished with the ropes and then shot Wolfgang a glance. "Well?"

"Well what?"

"What happened to your leg?" asked McVain. "You walk like a three-legged mule."

"Polio," Wolfgang said. "When I was eight . . . I was stricken with polio."

McVain didn't seem to care. He stood from the wheelchair, stumbled as if drunk, which caused a tiny squeal of panic from Susannah, and then righted himself against the trunk of an oak tree. He straightened his pajamas and ran his left hand through his orange hair. Wolfgang thought it funny that he'd used the hand with the missing fingers for such a duty.

"What's so funny?" asked McVain, doing it again.

"Must be like raking leaves with a pitchfork."

"What the hell are you talking about?" McVain looked up the hillside. The rooftop and bell tower of the sanatorium were visible between the swaying tree limbs. "Never thought I'd get kidnapped from a TB hospital in the middle of the night."

Susannah walked by his side, but not too close. "Consider it a field trip."

McVain gave Susannah an angry sneer. "Do I scare you, doll face?"

"It's Susannah, and no, you don't scare me, Mr. McVain."

Wolfgang pushed the empty wheelchair and McVain and Susannah followed. McVain kicked various rocks down the hill like a kid would probably do, and he walked with his hands in the pockets of his pajamas. He looked up when they neared Wolfgang's cottage. The lone window on the side of the house glowed with a fiery warmth not found in the hospital.

Wolfgang extended his arm. "Shall we go inside?"

McVain grunted. Susannah gripped his elbow and walked him inside. McVain didn't pull away from her touch. By the time they entered Wolfgang had already lit several more candles to go along with the snapping flames in the fireplace. It was warm and the windows were steamed.

"No electricity?" asked McVain.

Wolfgang lit a candle above the fireplace and caught a glimpse of

Susannah's right wrist, which had a purple ring around it. "Where'd you get the bruise?"

Susannah looked at Wolfgang. "Where did you get yours?"

Wolfgang touched his jaw and nodded toward McVain, who now wore a smirk on his face. "You're dodging my question. Your bruise?"

Susannah pulled her sleeve down to cover it. "It's nothing."

"It doesn't look like nothing."

"It happened this morning." She shook her head. "I was up on the rooftop. Something spooked Herman. I tried to calm him and he grabbed me. No big deal."

"Who's Herman?" McVain asked.

By "up on the rooftop" she was referring to the handful of rooms on the fifth floor used for the mentally ill. Susannah and Nurse Rita had the unfortunate job of tending to them daily and Wolfgang feared for their safety up there. So now he would worry even more. Herman was a loose cannon inside Room 502. Susannah was brave and she could hold her own with most men, but Herman was twice her size and slightly crazy.

"Was this the first time he touched you?"

"Who the hell is Herman?" McVain asked again.

"I'll be fine." She walked McVain deeper into the room and stood beside him in the center of Wolfgang's dwelling area—piano to the east, bed to the south, couch and fireplace to the west and kitchen to the north. She turned toward McVain. "He prefers candlelight to electricity. Which is probably why his eyesight is going bad. But it's all part of the nostalgia. Right, Wolf?"

"All part of the freak show," said McVain. "I half expect to hear some Gregorian chant coming from the dark corners of this cave."

"He told you about his cylinder collection?" asked Susannah.

"Nearly fell asleep." McVain finally pulled from Susannah's grip. "What am I doing here? I want to go back."

"And do what, McVain?" Wolfgang asked. "Sleep? Rest like

you've been doing for the past month? Go back to being a mute?" Wolfgang could tell he'd seen the piano but was purposely avoiding it. Wolfgang placed a candle on top of it, highlighting the rose beside it.

"This some kind of joke?" asked McVain.

"Therapy," said Susannah. "Therapy we think will do you more good than rest and fresh air."

Wolfgang held up a finger. "A happy McVain would do the entire hospital a favor."

"Breeze off, priest." McVain turned away from the piano and headed for the door.

Susannah blocked his path and stood rigid with her arms folded under her breasts. The quiver in her voice showed a slight fear but she didn't budge. "Please stay."

McVain clenched his jaw. "I hate both of you. You know that?"

"We can discuss your anger in confession," Wolfgang said. "But don't hate the music. Don't hate what you were."

"What . . . a criminal?"

Wolfgang propped a few sheets of music on the piano, sat down and began playing a Mozart piano sonata. He stopped and glanced over his shoulder at McVain, who looked sad and angry at the same time. His red hair was aflame in the candlelight, his deep-set green eyes rested in pockets of darkness. Wolfgang arose from the piano, urging McVain on with his eyes.

Slowly, McVain walked through patches of shadow and light, as if fighting a vice or a craving or an addiction he'd battled for years, approaching with small, shuffled steps—a prisoner finally set free and afraid to make a run for the light. Wolfgang watched him sit and wondered how long McVain had repressed the addiction. McVain coughed into his right fist, straightened his back and stretched his fingers. He touched a low key with the pinkie on his left hand. He waited until the sound faded and then struck another key with his left thumb. Again, he waited until the sound faded. He looked at the music and began to play. He hit a few clunkers and stopped after several more seconds of unsatisfactory playing. "Needs tuning," he said.

"Keep going," Susannah said.

"I'm missing three of my fucking fingers, Miss Susannah." McVain continued to face the piano. His shoulders relaxed. His tone softened. "I just can't hit the right keys."

Wolfgang stepped into the nimbus of light that shrouded the piano. "Then the remaining two fingers will have to work that much harder." Wolfgang had heard a glimpse of McVain's capabilities and what he'd heard only made him more persistent. "Please . . . keep playing."

McVain focused on the piano again. He played for ten seconds, messed up. He played again. The fingers on his right hand had begun to flow like oil over the black and white keys, gentle yet demanding, and he milked every note and tone for all it was worth. But his left hand lumbered along, stiff and plodding, his wrist at the wrong angle and way too tight. Wolfgang would have been hit atop the hand by his father's violin bow for such technique, but he could empathize with McVain's difficulty. Just as Wolfgang had learned to walk again, McVain would learn to play again, perhaps not in the same way but . . . he would learn to adapt. Wolfgang was sure of it. Everyone evolves when they have to.

Wolfgang tapped the sheet music. "Mozart's piano sonata in C minor."

"I know what it is." McVain pushed the music to the floor. "I don't need these. They called me a prodigy . . . " After another hesitation he faced the keys again, the determination evident in the glare in his eyes. His hands hovered above the keys at the center of the piano. First the right one dropped softly to the keys, then the left. He played for a good minute before his left hand lost pace again. He stared silently at the keys. His shoulders moved as if he were crying.

"Try to make the adjustment," said Wolfgang.

McVain raised both hands and brought them down as fists against the keys, hard. "How's that? Huh?" He banged his fists against the keys again and again, looking over his shoulder like a lunatic, his anger focused on Wolfgang. "How's this adjustment?" Bang. Bang. The shrill sound of the keys was painful to hear. Bang. Bang. Bang. And then slowly, like an ocean tide receding from the shore, he drew his arms in. He wiped his eyes, stood from the bench and faced his two kidnappers. He stood stoically with his hands by his sides as if ready to take a grand bow at any moment. "I'm ready to go back now."

"But—" Susannah started.

"I'm ready to go back!"

"Yes . . . of course." Wolfgang's arms were trembling. Blood coursed beneath his skin. "But if I may ask . . . how long has it been since you've played?"

McVain looked to the floor. "Since the war."

Wolfgang stared at McVain's left hand as he walked to the front door, which Susannah had already opened for him. Since the war? McVain hadn't touched a piano for more than ten years. Wolfgang hoped that, eventually, he would learn why.

8

WOLFGANG HAD FILLED the bathtub so full even the slightest movement sent water trickling over the lip and onto the bathroom floor. He rested the back of his head on the edge of the tub and placed his arms on the sides, doing his best to stay still and relaxed as the water sloshed over his body. A sliver of moonlight had found its way through the trees outside and into the bathroom, highlighting the foot of the tub, where the toes of his left foot protruded just out of the water. His right foot he kept hidden, even to himself. Only one person in the world had found that foot beautiful and she was dead now. Other than the moonlight, the bathroom was dark and quiet. Outside, the wind rustled loose leaves. A skunk had apparently sprayed an enemy somewhere close and the cottage's thin walls did little to keep out the stench. At least it would keep him awake while he soaked.

He stared down the length of the tub, over the surface of the water, thinking about McVain. Tonight he had opened the door. Tomorrow he would force his way through. Wolfgang closed his eyes as the bath water lapped around his neck and wetted the back of his hair. His thoughts turned to his childhood. He wondered what his mother was doing? Was she even alive? He hadn't seen her in so many years. Did she even regret the way they had parted? They'd fought so often after his father had died, neither trusting the other for unspoken reasons. There was a time when she'd been his security blanket. She was the parent that would hug him when he was scared, hold his hand when he was nervous, tell him stories at night when he couldn't fall asleep, and wash his wounds and kiss his bruises given to him by his father. Wolfgang truly believed she healed them with her kisses. One brush of her lips against any bruise would immediately start the healing process.

Wolfgang's first vivid memory of his childhood was a bath he'd taken after his father had bloodied his nose. He'd accidentally knocked Charles Pike's latest fugue from the Llewellyn piano, scattering the pages to the floor and completely out of order. That he didn't remember. His memory started from the bath. He was five years old and sitting naked in a tub of tepid water, shivering, his teeth chattering. He sat with his legs drawn in and his knees upright, his lowered chin resting on the bony plate of his right knee. He stared below at his penis as it buoyed in the water, not wanting to look anywhere else but down. He remembered having to pee but he didn't want to get out of the tub. The drip of blood from his nose hit the water in red swirls before spreading out between his thighs.

His mother, Doris, hovered above, washing him, leaning so far over the side of the tub that the tips of her long red hair grazed the water. Her red nightgown hung loosely from her body. The breasts he'd suckled for the first twelve months of his life drooped inches from his face, hanging in the shadowed folds of that nightgown he'd become so accustomed to smelling every morning when she'd hug him. He listened as his mother plunged the washrag into the bath water. She squeezed it and wet his hair, rinsing it free of suds. She lathered the washrag with a bar of white soap and washed his back, where there were no bruises. The water trickled down his spine and dripped into the water that rose just above his hips. His mother hummed one of her made-up tunes that calmed them both after one of his father's tirades, but she didn't speak about what had happened. She never discussed fault. She never questioned her husband's drinking, his mood swings and his ability to love one minute and become brutal the next. She never spoke about their bruises. She never blamed anyone, and eventually the bruises went away. Wolfgang was too ashamed to look up into his mother's brown eyes. He was sure she'd be smiling. But behind the smile he'd known there was sadness. Even at age five, he'd known.

WOLFGANG HAD GROWN up in a small Tudor-style home on the outskirts of Central Park. It was a two-story structure with stucco siding, a steeply pitched roof, decorative half-timbering, cross gables and an arched wooden door that made it look like a medieval cottage. It had small dormer windows and a prominent brick chimney that rose just above the highest point of the roof. Because of the sloping uneven rooftop, the two upstairs bedrooms were small, irregularly shaped, and the ceilings were set at severe angles, making the positioning of the beds and dressers a chore. Wood dominated the interior of the house. Old wood floors throughout both levels—floors with whorls, splintered planks and tiny holes and cracks throughout, most of which Doris had covered with various throw rugs. The wall separating Wolfgang's bedroom from his parents' room was wood as well.

Every sound and smell carried throughout the house—the smell of bacon frying in the morning, the smell of potato soup in the evening, the sound of his parents having sex on the other side of that flimsy wooden wall, and most certainly the sound of his father's hypnotic music. The sound of the Bach and Beethoven fugues he'd play on one of his eight violins. The smells and sounds Wolfgang remembered distinctly. But the two constants early in his life were music and his mother's dependable love.

Doris Pike was a pretty woman, slight of build and twenty years of age when she'd given birth to her only son in the summer of 1900. She was gentle but tough—tough enough to take the beatings without shedding a tear. Tough enough to cook and clean despite the pain of *her* hidden bruises. Wolfgang had hoped to one day acquire her toughness. He'd rarely even seen her cry.

Wolfgang knew she concealed bruises beneath her clothing. He knew his father beat her as well, mostly behind the closed doors of their bedroom. Wolfgang would watch through the hole in his bedroom wall. He'd watched his father slap her with the back of his hand after he'd had too much gin or wine. He'd never forget the look of malevolence that would mask his father's eyes and the quiver in his chin just before he'd strike like a snakebite, quick and potent. He'd watched his father tug on her skinny arms. She'd whimper in resistance and never hit back. She'd cower to his harsh words when they'd argue about their "business" or their "work" at the "factory" and sometimes Doris would verbally fight back. The verbal attack usually led to him striking her again, harder. On some nights Doris would sit on the bed alone with no shirt on, looking over her body, twisting her arms and arching her shoulders to count the bruises she would have to hide by morning.

But not all nights were made of anger. Wolfgang watched them every night from his bed. He'd lie on his stomach, prop his elbows atop his pillow, close one eye and peer through the hole in the wall. He was aware of the beating he would receive if his father ever found out he'd been spying, but he couldn't help himself. It was part of the thrill, the fun . . . the danger. His sanity required that he know the reason for the sounds. He became addicted to watching. Some nights Wolfgang watched his father lovingly hold his mother as they danced along the limited floor space of their bedroom—from the bed to the dresser, from the dresser to the bathroom door and then back to the bed—moving to a rhythm Charles would hum, smiling as he'd clutch her small hands and hold her close. Wolfgang remembered the sound of their feet shuffling across the dusty floorboards. Charles Pike was tall with a thick chest, strong forearms and a head of long black hair, always worn pulled back from his forehead. He had large droopy ears like an elephant. His eyes were brown and magnified by the dark bushy eyebrows that hung long and wild above them. Charles was always dressed in a suit of some sort, morning, day and night, changing only before bedtime. Otherwise he had on his trousers and coat, his cravat and polished shoes, his vest or suspenders so as to always look important and bigger than life. When they danced, Doris came up to his chest. Often Charles would rest his head atop her head, as they'd dance across the floor. Some nights they would laugh. His father would tickle his mother on the bed and they'd end up with their clothes off. Wolfgang would look away when they'd begin fondling each other and kissing each other in bad places. He'd clasp his hands over his ears until the grunting ceased and the sound of the bed springs settled. Every night, despite the events—whether made of anger or love—his father would kiss his mother on the lips, tell her he loved her and promise her they'd move to Vienna and live in luxury. It was only a matter of time, he'd tell her. Soon they would have enough saved. Only then could Wolfgang fall asleep.

CHARLES PIKE WAS a talented musician and composer, but never quite good enough at either to make an honest living doing what he truly loved. And that, Wolfgang had come to learn, had been the root of his anger. He was a man with brilliant ideas. The music in his mind rivaled Mozart and Beethoven, but there the brilliance stayed, buried and locked up forever. He'd become the most frustrated when he composed because it wouldn't come out the way it sounded in his head. He'd drink more, and the more he drank the more paranoid he seemed to get. The curtains that covered their downstairs windows were always closed, but Charles would peek out numerous times a night. At least twice every hour he'd walk away from his writing, push the curtain aside and watch the dark street, as if waiting for something or someone to come after him. The constant paranoia had sparked a line of questioning from Wolfgang by age seven.

"Dad, why do you always look out the windows at night?"

"Is someone coming over?"

"What do you and mommy do at the factory?"

"Why does mommy sometimes leave at night?"

He'd always give the same vague answers, quickly changing the subject or placing the Bible in his hands and telling him to read, or pushing him toward the instruments and telling him to practice. His mother was equally obtuse. In other words, it was none of his business.

"We make things at the factory, Wolf. That's all you need to know."

AT NIGHT, BEFORE his father would come to their bedroom and after his mother had read to him from the King James Bible, Wolfgang would get down on the floor of his own bedroom. On his hands and knees, he'd pull back the gray woven throw rug and peer through the cracks in the planks. The living room was directly below. It was his father's work area. Musical instruments were scattered everywhere, strewn about like discarded clothing— a piano against one wall, his eight violins sitting like little children across the cushions of the couch, two cellos propped against another wall, a trombone resting on the seat of a straight-backed reading chair, two clarinets and three flutes in the middle of the floor, and a piccolo atop the piano next to three lit candles and his well of ink. Atop his podium sat his latest symphony or fugue, his latest opera or requiem, all weighted down by a harmonica he'd play when all else failed. From the crack in the floor Wolfgang would spy on his father. He'd watch him dip the quill of his pen into the ink and carefully scrawl artistic notes on the page, his eyes wild in the candlelight. He'd write and stop abruptly, and then place the pen sideways between his teeth and lift one of his violins to play what he'd just composed. Wolfgang would watch him rant and rave, waving the bow of his violin around like a sword at imaginary attackers, frustrated, happy, or drunk. He'd shuffle around the cluttered floor, violently pulling and pushing the bow at every conceivable angle against the taut violin strings, sweating profusely, strands of hair coming undone from his hair clip and dangling over his unblinking and unfazed eyes, his face red with strain. The face of a crazed man, Wolfgang had thought. But that was also why he'd loved his father, because of the passion. Despite the bruises and the beatings, his father had given him music, and music moved his soul.

Wolfgang loved the feeling as well as the sound, the vibrations of the string instruments as they'd hum through the floor like current. The sound of the piano keys under his father's delicate fingertips, flowing like honey. The sound of the clarinet as it reverberated off every nook of the house. Wolfgang had fallen in love with it all at a very early age. The music consumed him. He liked baseball, but he couldn't live without the music. Charles refused to allow him to play baseball. Instead, Wolfgang spent his time indoors reading the Bible and learning how to play all the instruments. Wolfgang understood that the same passion that caused the bruises also caused the happiness in his heart. Without the music he would have been lost. Charles Pike was a flawed man but he'd given his son the best gift he could have given him. His time. Every day when he'd return from the factory he'd sit down with Wolfgang and the lessons would begin. That's when being close to his father wasn't painful, unless he'd hit the wrong key on the piano or strike the wrong string on the violin and Charles would slap the bow across his knuckles. But that was the acceptable type of pain. In those moments, Wolfgang understood how he both loved and hated his father.

So when Wolfgang would watch his father from the crack in the floor, he'd watch in awe. He'd observe with a warm heart and a feeling that bordered between nervousness and euphoria. He'd completely open his ears and mind and let the music replace all his fear and uncertainty.

Music had become Wolfgang's life. That was their bond. And then a few weeks before Wolfgang's eighth birthday, Charles Pike was murdered. Wolfgang had seen it all through the hole in his bedroom wall.

9

WOLFGANG SLEPT THROUGH the night. No nightmare of being suffocated ever arrived. His body was exhausted from wheeling McVain out of the sanatorium and down the hillside. His muscles were sore from the anxiety of pulling the plan off without being caught. His body was relaxed from the soaking bath he'd taken after he'd returned McVain to his fourth floor room. His mind was weary from churning up memories of his childhood, thought to be long buried.

His eyes didn't open until after the sun rose over the trees, and when he did open them it was to the sound of music, partially coming from his mind and partially coming from somewhere yet to be determined. What he first took to be birds sounded more and more like the sound of . . . a flute. It wasn't birds at all. It sounded like a flute. Wolfgang tossed the covers aside and swung his feet from the sheets. He felt the erection before he saw it. He reluctantly looked down and saw the crotch of his pajamas sticking out like a tent and immediately wondered from what kind of dream had the flute music lured him. For four years he'd been able to flip the switch and completely free his mind from any hint of his sexuality. With Rose dead, he'd been determined to focus on the Lord and helping people with his skills as a doctor and a priest. He'd become numb to the female body over that period of time.

He learned to squash any urges early on by working on his music, reading about the history of Catholicism, or drinking. Had one very brief look at an exposed breast undone it all? No, his mind cried. So why did his mind keep coming back to the hole Lincoln had told him about in the women's shower? A part of him, a deeply buried voyeuristic craving, wanted badly to check for himself, just as he'd watched his parents every night as a child. The addiction had returned. To step up on the log outside the nurses' dormitory, close one eye and peer through the hole with the other. Wolfgang forced himself from the bed and thought about birds, food, music, God—anything but a nude female.

He rubbed his eyes and blinked the heaviness from his lids. The flute music continued. He slipped on his bathrobe and tied it on his way to the door, where he was greeted with a cold burst of air. The Indian summer had come and gone, replaced instead by the frigid winter. The bright sun was only a tease, providing little more than a slight warmth on the skin. Swirls of white clouds floated quickly over the treetops. The flute music was louder and clearer.

Where was it coming from? Whoever was playing had talent, he thought. He surveyed the woods and eyed a cluster of squirrels as they sprinted down the hill, falling over each other and crisscrossing seamlessly around the trees.

Susannah came walking around the corner wearing a long brown coat over her white uniform. He looked over his shoulder and did a double-take before realizing what time it must have been. She giggled. "That's what you're wearing to work now?"

Wolfgang pulled the lapels of his robe together and instinctively checked his nether regions. He found no bulge. His erection had come and gone. His beard felt matted from his pillow. He wasn't used to such a solid night of sleep. "Do you hear the music?" He pointed down the hill where portions of the colored hospital were visible. "It's a flute."

Susannah folded her arms as if chilled. "Someone's been playing for an hour now. Come on. We're going to be late. Get dressed. And please do something with that hair."

WOLFGANG SKIPPED HIS morning coffee and wet his hair and beard down with handfuls of water from the sink. He brushed his teeth in a rush, pausing briefly when the flute music stopped. He finished, spat, wiped his face and met Susannah out near the tree line. The combination of wind and wet hair made his skull feel like an icy ball, but his brain was full of optimism. Susannah had to hurry to keep up with his pace, and then suddenly Wolfgang stopped with a fleeting touch on her arm.

"What would you think if I formed an orchestra here?"

She looked up through the trees. "At Waverly?"

"Not a full orchestra . . . " He continued walking. "Never mind."

"No, tell me."

"What if I taught the patients to play."

"They're not here long enough."

"Maybe some of them already know how," he said. "McVain triggered something. Ever since I was a child I imagined myself conducting. I'd stand at my father's podium and pretend I was leading an orchestra."

Susannah sidestepped a narrow dip in the ground where water had collected in a puddle. "What happened to your dreams?"

"We make choices," Wolfgang said. "Mine brought me here."

"Instead of Carnegie Hall?"

He looked straight ahead. He could feel her stare.

"You regret being here?"

"No." He walked for a moment in silence, staring at his shoes, and then his chin popped up again. "But watching McVain last night, it sparked ideas."

"I like the idea," she said, "but Barker won't—"

"I'll handle Barker. I'll sidestep him somehow. I just need to get McVain."

Big 15 made his way toward them, maneuvering his cart with his left hand while he popped something into his mouth with his right. He chewed and returned both hands to the grip. He passed right through the steam wafting up from his covered food, inhaling it as he angled the cart downward. "We got sausage this morning, Boss. Want one?"

Wolfgang waved. "I'll wait, thank you."

Susannah stepped away from them. "I'll meet you inside."

Wolfgang nodded and then approached Big 15. "I heard music coming from the colored hospital this morning. A flute."

Big 15 eyed Susannah as she reached the entrance portico and entered the sanatorium. "Heard it m'self, Boss."

"Who is it?"

"New patient, I reckon. Group of 'em come in yesterday."

"Could you get a name for me?"

"Sure could try."

Wolfgang patted his shoulder, lifted the towel from the cart and grabbed a piece of sausage. He half jogged up the lawn toward the sanatorium with crazy notions flirting with his mind. Only eleven patients attended his early mass. His heart wasn't in his shallow homily. He couldn't get the flute out of his head.

AFTER MASS HE reported to Doctor Barker's office. Summoned was more like it. Nurse Marlene, of all people, had been sent by Doctor Barker into the chapel to get Wolfgang to report as soon as Mass let out. He'd managed to avoid looking at her chest when she'd spoken to him. Foolishly he'd stared at her white shoes and shapely calves, and then her bare knees just below the bottom of her skirt. Finally he turned away as if something else had caught his attention. He'd thanked her and she'd moved on.

Wolfgang knocked on the large pane of frosted glass inside Doctor Barker's office door and waited for his boss' voice to invite him in, which he did after the third knock. Wolfgang stepped inside and stood there while Doctor Barker's gaze remained on a set of files spread out atop his cluttered desk. A toothpick danced across his teeth. Finally he looked up and stared at Wolfgang, although he said nothing for a good twenty seconds. He just sat there, gnawing on the toothpick, staring, as if trying to intimidate with his look alone. And then, "I warned you, Doctor."

"Sir?"

Doctor Barker leaned forward and slammed his right palm on the desktop. He nearly knocked over a framed picture of his wife. "Don't play games with me. I know what you did last night. You took a patient out of this hospital. A highly contagious patient. You deliberately—"

"I brought him back, sir."

"This isn't a joke." He took the toothpick from his lips and tossed it into the trashcan. "Is this the action of a priest? Deception?"

Wolfgang moved closer, placed his black bag of instruments on the corner of Doctor Barker's desk and sat down in a chair opposite Barker's. "I'd call it more of a revelation. McVain's speaking now."

Doctor Barker pursed his lips, ran his hands through his hair and sighed.

Wolfgang knew what he'd done was against the rules, but he didn't care. It wasn't as if he'd made a spur-of-the-moment decision to temporarily kidnap McVain. He'd thought about it for two days. It was a rule that needed to be bent for the mental wellbeing of a troubled patient, so he denied nothing.

"They need rest," Doctor Barker said, his tone rising a bit. "They need fresh air. They don't need to be walking through the woods in the middle of the night in the dead of winter." He stood from his chair and leaned with his splayed fingers on his desk. "You're too friendly with the patients. Too lax with our rules."

Wolfgang stood with him, eye-to-eye. "This isn't a prison. Maybe I've lost faith in our . . . medicine. I search for other options. I'm sorry if you don't understand music."

"I understand music, Wolfgang." Doctor Barker lifted Wolfgang's bag of instruments and tossed them out into the hallway. The piccolo rolled from the bag and against the hallway wall. "Don't tell me—"

"Then why do you fight me?"

Doctor Barker walked around his desk. "We're dealing with the most deadly disease of our time. We're losing more to TB than bullets killed in the Great War. Half of the city's schools have vacant seats. Churches are empty. Our people are afraid to leave their homes. My wife is afraid to be around me."

"Music is contagious too. It—"

"Don't speak to me of music. Speak to me of a cure."

"I'm closer to a cure than you, sir." Wolfgang spun away and stepped out into the hallway, where Susannah was bending down for his piccolo, most assuredly listening to the entire conversation and probably wondering if she was going to be next. "Thank you." Wolfgang took it from her, shoved it into his bag and zipped it up.

"I'm on my way upstairs," she said softly because Barker's door was still open.

"To check on Herman?"

"And the others."

"I'm going with you."

"It's not necessary, Wolf."

The bruise on her wrist was lurid in the morning light. "Yes, it is."

AT TIMES, THE wind on the rooftop was enough to knock over a well-balanced man if it hit the right way. Wolfgang was rarely balanced with his limp, but he managed to stay righted as he followed behind Susannah. His lab coat rippled in loud snaps. Susannah held onto her cap as she walked across the graveled floor of the roof and then onto the terra cotta tiles where most of the heliotherapy patients spent their time in the sun. Farther down the rooftop, inside the nurses' station and bell tower, Herman's bellow carried from the open windows of Room 502.

"I want my cakes! Give me my cakes!"

"I wonder what's got him wound up." Susannah approached a group of men lying on pool chairs. Three of them, despite the cold air, sat shirtless, their skin absorbing the sun's rays which, at the moment, remained hidden behind a cluster of puffy white clouds. The men looked up politely and either smiled or waved. A thin man with sunburned shoulders nodded toward Wolfgang. "Morning, Father." He tipped an imaginary cap toward Susannah and smiled. "Miss." Three of his front teeth were missing. She gave them all a warm smile, knowing how the men all looked at her. She was flattered. She worked a lot with the heliotherapy patients on the rooftop. Sun treatment was used for TB of the glands, bones, joints, skin, eyes . . . there was really no stop to where the white death could spread. The men spent nearly every sunny day on the roof, and when it rained some were treated with radiation by means of mercury lamps. Today they were in the middle of a game of cards, but they were struggling to keep the cards and chips on the table.

"Little windy for cards, Geoffrey." Wolfgang bent down, picked one up off the floor and handed it to Geoffrey's buddy—a chubby man with a sunburned belly named Cletus Winks, who, for whatever reason, winked at Wolfgang before he began to shuffle the deck. Wolfgang glanced at Susannah. Was that why he'd winked? Because he was always with Susannah? Had someone seen him enter the dormitory the other night? Had they heard of the incident with Marlene?

Herman screamed again. "My cakes, you bitches! Who stole my cakes?"

Wolfgang rolled his eyes. In the background over the ornately capped rooftop wall, the treetops danced with the wind. He tried to ignore Herman's ranting, which didn't sound too much unlike

his father after a night of drinking. Susannah and Wolfgang stepped
into the shadows of the bell tower and opened the door to the
nurses' station that housed rooms 502 through 506. What had
once been a sleeping station for the nurses now held a handful of
head cases, and Herman was the worst of them all.

"Susannah!" Herman screamed as she entered, as if he could
smell her. Nurse Rita sat pale and very still behind the main desk.
Her eyes seemed frozen in a daze across the room toward 502.
Wolfgang touched Rita's shoulder. "Rita . . . Rita!" Nurse Rita's
eyes didn't move from Room 502.

"I hear the music!" Herman shouted from behind the closed
door.

Susannah turned toward her fellow nurse. "Rita . . . Rita?"

Slowly Rita turned toward Susannah. The two young nurses
stood silently for a moment, one calm and unflappable and the
other completely on edge and too frightened to even talk. "Are you
okay, dear?" Rita looked back at Room 502 but said nothing.

Wolfgang lifted the food tray from the counter but Susannah
snatched it from him. "I'll get it." She walked confidently toward
Herman's room and, balancing the tray on one knee, unlocked
and opened the door. Wolfgang followed behind her. The room
had two beds and a large screened window. It smelled of urine and
feces. Herman sat naked on the floor, slapping his belly and hairy
chest repeatedly with the palms of his hands, which appeared to be
smeared with excrement. He looked like a deranged monkey. His
clothes rested in a bundle at the foot of the bed. He stood, fully
exposing himself to Wolfgang and Susannah. Wolfgang wanted
to cover Susannah's eyes but she remained calm and unfazed, despite the horrible stench. Her eyes didn't waver as she pointed at
Herman. "It's time to eat, Herman. Put your clothes on."

Herman looked toward the door for a split second, just long
enough for Wolfgang to catch a glimpse of his crazy, dark eyes
that reminded him a little of a rat he'd seen scurrying across his

bathroom floor early in the spring. Herman's tangled hair fell against his heavily freckled shoulders. His scraggly beard hung down toward his hairy chest in one matted plait. Somewhere within the growth was a mouth that, when it moved, caused the entire hairy contraption around it to move as well.

"Can you hear the train coming? Rita can hear it." Herman hunkered down again, moaning and smearing feces against his chest, the flesh around his eyes turning red, the wrinkling of the crow's feet accentuated by some hidden strain. "The train's a-coming." He moaned, stopped abruptly, and then slumped over toward his bed.

Susannah finally did look away. Wolfgang could have strangled him for putting her through such a scene, but the fact that she was unnerved by the entire episode interested him in a way he couldn't truly explain. Susannah looked toward Wolfgang, and when she saw him watching her she quickly averted her eyes. Herman wiped his shit-covered hands on his bed sheets, coughed and spat at the window. Yellow phlegm dripped slowly down the screen, filling the tiny holes with pockets of his saliva. He sat up with his back against the pea-green wall and faced them, smiling. "Enjoy the show?"

Susannah had her stern face back on. "Clean yourself, Herman. And put your clothes on now. You're going to wake up Benson."

Something moved beneath the covers on the other bed and a high-pitched voice emerged from the tangle. "Shut up . . . shut up . . . shut up . . . shut up . . . No, I cannot hear the train. I do not hear it coming down the tracks . . . I love my dog . . . I would never hurt him . . . her . . . hurt her . . . so shut up, Herman. Shut up—"

"I want cake for my birthday!" Herman screamed.

From Room 504, Maverly Simms joined in on the madness, shouting as if in competition. "Maverly at Waverly. Maverly at Waverly. Maverly at Waverly . . ."

"It's not your birthday, Herman," said Susannah.

"When *is* his birthday?" Wolfgang asked. "And why do they never use the bathroom up here?"

Benson stuck his bald head out from the covers, then quickly ducked back under. His words faded to a whisper. "Shut up . . . I let the dog out . . . shut up . . . "

"Maverly at Waverly . . . Maverly at Waverly . . . "

"I can't believe you deal with this," Wolfgang said out of the side of his mouth. He had reason to fear for her safety. The nurses weren't trained for these patients—the look in Rita's eyes proved as much. Herman was a huge man with a thick chest and a deep, powerful voice. His hands and feet were huge, probably second only to Big 15's on the entire hillside. Although fat hung in rolls beneath his droopy chest, his arms appeared toned. He could easily pick Susannah or Rita up and throw them, or worse.

Susannah stepped farther into the room with Herman's tray of food. Wolfgang grabbed her arm. "What are you doing?"

"I'm taking him his food."

"Just leave it there on the ledge."

"He won't eat it unless I bring it to him." Susannah carried the tray to the bed and placed it where the covers weren't rumpled. Herman's beady eyes watched her like she was a rabbit and he a jackal. She kicked his clothes toward him. "Get dressed."

"No one listens."

Susannah moved toward the door. "I listen plenty, Herman."

"But you don't hear me." Herman looked directly at Wolfgang. "I'm like you, Father. I have secrets." A sinister laugh emerged from Herman's mass of hair and lips.

His odd words reminded Wolfgang of the guilt he felt every day, an increasing guilt that was rooted so deeply he couldn't pinpoint where or when it had started. He only knew it was there, and the feeling only eased at night when he took off his clerics.

Wolfgang turned away from Room 502, wondering what Herman could have meant. When he looked back over his shoulder before exiting the nurses' station, Rita's eyes were following him.

THE CAFETERIA AT dinnertime was alive with chatter, coughing and silverware clanking off plates piled high with meatloaf, mashed potatoes and green beans. Wolfgang sat with Susannah, Abel and Lincoln at a table near the back of the cafeteria, where most of the staff preferred to eat. The rest of the vast space was scattered with patients mobile enough to come down to eat on their own. Fifty tables with six chairs per table. A quarter of the chairs were occupied. The cafeteria was a picture of cleanliness, white and bright and optimistic. Proper diet was essential to beating tuberculosis and they'd designed the cafeteria to be as welcoming as possible. It was open at all times. The walls were decorated with paintings and drawings made by the patients themselves.

Abel attacked his food as if he hadn't eaten in days. Susannah watched him proudly, knowing that a healthy appetite often meant improved health. His exuberance was starting to show more every day. His color was better. If only the adults had the same success rate as the children, Wolfgang thought. One day it would happen.

Between bites of meatloaf, Lincoln puckered his face and furrowed his brow in a crude imitation of their boss. "Stop wasting your time on tunes, Wolfgang." Susannah laughed, then gave Abel a quick glance. He laughed as well. Doctor Barker had yelled at Abel a few times in the past, in his case for being up too late. Having gotten one laugh, Lincoln ratcheted it up a notch. "I bet his wife is a stiff too."

"She's a nice woman," said Susannah. "I hear they're having trouble though."

Lincoln took a bite of potatoes. "Shocking."

"Barker is a decent man," Wolfgang said. "He has a stressful job here." He offered no more explanation for why he'd just backed his nemesis, unsure why he'd done it himself. Still they watched him, as if waiting to see if he'd go on.

Lincoln put his fork down and wiped his mouth with a napkin. He looked over his shoulder and then leaned forward over the table. "Brought some hooch up the chute this morning."

Susannah rolled her eyes. "How on earth do you get this whiskey?"

"I got my ways."

"That he does," said Wolfgang. "He got roses to bloom in the dead of winter."

"But don't tell Barker, Susannah," Lincoln said. "He doesn't know we borrowed his stuff."

"You scare me, Lincoln." Susannah leaned back in her chair and folded her arms. "Somehow, Prohibition doesn't affect you and I don't care to know the reason why."

Lincoln winked at Wolfgang. "Prohibition doesn't affect you either, does it, Father?"

"Bootlegging is illegal," Susannah said.

"I got plenty of ciggies too."

Abel put on a miniature man-of-the-world face. "That's not illegal."

"That's all we need," Wolfgang said. "One of our staff smoking in a TB hospital."

"What's that got to do with anything?" asked Lincoln.

Susannah placed her hand on Wolfgang's shoulder. "Wolf thinks those cigarettes you smoke kill your lungs."

Lincoln waved a hand at them. "Horsefeathers." He leaned forward with his elbows on the table. "I heard Al Capone and some of his gangster friends frequent the Seelbach downtown. They've been pushed out of Chicago, so they do their bootlegging down here. Chicago of the south."

"Nonsense," Wolfgang said, more for Abel's ears than anything else. It was a common belief that Prohibition had caused more problems than it had solved, and crime was a major product of it—a new type of crime that was organized and frightening.

Jakes walked by with a tray of food.

Lincoln spotted him. "Hey, Jakes, find out how those pigs are escaping yet?"

Abel snickered, hanging on Lincoln's every word. Jakes ignored them and walked on. Lincoln looked across the table at Abel. "Hey, little fella, what are you doing here anyway? Aren't you supposed to be with the other children?"

Abel lifted his chin. "Miss Susannah said I could be here."

Lincoln stared at him. "Not contagious, are you?"

"He's fine," said Wolfgang.

Susannah sipped her tea. "Leave him be."

Lincoln let it drop. Wolfgang could tell Lincoln was getting on Susannah's nerves. He always did. He fidgeted in his chair, looked around the cafeteria until he found Rita sitting at a table all alone. Her food was untouched. She stood, left her tray and hurried out holding her mouth clamped shut as if trying not to throw up. Lincoln shook his head. "What's up with Rita lately? She's a pretty girl."

Susannah sighed. "She must be depressed."

Lincoln was dubious. "She hasn't been here long enough to get depressed."

"It doesn't take long in the mental ward," Wolfgang said, knowing where this was going.

"Try working in the Death Tunnel all day."

"This isn't a competition," Susannah said.

"What's the Death Tunnel?" asked Abel.

"You bring Herman his birthday cake yet, Susannah?" Lincoln laughed, picked at his teeth. "Benson let his dog out?" Another laugh. "Maverly at Waverly. Maverly at Waverly."

"Grow up." Susannah stood and slid her chair back. Abel followed her to the counter where they deposited their trays and left the cafeteria.

"When *is* Herman's birthday?" Lincoln asked Wolfgang facetiously.

"Good job," Wolfgang said.

"What?"

"It can be dangerous up there on the roof," Wolfgang said. "Make jokes if you want, but those women have a tough job." Lincoln stared over Wolfgang's shoulder as he chewed another bite of meatloaf, and eventually his eyes settled on Wolfgang. An unreadable smirk crossed his face. "What?" Wolfgang asked.

"Susannah . . . she laughs at everything you say."

"So?"

"You're not that funny of a guy, Wolf."

Wolfgang put his fork down with a clank as his thoughts turned to Rose. Lincoln looked back down to his plate. They remained silent for a few seconds. Some kind of border had been crossed. A lump formed in Wolfgang's throat. When Lincoln dug into his food again, Wolfgang excused himself from the table. Out in the hallway he passed a patient, a frail woman with gray hair. She smiled at him. "Hi, Father." Wolfgang smiled back and continued on.

Father, bless me for I have sinned.

He heard the statement countless times a day.

Father, what is Heaven like?

The question, and the many derivatives of it, had haunted him from childhood to present. His father had died when he was young. Rose had died when he was in his mid-twenties. He talked to them still, but they never answered back. Perhaps that was the reason he'd come to live his life on the hillside, secluded and surrounded by death. To answer their questions before they exhaled their final TB-infected breaths. He'd chosen a profession that allowed him to answer their questions despite the fact that he knew none of the answers.

10

THE NEXT EVENING Charlie Chaplin's silent film *The Circus* was the Waverly movie of the week. A couple dozen patients and a handful of staff members sat in the dark theater. One center aisle split ten rows of comfortable chairs and faced a wall where the picture was shown, and except for a few coughs and bits of contained laughter the first floor theater was indeed quite silent as everyone focused on the screen. Chaplin's Little Tramp character was being chased by a policeman at a circus and the ringmaster thought his antics were hilarious. Wolfgang stood with his arms folded, chewing his lower lip, eyeing the clock on the wall. Susannah stood beside him, stifling her laughter with a closed fist. She looked at him. "You're not laughing. What's wrong?"

"Nothing." He kept his eyes on the screen. "I'll be back."

"Where are you going?"

Wolfgang pretended not to hear her and ducked out into the bright hallway. Someone down the hillside was playing the flute again. He could hear it more clearly as he approached the exit and stepped out into the cool air, where the sun barely lingered in the west, smearing the sky in swaths of purple and gold. He inhaled the fresh air as he entered the line of trees and hurried through the woods. It was dark amidst the trees but he knew the paths like the back of his hand. He hummed along with the flute. It sounded like Mozart's *Requiem*.

About forty yards downhill and northwest of the main sanatorium, Wolfgang stopped at a two-story clapboard building where the colored workers lived. He tossed a pebble up at a closed, grimy window. It sailed several feet from its target and bounced off into the undergrowth. He found another pebble and threw it. Whether by luck or skill it hit the edge of the window. Moments later the window opened and Big 15 stuck his head outside. "Boss, that you?"

Wolfgang stepped into a small clearing next to the foundation where the ground was hard and free of grass. "You hear the flute?"

"Course I do."

"Will you take me to it?"

Big 15 sighed. "Be down in a minute, Boss." The window closed with a thwack against the dry-rotted frame. A few minutes later Big 15 stepped outside, buckling a large black belt that cinched his overalls at the waist.

The colored hospital was another thirty yards down the hillside and the flute became louder as they neared the entrance to the two-story brick building. The crisp breeze that had refreshed him moments ago now chilled him. His breath crystallized. The temperature had dropped quickly with the sunset. The entrance was little more than a slanted tin roof with sagging gutters held up by four wooden posts—a glorified lean-to. Two folding chairs flanked the double glass doors. A stray cat looked up from the right chair and meowed as they passed. Wolfgang ruffled the fur behind the cat's ears. Big 15 opened the door and ducked inside, where the air was thick with the damp vapors of mildew. The colored hospital had taken the brunt of the rainfall weeks ago. Not only had it been soaked because of the holes and crevices in the weathered roof, but the basement had quickly flooded from the rain and mud streaming down the rest of the hillside. Mud, water and remnants of backed up sewer gunk had stood three feet high against every wall, taking weeks to be emptied by a bucket-by-bucket chain gang. Pungent odors had emanated from the cesspool, making recovery from TB nearly impossible. Much of the first floor had flooded and pools of water still remained on the lobby floor. Too many patients at once and not enough time or space to clean what the flood had brought with it.

Instincts told Wolfgang to hold his nose upon entry but he resisted the temptation. The colored patients breathed it in so why shouldn't he? Lack of ventilation and poor air circulation made it uncomfortable to breathe the air, which was senseless to the cause they fought daily. The floors were so overcrowded that the newest arrivals had been placed in the cramped lobby. The lighting was poor and dim. Every nimbus of light that hung from the peeling ceiling—marked with brown stains from the leaks of the heavy rains—showed tiny dust particles unmoved by poor circulation.

Wolfgang felt ashamed. If the fresh air was so important, he thought, then why weren't they up higher on the hillside with the white patients? If he were to close his eyes, the moaning and groaning and sputum-filled retching and coughing would have sounded much like up in the main sanatorium, but seeing it made it worse. Beds in the shadows. Children sleeping in dark, musty corners while the vermin skittered along the walls. The modest sleeping porches were too crowded to fit everyone, so they shared. They took turns breathing the fresh air. During the flood some often slept outside the building on cots to escape the crowd and stench that wafted up the stairwells from the basement.

Big 15 took it in stride as he passed through the lobby. Three black children jumped up from the shadows and excitedly shouted his name and Big 15 smiled and waved, slapping fives like some hero. He was a hero. He was a strong, strapping TB survivor who had come back to help his "people" as he so often called them. His presence alone gave them hope while the main sanatorium loomed over the trees like an unattainable beacon of light.

Wolfgang followed Big 15 up a narrow stairwell, where they sidestepped a skinny man blowing his nose into the sleeve of his yellow pajamas. A gnat landed on the man's left arm. He smacked at it, looked up and gave them a kind smile as they passed. Wolfgang touched his shoulder and gave it an affectionate squeeze. He was reminded of the writings of Charles Dickens and the squalid rookeries and tenements of London, where poverty and sickness ruled the streets.

Finally he felt the air again near the top of the stairwell where the steps gave way to the second floor sleeping porch. It was much smaller than the porches up the hill, but at least the air was moving. Cool fresh air. Dozens of beds filled the brick-enclosed porch. Screens kept the biggest insects out. Spit buckets sat beside each bed. The patients were either asleep or resting with their eyes open, listening to the flute, which appeared to be coming from a room about twenty yards ahead to the right. Wolfgang had been to the colored hospital on many occasions to attend to the sick and to hear confessions, but not usually at night, so they viewed him with curiosity as he and Big 15 made their way down the porch. They had their own doctors . . . so why was a white one coming down the hillside? Wolfgang could read the questions in their furrowed brows.

A middle-aged woman watched him with sorrow in her eyes. An older man smiled with bright white teeth and bowed as if the Pope himself had arrived.

If my father could see me now, thought Wolfgang.

Big 15 ducked into one of the rooms on the right and left Wolfgang standing next to an adolescent boy in a white T-shirt and baggy tweed trousers. He had big brown eyes and dark skin. His black hair was cut close to his scalp. He had a warm, toothy grin that oozed confidence.

The kid tugged on Wolfgang's lab coat. "You like baseball, Father?"

Wolfgang motioned toward his right foot, where the toes of his black shoe angled to the floor while the heel remained raised. "Never been much of an athlete, but yes, I do follow baseball."

The kid lifted his right thumb and pointed to his chest. "I'm gonna play pro ball some day. Soon's I get outta here and well. I'm gonna be the black Babe Ruth."

Wolfgang knelt beside the bed and rubbed his hand over the kid's coarse scalp. "I'll pray that you do." Wolfgang looked him in the eyes. "What's your name?"

"James. Friends call me Smokey."

Wolfgang patted the kid's shoulder and stood up. "Alright, Smokey. Perhaps one day they'll make a Louisville Slugger with your name on it."

Smokey smiled large and proud and leaned back on his pillow. The flute music stopped. Somewhere a baby wailed. Coughing mixed with the wind. Big 15 ducked out of the room and beside him stood a squatty black man in blue and red checkered pajamas under a brown coat. The man had short hair and a chubby face free of stubble. At a glance he appeared in his forties, although no wrinkles or age marks marred his caramel skin. He smiled, but Wolfgang sensed a twinge of reluctance behind it.

"I'm Doctor Pike."

Big 15 patted Wolfgang on the back. "He likes to be called Boss."

"I'm Rufus." He sat on a wrought iron bench, started to offer his hand but then pulled it away. "I've heard stories of you. You play music for the white people. They call you Mozart."

Wolfgang sat beside him. "They call me all sorts of things." Wolfgang spotted the flute in Rufus' thick, calloused hands. "You like Mozart?"

He nodded.

"I heard you playing his *Requiem*."

"Seems to fit this place."

Wolfgang looked out toward the woods. "A requiem for the dying."

Rufus put the flute to his lips and played a few bars. His enormous cheeks expanded like a puffer fish. His pudgy fingers and hard nails danced effortlessly over the keys. He slowly lowered the instrument.

"I play the piccolo," Wolfgang said. "But not anywhere close to the perfection with which you do."

"It's peaceful out here on the porch." Rufus rotated the flute in his hands. "The music carries."

Big 15 sat on the edge of Smokey's bed and yawned. Smokey was still smiling, staring up at the ceiling with his hands behind his head.

Rufus turned his head and coughed into his fist. "Excuse me." He wiped his mouth. "Luckily I still have some power in my lungs. Don't know what I'd do without this."

"Where . . . where did you learn to play?"

He chuckled and his belly shook. "Thought I'd like jazz, didn't you? Or ragtime? My grandpappy was a slave for a family in Georgia. The owner treated them well. Taught them to read and write. Gave them this flute when they let them free."

"Can I see it?"

Rufus hesitated. "Don't you worry 'bout getting TB?"

"Not anymore." Wolfgang took the flute, turned it in his hands, tried the keys and gave it back. "Good instrument."

"He taught my grandpappy to play. And my father when he was a boy."

"If I call on you to play one night, will you come?"

"Where?" Rufus looked skeptically up the hillside and pointed toward the main sanatorium. "Up there? Oh, no, sir." He shook his head. "We're not supposed to."

Big 15 stood from his seat on Smokey's bed. "Boss seems all proper 'cause he's a padre. But he ain't a stickler for no rules. He ain't got no problem with colored folks."

"I don't know . . . Why can't we play here?"

Wolfgang patted his knee. "I've got someone I'd like you to meet. He's a pianist."

"Up there?"

"Will you come play with him?"

Rufus rotated the flute in his hands. "I think I'd like that."

"That means you'll do it?"

Rufus stood with a grunt. "It means I'll think about it. How would you like to be the only white man in a building full of Negroes?"

"Isn't that where I am now?"

"It isn't the same." Rufus turned away and disappeared into his room. Seconds later he began playing again.

He was right, Wolfgang thought, it wasn't the same.

WOLFGANG WASTED NO time deliberating how he'd make the proposition to McVain, convinced that planning a conversation with someone who was completely unpredictable was an exercise in futility. He marched up to the fourth floor solarium porch, clutching his lab coat tightly against his chest as the evening temperature continued to plummet. The purple clouds above moved quickly, unnaturally fast, across the dark blue sky.

He found McVain on his bed, sitting up. Wolfgang immediately told McVain about Rufus, unsure why he failed to mention that Rufus was black. Wolfgang waited for an answer he feared would never come.

"Well?"

"What?" McVain looked at him as if he truly didn't remember what Wolfgang had just asked him.

"Would you consider playing with someone else?"

"What does he play?"

"I told . . . the flute. He plays the flute. I'm sure you've heard it."

He grunted, stretched his legs out on the bed.

"You were a concert pianist, right?"

McVain exhaled a deep breath and glanced over at Weaver, who had his eyes closed and earphones over his head. "I wrote three symphonies before the age of twenty. And had them performed. I was a different man back then. I don't play anymore."

"You played the other night," said Wolfgang. "And you *will* play again."

"I was terrible."

"But with more practice—"

"That quack Barker isn't going to let me out those doors again," McVain said. "What you did was cruel—*Father*. You dangled the carrot. You probably give drunks a spoonful of booze, then smash the bottle." He held up his fingers. "Might as well cut the rest of them off. I'm going to die here. Neither your God or your confessions can help that."

"I wasn't planning to—"

McVain held up his mangled hand, palm stiff, his two fingers spread, nubs suspended. It was a powerful enough move to back Wolfgang off. He stood, frustrated, and turned away, disappointed but not finished. He checked Mr. Weaver's charts. Down in the solarium he spotted Susannah hurrying into the stairwell. Children screamed from the rooftop. He took off after Susannah and caught a glimpse of her calves as she bounded up the stairs to the next platform leading to the rooftop. His eyes followed her flesh to just above the back of her knees where the hem of her skirt fluttered in waves as she sprinted upward.

"Susannah!"

She looked over her shoulder and down. "Something's happened with Herman."

"What?"

She continued on and Wolfgang chased behind her. "You know you don't always have to accompany me up here."

A dozen kids had gathered near the swingset. Nurse Marlene stood in the middle, calming them. Two of the kids spotted Wolfgang and Susannah and pointed to the bell tower and nurses' station. A few snowflakes spiraled through the air, abused by the wind. Herman was out and standing next to the ledge beside the tower, staring off toward the trees behind the sanatorium. His hair blew back from his head in wild strands. His beard clung to his chest.

"My cake!" Herman screamed.

"What on earth is he doing out?" asked Wolfgang.

Susannah shook her head and slowly approached Herman. He craned his head and stared her down. "My cakes!" Saliva dabbed the corners of his lips. Moisture pooled in his eyes. He faced the bell tower. "Miss Rita . . . The train finally came for her."

Susannah took a cautious step toward him. "What about Miss Rita, Herman? Herman?"

"Her feet don't touch," Herman said softly.

Wolfgang gripped the large man's right elbow and led him along. "Let's get you back inside."

Herman kept his wild eyes on Susannah. He gnawed the fingernails on his left hand, smashing them in, his fingers lost in the growth that concealed his mouth. "Her feet don't touch."

"Did you do something to her?" Wolfgang asked.

Susannah opened the door to the nurses' station and screamed. Wolfgang was directly behind her and saw over her shoulder. Nurse Rita hung by a rope from the ceiling pipes. Susannah lurched backwards, covering her mouth with her hands. She fell into Wolfgang's arms, knocking him slightly off balance. He braced their weight with his stiff left leg and then walked her inside.

Herman entered behind them. "I told you. Her feet don't touch the floor."

Rita's white shoes dangled a few feet from the floor, swaying slightly under the weight of her body. The chair she'd used lay on its side a few feet away. Her eyes stared straight ahead. As the rope crinkled and slowly twisted, Rita's gaze met Wolfgang's for a moment and then passed on. The sound of the rope twisting and pulling against the pipes was like an ice shelf preparing to crack and float away. Benson was out of the room as well, walking in a daze around the station, passing Rita's body as if nothing had happened, as if she wasn't even there. "I let the dog out. He didn't shit on the carpet. He didn't. He didn't. The train won't come for me. Because I let him out. He didn't shit on the new carpet."

Wolfgang covered Susannah's eyes and they both hunkered down against the wall. Her tears trickled through his fingers. He wiped her cheeks and hugged her shoulders and told her repeatedly that it was going to be okay. He couldn't take his eyes off Rita's body. Such a young, pretty girl.

Herman stepped closer to her swaying body. "Benson, you shut up. Her feet don't touch! Can't you see? She'll never bring me my cakes."

Maverly Simms stood at the doorway to her room. "Maverly at Waverly," she said, lacking the enthusiasm of her typical ranting. "Maverly at Waverly."

Wolfgang took it all in and then screamed louder than he'd ever screamed in his life, as if the stress and pain from decades had come out in one giant burst. "Be quiet!" Both Herman and Benson froze. Wolfgang pointed at both of them. "You did this. You drove her to this." He pointed toward Maverly. "You did this. There is no train! Now get back into your rooms."

Herman inched his way back into Room 502 and Benson followed, crying and still mumbling. Their door closed. Maverly backed away and slithered into her dark hole where pissing on her own leg was the norm.

Wolfgang held Susannah close. He felt Susannah's warm breath against his neck. "Cut her down, Wolf. Please, cut her down."

* * *

Susannah didn't stay to watch Wolfgang saw the rope that held Rita tethered to the ceiling. The rope was too thick to cut with a knife, so Wolfgang had to go into the basement for a tree saw. He'd acquired Lincoln's help. Herman, Benson and Maverly were quiet as mice as they worked. Lincoln held Rita around the waist as Wolfgang stood on the chair she'd used and sawed the rope about a foot above her head. Lincoln didn't complain. Wolfgang could see guilt in his eyes. He'd probably regretted the comments he'd made about her and now she was dead. The final fibers of rope snapped and Lincoln held Rita's dead weight. Together they lowered her body to the floor. Her neck was blue and swollen, broken where the rope had rubbed and burned against her skin. Her face was pale. Her hands and legs appeared blue and bloated from where her blood had begun to collect in her lower extremities—gravity's patient now, no longer pushed by the pumping of her heart. Another body for the Death Tunnel. Wolfgang could still see her blank eyes staring him down as she'd held Susannah on the floor, staring at him as if he could read her final confession in the reddened sclera of her eyes.

Father, forgive me, for I have sinned . . .

Wolfgang touched her dark hair and thought of Rose. He'd held her in much the same way. He closed Rita's eyelids and whispered a quick prayer for her soul.

Lincoln stared at Wolfgang's right hand with a deadpan look. "You still wear your wedding ring."

Wolfgang shielded it from him by covering his right hand with his left, and then he moved it away. He knew Lincoln had seen it many times before, yet he'd chosen this particular moment to ask about it. Wolfgang turned the gold band on his right ring finger, slowly rotating it. "After I joined the priesthood I moved it to my right hand." Lincoln nodded, found himself holding Rita's limp hand and carefully let the dead weight slide to the floor. Wolfgang rotated the ring again. "I refused to stuff it in a box or some dusty drawer." He sat up straight and touched Rita's hair again. "Let's get this over with."

AFTER TAKING RITA'S body to the morgue, Wolfgang stopped by Doctor Barker's office but his boss wasn't there. Surely he'd heard the news. Wolfgang made his way to the chapel, walking slowly, not ready to confront anyone. His guilt had returned. It rested undigested in the pit of his stomach. He grieved for Rita. He prayed for her soul. But all he could think about was how it had felt to have Susannah in his arms. The weight of her slender body cradled against him. The fresh smell of her hair against his cheek. His fingers interlocked and holding tight against her stomach. How the buttons of her dress had brushed against his palms. His mind fondled the memory. He hadn't been that close to a woman since . . .

His pace quickened. *What am I doing?* he thought. Guilt drove him into the chapel at the corner of the second floor where the east wing joined the north. The only light came from candles that ran the length of the room on both sides. They rested on a wooden sill. Dozens of them had been lit by patients honoring the dead or praying for someone still living. The flames flickered, casting phantom-like, shape-shifting shadows against the white Roman support columns that melted into the white plaster ceiling. Wolfgang leaned against a column, arms folded. He wasn't alone in the chapel. Doctor Barker stood in the center aisle facing Susannah. He spoke in a hushed voice, placed a supportive hand on her right shoulder and then gave her a quick hug. Susannah didn't return the sudden embrace. Instead, her arms hung to her sides. Doctor Barker let go and left her alone, his footfalls echoing off the tall quiet ceiling. Wolfgang hid behind the column as Doctor Barker exited. He ducked his head outside and watched until Doctor Barker was gone.

Back inside the chapel Susannah was on her knees, facing the life-size crucifix on the back wall, her hands folded on top of a pew. Her shoulders moved as she cried. Wolfgang gave her a moment alone before limping down the rug that stretched the length of the center aisle. She sobbed silently. She'd lost a dear friend, a friend who wasn't sick with disease but apparently was sickened by it. Susannah didn't turn around. Perhaps she didn't hear me, he thought. She continued to stare at the crucified Jesus while Wolfgang purposely looked everywhere *but* at the cross. He reached out for her shoulder but stopped inches away. His hand hovered for a few seconds and then he reeled it back to his side. Instead, he knelt beside her. They said nothing for a while. She stared at the cross while he stared at the floor. Finally he spoke. "I'm sorry."

Susannah glanced at him and then faced the crucifix again. "Thank you."

Wolfgang stood and left her alone.

They walked home together as usual just before ten o'clock. They remained silent until they reached the line of trees. Susannah spoke softly. "I don't think I can sleep alone tonight."

Wolfgang hesitated just long enough to make it awkward. "You . . . can sleep on my couch."

She found a way to smile. "Thank you."

Paranoia swept over him. Wolfgang peered over his shoulder as they walked deeper into the woods. He convinced himself that he was doing the right thing, comforting a dear friend in a time of need. She'd witnessed something terribly traumatic. Wolfgang's heart was fluttering. His palms sweated despite the cold.

"You look nervous, Wolf."

"Just cold." He hugged his arms. "Should have worn a heavier jacket."

As soon as his cottage was within sight he hurried ahead and unlocked the door. Inside he lit several candles. He took her coat, hung it up in the closet, lit two more candles, glanced into the kitchen and closed the bathroom door, stretching out the mundane actions to fill the time.

When he stepped back into his living quarters she stood inches from his face. She was only slightly shorter than Wolfgang, her eyes slightly elevated to find his. She reached up to his collar. "You seem tense."

"What are you doing?"

She removed the white clerical collar from his black shirt and handed it to him. "Trying to get you to relax." He unbuttoned his top shirt button and stepped away. She sat down on the couch. "Maybe some wine would help."

He quickly disappeared into the kitchen, moving as if he'd prayed for such a request. He leaned against the counter and took a deep breath. He pulled a bottle of unmarked wine from a rack beside the sink and twisted the top off. He poured two glasses of red wine. His hands were unsteady and he spilled a few drops on the counter. He wiped them up with a towel. He lifted the glass and turned away from the kitchen. In the other room stood his piano against the wall and beyond that was his bed. He eyed the made part of the bed. Rose's side. Was this why he'd joined the priesthood? So moments like these could be reconciled with a single statement and oath? So he could not be tormented by his promises to Rose?

"Wolf?"

She was just around the threshold and to the right, sitting on the couch. He wondered how she was positioned. Both feet on the floor? Legs crossed? Had she taken her shoes off to get comfortable in his chilly, humble abode? He entered with both glasses in front of him. She had indeed taken her shoes off and she sat with her right foot on the floor and her left foot up on the couch cushion and tucked delicately beneath her right leg. She had small feet and toes.

"Can we light a fire?"

"Of course." Wolfgang handed her a glass of wine. "Of course." Then he dove into another distracting chore, adding logs to the fireplace, stuffing newspaper under them, igniting the paper and logs with a candle from the mantel. Within minutes the wood, slivers of which had already begun to glow a shade of amber, began to snap and pop. The warmth was immediate.

Susannah took off her cap, rested her head on the arm of the couch, took a sip of her wine and then closed her eyes. She opened them again and swirled the wine in her glass. Her technique was good, Wolfgang noticed, wondering how often she drank. She smiled at him. "Lincoln winked at you when we spoke of bootlegging."

Wolfgang laughed, still standing in the middle of the room. "Sacramental wine is exempt under the Volstead Act."

Susannah sipped her wine and licked her lips. "Is . . . this . . . sacramental wine?"

If it were, he thought, would it sanctify the moment for her or make him seem a piker? "Let's call it leftover and leave it at that." Wolfgang turned away and poked at the logs.

"How's your requiem coming?"

Wolfgang squatted near the fire and continued to poke and prod the logs. He looked to his left. Her lips touched the rim of the glass. Red wine wet them and entered her mouth. In the seminary fellow priests discussed past friendships with females. Women were often open and rather forward with priests because they didn't threaten them. In a way it made Wolfgang feel used. Was that what this was about?

"Wolf—your requiem?"

He stood. "I'm afraid I'll never finish."

"Rose wouldn't have expected perfection." Susannah sat up on the couch, both of her feet flat on the floor.

"But I'll accept nothing less," he said. "It'll be the best piece I've ever written."

Susannah sipped her wine and surveyed the bare walls. "You took her portrait down."

"I still have it."

She spotted his Edison phonograph beside the fireplace. "They have newer ones now, much larger."

"And they play longer too. But this works fine. It was my father's."

"As were all your instruments," she said. "You loved him?"

Wolfgang sat on the piano bench and scratched his forehead. "It's complicated. He was a tough man. He beat me and my mother."

Susannah's mouth froze with her lips slightly parted.

"It's okay," Wolfgang said quickly. "He drank a lot. I'm not excusing his actions . . . He wasn't a bad person. I do think he loved me."

"And you?"

"I fear that I love him more now that he's gone." Wolfgang chuckled. "I was to be a famous musician."

"And you think you let him down?"

"No. I'm putting my music to good use. I let my mother down by running off with Rose."

"She didn't approve?"

Wolfgang was beginning to feel the warm, familiar rush from the alcohol. His tongue loosened. "Rose was a flapper. A modern woman. Short dresses, bobbed hair."

"I know the look," she said. "Why did she disapprove?"

Wolfgang stared down into his wine. "She disapproved of me becoming a doctor. She knew I became a doctor to spite my father. He detested science. He believed only the Lord could heal."

"Why did you become a doctor? Out of spite?"

Wolfgang pointed to his withered right foot. "For answers. To help cure disease. Out of spite. Not because of my father, but my mother. She was Protestant. I was raised Protestant. Not just Protestant but anti-Catholic. My parents were true Natives, descendents of Know-Nothing party members. Equated the Pope with the devil. She wanted me to become a Protestant preacher."

Susannah's left hand touched her mouth in shock.

"I was determined to torture my mother throughout my adolescence and young adulthood." Wolfgang finished off his glass of wine and noticed that Susannah had only managed to down half of her wine. "Rose was Catholic. She deepened my love of the Catholic Church. We met at the Cathedral of the Assumption."

"So after she died you ran to the priesthood?"

"I . . . " Wolfgang buried his thoughts with the tipping of his empty glass. He tilted it until the last drop hit his tongue.

Susannah cleared her throat and winced as if her head ached. She looked tired, her eyes finally touched by the wine. "Will you play for me?"

Wolfgang spun quickly around and faced the piano. "Love to." He looked over his shoulder and noticed she'd stretched out on the couch, lying as if ready to be painted. "What shall I play?"

She closed her eyes. "I don't care. You choose."

Wolfgang played bits of Beethoven, Bach and Chopin for nearly an hour, occasionally checking over his shoulder to see if she was asleep. Her eyes stayed closed, but every so often she'd shift and give off the slightest sound. Her glass of wine rested empty on the floor before the couch. He wasn't sure when she'd finished it. The firelight cast a halo around her torso and head. He smiled and faced the piano again, and just before his fingers eased down on the keys once more, she spoke.

"Wolf, how did your father die?"

11

WOLFGANG FIRST NOTICED something was wrong with his father in May of 1907. Charles Pike was an energetic man who could play his violin four hours without tiring. Wolfgang wasn't used to seeing him rest. Three days in a row his father had slept in late. Wolfgang had watched him from the hole in the bedroom wall, wondering when he would awaken. When Charles did finally get up he failed to get dressed. Instead, he sat at the kitchen table for an hour, drinking coffee. When Charles came home from the factory, sweating and holding his stomach, Wolfgang had known something was wrong. Charles took the time to remove all eight of his violins from the couch, one at a time, and lean them against the far wall. He dropped to the cushions and stretched out while Wolfgang, seven years old, watched from the opening to the dining room. Charles blinked as he stared at his son, and then doubled over into a fetal position.

Wolfgang took a step toward the couch. "Daddy? You okay?"

Charles grunted, straightened slightly but stayed on his side, wincing. "Play the piano, Wolfgang."

Wolfgang stopped in mid-stride. He sat on the piano bench, still watching his father, a man who had shown him nearly every emotion in his life except for pain. Seeing him in pain made Wolfgang want to cry. Often Wolfgang had wished pain on his father, when Charles would slap him across the face or grip his arm and yank until pulses of pain shot from his shoulder. Or when he'd kick him in the rear to get him to move faster. Wolfgang would secretly wish some kind of pain on him, nothing specific. He could never manage to conjure up anything exact—just some kind of pain so Charles would know what it felt like to be hurt. Had the pain arrived? Wolfgang looked to the cross on the wall above the piano and held back tears. What had he done? Never again would he pray to God and ask for pain.

"Play, Wolfgang," his father said from the couch, wincing as another wave of cramps shot inside his stomach.

Wolfgang focused on the white and black piano keys before him. He started to warm up with scales.

"Good," coached Charles. "Good . . . tempo . . . tempo . . ." He screamed out again. Wolfgang's mother wasn't home from the factory yet. It was just the two of them. Charles gripped his stomach. His eyeballs bulged.

Wolfgang didn't know what to do as he watched from the piano. Tears formed in his eyes. "Daddy . . ."

"Keep playing," hissed Charles Pike. "God damn it. Watch your tempo."

Wolfgang looked to the cross above the piano. Stop it, his mind cried. Stop the pain. God, please stop my father's pain. I take it all back.

"Damn it!" Charles screamed.

"Daddy . . ."

"Keep playing . . ."

Wolfgang glared at the cross. "Stop it . . . stop it . . . stop it . . ."

THE NEXT WEEK Charles seemed to improve. The lethargy had passed. He stood with Wolfgang in the center of the living room floor. Wolfgang had the violin craned between his neck and left shoulder. He held the bow in his right hand and awaited the next instruction. Charles had his hair down and it fell over his shoulders and hid his loopy ears. His red cravat hung loose around his neck. He'd taken off his jacket and vest so all that remained was his fluffy white shirt rolled to his elbows. In his left hand was his favorite violin, the one with the carefully burned letter P on the base of the wood—a signature type letter, sprawling and slanted. A letter he'd spent hours practicing the precise way to pen. It was how he would sign all of his instruments in his Vienna music store. The violin in his left hand was a model of his dream come to fruition. In his right hand dangled the bow that went with it. He slapped it across Wolfgang's knees and warned him about his posture.

Just as Wolfgang raised his bow across the strings he noticed a look in his father's eyes. The same look he'd seen on the couch the previous week. Charles dropped his violin and bow, doubled over and ran that way into the bathroom down the hall. Wolfgang, still clutching his own violin, followed his father until the bathroom door slammed in his face. Wolfgang put his ear to the door. He heard Charles pass gas. On any other day the sound would have caused a chuckle from both of them, but this sound was different. On the other side of the door Charles grunted in discomfort and breathed heavily. Wolfgang heard something heavy drop into the toilet and with it the foulest stench he could remember slithered under the door. A minute later Charles screamed. "Jesus. What the . . . Doris! Goddamn. Doris!"

Doris ran down the hall wiping her hands on a dishtowel. She backed Wolfgang away from the door and tried the knob. It was locked. "Open up, Charles." The lock clicked. Doris Pike opened the door, disgusted by the stench, and forced her way inside. Next, Wolfgang heard her gasp: "Charles, you're bleeding . . ."

FOR THE NEXT several months Charles lost weight at the rate of three pounds a week, and by the end of the summer he'd dropped fifty pounds. The bloody stools and stomach cramps continued. At one hundred and sixty pounds he was a mere shell of the man he had been. His face showed the angled form of the skull underneath the skin. His face was pale and gaunt. His eye sockets darkened. His hair began showing signs of gray. Still he refused to see any doctor. "The Lord will heal me if he so chooses."

WOLFGANG CURSED HIS father's stubbornness. By November Charles had stopped going to work at the factory. He was too weak to play his instruments. He and Doris fought over lack of money. They fought over his declining health. Every day she urged him to go see a doctor, but still he refused. His clothes hung from his thin frame. He'd had Wolfgang cut a new notch in his leather belt to keep his suit pants from falling. Charles spent most of his evenings in bed, especially after the nausea began to set in. He'd lay with his legs under the covers, his composition on his lap and his inkwell propped in the folds of the bed sheets beside him.

One night Wolfgang gathered up the courage to knock on their bedroom door. His mother was in the kitchen and would have scolded him had she known he was going to disturb Charles while he was writing.

"Come in," he said weakly.

Wolfgang slid inside the cramped room that had begun to smell more and more like sickness—the air thick with sheets that needed to be washed, clothes that needed to be cleaned and pillows stained with the drool that had been leaking from his father's mouth while he slept. Charles gave Wolfgang a warm smile and beckoned him closer with a flick of his long, limp hand. His fingernails needed to be clipped. Wolfgang approached slowly, staring at the man he'd once known as his father. Charles put his pen on the top page of his work and ruffled Wolfgang's hair. "The greatest fugue ever written." He tapped his work with the crooked index finger on his left hand. "Right here." His favorite violin, the model for Pike Music, rested on the pillow beside him.

"Yes, father." It was during the time of sickness that Wolfgang had begun to call Charles father instead of daddy. This sick man wasn't his daddy. "Did God make you sick?" asked Wolfgang.

Charles nodded. "Yes, he did. But he had his reasons, Wolfgang. He always has his reasons." He ruffled his son's hair again. "Do you have dreams?"

Wolfgang shook his head.

"Someday you will."

Wolfgang stared at him, confused.

THE VOMITING STARTED in December. And the fevers after that. His mother cried a lot when she knew Wolfgang wasn't looking. Sometimes she'd cry at night, knitting in a rocking chair next to their bed while Charles worked by candlelight. Wolfgang would watch them from the hole in his bedroom wall. Whenever his father would lean his head back against the headboard and moan, she would stand up and wipe his brow with a wet cloth. When he'd lean over the side of the bed and vomit into a metal pail, she'd empty it and wipe his mouth. Sometimes his mother would leave at night and return a few hours later with food. Fruit and vegetables. She'd fix him a plate of carrots and celery, apples and oranges, and she'd take them up to their bedroom so he could nibble on them while he composed. One night Wolfgang heard her feet on the stairs. He knelt on his mattress, peered into their room through the hole and watched her enter with a plate of vegetables. It was all she could get him to eat. She placed the plate on the bed beside him, but she was clumsy taking her hand away. Her fingers clipped the well of ink, spilling some of it on the sheet. A few spots splattered on his work. He grabbed her hair, yanked her down and shoved her nose in the spilled ink. He slapped her with his left hand. He lifted the inkwell and rammed it against the side of her head, cutting her above the left eye. She staggered back with ink covering her face.

Twenty minutes later Charles vomited. Doris cleaned it up. Before they went to bed he kissed her forehead and told her he loved her. And that they would jump on a boat and sail to Vienna as soon as they had enough money stashed away. He would open his own music store. Doris nodded obediently, some of the ink still staining the creases of her face. Charles lovingly moved a strand of her red hair from her eyes, kissed the cut he'd made above her left eye and tucked the hair behind her left ear. "You've got ink in your hair."

As if he never remembered beating her.

Four days later Wolfgang entered the bathroom soon after his father had left it. The darkest urine he had ever seen rested in the bowl, brown with swirls of amber, and the stench was nearly toxic. That night he looked into his parents' bedroom and witnessed something his young eyes and mind would never completely fathom. It was a night that would completely change his life and how he looked at his mother. His father lay in bed with the covers tousled around his torso and down to his knees. His inkwell and stack of papers were still on the bedside table. His feet were bare, the bottoms facing Wolfgang and his hole in the wall. For a moment his mother was out of sight, but then she appeared with a pillow in her hands. She stuck her head out into the hallway and then quickly ducked it back inside. She closed the bedroom door, paused for a moment with her nose against the grains of the wood, and locked it. She approached the bed and kissed Charles on the forehead. Then, with all her strength, she pressed the pillow down over her husband's face with both hands. She let out a soft grunt as the muscles in her arms flexed. For leverage she stood on her tiptoes. Her calf muscles strained as her slight body pressed down on the pillow. Charles moaned and grunted against the pillow as he suffocated. His fingers clutched the tangled bed sheets. His arms didn't fight but his legs kicked. His bare feet raised several inches off the mattress, kicking and falling, kicking and falling, until finally they stopped moving.

Wolfgang watched in horror. What was she doing? He couldn't believe what he'd just seen. Wolfgang's mouth was open, his lower jaw slack, his trembling hands pressed together as if praying, index fingers to his lips. He tried to scream but the sound got caught up inside his throat. He froze. His mother moved the pillow from his father's face and dropped it to the floor. She checked for a pulse at his father's neck. She knelt to the floor, rested her face against his chest and started crying.

Wolfgang forced himself away from the wall, completely numb. She'd just killed his father. Her husband. The man who had beaten her since the day they'd married in the last year of the nineteenth century. The man who had loved her since that same day. Wolfgang lay on his back, pulled his covers up to his neck and stared at his ceiling. He listened to his mother crying on the other side of the wall. She cried for hours. He watched the tree limbs outside his bedroom window. Shadows moved everywhere. His eyes were too adjusted to the dark. He was too scared to close his eyes. Too shocked even to breathe correctly. He felt like he was wheezing. He waited all night for his bedroom door to creak open, and for his mother to walk in his room with a pillow and smother him until he suffocated to death. He waited but she never came. He fell asleep for five minutes in the middle of the night and startled himself awake with a nightmare of being suffocated by his mother's pillow.

Do you have dreams? Someday you will . . .

Wolfgang stayed in bed until the sun came up the next morning, watching his bedroom door the entire time. Even after the sun shone into his room he was slow to get up. He refused to look through the hole in the wall. He'd convinced himself that it had all been a dream. A terrible nightmare. There was no way he'd seen what he'd seen. He'd rather be beaten by the back of his father's hand than watch him buried. He envisioned his father would be alive and writing in the living room when he came down the stairs. His favorite violin would be tucked to his neck, the bow limp in his grip, his arm moving maniacally back and forth over the strings while strands of his hair danced over his possessed eyes. But the living room was empty . . . and silent. Wolfgang found his mother sitting alone at the kitchen table. Maybe he'd gone to the factory? He'd left early for work?

Doris Pike sniffled into her fist as Wolfgang showed himself. "Come here, honey." She patted her right thigh as if she wanted him to sit there. Her eyes were red and swollen from crying. Wolfgang didn't budge. He stood ten paces away from her and stayed there. She sniffled again. "I'm sorry, honey, but you know how sick your father was?"

Wolfgang nodded.

"Well . . . he passed away during the night."

WOLFGANG SAT ON the piano bench with his elbows on his thighs and his hands folded between his parted legs, staring down at the floor of his cottage, the splintered slats between his boots. Only Rose had known what he'd seen his mother do to his father. And now Susannah. Wolfgang waited for her to say something but the room remained silent. She sniffled much like his mother had that morning in the kitchen. The flames popped and snapped against the charred stones of the fireplace. His face felt slack. Behind his eyes he had that dry, drained feeling he would get after a good, cleansing cry, yet the first tear had yet to fall down his cheeks. Still, he didn't look up, afraid that if he looked into Susannah's eyes that the tears would start, and he didn't want to cry in front of her. After his father had died . . . after his mother had killed him . . . he'd promised himself that he would never cry in front of her again. His childhood innocence had been lost that day. He'd never give her his love. He'd never show his fear, so as never to invite her comforting touch. He would cry sometimes at night, when he was sure she couldn't see or hear him, but only then. Rose was the only woman he'd felt close enough to allow his emotions to come forth, and he was afraid to look at Susannah. He was afraid what the emotions would mean. Instead he stared at the floor and waited for her to say something.

Susannah sniffled again. The couch creaked as her weight shifted from it. He listened to her bare feet pat against the wood floor, coming closer, her shadow combining with his own. She stopped before him but still he didn't look up. She hugged him, draped her arms around his shoulders and kissed the top of his head. He fought back tears as his face brushed against the buttons of her dress, the left side of his face pressed against her chest. Just on the other side of the fabric her breasts rose and fell. Her heart beat into his ear. She held him much like he'd wanted his mother to hold him after his father had stopped breathing, but he wouldn't let her. Susannah held the embrace for about thirty seconds, sniffling as she rubbed his back, and then she let go. She touched the top of his head. Her fingers sunk into the fluff of his hair. She turned and moved back to the couch. Only then did he look up, and he did so with a warm smile on his face, watching her from behind—the way her sandy hair fell in curls between her shoulders, the way her nurse's dress conformed to her narrow waist, the way her hips moved beneath it . . . He turned to face the piano just before she sat on the couch again.

"Shall I play some more?"

She sniffled. "Please."

Wolfgang felt a sense of freedom as he faced the piano keys. His arms relaxed. His shoulders sagged. He felt as if a tremendous weight had been lifted from his soul. It was the second time he'd told the story to anyone. He'd thought that the pain had been lifted after he'd told it to Rose, but it seemed as if it had gained momentum since she'd died, building over the months and years when he'd bottled himself up as he had with his mother. It felt good to talk to someone. He'd spent so much of his life alone.

He went from Mozart to Beethoven and back to Mozart before pausing to see if Susannah had fallen asleep. Before even the last note had drifted to silence, Susannah's soft voice came from across the room. "Keep playing."

He could have played for her all night. He touched his fingers to the keys again, periodically glancing toward the rose atop the piano. For the next hour he played Chopin, Liszt and Brahms, and finished with the Mozart *Fantasia* in D minor. After the sonority of the final chord faded to nothing, another soft sound found his ears.

Susannah snored on the couch. He turned on the bench and watched her for a moment. No hole in the wall here, he thought. She was right in front of him, lying on her side, her chest rising and falling in rhythm with her snoring, her left hand resting on the curve of her left thigh, her legs bent at the knees. Wolfgang opened his closet and found a heavy blanket. He covered her from shoulder to foot and then got himself ready for bed. He brushed his teeth, contemplated changing into his pajamas, but decided against it. He'd sleep in his black pants and shirt in fear of becoming too comfortable with the situation. He blew out all the candles, waited a moment for his eyes to adjust to the dark and then limped his way to his side of the bed. He watched the fire dwindle to ash. He stared at the ceiling for a while. He glanced at the couch from time to time as the wine continued to work on his brain. His hands fondled the bed sheets. The guilt returned. He had another erection. His right hand slid from the sheets to his pants, where it slithered carefully beneath the raised waistline. What was he doing? He'd spent four years becoming immune to the subtle sexuality that oozed from certain women. Now he was helpless to stop it. He turned on his right side and faced the made-up side of the bed. More guilt. He quickly turned away, rolled to his left side and faced the wall. He thought of the patients on the hillside, black and white. He thought of the brick flying through his window. He thought of McVain and Rufus, and an idea suddenly hit him like a fist in the face. An incredible idea that would have to wait until tomorrow night. His erection had come and gone. He closed his eyes and blocked out Susannah's breathing.

Finally, he slept.

12

THE ANTICIPATION OF *seeing her face drives me, and the intoxication of the moment still holds the same feeling of giddiness I'd had the first day I'd met her outside the steps to the Cathedral of the Assumption. Rose had saved me from a life of solitude—a life void of the pleasures I would come to partake in daily. The pleasures of love, the pleasures of communication and trust, and the pleasures of intimacy thought impossible for a sexually naïve young man with an impenetrable façade and a gimp foot.*

It was the limp from that polio deformity that had first drawn her attention to me. Without it I would have been like everyone else standing outside of that church. With that limp she saw character. With that limp she saw a story that needed to be told. She saw a frightened boy stuck in the body of a twenty-year-old man.

Rose is a brash young woman with an affinity for anything out of the ordinary, and she'd wasted no time in introducing herself. She'd later told me she'd been drawn to my innocence, the innocence I thought had vanished the night my father was killed. But I remained convinced it was my limp. It was the first time I'd thanked God for the polio that had nearly rendered my legs useless during my eighth year on this earth.

I treat her like a queen, and after three years of marriage I finally feel like the King she deserves. So as I pull my Model-T Ford onto the winding gravel driveway that leads to our home, I pray the sound of the smashing rocks beneath my tires does not warn her of my arrival. I stop the car a good thirty yards from the house and walk the rest of the way, the toes of my right boot scraping a narrow groove in the rocks as I drag it along. I'm not ashamed of it anymore. It has given me a clumsy gait all to my own—a uniqueness in my hurried step that Rose has come to call my gallop. So I gallop along the driveway, creating tiny clouds of dust in the wake of my right boot, watching the pink leaves of the dogwood trees that line the side of the small brick house and shade the uncovered back porch. I hope the door does not open. It makes my day to surprise her after so many hours of visiting the sick.

I'm home early from work. My last patient never showed. The birds are singing on this warm spring day. I loosen my tie as the sun beats down on my shoulders. The azaleas are in bloom in front of the house, flowering in purple and red. I pass the dogwoods and porch, and on the other side is a garden of roses, planted and kept by my wife during our first year of marriage. There are so many to choose from, all of them red and bright and full. I spot the perfect one and tug the stem low to the ground, snapping it carefully. Today's rose. Tomorrow I shall choose another. It is childish, I know, but it is a ritual I will not soon get rid of.

I hold the rose upright and steady, and quietly open the back door. I spot her from the laundry room. She sits on a chair in the kitchen with her back to me, reading. I tiptoe across the linoleum floor of the kitchen, where sunlight abounds and purple flowers and green vines border yellow wallpaper. Rose's hair has grown out since the day we'd first met. It is dark, curly and pulled back in a tail that shields most of her ivory neck. Her dark hair has a red bow in it. I'm sure she has heard my right foot sliding across the floor but her heart is too large to spoil the fun for me. And then suddenly she closes her book and stands in her yellow summer dress that sways around her knees. Her shoulders are slender, her neck long. She turns slowly toward me.

"A rose for a Rose," I say.

She smiles at me behind tired, blue eyes. She smiles as if she's happy. So why is she crying?

* * *

WOLFGANG'S EYES SHOT open just before the pillow enclosed his sleeping face. It was morning. The sun shone onto the floor in between the bed and his piano, but the room still held onto a chill that had crept in after the fire had died out. Wolfgang glanced to the wall clock. It was seven o'clock. He had a slight hangover from the wine.

Susannah?

He looked to the couch and found it empty except for the neatly folded blanket she'd left on the arm. He hurried from the bed and noticed a note lying on top of the folded blanket.

> *I'll be back at 7:30. It's a workday, you know.*
> *S.*

Wolfgang lowered the note, thought about tossing it into the trash can in fear of it being seen by someone, namely Lincoln, who would have a year's worth of fun taunting them if he were to find out she'd spent the night in his home. Instead, he slid it beneath a stack of music atop his piano. He'd decide what, if anything, to do with it later. He took a quick bath and readied himself for another day of confessions.

WOLFGANG STARTED THE morning off with a baptism in the chapel. A thirty-year-old man in the final stages of TB had lived what he'd called a faithless life—a moral but faithless life. He'd never believed in God, and the closer he got to death the more he began to wonder, as they all did, what would happen after his death. Where would he go? Was there really a Heaven? And so he asked to be baptized so he could enter that mysterious void as a pure soul.

"You have doubt?" Jesse Jacobs had asked him with Wolfgang listening from behind, preparing the baptismal water.

"Yes," the man said.

"Faith is doubt, my friend," Jesse said, patting the man's shoulder.

Wolfgang stepped in. "Very well put, Jesse." And so Wolfgang baptized the man Catholic with Jesse there to witness. They'd managed three pieces of cake and three glasses of milk from the cafeteria as a celebration before Jesse and the newly baptized man returned to their solarium porches.

Wolfgang went up to the fourth floor to check on McVain and found him standing on the solarium porch, his face inches from the screen and staring down as Jakes chased two pigs across the lawn. "Fool. Can't keep a pig in its pen." He sat down on his bed with a dramatic sigh. "What do you want, Amadeus?"

Wolfgang reluctantly handed him a stack of music.

"What's this?"

"The requiem I'm writing. It's called *The Requiem Rose*."

McVain flipped through it carelessly and then tossed it on a chair beside the bed as if it were junk. He rested his head on his pillow. "I'm tired and nauseous."

"I've got a surprise for you tonight."

"Sending me home?"

"No, but it should keep us both out of trouble."

McVain closed his eyes. "Can't wait."

By MID-AFTERNOON, THE sun ducked behind the clouds and the temperature dropped several degrees. Wolfgang found Big 15 sitting outside on a concrete stoop outside the storage room, eating a hunk of bread with ham on it. Beside him was a bottle of milk. He chewed and watched the woods. A deer sprinted through the growth and then jumped over a small ditch and out of sight. Big 15 looked up as Wolfgang approached. "You see that deer, Boss?"

Wolfgang nodded. "I've been looking for you."

"Just eatin' lunch."

"Come join us."

Big 15's eyes grew large. "Not s'posed to."

"To hell with that." Wolfgang waved him along. "I need your help with something tonight. You know every trail, path and undulation of this hillside."

Big 15 followed Wolfgang into the cafeteria and nodded sheepishly toward every set of eyes that stared him down. Some offered kind smiles but others, Wolfgang could tell, wondered what he was doing there. "Ignore them." Big 15 sat beside Lincoln and across the table from Wolfgang and Susannah and he listened intently as Wolfgang revealed his plan. Susannah rolled her eyes throughout in obvious disagreement.

Lincoln leaned over the table. "Count me in. Your place, midnight."

"Me too, Boss."

Doctor Barker walked by their table and eyed Big 15. "Lincoln. Room 218 needs to be prepped." He gave Wolfgang an extra long glare and moved on.

Lincoln got up from the table and Big 15 took that as his cue to leave as well. He was obviously uncomfortable. It wasn't Wolfgang's wishes to put him in that situation but he hated seeing his friend eat outside, despite the fact that Big 15 had told him on numerous occasions that that's what he liked to do—to eat and watch the woods.

After they'd gone Susannah spoke up. "You'll get yourself killed." She dropped her ham sandwich to her plate, having only eaten two bites from it. "It's a foolish idea."

"You haven't eaten much," said Wolfgang.

"I don't have much of an appetite."

Wolfgang watched her. "Don't worry . . . we'll have plenty of muscle."

"Who . . . you?" She looked away. "How much can you lift on that foot of yours?"

They sat silent as Wolfgang sipped his vegetable soup. He wondered if she was thinking of Rita again. "What did her note say?"

Susannah wiped her mouth with a napkin. "She was depressed. She felt suicide was the only way out."

"It seems . . . "

"What?" she snapped.

"A bit selfish." Wolfgang wished he hadn't finished his thought. He was out of practice reading women's moods. "All these people here, dying. Sick people fighting until the end, freezing on the porches at night in hopes of getting well."

"I forgot," she said. "You're a man of the cloth now. What she did was a mortal sin. Completely unforgivable."

"Susannah—"

"She felt trapped, Wolf."

"We all do at times."

She dropped her napkin. "Why do you stay?"

Wolfgang looked away. "This is my work."

"There's more to it than that."

"Like what?"

Susannah rubbed her eyes and sighed deeply. "Rita was pregnant."

Wolfgang's heart thudded in his chest. Rita had killed two with her actions.

"She was afraid to have a baby out of wedlock," Susannah said. "She was afraid for the baby's health because she worked here. She made a terrible mistake, but don't condemn the poor girl."

"I'm sorry."

Susannah folded her napkin, then unfolded it. Folded it, unfolded it.

"You feel trapped here too, don't you?" asked Wolfgang.

"I can't stop thinking of her unborn baby." Susannah glanced to her side, where Wolfgang sat running his spoon through his soup.

She looked straight ahead toward a table of patients. "You speak of your dreams, Wolfgang. To be a great composer. To write the perfect requiem. To stand before an orchestra and lead them. But you've never once asked me of mine."

"What's your dream?"

She chuckled sarcastically. "One day I'll get married and have a family. With a washer and refrigerator and a Model-T in the driveway."

"What's stopping you?"

"What a stupid question. How am I supposed to find a husband here, on this hillside, surrounded by death?" Wolfgang had no answer for her. She stood up, waited for a nurse to pass and then stepped closer. "All you do is spend time at that piano, writing something you'll never finish. I'm sorry about your father . . . and for Rose. But all your life you've been searching for an answer you won't get until you die. I'll give you the answer, Wolf. No one knows. That's the answer. Running to the priesthood brought you no closer to the truth."

Wolfgang's mouth dropped open. What had happened since last night? "Have I said something to upset you?"

"You're infatuated with Mozart. You live by candlelight. Everything about you is stuck in the past." She started to walk away but stopped to look over her shoulder. "Do be careful tonight."

"MOTHER, WHERE DO we go when we die?" It was the first question Wolfgang had asked his mother after nearly a week of not speaking since his father's funeral. They sat at the kitchen table eating bread with butter.

"We go to Heaven, son." She took a bite of her bread and wiped a spot of butter from the corner of her mouth. "To live with the Lord."

"So father is in Heaven?"

Tears welled in her eyes. "Yes."

He couldn't believe the tears to be real. She was always so confident with her answers. So sure of it all. For so many years her confidence had nurtured him. Her warm embrace had strengthened him. He would never forget the smell of her nightgown when she'd hug him. But never would he allow her to get close to him. His cold shoulder would push her away until eventually she would give it right back. The house would become a cold place where they did nothing more than sleep and eat. Nothing meaningful would be shared. He'd play the music, not because she asked him to but because his father would have wanted him to. He cut the grass and did the chores because he was taking his father's place in the household. She insisted he attend church to repent for his increasingly belligerent attitude toward her, and eventually he would rebel at that too.

Wolfgang watched her eat the buttered bread, wondering even at his young age if she ever had his doubts—his thirst for more than just faith. What was faith? Why did he believe? Because his father had faith, and his parents before him, and on and on.

"Can father hear me when I talk to him at night? Even if I talk to him in my head?"

"He hears you, Wolfgang."

"Then how come he never answers?"

He saw the same hesitation at age six when he'd asked her how babies were made—like she knew but was baffled as to how to go about telling him.

"He answers you, Wolfgang." She'd attempted to touch his extended hand but he'd pulled it away. "He hears you in ways that you just can't see."

EVEN NOW, WOLFGANG wondered. "Show me a sign?" he said softly. A knocking on his door moved him from his reverie. He sat up in bed, his boots already on and laced. The room was lit. The knocking again. It was midnight. Wolfgang's veins pulsed with adrenaline although much of his heart sagged with the thought of Susannah's disapproval and subsequent fight in the cafeteria. She'd avoided him the rest of the day and evening, claiming she had to work late when he'd asked to walk her home.

Wolfgang opened the door, ushered Lincoln and Big 15 inside and then quickly closed the door. "Did anyone see you?"

Lincoln moved to the left side of the piano. "Relax, it's not like we're stealing anything." He squatted, lifted the side of the piano a few inches off the floor and then dropped it with a clang.

"Careful," said Wolfgang.

"This baby's heavier than I thought."

Big 15 took the other side of the piano. "Ready, Boss? I gots to get up b'fore the sun does." He hunkered down, laced his thick fingers beneath the wood of the piano bottom and lifted his end with an ease that challenged Lincoln to roll up his sleeves and try again.

Lincoln grunted. "You are twice my size. You know that, Hercules?"

Lincoln and Wolfgang lifted the left side while Big 15 handled the right, and together they side-stepped, shuffled, limped, grunted, moaned, cursed, grimaced and nearly fell getting the piano out the door, down the steps and up the incline under the trees. After ten minutes of lugging it through the woods, Wolfgang came to believe that he'd set an insurmountable task, one that would more than likely have them leaving the piano for the forest animals to play on. The incline up into the trees was tough enough on foot. He'd been foolish to think the three of them could carry the piano. He'd already come close to dropping it when he'd gotten his right foot snagged on a patch of brambles, but luckily Big 15 had righted the ship, catching most of the weight on his knees. He'd been limping slightly ever since, but he'd yet to complain.

Lincoln breathed heavily, sitting on the ground with his back against the sappy bark of a pine tree, complaining about the cold temperature and his aching fingers. Big 15 seemed ready to move again. He cleared sweat from his forehead and breathed out plumes of air from his nostrils. Wolfgang felt guilty for having him out here. Not so much for Lincoln. Big 15 tapped the top of the piano, clearly in thinking mode. Or maybe in annoyance?

Wolfgang couldn't get his mind off the creaking sounds that had come from the piano every time they heave-hoed it up the hill. The strings vibrated with every little shift and tug. Something rattled inside every time they lifted it unevenly. One of the wheels had cracked. He feared it would split apart any moment. The instrument was too old for the stress they'd already placed on it.

Lincoln mumbled from the ground. "Work smarter, not harder. Smarter, not harder. Smarter—"

Wolfgang stared him down. "That your motto?"

"Smarter, not harder." Lincoln popped up with a sudden burst of energy. "The tunnel. We take this baby up the chute. The winch system works both ways."

Big 15 leaned against the back of the piano. Something groaned inside. "He's got a point, Boss."

"We'd have to take it down the hill to get it to the bottom of the chute."

"Lot easier than moving it up," Lincoln said.

All in agreement, they started down the hill. It took them nearly three hours and about a dozen stops before they got the piano down through the woods, up the chute and into the first floor of the sanatorium, but the winch system had worked like a charm. Lincoln had been happy to use the chute for what it had initially been designed, as a supply tunnel, instead of a slide for dead bodies. Big 15 had braced himself behind the piano as it ascended the chute, holding it in place in case it decided to shift or slide backward. Lincoln and Wolfgang followed beside it up the elongated steps. By the time they entered the north wing of the first floor they were all near collapse, even Big 15, who eventually complained that it was way past his bedtime. The joints of Wolfgang's fingers ached as if someone had taken a tire iron to them. His legs were sore. His right foot from the shin down to the toes throbbed with every beating of his heart. His wrists were scraped and scratched and near bleeding and his back had begun to tighten up. Lincoln was on the floor in the middle of the hallway, on his back, moaning and cursing under his breath. Big 15 sweated profusely as he leaned against the piano but appeared ready to move on.

Lincoln looked up from the floor. "Father, I hate you for this."

"He don't mean that, Boss. He's smilin' when he said it." Big 15 started pushing the piano down the hallway, broken wheel and all.

"No, I meant it." Lincoln walked beside Wolfgang, pushing along with them.

Wolfgang pointed down the hallway. "To the elevators."

McVain's eyes opened and followed the squeaking sound as Wolfgang and Lincoln grunted and moaned their way across the fourth floor solarium porch, pushing the heavy piano, which, by now, had developed an annoying rumble near the base. The left side partially scraped the floor. Big 15 had left them at the elevators, determined to get a few hours of sleep before he had to get up and push his food and supply cart. He was also nervous about being seen too often in the main sanatorium. Wolfgang and Lincoln took it the rest of the way. A few patients were awake and they watched amusingly as they passed. One man said aloud: "Am I dreaming?" "No," Wolfgang answered. "This is very real." They parked the piano near the foot of McVain's bed and in front of the bricked-in screen window. Wolfgang stood at one end, quite proudly, and Lincoln stood on the other, hunched over at the waist and breathing heavily.

"So this is the surprise?" McVain's head never lifted from his pillow. His lips quivered in the cold.

"What do you think?" Wolfgang asked. "It'll need a few cosmetic repairs but you can play whenever you need to."

"You wasted your time."

Lincoln shook his head and hobbled away.

Wolfgang pointed toward Lincoln, who had already disappeared into the shadows. "They risked injury bringing this piano here—for you."

"I didn't ask them to."

Wolfgang bit his lip. He was physically and mentally exhausted. "You stubborn mule." He pointed a finger at McVain. "Stare at it all night for all I care. It couldn't make you any more bitter." He started to walk away.

"Why do you care? What does it matter if I ever play again?"

"I don't know, McVain. Why should I care about an ungrateful man like you? I can't answer that. It sure isn't pity. But there's something forcing me to press on and I can be one stubborn son of a bitch. So get used to it."

THAT NIGHT IN bed Wolfgang couldn't sleep. His mind jumped from pain to worry and back again. Would Susannah knock on his door in the morning? He couldn't sleep knowing she was still mad at him. It ate away at him like a virus. Would McVain ever get up from his bed and approach the piano? Only time would tell. His body ached too badly to compose anything. He looked across the room, and beyond the patch of moonlight the wall was empty without the piano. His candle and vase stood on the floor. He stared at the ceiling and tried not to move. Every movement caused a different kind of pain. The only constant was that every movement sent pulses down his right leg and into his withered foot. He hadn't felt so immobilized since polio had kept him bed-ridden for nearly six months when he was eight years old.

It had started three months after his father's funeral. His mother felt sure he'd gotten it from another child at school. It started with headaches and a fever. His neck became stiff, his muscles sore and painful to the touch. He was convinced he'd come down with the same thing his father had, and the fear had prompted him to ask his mother. She'd told him repeatedly that it was not, but he wondered how she could be so certain. His father didn't believe in doctors and she showed little evidence that she would ever take him to one. He rested day and night as the fevers made him feel like he was dying. He was too exhausted and weary to fight her when she held damp washcloths to his forehead.

A few days later he fell to the floor on his way to the bathroom and couldn't gather enough strength in his legs to stand back up. His mother had gone off to the factory, promising to be back soon. He'd crawled along the floor like a slug for about ten feet before giving up. He punched his thighs and slapped his legs but felt very little sensation. His bowels let loose right there in the middle of the living room floor and he could do nothing about it. He lay in the foul, putrid filth until his mother came home an hour later. She screamed and hurried to him and nearly vomited when the smell hit her nostrils. Finally she brought in a doctor, a sterile man with narrow eyes, white hair and a small, white mustache. While his mother had opened up the windows to ventilate the stench of Wolfgang's feces, the doctor confirmed that he'd been infected with polio. He'd know more after analyzing the stool sample Wolfgang had deposited in his pants, but after listening to Doris Pike explain the symptoms he felt sure it was polio.

"He could continue to shed the virus in his stool for the next three to six weeks," the doctor had said. "Until then he needs to rest. Drink a lot of fluid."

Is that it? Wolfgang thought.

Doris managed to get him up to his bedroom after she'd cleaned him up. The polio virus had attacked the nerve cells that controlled the muscle movements in both of his legs. Only time would tell if the paralysis would be temporary or permanent. Wolfgang had no choice but to let his mother get close to him. He couldn't push her away. His arms were too tired and his legs couldn't move at all. She was that same loving woman on the outside but he knew that inside dwelled a monster. He felt helpless just as his father had been helpless. He was convinced that any night she could enter his room and smother him with her pillow. Every time his bedroom door opened and she walked in with a tray of food or juice he feared the pillow. At night he'd awaken from nightmares of being suffocated. On several occasions he'd fallen out of bed in meager attempts to run, forgetting that his legs no longer worked. But the suffocation never came. The pillow never darkened his vision.

Instead, his mother took care of him with frequent baths of water and almond meal, mustard applications and physical therapy and massages. Two months later he started getting some feeling back in his left leg, first the thigh and then a few days later below the knee and into his foot. Sensation started to come back in his right leg days later. The following week he tried to walk but collapsed on his bedroom floor. His mother helped him back into bed and told him he may never walk again. He was determined to prove her wrong. So many weeks he'd slept on his back with the hole in the wall above his head, but he'd been unable to get up on his knees and look through it. He could hear his mother crying at night. Did she cry for him? For his father? Did she feel guilty for what she'd done?

His left leg recovered fully but some of the nerve cells in his right ankle and foot had been completely destroyed. They tried splints, rigid braces and uncomfortable corrective shoes but nothing worked. He'd developed what the doctor called equinus foot. The muscles in his right leg that pulled the toes downward worked, but the muscles that pulled it upward did not. So his foot tended to drop toward the ground. His Achilles tendon at the back of the foot had retracted to the point where his foot couldn't take on a normal standing position. His left foot could stand flat on the floor but his right foot could not. He couldn't put his right heel on the ground, so it remained permanently raised. He'd walk on his right toes for the rest of his life and drag them when he tired.

But he'd survive, and with the help of a cane and thousands of miles of pounding the streets with it, he'd learn to walk again.

He still kept the cane in the closet as a reminder of what he'd endured. As Wolfgang lay in bed he contemplated getting up for a glass of wine. If the soreness from moving the piano remained by sunrise, he feared he would have to use that childhood cane to get up the hillside. Just as he started to slide the covers from his limbs, something caught his ear.

Piano music.

It carried magically down the hillside from the fourth floor solarium porch. Wolfgang got back into bed and listened with a broad smile etched into his face.

He knew McVain would cave.

13

WOLFGANG WAS UP before sunrise the next morning, having stolen two hours of sleep after he'd heard McVain playing up the hill. The soreness from the previous night's activities had gotten worse while his eyes were shut. He felt as if his muscles had atrophied for his first few uneven steps across the room, but he'd managed to gain his balance by the time he made it to the bathroom. He braced his left hand against the wall as he urinated. He couldn't stop thinking of Susannah and the disagreement they'd had. He winced as he dressed, but the more he moved, the more his muscles loosened up. He ate an apple, drank coffee, sat on the couch and stared at the front door.

At seven o'clock he heard Susannah's familiar rapping on the door. Not only had she come, but she'd arrived early. He jumped up so quickly he nearly spilled his coffee down the front of his lab coat. He opened the door. She stood at the bottom of the steps, as always, smiling.

"Morning, Wolf."

Wolfgang pulled his door closed and locked it. They walked side-by-side into the woods and he did his best not to appear too stiff.

"I want to apologize for the way I spoke to you yesterday," she said. "I was emotional."

"Think nothing of it."

"Rita got me thinking of my family."

"Of course." Wolfgang knew of Susannah's history and the unfortunate demise of her family. Both of her parents and both of her brothers had been taken by tuberculosis, all within a span of seven years, all but her father passing away at Waverly Hills. She was the only one not infected, and because of it felt a calling to help those that were infected. It was another reason she felt so attached to Abel. Both of her brothers had been younger.

Susannah grinned on their way up the hill. "You're hobbling."

"It's nothing . . . well, all right." Wolfgang gave in and allowed his shoulders to sag. "I'm in severe pain and my back is so stiff I could hardly tie my shoes. I'm sure I'm quite a sight at the moment."

She giggled. "So the piano's up there? No one got hurt? Arrested? Fired?"

"Not yet," Wolfgang said. "Lincoln survived."

"Not without a few complaints, I bet."

"We never would have made it without Big 15."

Susannah folded her hands as she walked. "He always seems helpful."

Wolfgang did his best to keep up with her but his legs were not dependable. Her comment about Big 15 surprised him. She'd barely spoken a few words to him in all the years she'd known him. Wolfgang knew it wasn't prejudice. She didn't have a hateful bone in her body, but he'd noticed the way she carried herself—the way she became withdrawn over the years whenever they ran into a Negro.

"We're early, Wolf."

"Yes . . . yes, I've noticed."

"The other night I wanted to show you something that I've been working on."

Wolfgang rubbed his forehead. "Yes, and I've been too pigheaded and self-involved to remember."

"I can't deny that."

"But it did take me time to get over seeing Marlene."

"Marlene's already at the sanatorium," she said. "The dormitory should be clear. It wouldn't take me a minute to show you."

Wolfgang extended his right arm. "Lead the way."

After they traveled half the distance to the nurses' dormitory, Susannah caught Wolfgang smiling. "What are you thinking about?"

"Barker's reaction when he sees that piano."

Susannah was right. The dormitory was empty when they arrived. No one emerged from the showers. No one watched him suspiciously as he walked inside, but it didn't stop the butterflies from swirling when they climbed the steps to the second floor and entered her room. Unlike his room, her walls were decorated with pictures of her family members and a few oil landscape paintings. He would have liked to have known her family if she was any example of their character. Her bed was neatly made and fit snugly in the corner next to the window. Beside it was a wooden dresser painted white and covered with more pictures and two stuffed animals—one bear and one puppy dog with a missing left button for an eye. She grabbed his arm and walked him across the room to her desk, which was cluttered with stacks of paper, pens and medical books. A large black typewriter—the kind in which the type bars strike upward and the typist could not see the characters they'd hit until the subsequent lines scrolled into view—took up much of the desk's surface.

She pulled out her chair and lifted a stack of pages that was about two inches thick. She appeared nervous as she handed it to him. "I'm not finished yet, but that's most of a first draft."

"What is it?" Wolfgang flipped through, perusing it with interest before coming back to the top page again, which read: *White Death, by Susannah Figgens.*

"Is this a novel?"

She shook her head. "No . . . it's a book on tuberculosis. I've been working on it for five years, reading medical books, studying treatments . . . I'd like to eventually publish it after I find a cure. But I'm not there yet."

Wolfgang flipped through it again, read a short passage about sun treatment, and closed it. "This is wonderful. I had no idea."

"I'd like to become a doctor."

Wolfgang smiled.

"I know . . . you laugh—"

"No . . . no . . . I'm not laughing. I think it's great. I'm just shocked is all."

She took the manuscript from him, placed it back on the seat of her chair and pushed the chair back in the well of the desk. "Well, now you know."

"I'd like to read it sometime."

"Give me a few more months." She looked at the clock on the wall. "We better get going. Barker's probably thrown the piano overboard by now."

DOCTOR BARKER STARED at Wolfgang pensively from behind his desk. His deep-set hawkish eyes glared through his thin glasses. Wolfgang waited for the eruption, but what came instead was an attempt at a controlled temper. "Need I ask what your piano is doing on the fourth floor solarium?"

"An act of God, sir."

"Don't mock the Lord. You of all people." Now the eruption. He stood and pointed at Wolfgang. "You did this behind my back."

"Look, you refused to let me take him to the piano, so I brought the piano to him. What else could I do?"

"I'm sure Lincoln had a hand in this as well?"

"It was my doing."

"And Susannah?"

"She was against it."

"Big 15?"

"Just me."

"Why does he call you Boss?"

"Maybe he calls everyone Boss." Wolfgang knew that he addressed Barker simply as doctor. "Repairs are badly needed at the colored hospital. It's overcrowded, dark, and—"

"Do you think I don't know that, Doctor Pike? I can't do anything without more funding." Doctor Barker sat on the corner of his desk. "We can't have McVain playing in the middle of the night, not when everyone is trying to sleep."

"See if his mood doesn't improve."

"Don't play innocent. You know this isn't only about him. We have hundreds of other patients to worry about. We have occupational therapy, movies, all kinds of activities—"

"But not a piano."

Doctor Barker pounded his fist against the top of his desk. Papers scattered to the floor. "God damn it, they need their rest. We can't have him playing at all hours of the night."

Wolfgang stood eye-to-eye. "McVain already has fans. When I arrived this morning, dozens of smiling patients asked me who was playing the piano and if he'll continue."

Doctor Barker turned away. "Don't bank on it."

Wolfgang gripped Doctor Barker's elbow and spun him back toward him. Doctor Barker pulled away violently and shoved Wolfgang against the wall, where his head hit a picture of Barker's wife, Anne. The picture dropped to the floor, cracking the glass inside the frame. Barker gave it no attention. Instead he stuck his finger in Wolfgang's face. "Don't tempt me. I've got ways to control you if it comes to it. The church doesn't make you invincible."

"What is it about me? What have I done?"

"We have rules."

"It's more than that!" screamed Wolfgang.

Doctor Barker sidestepped Wolfgang and stopped next to his door. "Don't involve Nurse Susannah in this. She has aspirations that go higher than mere music. Don't bring her down with you."

"What do you know of her aspirations?"

Doctor Barker smirked. "You're lucky the piano didn't crush you."

"The piano stays." Wolfgang slammed the door and left.

SNOW FLURRIES SPUN frantically in the wind. The night's frost had settled in and the wet grass hardened to a crunch underfoot. Wolfgang navigated the downhill by himself, using his Babe Ruth Louisville Slugger as a makeshift cane. In his other hand he held his black bag of instruments. He found the colored hospital only slightly less depressing than he had the other night. The cold temperatures seemed to dampen the stench and bring with it a false facade of crisp cleanliness.

He played the piccolo on the solarium porch for a group of about two dozen patients while Rufus followed along with his flute. His reason for playing was two-fold. To give the colored patients the same musical pleasure he gave the whites up the hill, and to make McVain jealous. Off to the side and standing atop his creaky bed, Smokey playfully swung the Babe Ruth baseball bat, repeatedly, probably hitting a hundred imaginary home runs in the short amount of time that Wolfgang and Rufus had played together.

Wolfgang lowered the piccolo from his lips. "Cold."

Rufus stared up the hillside. "I heard him playing last night. He's not bad."

"He's missing three fingers." Wolfgang held up his left hand and wiggled his middle three fingers. "He's learning to adjust."

"What happened?"

"That's what I'd like to find out." Wolfgang spotted Smokey on the bed. "A charming boy."

Rufus nodded. "Your offer still stand?"

"My offer?"

"To play up there."

Wolfgang's eyes lit up. He stood from his seat. "Of course. We can go now if you'd like. Doctor Barker has left for the night."

"What should I wear?"

Wolfgang viewed Rufus' attire—plaid pajamas, a brown coat and black boots. "Come as you are, my friend. Come as you are."

Wolfgang started down the porch, thanking several of the patients for letting him come down and play. He checked over his shoulder to make sure Rufus was still coming. Rufus was slow, hobbled by a limp of his own, and burdened by his hefty size.

When they passed Smokey's bed, the kid held the bat out for Wolfgang to take back. "Thank you, Father."

Wolfgang gripped the barrel of the bat and pushed it gently back Smokey's way. "Oh no, Smokey . . . it's a gift. The bat is for you. Go and become the . . . the black Babe Ruth is what you called it?"

"Yep, the black Babe Ruth." Smokey swung again. "That's right, Father."

No COLD FEET for Rufus. He played the flute as he walked. Once he'd decided to journey up the hillside and throw fate into the wind, he moved at a brisk pace, stopping only when they'd reached the entrance to the Grand Lobby, where he stood in awe of the beautiful décor and pillars that stretched from floor to ceiling. He tested the shiny floor with his shoes, swiping over it like a baseball player clearing the dirt in the batter's box. His reaction made Wolfgang feel ashamed of the vast differences between the two hospitals.

"It's huge." Rufus waddled beside Wolfgang, his flute tucked under the weight of his right arm. The first floor hallways were clear. Wolfgang took Rufus on an elevator to the fourth floor. On the way up Rufus nervously drummed his fingers against the length of his flute, his eyes darting, ears perked by the mechanical sounds of the elevator. The door opened and Wolfgang was the first out to the fourth floor solarium. Again, Rufus moved behind him in awe, peeking through the screened window and down to the lawn four floors below. McVain was playing the piano from his spot down on the porch. Many of the patients slept. Others seemed to be relaxing to the sound of McVain's playing. A few gave Rufus unfriendly looks as they passed the foot of their beds.

"I feel like I shouldn't be here," said Rufus.

An old man lifted his head from his pillow and hissed. "What's the Negro doing here?"

"Ignore them," Wolfgang said, quickening his pace. "That man's in the minority here, I assure you." As they approached McVain and the piano, Wolfgang had Rufus wait in the shadows. Susannah stood next to the piano, turning pages for McVain as he flew through a piece by Chopin. When he stopped playing, several of the nearby patients applauded. McVain shrugged off the attention and turned to face Wolfgang.

"You know Chopin was a victim of tuberculosis," said Wolfgang.

"I'm tired," said McVain. "What did you want to show me?"

Wolfgang extended his hand and Rufus stepped toward the piano, gripping his flute like a child would hold a blanket. He nodded politely. "McVain, meet Rufus. He plays the flute like he invented it."

McVain stared at him like he was an alien. "He's a nigger."

"So?" Wolfgang said.

"So they've got separate hospitals for the jigaboos."

Wolfgang crossed his arms. "I should have known."

"He's no different than you," Susannah said. "He's here because of TB. You're no better because you're higher on the hill."

Wolfgang was proud of her.

And then she added, "You're both probably dying."

"And you both love music," Wolfgang said quickly. "McVain, you played Bach earlier. Rufus, you know any Bach?"

"I do, but I'm perfectly content playing by myself . . . down with my own." Rufus turned away and began walking back down the solarium toward the elevator.

McVain called after him. "Stop by the cafeteria on your way out. Have a banana on us."

14

THE SUN MADE an appearance the following morning and the rooftop was crowded with sunbathers. Men with their shirts off, playing cards and shivering in the cool air. Women with their sleeves rolled up, huddled together and playing some kind of dice game on the terra cotta. Even Herman requested an hour outside, which he spent alone, facing the swings, watching the children play. He'd been on his best behavior since Rita's death. Wolfgang had begun to believe there was a real person inside that confused mind. Every time Wolfgang came near, Herman would watch him with an unreadable gaze, which, had he known better, could have been mistaken for some kind of jealousy.

Wolfgang had spent most of the morning avoiding the fourth floor, but when it was time to add shot to Weaver's bags, the confrontation with McVain was unavoidable. He'd been so angry at McVain last night that he'd felt his blood pressure rise and his heart palpitate. Wolfgang had felt uneasy for hours after Rufus had left, and the walk home with Susannah had barely managed to calm him down. The wine would do the job later. How could one man have so much hate? he'd asked Susannah. But she didn't have an answer.

So as Wolfgang worked on Mr. Weaver he did his best to avoid looking at McVain, which proved difficult because Weaver's bed had been pulled out closer to the solarium window. McVain's bed was closer to the room, in the shadows for some reason, away from the piano and constantly in Wolfgang's line of vision. He couldn't help but notice when McVain rotated on his side, reached across to his chair and grabbed Wolfgang's requiem from the seat. He had his attention then. McVain was a sly creature. He'd even glanced up to see if Wolfgang had noticed, and for a brief instant their eyes locked. Wolfgang looked away as if repelled, still fuming from how McVain had treated Rufus. McVain flipped through the pages, loudly, methodically. Wolfgang was furious and anxious at the same time. No one had ever seen his work before. Doubt crept in, not only because he feared the quality of what McVain was seeing, but he started having second thoughts on whether the bully should even be seeing it. But the requiem needed to be perfect, and for it he would swallow his pride and take any criticism given, however harsh, from the likes of McVain, who couldn't sugarcoat a chocolate morsel if it fell directly onto his bitter tongue.

Mr. Weaver was hot with fever and rather quiet, probably aware that Wolfgang's attention had been turned elsewhere. Wolfgang finished with him and moved on toward McVain.

"The Requiem Rose," McVain said obnoxiously loud. He flipped through the pages some more, shaking his head at random parts, quite aware that he had Wolfgang's full attention now. "It's choppy . . . like here . . . " He pointed to a page near the beginning. "And here."

That was it? Choppy? Wolfgang stood there like some damn fool. Years of work condemned for choppiness?

McVain tapped the front page. "The harmony needs filling out. More notes."

"I'm happy with everything but the ending," said Wolfgang.

"Do you want my help or not?" McVain asked. "And what ending? You have no ending. It just rambles on to this . . . this . . . "

Wolfgang pursed his lips. "Go on."

McVain began leafing through the pages again without preamble. "I've marked places where it needs more improvement, and there are many. The second movement . . . I think needs a double bass to give it a darker feel." McVain sighed, placed the requiem on his lap and rubbed his eyes. "I'll help, but we'll need to start over."

"Start over. I've spent nearly four years on this. That's crazy." Wolfgang stared at him but McVain didn't budge. If he wanted McVain's help the project would have to start anew. It was too much for Wolfgang to grasp. He turned away.

"And get that damn piano tuned!" shouted McVain. "It sounds like a pig at a slaughterhouse. A tone-deaf pig."

Wolfgang fumed his way down the solarium, staring down so the patients could not see the frustration in his eyes. Four years of work . . . Up ahead it was hard not to notice Nurse Cleary and her considerable bulk waving her arms and calling his name.

"Father Pike." Nurse Cleary waved both arms, apparently excited about something. Father Pike. Doctor Pike. She was the only one who never stuck to one name. He could count on her to alternate between the two depending on the weather or the time of day. And sometimes just to throw him off she'd utter both within a ten second span. "Doctor Pike. Father Pike. There's a patient on the second floor who wants to see you. His name is Josef Heinz. Room 218."

Wolfgang hurried down the stairwell, clip-clopping to the second floor solarium porch. Josef Heinz. The name sounded familiar to him. Wolfgang had met nearly every patient in the building, but with the high turnover, meeting them all was becoming increasingly difficult. Inside Room 218, an old man lay on his bed. Wolfgang knocked on the door frame. "Josef Heinz?" The old man pointed out toward the solarium. Outside, dozens of beds clustered together in a bunch for maximum sun exposure and warmth. "Josef Heinz?"

A slender man with long arms and yellow hair raised his right hand. He appeared to be about forty years old, possibly younger. Tuberculosis had a way of prematurely aging the skin. Wolfgang maneuvered among the catty-cornered beds and stood at the foot of Mr. Heinz's, on which a newspaper lay open to the cartoon comic strip "Thimble Theatre."

"One of my favorites," Wolfgang said. "I like the new character. Popeye the Sailor." Wolfgang was convinced that laughter and happiness were strong remedies for pain, regardless of Doctor Barker's beliefs. Mr. Heinz's toothy smile was kind and inviting. He held a small chalkboard on his lap and a piece of chalk in his right hand. Wolfgang sat beside him on the bed. "I believe we've met before. TB of the throat?"

Josef Heinz nodded. Physically he could still speak, but the doctors and nurses didn't permit it except for emergencies. They preferred he used his chalkboard for all communications to allow his throat to heal.

"You asked to see me?"

Josef wrote one word on the chalkboard: Piano?

"You heard him playing?"

Josef nodded.

"Two floors up," said Wolfgang. "He's a patient here. Tad McVain."

Josef wrote: Talented.

"You're one of several fans."

Josef erased his board with a corner of his bed sheet and wrote another word: Flute.

"You've got quite an ear, Mr. Heinz."

"Josef," he hissed.

"Use the board. But Josef it is."

Josef wrote: I'm a concert violinist. Do you have one?

Wolfgang couldn't believe what he'd read. The coincidence was starting to border on weirdness. "At home . . . I have several in fact. I could bring one to you. Will you play with us?"

I'd be honored.

*   *   *

WOLFGANG'S FIRST INCLINATION was to march Josef Heinz up to the fourth floor and have him meet McVain as soon as Doctor Barker left for the night, but minutes before his boss had left, Wolfgang thought of a better idea. He'd take Josef down the hillside to the colored hospital to play with Rufus. Josef was excited about the clandestine trip and greeted Rufus and Smokey with the pleasure of long-lost friends.

Smokey sat on the edge of his bed with his Babe Ruth Louisville Slugger propped against the inside of his right thigh, listening as the duo played the violin and flute with beautiful harmony and richness. Wolfgang sat beside him with his piccolo on his lap, declining to play with them, preferring instead to listen and take it in. The violin he'd given Josef was one of his father's old violins, not the famous *P*, but one of the better ones. It warmed Wolfgang's heart to hear music coming from his father's instrument again— quality violin music and not his typical ramblings. The violin had never been his strongest tool. Rufus and Josef finished a short piece by Brahms and the small crowd that had gathered applauded.

Wolfgang stood and clapped as well. "Bravo." He pointed up the dark hill to the main sanatorium. "Now louder. Let's play louder. I want McVain to hear. Stick the dagger in and twist it."

JANUARY WEATHER IN the Ohio Valley was unpredictable. The sun that had bathed the sanatorium in warmth yesterday had never even showed its face the next morning. Instead the sky was crowded with dark, billowing clouds that appeared confused about whether to rain or snow or sleet as they rolled in so low toward the tip of the bell tower. The temperature hovered near the freezing mark, so it was only a matter of time before they all got to see in which form the precipitation would fall. It looked as if the bell tower would puncture the fluff like a knife against canvas, ripping as the clouds coasted along, spilling the moist guts.

Shortly after lunch, the first drops fell as sleet and pounded against the tiles of the rooftop, snapping and dancing like the dice that the rooftop ladies used for their games. The patients cleared out and headed for their respective solarium porches. A light rain they could withstand, the hard-driving stings of the sleet they could not.

Wolfgang could hear the tumult from the fourth floor and minutes later he noticed several of the beds that had been empty thirty minutes prior suddenly becoming occupied as the patients returned seeking shelter from the sleet. It was a soporific sound, the rain falling as ice pellets. All across the woods, the boughs and branches cowered and swayed. The grounds became covered with dancing shimmers of silver, and then it all changed into a cold rain. Wolfgang approached McVain's bed on the solarium for the first time of the day, determined not to say anything about last night's party at the colored hospital.

McVain was the first to speak. "Hey." Wolfgang continued to walk along as if he hadn't heard. "Hey."

Wolfgang stopped. "I'm busy, McVain. What is it?"

"I heard the flute last night. And a violin."

Wolfgang squashed the smile that so badly wanted to come out by clinching his jaws together. "You refused to play, so I found someone else."

McVain stared at him for a few seconds, scratched his chin with the two remaining fingers of his left hand. "Tell the nigger I'll give him another chance."

"His name is Rufus."

"Okay, Rufus then. But get that piano tuned first."

WOLFGANG TUNED THE piano himself as he'd learned to do from his father so many years ago. McVain listened as Wolfgang tested the keys and after an hour of tinkering they both seemed satisfied with how it sounded. The rain and sleet had decreased as the night moved in, finishing as sprinkles and then snow flurries. The grounds were covered with a slight dusting by the time all had stopped.

Shortly after ten o'clock the coast was clear for Susannah to escort Josef up to the fourth floor while Wolfgang retrieved Rufus from down the hillside, where they'd waited at the fringe of the trees for Doctor Barker to start his jaunt through the woods on the opposite side of the sanatorium to his cottage. Introductions were brief. They had one who wasn't allowed to speak, one who was afraid to speak and one who, when he did speak, put every one on edge as to what might come from his dirty mouth. The most eloquent moment was the expression on Josef's face when he first saw McVain's left hand. Luckily McVain hadn't seen him staring or the night might have been called off before it had even started. Their music was their conversation and it didn't take long for them to mesh, with McVain as the centerpiece in the three-man ensemble—four-man, if you counted Wolfgang as the humble conductor.

For half an hour they played different movements from Mozart's *Requiem*. Although the piece was written for an entire orchestra and chorus, the three of them made it sound full and complete. At some point, and for no longer than a few minutes, each took a solo before the other two would join back in. They spoke with their eyes, their hands, by nodding their heads, never breaking stride, and the awed audience grew by the minute, crowding the fourth floor solarium with what seemed like most of the healthiest patients in the sanatorium.

It all came to a halt when McVain suddenly stopped playing, apparently needing a break to flex his fingers, roll his bullish neck and rotate a kink from his lower back. He pushed away from the piano and looked toward Josef, who was standing beside the piano and smiling as he lowered the violin from his shoulder. Wolfgang watched McVain's eyes and they immediately made him nervous.

"So what kind of a name is Heinz?" asked McVain.

Josef rested the violin against the side of the piano and grabbed his chalkboard. He wrote: German.

McVain stood abruptly.

Wolfgang grabbed his arm. "What is it now?"

McVain wrestled his arm away from Wolfgang's grip. "First a nigger. Then a Kraut. Next you gonna send me up a Jew?"

"If I could find one," said Wolfgang.

McVain stomped off toward his room, his face red. As he passed, Josef showed him a new message. I am a Jew.

Rufus grinned. Susannah chuckled. As much as he tried not to, Wolfgang burst out laughing.

McVain stormed off.

15

THE FOURTH FLOOR solarium, despite the cold winter and the sounds of sickness, was Wolfgang's new office. He couldn't complain because it was his own doing, and he'd convinced himself that the cool temperatures helped him think more clearly. Perhaps that and the absence of wine. The coughing proved motivational, the rigidity of his cold fingers on the keys just another obstacle to overcome. His frozen earlobes only pushed him to focus more closely on sound. He'd come to grips with completely reworking the requiem, and after starting it over, his mind began to flow with the optimism that the work would most certainly be improved because of it. Hearing the three men play had helped rejuvenate his creative spirit and he'd decided to return to the sanatorium after walking Susannah back to the nurses' dormitory.

Near midnight a quiet snow began falling, drawing his attention from the requiem only momentarily for a quick glance toward the woods. Wind blew flakes against the screen and a few of them filtered in through the tiny holes and melted on the concrete solarium floor. McVain lay behind Wolfgang and the piano, fountain pen in hand, reworking a portion of the requiem. Wolfgang blew into his hands, rubbed them together and softly played the new opening, which was to begin with the deep, rumbling tone of a bow gliding across the thick strings of a double bass. Minutes later a viola would enter, and then the three would blend into a piano trio.

Wolfgang imagined a woman's soprano voice singing the introit. He could hear it clearly. He mouthed the words as he played—a song for the angels. A song for Rose. He glanced over his shoulder and found McVain crossing out and scribbling. He'd said very little since his abrupt exit from their ensemble earlier in the evening. If he felt any guilt over his treatment of Josef and Rufus, Wolfgang couldn't see it. He acted as if nothing had happened.

Wolfgang checked his pocket watch—two in the morning. His eyes were getting heavy. Just as he was about to stand he heard someone shuffling through the shadows, where Josef emerged in slippers and pajamas, walking slowly with his chalkboard hanging from a string around his neck.

Wolfgang jumped up. "Josef, it's late. What are you doing up here?" He stood between Josef and McVain in case they started an argument that could potentially ignite into blows.

McVain dropped the requiem to his lap and glared at Josef. "Scram, Kraut."

"Blarney," Josef hissed. Upon his board he'd written a long message: Let me guess. You were a soldier in the Great War. A German blew your fingers off.

McVain read the board and looked away, neither confirming nor denying what Josef had written.

Josef erased the board with a rag he'd brought with him and wrote again: I fought for the Germans. I'm an American now.

Wolfgang said nothing. It was between McVain and Josef. He would not step in unless McVain made a move to strike. Perhaps he was softening?

Josef didn't give up: Where are your parents from?

McVain stared at him with his ornery green eyes before finally speaking. "Ireland."

Then we're both immigrants. He erased and wrote again. And

we're both dying of TB. He erased, wrote. I'd be honored to play with you in the meantime.

McVain grunted, looked away, fingered the bed sheets that he'd pulled up to his waist. "Same time tomorrow. And bring Rufus." He rolled over in bed and faced the other way.

Josef leaned down toward McVain's exposed left ear. He'd saved his throat for the final, strained words. "Make peace with Rufus. Bullets don't care what color the skin is." And then Josef disappeared into the shadows.

THE NIGHT WAS half over when Wolfgang stumbled wearily down the hillside to his cottage. As tired as he was, he tossed and turned in his bed, thinking of everything except sleep—his requiem, conducting his own orchestra, McVain, Josef and Rufus. Their harmony was amazing. He thought of anything to keep his mind off Susannah. His mind wanted to keep drifting to glimpses of her body, glimpses he'd taken many times in the past but was only now allowing himself to see. Her legs as he'd looked up toward her on the stairwell. Her bare knees slightly bent on his couch, the curve of her hip as she rested her head on the cushions, sleeping softly, her chest gently rising and falling to the flow of his piano music. Her eyes fluttering behind closed lids, lips slightly parted.

He thought of her in the shower. The hole in the nurses' dormitory wall called to him, beckoning him from his restlessness. He fought it, determined not to return to that addiction of his childhood. He wondered how his life would have been different had he never looked through that hole in the wall that divided his room from his parents. He never would have seen his mother place the pillow over his father's face. And the next morning when she'd told him in the kitchen that his father had passed away . . . he would have believed her. He never would have turned against her, wrecking their relationship for the remainder of their lives. Would he still have rebelled and sought solace under the folds of Catholicism had he not thought his mother a murderer? Then he may not have ever met Rose. In essence, spying through that hole had traded his mother's life for Rose's. Perhaps he would have become that Protestant preacher she so desired.

Wolfgang had no regret. He would not have traded Rose for anything or anyone, including his parents. What would Rose think of Susannah? His thoughts of spying on her through a hole in a shower wall? Wolfgang forced it all from his mind. It was four in the morning. He felt chilled. He was a priest, for Christ's sake. A man of the cloth. He grabbed his rosary beads from the dresser, knelt beside the bed and began to pray. "Hail Mary, full of grace, the Lord is with thee . . ."

Something thumped against his front door. Not a knock, but a heavy thud followed by a splat. Then laughter. Wolfgang tossed the rosary on the bed and ran to the door. He opened it and jumped back a step as blood trickled through the cracks in the porch, streaming in rivulets from a puddle of more blood. The severed head of a pig faced him, resting in the center of the blood puddle. A knife had been stuck in the animal's skull, pinning a piece of paper to the muddy flesh on top. Its eyes were open and slightly yellowed. Its ears had been sliced off and the tongue cut out.

Wolfgang hurried into his shoes and searched for his baseball bat. After realizing that it was Smokey's bat now he stepped outside, over the pig's head, and ran down the porch steps. A few yards from the porch lay what could have been the pig's missing tongue but Wolfgang wasted no time examining it. Footsteps sounded up the hillside, crunching over the dusting of snow, amidst the dark trees, fleeing, but Wolfgang was determined to catch them. If they were indeed patients, he should be able to catch the tuberculosis-ridden misfits, even with his gimp foot. He half-sprinted and half-hopped into the trees, ignoring the soreness that still lingered in his legs from moving the piano. The footsteps scattered. Laughter. Male laughter from two different angles. Flashes of white confused him and before he could react one was upon him. He wore a white garment not too unlike the vestments Wolfgang wore at Mass, yet atop the attacker's head, covering his face and most of his neck, was a pointed hood with holes from which two shifty eyes peered outward.

"You're gonna die, priest."

The second, dressed in the same white attire, jumped at Wolfgang from the opposite direction. One of them hit Wolfgang hard in the stomach with a thick club. He doubled over. A knee collided with his jaw. He saw stars and tasted blood. It felt as if a couple of teeth had come lose. Unable to fight back, he dropped to the ground to protect himself.

Another voice bellowed from down below. "Hey, Boss! Hey! What the hell?"

Upon hearing Big 15's voice, and most assuredly upon seeing his great size and strength, the attackers took off into the darkness. Instead of giving chase, Big 15 stopped next to Wolfgang, knelt by his side and rolled him over. "You okay, Boss?"

Wolfgang leaned on his right elbow and dabbed at the blood running from his lips. "KKK." He saw a look in Big 15's eyes that he'd never seen before. A look of hate and revenge. Wolfgang made it to his feet with a moan.

Big 15 helped him up. "There's a burnin' cross down by the colored hospital."

By the time they made it to the colored hospital, the flames had been doused with water. A black, charred cross, built crudely with two planks of splintered wood, stood on the grassy rise before the hill plummeted down to the hospital. Wolfgang stopped about twenty yards away, clutching his stomach. Acrid black smoke spiraled from the burnt cross. The grass at the base of the cross was wet. Four buckets rested on the hill. The boards used for the cross looked like those Wolfgang had seen on the woodpile next to the maintenance shed, which supported his theory that the culprits

could have been two of the Waverly patients. Or possibly employ-
ees?

Big 15 kicked the makeshift cross. It held together stubbornly
with a few bent nails. He kicked it again and the planks dropped
to the wet grass. Dozens of patients stood outside the entrance to
the hospital, staring at the broken cross as if to say, how could this
happen to us? Smokey leaned on his bat, his trademark smile nonexistent.

Wolfgang attempted to straighten. "We'll find who's responsible." Wind shifted the smoke away from the hospital. Wolfgang
choked, slumped over and threw up in the grass. He waited there
with Big 15's hand on his shoulder, fought back a couple of dry
heaves and then wiped his mouth. Only then did he realize how
cold he was out there in his pajamas. Big 15 helped him to his
feet. Wolfgang leaned against the wet bark of a tree and collected
himself with some deep breathing. He tasted bile and his tongue
begged for water. "Find out if anyone saw anything." He stared at
the smoldering wood planks on the ground. "I'll ask around up the
hill in the morning. Might even do a room-to-room search."

"Why they afta' you?" Big 15 helped Wolfgang back to the footpath, gripping his elbow the entire way.

"The new Klan is radically anti-Catholic," he said. "I think they're
patients here."

Big 15 chuckled. "Then maybe they gonna die soon."

THE PIG'S HEAD was still on the porch when Wolfgang returned.
The wide yellowed eyes watched him up the steps. Removing the
knife lodged in its skull proved to be more difficult than he'd expected. TB patient or not, at least one of them still had some
strength. He yanked the note from the knife, nearly ripping it in
half. A message had been written in large blocked letters.

ONLY WARNING, PRIEST.
NO MORE NIGGERS IN THE HOSPITAL.

"Cowards." Wolfgang crumpled the paper and stuffed it into his pocket. "How could anyone have so much hate?" And then he thought of McVain. No, it wasn't possible, he thought. He couldn't have done this. Neither attacker had been McVain's size. Wolfgang squatted down over the pig's head and pondered the task before him. After a few awkward seconds of twisting, pulling and jangling, Wolfgang managed to pry the knife free and set it aside next to the cottage wall. He lifted the head in both hands and heaved it into the brush. He watched it roll down the hill for about ten yards until it stopped against the trunk of a tree.

He wiped his hands free of the blood and frost and limped inside, where he sat by the fire until his hands and feet thawed. He could have fallen asleep right on the floor he was so tired and sore. But his face was a swollen, bloody mess. He didn't have the energy to clean it. He crawled on his hands and knees to the front of the couch and pulled his weary body up to the cushions. He convinced himself that he would go into the bathroom later and clean up. He just needed to close his eyes and rest.

He was down for about ten minutes when someone knocked on the door. His eyes shot open. His mouth felt more swollen than it had before he'd closed his eyes.

"Who is it?"

The door creaked open and Susannah's head popped in. She stepped quickly inside and closed the door behind her. "Oh, Wolf, look at you." She knelt beside him. "I came over as soon as I heard." She sniffled as if she'd been crying.

"I'll be fine." He attempted to get up, but her hands pressed firmly against his chest and forced him back down to the cushions.

"Rest." She slowly raked her fingers through his hair and down the side of his beard. She leaned down and kissed his forehead. He was reminded of his mother's kisses when he'd been paralyzed from the polio. He blinked, swallowed a mixture of saliva and blood, and then followed it up with a heavy cough that brought back the bile taste. Susannah was up in a flash, her navy blue skirt swirling behind her as she turned for the kitchen. She was back in an instant with a glass of water. She eyed the bed on her way and decided to reach across Rose's side to snatch Wolfgang's dented pillow instead of the closer one. She handed him the water, lifted his head and stuffed the pillow behind his neck. She helped him with the water. It was cold, but it felt good going down. He was sure he could have managed to hold the glass of water to his lips, but he didn't stop her. He swallowed two large gulps, winced and then grunted.

"Enough?"

"Yes, thank you."

Susannah placed the glass on the floor and re-entered the kitchen. Cabinets opened. Dishes and utensils clanked. The faucet turned on. She returned with a bowl of water and a washrag. His throat felt raw, the taste in his mouth was rancid, his mouth pulsed with pain and his mind worried for the safety of everyone on the hillside, yet he found enjoyment in the moment. Susannah was taking care of him. He told himself it was harmless. She was simply a nurse who had aspirations of one day becoming a doctor tending to a wounded patient. Nothing more. Then why the goose bumps? He wondered if she'd noticed the hair standing up on his arms. He *was* shivering from the chill of exposure. His tongue moved around the cavern of his closed mouth and for the first time he realized he had a tooth missing on the lower left side.

Susannah dabbed the wet cloth to his chin, leaning close enough for him to see the slight imperfections in her skin—a few freckles, a tiny white scar about a half-inch long above her arched left eyebrow, a couple tiny pock marks on her right jaw line. Her eyelashes were longer than he'd thought.

It took her six tries to get the congealed blood off his face, and when she did, she dried his chin with a clean washrag. "Open your mouth," she said. "Oh my, your lip is swollen." He opened his mouth. She leaned closer to examine. He gazed into her eyes, noticing for the first time the tiny flecks of blue around her pupils. He felt the gentle pushes of breath coming from her nose, and he truly believed, despite his pain, that he could have stayed in his current position all night. "Your tooth is definitely missing." She handed him the glass of water. "Wash your mouth out with this."

Wolfgang took a mouthful, swished it around and then spat into the bowl. She dried his neck and then combed his hair with her fingers again. She caught him staring at her face, which was perfectly framed by her wavy blonde hair. She looked away. Wolfgang found the spot against the wall where his piano had been. Rose's vase rested on the floor next to a lit candle. "Thank you."

Susannah scooted down the couch toward his feet and removed his left shoe and sock. He flinched when she began to remove his right shoe. "Please," he said. "Leave it on." At first she appeared hurt by his insecurity, but she gave him a quick smile and lowered his foot back down to the cushion. Rose was the only woman other than his mother who had seen his withered right foot. He didn't feel like showing it now.

He reached down and tugged the note free from the pocket of his pajamas. "This note was left."

Susannah unraveled it, read it and immediately crumpled it again. She dropped it to the floor. "I assume they mean Rufus? It's harmless, isn't it, him playing for a few hours a night?" Wolfgang shrugged. Susannah carefully lifted his legs, sat on the couch and then dropped the weight of his feet on her lap. She massaged his bare left foot. "You'll warn Rufus?"

"Of course."

"And Barker?"

"I don't know."

"He's sure to know what happened."

Wolfgang lifted his head. "But he doesn't have to know about that note." He watched Susannah's hands and slender fingers rub the top of his foot. "Perfect excuse to shut us down for sure."

"You'll be taking a chance, Wolf. It worries me." She stopped rubbing. "I'll talk to every patient if I have to until I find the hoodlums who hurt you."

"I'll live." He rested his head back on the pillow and peered down the length of the couch, where his left heel sunk slightly into the meat of her thigh beneath her skirt. "I'll leave it up to Rufus if he plays or not. He'll be my only concern."

"And you?"

"I'll take my chances." He wondered if it was wrong to take a chance on something that was becoming so right? In a lifetime of searching for proof of his faith, the trio of musicians was the closest thing he'd ever seen to God's intervention. He felt as if He'd placed them all here for a purpose. "I won't allow the threats of the weak to interfere with my plans. Perhaps it is selfish, but I want it for the three other men as much for myself. They're dying. They need it."

Susannah started to argue but stopped. Her grip on his foot became stronger. He turned on his right side to hide his arousal.

"What is it?"

"Nothing." He hoped she would continue to touch him. She did. He stared at the rosary beads he'd tossed on the bed what seemed like hours ago. He felt like a sinner in more ways than one. Was God watching? Was this worse than wearing a white hood and beating a priest? Or burning a cross? He wondered if Rose could see him? Could she hear his impure thoughts? Susannah closed her eyes and eventually fell asleep with her hands on his legs. He watched her for the longest time before his eyes grew heavy, and he too succumbed to slumber.

At some point in the middle of the night he felt Susannah's lips on his left cheek. "I'll be back in the morning," she whispered. And then she was gone.

16

When Wolfgang awoke the next morning, his underwear was cold and recently wet with the same residue that had first startled him on a rainy Friday morning shortly after his twelfth birthday, something his father had been unable to explain to him, something he slowly learned about through ridicule and laughter when he'd asked a few questions of some boys in the schoolyard. The wet sensation reminded him that he'd never kissed a girl until he'd met Rose. He'd avoided them like the plague, knowing deep down that there was no way a teenage girl could be attracted to a boy with such a noticeable limp. At that age they looked for strength and agility, a flippant attitude and a tough demeanor, a cool tongue and a confident gait. Not a disfigured, shy and sheltered boy who preferred internal conversations with himself to any type of talk with his own mother.

In the bathroom, after he stepped out of his clothing, he contemplated what to do with his wet underwear. When it had happened to him as a child he'd stuffed his underwear deep down to the bottom of the dirty clothes, wondering what had happened to him during the night. Was he sick? Had some form of polio returned? He understood now, as a man, which was exactly why he was racked by guilt. After a long, soaking bath he dressed in his drab black clothing, thought about wearing a Roman cassock, but decided on his white lab coat instead. No amount of vestment could overshadow the thoughts in his head. He bundled his soiled clothes and left them in the corner of the bathroom next to the toilet. Perhaps he'd burn them, marred as they were with remnants of pig blood and semen. There was no need to hide them from his mother now. In the mirror, he saw a reflection of tired eyes and a swollen lip that was more or less concealed by the hairs of his beard.

Wolfgang skipped his coffee and said very little to Susannah on their walk up to the sanatorium, his thoughts now centered on an unavoidable confrontation with Doctor Barker. He searched for footprints but the night's dusting of snow had already melted. The cows were especially loud, agitated for some reason or another, mooing, some in unison, some in alternating pitches and starts.

"They actually sound quite good," Susannah said.

"Who?"

"The cows."

Wolfgang laughed. He waited until after Mass to see Doctor Barker, and when he did he heard Susannah's voice inside his office. He'd evidently called her in as well because he doubted she would have ever gone up there voluntarily. Wolfgang waited just outside the door and listened.

"I saw you last night," Doctor Barker said accusingly to Susannah. "Entering Father Pike's cottage."

"He was assaulted," said Susannah. "I went to check on him."

"People will talk, Susannah."

"Then let them."

"Wait." He paused. His tone softened. "Wait. Perhaps when you're finished with your book . . . I can be of some help in getting it published. Maybe a medical journal."

"You would do that?"

"If the work merits it," he said. "We can both work on it. I'm going out of town for a week, but when I get back I'd like to see it."

"Oh . . . okay. Really?"

Wolfgang stepped closer to the open doorway.

Doctor Barker sighed heavily. "What should I do with Wolfgang? He continues to defy me."

"I'm not sure I'm the one you should be asking," said Susannah. "I'm in favor of what—"

"He's giving them false hope."

"He's lifting their spirits. And it's taking his mind off of Rose."

"And you think that is important?"

"He truly believes God has sent him those musicians. It can't stop now, sir."

"But this isn't about him. It's about the patients."

"Exactly, Doctor Barker. The patients."

She gave Wolfgang no time to backtrack down the hallway, leaving as abruptly as she did after her last comment. So instead of pretending he hadn't heard their conversation, he gave her a smile on her way out and then knocked on the door frame.

Doctor Barker looked up from his desk and waved him in. He carefully placed a stack of files inside a briefcase as he eyed Wolfgang. "I'm sorry this had to happen. How's your face?"

Wolfgang touched his lip and chin. "Sore."

Doctor Barker snapped his briefcase closed. "We'd hoped the brick would be an isolated incident. I've contacted the police."

"I believe the two attackers are patients here."

"What makes you think that?"

"One of them has a TB cough." By the light of day, Wolfgang's decision not to risk the music by telling him about the note seemed irresponsible but irrefutable. "I've heard it on both occasions."

Doctor Barker grabbed his briefcase from the desk and held it with a military-type stiffness by his left side. "I doubt anyone at Waverly is affiliated with the KKK."

"TB infects the wicked as well as the good," said Wolfgang. "We'd be naïve to think that everyone here is a saint . . . sir."

Doctor Barker walked past Wolfgang to the door. "I have to go out of town for a week. My mother is sick."

"I'm sorry."

"I think she'll be okay, but she says my presence comforts her."

"Is Anne going with you?" Wolfgang was unsure why he'd even asked about Doctor Barker's wife.

"No," he said softly. "See to it that there are no problems while I'm gone."

As THE DAY drew on, Wolfgang tended to the sick. He listened to confessions and played bedside music for those who requested it. It was a gray winter day with nothing other than freezing temperatures to offer, the type of day where all the plants, shrubbery and grass seemed to shrink as if curling up to preserve heat. More snow flurries fell—the clouds full of uncertainty. Snow appeared imminent, but the clouds had yet to deliver. Snowfall gave the cold weather meaning, a purpose, and it was aesthetically pleasing to the patients.

Sometime after lunch, Wolfgang got word from Lincoln that Big 15 had found the rest of the pig's body in the woods, not far from where the cows were kept. The cows had evidently spotted the carcass and they'd mooed until someone came to find out what the commotion was about. On the attackers, no one had seen anything of significance last night. Susannah had been true to her word and she'd questioned nearly every patient in the sanatorium by sundown. Wolfgang asked questions, snooped around and eyed certain men who could have been close to the heights of his attackers, but everyone seemed innocent and sick. He felt guilty for even suspecting them. He began to wonder if he was way off base. As the night went on his thoughts returned to the music. The boss was away so the mice came out to play.

As Wolfgang had expected, Rufus refused to let the note scare him or stop him from entering the sanatorium and playing with

McVain and Rufus. He'd been given a dose of musical medicine, he'd told Wolfgang, and his soul craved more. When they'd arrived, McVain and Josef were already playing, McVain apparently warming up ever so slightly to his German chalkboard-writing enemy. Susannah listened under the warmth of a wool quilt while Wolfgang conducted at his podium. Maverly's cries carried from her room on the rooftop, but she was mostly ignored, her voice drowned out by the music. The ensemble played for two hours and stopped only because they were exhausted.

McVain blew into his cupped hands. "Can't feel my damn fingers."

Rufus lowered his flute. "And you haven't got that many to feel."

"Well it's fucking cold, I know that much."

Josef flexed his right fingers but said nothing. He wrote **Goodnight** on his chalkboard and stood to leave. Rufus was the next to go. Wolfgang escorted him to the fringe of trees, walked Susannah home and then returned to the fourth floor to work on his requiem. The cold helped to numb his busted lip.

He found McVain still sitting at the piano with a blanket draped over his shoulders. At first he appeared asleep, but as Wolfgang approached, McVain looked up from the keys, eyes red. He shivered in bursts. His red hair squirmed in the breeze. His breath came out in two distinct plumes from his nostrils, which were running with clear snot. He wiped his nose on the blanket. The skin above his upper lip was red and chapped.

"It wasn't me," McVain said.

"What do you mean?"

"The burning cross." McVain faced the piano again and ran his left pinkie across one of the black keys. "It wasn't me."

Wolfgang sat on the edge of McVain's bed. "I never said it was."

McVain turned to face him. "I saw it in your eyes this morning. You wear your emotions on your sleeve, Wolfgang."

It was the first time, to Wolfgang's knowledge, that McVain had called him by name. "Perhaps for a second." He noticed that beneath the blanket McVain had changed into pants, a nice white shirt and a pair of Buster Browns. "Going somewhere?"

"Take me to the colored hospital."

"Why?"

"Because I don't know how to get there, that's why." McVain stood from the piano bench and lifted a brown sack from the floor.

It was the second time Wolfgang had escorted McVain from the sanatorium, but now he walked on his own and Doctor Barker would know nothing about it. McVain had begun to open up, but he was still far from the conversationalist Wolfgang had hoped he'd become. He never offered up what he carried inside the brown paper sack in his right hand, and Wolfgang decided not to risk spoiling the mood by asking. McVain's eagerness to reach the colored hospital was a pleasant shock, and he didn't hesitate to stand beneath the lit porch and wake up whoever was sleeping above.

"Hey . . . Rufus!"

Wolfgang stood in the shadows and leaned against a tree. It was McVain's business. He would give them privacy to talk unless invited.

A portly lady with caramel-colored skin pressed her face against the screen and called downward. "My land, man, what could you possibly want this time of night?" She glanced over her shoulder and spoke to someone. "It's a white man."

"I'm looking for Rufus," called McVain. "Is he there?"

"What's in the bag there, mister?" the lady asked.

He raised the brown bag. "Beer."

"Got one for me?"

"No."

McVain waited for a moment under the single, elevated porch. The wet grass glistened in the moonlight. Crickets chirped. One minute passed, then two. Just when McVain appeared ready to give up and return up the hill, Wolfgang delayed by engaging him in conversation.

"How'd you get the beer?"

"Lincoln." McVain glanced over his shoulder. "Said he can get anything up the tunnel."

"So you know about the tunnel?" Wolfgang asked. McVain nodded. "Lincoln seems to have a limitless supply of giggle water."

McVain grunted. "He's infatuated with Al Capone. Says he hangs around the Seelbach Hotel. I think he's full of all kinds of shit, personally."

They shared a laugh.

Just when the look of dejection began to resurface, Rufus stepped out in his pajamas, slippers and a dark coat. "What do you want?"

McVain held up the brown bag and removed the two beer bottles. "Could only manage two."

Rufus watched him for a few seconds. McVain stood only a few paces from where the cross had burned. As if he'd read his mind, McVain looked down, spotted the charred grass and respectfully stepped aside. Rufus took a few cautious steps forward.

McVain handed Rufus a bottle that had already been opened. "No problem keeping it cold."

Rufus grinned, barely, and took a swig. He wiped his mouth with the sleeve of his coat. McVain walked down the slope and sat on a concrete bench next to the brick building. Rufus found room beside him. Wolfgang sat down in the grass about twenty feet away. Their voices carried.

McVain took a swig of beer. "My father hated Negroes."

Rufus drank. "My father was a slave. I don't punish you for it."

"It was all I knew," said McVain. "I've never had a friend that wasn't white. I sure as hell didn't plan on starting here."

"I didn't expect to meet the likes of you either."

McVain sighed, took a swig and coughed into his left hand, which did little to stop the mist that flew from his mouth.

Rufus lifted his pajama shirt and showed McVain a circular wound on the left side of his stomach. "I was shot at St. Mihiel."

Wolfgang knew that McVain was in the war, and that he'd probably lost his fingers there. It was the perfect opportunity to offer how he'd lost them, or where, but McVain offered nothing. But their conversation rolled on. Rufus and McVain, drinking bootlegged beer given to them by an orderly with an affinity with speakeasies and Al Capone, talked for nearly two hours. After their defenses had lowered they'd invited Wolfgang over, making room for him on the bench.

Rufus was one of nearly two hundred black soldiers to receive the French Medal of Honor. He was in the 93rd Division of the United States Army, an all-black division that was kept apart from the white soldiers. Instead they were sent to France, wearing U.S. uniforms, to fight side-by-side with the French troops. They fought with honor. They'd volunteered by the thousands to fight for a country in which they desperately sought inclusion. It was their opportunity to express patriotism and bravery, said Rufus with passion. They fought in the battles of Argonne, Chateau-Thierry, St. Mihiel, Champagne, Vosges and Metz, yet Uncle Sam never saw them as equals. Out of nearly four hundred thousand black soldiers in the army, only ten percent had been assigned to combat.

McVain and Rufus talked about music, about the war, about buddies killed in action and about war stories thought long buried. But every time the conversation began to approach the end of McVain's service in Chateau-Thierry or its aftermath, he quickly changed the subject.

Long after the beer was drained, Rufus wished them goodnight and returned to bed. There were no handshakes involved in the departure, but it was obvious that a corner had been turned and barriers of pain had been hedged. Wolfgang helped McVain into bed. He'd been so exhausted after hiking up the hill that Wolfgang nearly had to drag him across the solarium or find a wheelchair.

McVain tugged on his bed sheets. His lips quivered. "I was set to travel all across Europe to play for royalty, not to kill."

"The Selective Service Act stole your life," said Wolfgang. "I'm sorry."

McVain mimed Uncle Sam's stern poster expression and pointed at Wolfgang with his mangled hand. "I want *you*." He lowered his hand. "Son of a bitch."

Wolfgang listened to McVain's labored breathing for a moment. "What was your wife's name?"

"Jane."

"Where is she now?"

"We divorced years ago. She moved to Virginia. Remarried." He stared down at his fingers. "I would have given both of my legs to keep my fingers."

Wolfgang patted his shoulder. "Your playing is getting better."

"It's terrible." McVain folded his arms. "I'll never play like I used to." He flicked a crumb from his bed sheet and closed his eyes. "I wonder if you'd be so damn friendly if you knew my sins." He opened his eyes. "I was prepared to die on this hillside, you know. I was ready to end it all."

"But now?"

He stared, but said nothing.

17

DOCTOR BARKER'S ABSENCE was like a vacation. McVain, Rufus and Josef played every day and night to near exhaustion, taking breaks only when Wolfgang would demand it. Extra medical duties had fallen in Wolfgang's lap and he'd shared them with Susannah. He allowed her to assist on a nerve crush. She'd been by his side when he'd removed two rib bones from a woman who'd been a patient at Waverly for seven months and her lungs had stopped functioning properly. For the days Barker was gone, Susannah was used as an extra doctor. They kept so busy they rarely had time to join the ensemble, but the music carried on. Patients on every solarium listened to their playing. The days passed quickly. Bouts of snowfall graced the sanatorium every day, but nothing sustained enough to cover the grounds.

Patients healthy enough ventured up to the fourth floor to get closer to the music. The audience grew daily. The trio played Mozart and Haydn, Beethoven and Schubert, Baroque and Classical, Renaissance and Romantic, and by the fourth day of Doctor Barker's absence, they'd begun to dabble with their own original pieces. No longer restricted to playing at night, the trio flourished. Three instruments became one. Their minds fused. Josef's wife Steffi brought chocolate-chip cookies. They played for her and between pieces she told them stories of Josef's past—about his clumsiness in the war, his inability to fire a gun the first time he'd tried, his violin performances in Austria, his playing on stage in front of hundreds, embarrassing moments in their fifteen happily married years, and their immigration to the United States and how he'd thrown up seventeen times on the boat trip across the Atlantic. The Great War had crippled Germany's economy. Josef's Berlin music store had gone out of business. Propaganda began to circulate through the cities, some of it blaming the German Jews for losing the war and for the state of the country afterwards. They'd fled the growing anti-Semitism and come in the summer of 1925—the year of Rose's death—to a new life in America.

McVain listened intently to every word that flowed from Steffi's mouth, no longer disgusted at the aggressive German accent. He looked at Josef as a fellow survivor, thrown into a war just as he had been, fighting scared. For the first time since the war, McVain had made new friends, and he'd chosen them from his enemies.

No new threats had come from Rufus' daily presence in the sanatorium, which prompted Lincoln to half jokingly accuse Doctor Barker of wearing the KKK robes. The attackers, if they did indeed live on the hillside, were keeping a low profile, possibly waiting until the fear died down. Wolfgang didn't drop his guard. Every night he worked on his requiem, collaborating not only with McVain but also with Rufus and Josef, both of whom proved valuable when it came to the rewrite. But McVain was the catalyst. His fingers had been lost to some mysterious accident in the war, but his mind had not been touched. His creativity had been building for years, untapped by his refusal to even look at a piano for ten years. Wolfgang was convinced that McVain's touch would make it a masterpiece. He was the teacher and Wolfgang the student.

Wolfgang took the requiem home with him every night to continue working on it. Once the piece had begun to gain some momentum, he found himself unable at times to push it aside.

His wine consumption increased to a bottle a day. It was becoming increasingly more difficult to separate music from work. On the fifth night of Doctor Barker's absence, he paced the floor of his cottage, his hands moving to the sound of music in his head—violins and violas, flutes and clarinets, double bass and piano, woodwinds, strings and brasses together. Rose would get nothing short of perfection. Just as his mind had nearly become lost in a violin solo, a knock at the door interrupted.

"Who is it?"

"Open up, it's freezing out here." It was Susannah.

Wolfgang unlocked the door and opened. He'd escorted her to the dormitory less than an hour before and nothing in the way she'd said goodnight gave any hint that she might suddenly drop by at ten minutes past midnight waving a newspaper ad in his face.

"What is it?"

"Hello to you, too." She pushed the ad in his hands. "New Steinite Radio. Thought you might want to take a look."

Wolfgang perused the ad. "A hundred and eighteen dollars. I can't afford this."

Susannah snatched the ad back from him. "Start saving." She pointed to the small table beside the fireplace where his phonograph rested like the fossil it had become. "It would look great in place of that monstrosity." She sat down on the couch. "Think how it would sound."

"Rose loved that phonograph."

"Of course she did."

Wolfgang sat beside her on the couch. "Susannah . . . what are you doing here?"

"You want me to go?"

"No, no, I just mean . . . it's late."

She clapped his shoulder and stood. "You stay up all hours of the night working. It's not late for you and I'm not tired."

"Have you been drinking?"

She rolled her eyes and spotted the open bottle of wine on the floor. "No, but I see that you have."

Wolfgang walked to the window and leaned against the sill. A cool draft blew over his hands. "Did anyone see you?"

"What does it matter? What do you care what others think?"

"I'm a priest . . . and you're a woman."

Susannah sat back down and crossed her legs, showing bare knees and calves. "But that shouldn't matter to you, right?"

"Of course not."

"This is just an innocent night with a friend."

"Exactly."

"And if you feel nothing for me as a woman, then what are you worried about?"

Wolfgang nodded in agreement. "This is as harmless as if Lincoln visited me in the middle of the night."

Susannah looked offended for a second, but her smile quickly returned. "What were you working on? Rose's Requiem? Can I hear some of it?"

Wolfgang hesitated before grabbing his father's P violin that rested on the stone hearth of the fireplace. His eyes drifted to the swell of her breasts beneath her red dress, and then he focused again on the violin. He fit it between his shoulder and neck and lifted the bow. "I'm not terribly good at the violin."

"Just play."

He played. It sounded much better in his mind than what resonated from the instrument's f-holes, but it was a work in progress and he was far from a virtuoso on any of the string instruments. He stood in the middle of the floor, lightly tapping the toes of his left foot against the floor while maintaining his balance on his right leg. He focused on the fingers of his left hand as they danced over the strings. He concentrated on his right arm, making sure the bow slid across the strings at the correct angle on every touch. Susannah didn't seem to mind his awkwardness on the violin, wincing only once when he hit the wrong note. What stole Wolfgang's attention, five minutes into his playing, was when Susannah closed her eyes, leaned back on the couch and began to hum. Her humming turned into soft singing. Her voice was lovely. He couldn't take his eyes off of her. He pulled the violin from his shoulder.

She opened her eyes. "I like it."

"I didn't know you had such a nice voice, Susannah."

"Sorry, it just came out."

"I had no idea you could sing."

She sat up straight. "I can dance too. And cook. And sew."

And then it hit him. His eyes widened nearly as much as his smile.

"What is it, Wolf?"

He sat next to her on the couch, not completely unaware that their legs were touching. She didn't move away. "I write piano parts and violin parts and flute parts," said Wolfgang, "but in my head I always hear a soprano singing the words. And now you've given it a voice. What's a requiem without a choir? But enough of my requiem. Our little ensemble needs a choir . . . a chorus."

She leaned away from him playfully. "And where will you find a choir, Wolfgang?"

"From the patients, of course."

THE NEXT MORNING was the sixth day of Doctor Barker's absence. Finally the snow had fallen, covering the grounds with an inch of accumulation. It was a wet snow that clung to the top of every tree branch and rested in the pockets of every bough. The mood was optimistic on the hillside—the perfect atmosphere for recruitment. Wolfgang and Susannah, along with Lincoln and Abel, spoke to every patient and staff member, searching for people who were willing to sing and still had the lungs to belt out a tune. Chatter grew throughout the day until talk of a choir was on everyone's lips.

By nighttime, they'd collected twenty-seven volunteers, two of whom Big 15 and Rufus recruited from down the hill—a man and a woman—and Abel had grabbed five eager kids from the children's pavilion. The turnout was better than Wolfgang had expected. They gathered on the fourth floor solarium. Several neighboring patients, including an ailing Mr. Weaver, had volunteered to scoot their beds to make room for everyone. Susannah arranged them in groups—men, women and children—and positioned them to the right side of McVain's piano. Josef and Rufus stood to the left of the piano while Wolfgang took a position in the center so that all eyes could follow his conducting, knowing going into it that most of them would not have a clue what each movement of his arms would mean. He would teach them.

Susannah situated a ten-year-old girl next to Abel in the front row and then bounced over toward Wolfgang. "They're ready. A few have really lovely voices."

"And you shall lead them," he said.

Susannah spun away to join the women's section on the right side of the choir. The men stood to the left. Wolfgang faced them all and spoke over the bitter wind that fought for inclusion through the screen windows. "I admire everyone's courage on this cold winter night and I welcome you all to what I believe will be a beautiful and healing process." They stood silent, focused on every word. "Don't be shy with your voices. I understand that some of you simply want to be involved and admit not to be the best of singers, but that doesn't matter to me. The fact that you're here is all that counts."

The patients stared back at him with haunted TB faces. Some had sunburned cheeks, others were deathly pale. A few scattered coughs filtered through the choir, but something new now burned in their tired eyes.

Wolfgang raised his arms. "We'll start with the *Cantate Domino* of Hans Leo Hassler." They continued to stare at him, even Susannah. McVain rolled his eyes. Josef, without hesitation, gripped his bow and readied himself. "I'm kidding," said Wolfgang. "We'll get to that eventually. We'll begin by warming up our voices with some simple scales." He nodded to McVain, who began playing the scales on the piano, apparently bored by the simplicity and sitting there slumped over like a hunchbacked troll. "Women first," Wolfgang shouted.

The thirteen women opened their mouths to sing. They started slowly, reluctantly, struggling to sing in the freezing weather, but after a few minutes their voices began to thaw and what came out of their weakened lungs became warm and lyrical. Clouds of steam puffed like smoke from every opened mouth. After the women, the men sang, and finally the children. When Wolfgang had them all sing together and began to tinker with different ranges and parts and to experiment with different combinations of voices, it all started to come together. They had several sopranos, a few tenors and a couple of baritones, but they lacked that one deep, bass that would have made it perfect. Nevertheless, the choir, after only a few hours of practice, had already passed Wolfgang's expectations and showed an eagerness to learn more.

Just before ten o'clock, when Wolfgang was ready to rehearse a short section of a Mozart mass, Lincoln hurried by his side. "Barker," he said, breathing heavily. "He's back early."

It took a second for the words to register, but when they did Wolfgang moved frantically, motioning for the patients to return to their rooms. But it was too late. Doctor Barker's voice boomed from somewhere on the solarium. The crowd of spectators parted like the Red Sea and Moses walked on through.

"What's the meaning of this?" Doctor Barker stood a few feet away from Rufus and Josef, who quickly stepped aside.

Wolfgang nodded toward Susannah and the choir. With Susannah directing them, they began to return to their beds and floors. Doctor Barker stared at him with contempt. Before berating

Wolfgang, Doctor Barker allowed everyone to clear out, all except McVain, who simply stood from the piano, shuffled to his bed and pulled up the covers. So much steam came from Doctor Barker's facial orifices that one would have thought a fire smoldered inside his head. "I want the piano taken down."

"It's too heavy," Wolfgang said. "And we recently had it tuned."

Doctor Barker pointed a rigid index finger in the air. "Sick patients standing out in the cold . . . in the middle of the night? In the heart of the winter? They'll die. And you call yourself a doctor? Or a priest?"

"They'd be lying in their beds in this same cold air. At least the singing keeps them warm."

"The standing puts strain on them."

"We'll get them chairs."

"And what about those children? This is a school night."

"Do you think these children worry about school, Doctor Barker?" Wolfgang pointed to where the children stood moments before. "They're here because they're sick. They care more about figuring out how *not* to die on this hillside. The children are the strongest we have."

Doctor Barker stepped closer, as if ready to physically attack. "Our entire city is in a panic. This is the most sought-after TB hospital in the country. And not because of the music. I won't have you damaging our reputation—or our patients. Prove to me that music can cure TB."

"Prove to me that it doesn't."

"I studied at Johns Hopkins—"

"Did you see their faces?"

Doctor Barker clenched his jaw. "They're tired."

"It makes them feel good," Wolfgang said. "You can't deny them this luxury."

"How dare you speak to me this way, Father." He glared at Wolfgang's white collar.

"Miss Schultz asks me every day . . . where do the bodies go? I lie. I change the subject. I don't tell her about Lincoln's Death Tunnel."

"They need rest and fresh air."

"That's what we tell them, but they're still dying at the rate of one per hour." Wolfgang stepped dangerously close to him, daring Doctor Barker to shove him—both of them too irate to stop and think about how unprofessional and disruptive their public argument was to the patients' well-being. "We have no cure. My only cure is to heal their soul. Make them happy. Make them look forward to opening their eyes the next morning. That is my mission now."

Suddenly, McVain's voice came from his bed. "Shut us down and you'll regret it."

Doctor Barker spun to face him. "Are you threatening me?"

McVain sat up in bed, resting his weight on his elbows. "I've done much worse things in my life than threaten someone. But if I have to I will."

Doubt began to flood Doctor Barker's face and Wolfgang didn't give him time to muster a retort. "Do you realize the talent we've stumbled across here? This is no coincidence. This is fate." A notion hit Wolfgang—an ally whom Doctor Barker couldn't touch. "God has put these people here. The music is from God. The music is religious. The choir has a calling from Him."

"Don't try to hide behind your collar." Doctor Barker shook his head. "That's sacrilege."

"You can tell me what to do as a doctor, but not as a priest." Wolfgang pointed down the solarium. "We have over four hundred patients here, and behind every one of them is a story. We need to learn from them. Connect with them. The music will bring them life." Wolfgang softened his expression, lowered his voice. "Don't be their enemy, sir. Death is their enemy."

Doctor Barker started to turn and then stopped. "I'll go to the archdiocese."

"On what grounds?"

"Prohibition keeps you from buying your wine in stores." Doctor Barker pointed to his chest. "I track every order that comes into this place, *Father*. It seems the consumption of sacramental wine has risen quite substantially since you've been here. Yet the church attendance is falling off." He stormed off without another word.

WOLFGANG STAYED ON the fourth floor solarium porch that night and played as if for the last time. He played for the patients. He played for Rose. He hoped she could hear him from somewhere. He played for McVain, who attempted to sleep in his bed behind the piano. He appeared restless, tossing and turning, the mattress springs groaning with every shift of his weight. Every ten minutes McVain would punch his right fist into the center of his pillow and then plop his head inside the dent. Nothing seemed to work.

Wolfgang's fingers ached, his joints stiffened. He was too unfocused and uncomfortably cold to work on the requiem. How dare Barker accuse him of abusing the system? Prohibition had decimated the wineries across the country. Making sacramental wine was the only way that some of them stayed alive.

Wolfgang stood from the piano with reluctance, fearing that it could be gone in the morning. He walked the requiem over to McVain's bed and locked the manuscript in its black case to which only he and McVain had a key.

McVain's eyes were open. "You really believe this is fate?"

Wolfgang flinched. "I thought you were asleep."

"It's twenty-five degrees out here and you expect me to sleep? I asked you a question."

Wolfgang dropped down on the cold folding chair beside the bed. "What do you think?"

"Coincidence," said McVain. "There's no other explanation. You believe in God because it makes you feel better about where you're going after you die." He looked Wolfgang straight in the eyes. "We're going nowhere except the ground we're buried in."

"You don't believe in God?"

McVain laughed. "Do you? I mean really?"

"Of course."

"Then why the look in your eyes?"

"What look?"

McVain sighed and laughed a silent, cynical laugh. "Why did you join the priesthood after your wife's death?"

"It was a calling from God."

"You say that as if you rehearsed it, Father." McVain's breathing was labored, pushed out in shallow bursts followed by bouts of calm. "What about Heaven and Hell? Do they exist?"

Wolfgang paused, stared down the solarium. "There is a Heaven, McVain, and one day I'll see Rose in it."

"With the angels, huh? Floating around above the clouds in pure bliss with wings and shit?"

Wolfgang stood. "Goodnight, McVain."

McVain held his head upward, his voice strained. "Do you really think there's a Hell?" His head settled on his pillow again. "A place of fire where the bad people like me go? Or was it concocted to keep people straight. Be a more dangerous world without the fear of consequence, wouldn't it?"

"What have you done that's so bad that you should go to Hell?"

"Maybe one day I'll tell you," he said. "Maybe one day I'll pour my confession out to you. But what would it matter?"

"It would empty the bitterness in your heart."

"Don't you have bitterness? You haven't spoken to your mother in ten years." Wolfgang opened his mouth to speak but nothing came out. McVain smiled. "The bitterness keeps me going. I wouldn't know what to do without it." Wolfgang started to leave but again McVain stopped him with another question. "Would God keep a moral man from Heaven's gates?"

"I shouldn't think so."

"Even if he doesn't believe in God?" Where was this heading, thought Wolfgang? McVain said, "There was a time when I thought I'd been blessed by God because of my talents."

"When did you lose this belief?"

McVain held up his left hand and wiggled his pinkie and thumb. "Was it coincidence that sent me to European soil? Or was it fate?"

"I don't have all the answers, McVain."

McVain's jaw tightened. His eyes glazed over with moisture, not from tears but from some buried pool of pain that wanted badly to come out. "I made a decision while I was over there, Father. I lost these fingers as a result of it. If it was a punishment from God, then I hate Him for it."

"God doesn't punish—"

"It's easier just not to believe," he said. "What kind of God would give something like this and then take it away?"

Wolfgang immediately thought of Rose. "Goodnight, McVain. I'll pray for your answers tonight." He turned away, unable to shake the vision of Rose from his mind—how she looked, how she talked, how she breathed when she slept, how she smelled, how she tasted, the feel of her skin . . .

You'll never walk again, Wolfgang . . .

Wolfgang referred to the years after he'd recovered from his polio paralysis as the "walking years." During his polio recovery, he started off with the upper floor, walking down the hall with the aide of a wooden cane his mother had come home with the day after he'd insisted he get out of his bedroom. He wouldn't allow her to baby him anymore. He'd used the cane so often that the grooved feel of it would always be ingrained in the palm of his right hand. Next he'd used the stairs to strengthen the muscles of his legs. Up and down he'd travel them, twenty times a day, before and after school, from the living room to his bedroom until he'd begun to wear the shine from the wood on the middle of each uneven step. He'd step up with the left foot, drive the cane down on the same step and then lift the right foot up next, the sound of each movement distinct, like a ritual, like a song. He pounded every inch of the sidewalk up and down their street, his daily presence as common to the neighbors as the milkman and mail carriers. Neighbors would wave, and sometimes, depending on his focus, Wolfgang would wave back. Mostly he'd nod and keep to his business, venturing outside more than he ever had in his life, loving the freedom of it, away from his mother's increasingly extremist remarks and teachings of her religious thinking.

In high school he was allowed to venture down the road to Central Park, where the famed architect Frederick Law Olmsted, of New York's Central Park fame, had designed a large open-air shelter with a colonnade built on top of the hill where the art museum had been. Wolfgang had watched the construction as he'd walked the seventeen acres of the park throughout each week, he and his cane clip-clopping around the winding walking trails, careful not to place the end of his cane in any patches of sunlight that bled through the overhanging tree limbs. It was a game. His cane couldn't touch the sunlight and his feet couldn't step on any crack. On some sunny days he'd appear to be dancing as he side-stepped and maneuvered his way around the patchwork of light and shadow, watching the squirrels and dogs chase each other, watching the women push babies in strollers, and waving to the horse carriages. Some days he'd stop to skip rocks across the wading pool or stare at his reflection in the shimmering water, sighting the first curls of black hair on his chin that would later become the beard he would never shave from his face.

After several years of walking the park, it was time to expand his horizons. Adolescence had made him curious and a bit adventurous. He'd finally gotten rid of the cane and decided it was time to venture further downtown. He stretched it a block or two every day until his daily jaunt had reached nearly ten miles. He'd packed a canteen full of water on his trips, sipping and rationing it out so as not to run dry too early. He'd hurry across streets and then his pace would slow on the sidewalks. It would slow even more when he'd curiously pass a bar or whorehouse on Green Street, where the men liked to drink to crudeness and dirty crib girls were known to give themselves for money. He'd imagine them in the throes of passion and then hurry on, snickering inside his head at the dirtiness of it all. He liked to pass storefront windows and watch his limping reflection, a boy without a care, a boy with no destination.

Until he hit Fifth Street on a summer day of his seventeenth year and noticed the tall spire extending from the pitched roof of a glorious building down the way. Clouds passed above it, moving with the wind. And Wolfgang followed with his heart pumping with an adrenaline he couldn't yet explain. Something seemed to be calling him, a throbbing in his gut, a warm feeling he could only compare to that which he'd get after his father would occasionally pat his back after he'd played a complete piece on the piano without screwing up. His pace quickened as he limped toward the building. He walked so fast his right foot began to drag, the toes of his black shoe like a broom sweeping across the dirt-covered concrete. A horse carriage rumbled down the street. He pretended to race it.

When he reached his destination, he stood for a moment with his hands on his knees, staring at the tall facade and large arched doors. Two women in pretty dresses and carefully-put-together hairdos walked up the wide steps and opened the massive doors, and what emerged from the belly of the building was the angelic singing of a choir, singing in a language he'd never heard before yet felt drawn to. He took out his canteen and drank more water. He stared at the building for a good five minutes before inching closer to the steps. A man in a top hat brushed past him and apologized on his way into the building. Wolfgang knew it was a church of some sort but he wasn't sure what kind. He surprised himself by speaking out at the man.

"What place is this, sir?"

The man stopped on the church steps and faced Wolfgang with a grin. "Why, this is the Cathedral of the Assumption."

"Cathedral . . . Is it Protestant?"

The man chuckled in a friendly way. "No . . . it's Catholic. Try coming in some day." He tipped his hat. "Good day." Wolfgang watched the man disappear into the church. He spent the next two hours sitting on the steps, contemplating entering. On that day he didn't, and when he got home he spoke nothing of it to his mother. Over dinner she said to him, "You have a smile on your face, Wolfgang. I'd like to know the cause, but I'm sure you won't tell me."

He simply nodded with that same smile and eventually she dropped it and focused on her plate again.

Four weeks later he did enter the cathedral. He arrived at a time when there was a rush of people entering daily mass. He limped hurriedly to funnel inside with the herd, and once he entered he knew he'd found the part of his life he'd been missing. He was swept away by the vastness of the building, the grandeur of the architecture, the colors of the tall stained glass windows that dominated the side walls, the height of the ceiling that hovered over what he would later learn to be the nave. Upon entering, he stopped without thinking to gawk and was nearly trampled by the incoming people. He stumbled back toward the baptismal pool and font that stood before the length of the center aisle, the pool where he would become fully immersed in water during his baptism into Catholicism two years later with Rose by his side. He righted himself and sidestepped out of the way, watching as the people poured in and the choir practiced singing in the choir loft above the entrance. Everything looked so different than the church he'd grown up attending with his parents, which was miniscule in comparison. Wolfgang faced the body of the church. So many seats filled the expanse. Marble and granite everywhere. One large center aisle flanked by two side aisles. Giant pillars stood like endless tree trunks along the center aisle, stretching up to sweeping arches and a curved rooftop highlighted by a painted fresco of cherubs surrounding Mary at the time of her assumption into Heaven. At the far end of the church behind the altar was the massive Coronation window that took up much of the back wall. Sunlight penetrated the stained glass, illuminating the purple, gold and deep blue colors that dominated the window. The colors shone brilliantly, prism-like, across the altar and marble floor. Dust motes hovered in and out of the light. Mary was being crowned as Queen. God took her body into Heaven—she was a sign of the eternal goal. He would dream of that window at night and the vision would save him from the pillow that suffocated him in every nightmare.

Wolfgang sat in the back row of the cathedral, captivated by that window. He listened to the priest at the pulpit, how his voice reverberated off of everything it touched. Later, during a silent lull in the mass, he asked a neighboring woman, "What language is he speaking?"

"Latin," she said. "The priest is speaking Latin."

Latin . . . He'd heard his parents refer to the language during several of their rants on the Catholic Church and the Pope and Rome's influence in the states. One day, he thought, perhaps one day I will speak Latin and preach from a pulpit while others listen.

He kept his daily walks a secret for nearly two years, until one day Doris had decided to follow him. She followed him around Central Park and eventually to the cathedral, where he'd bounded the steps with an enthusiasm that had nearly made her nauseous. When he'd exited the cathedral after Mass, she'd stood horrified on the sidewalk, so angry she couldn't look him in the eyes.

"Hi, mother," he'd said in passing. "I've found my calling. I'm going to be a Catholic priest."

Doris Pike dropped to the sidewalk and wept.

18

Sʜᴇ ʟᴏᴠᴇs ᴍᴇ . . .

She tells me as much every time we meet, claiming it had all started with a glance on the church steps when I'd simply held the door for her. But in truth my love for her started weeks before, when I'd taken my normal seat in the back of the cathedral and spotted her arrival. In fact I'd heard it.

She arrives a few minutes late and the sound of her heels clicking against the marble floor immediately draws my attention to her, and after she's gotten my attention, she claims my heart. Her fingertips and red nails ease into the baptismal pool and I follow them as they gently touch her forehead, the dip between her breasts, her left shoulder and right shoulder, as she motions the sign of the cross. She wears a red dress that conforms to her shapely figure and ends just above her knees. Her black hair has swirls of brown—cut in a bob that hovers like a small curtain above her slender neck. She hurries to the row in front of me, genuflects, and then sits in the first seat. I watch her the entire Mass. I watch her lips move as she sings along with the choir. I watch her movements as she stands, kneels and sits. I'd given up on women, coming to the realization that my shyness, my temperament and my deformity had me destined for a lifetime without the opposite sex. I was convinced that God was my calling until she walked into my life.

Two weeks later on a Sunday, a light rain falls. I hurry along the slick sidewalk without an umbrella, hobbling more because of the rain, and my left foot gets too far ahead of my right. I fall just before the church steps and barely manage to catch myself with my outstretched hands, feeling like a fool. I quickly brush them off on my pants, lower my head against the rain and walk up the steps. When I open the church door I turn and spot her coming up the sidewalk, moving quickly in a blue dress and high heels, protecting her hair from the rain with a small black umbrella. I hold the door for no one for a few seconds as rain blows into the church. Finally a cluster of people move inside, thanking me as I soak myself in the rain for them, but I'm not holding the door for them.

She lowers her umbrella when she reaches the first step. I watch her hips move beneath the tight blue dress and an urge to reach out and touch her sweeps over me. Somehow I resist.

I never expected her to talk to me. She looks up and we lock eyes. "Are you okay?"

"Me? Yes . . . "

"I followed you up the street." She holds the umbrella to her left side, clutches my left forearm with her right hand and leads me inside. "I saw you fall."

"I'm fine, thank you."

She runs her hands over the front of her dress, flicking off tiny beads of water. She shakes her head of hair and smiles at me. Her eyes are piercing, her lips full and her smile framed by dimples.

I stand not knowing what to say, but that silence doesn't last long with her. She immediately senses my discomfort and fills the silence with her lovely voice. "There was a time when you could have closed the door . . . earlier."

I stare at her like a mute.

"You waited just for me, didn't you?" She smiles again and touches my forearm. "That was sweet."

I look to the floor.

She extends her hand. "I'm Rose."

"Wolfgang." I shake her small hand and feel the tiny bones of her fingers.

"You mind if I sit with you?"

My heart races. Sweat begins to clear away the residue left from her grip and I curse it. "Sure," I say, heading off to my seat in the back. She continues to hold onto my arm as we move, sliding her grip slightly up toward the crook of my elbow. I look down at my right leg, self-conscious about our pace and the awkwardness of our steps.

"Don't be ashamed, Wolfgang. I like your limp."

"You do?"

"Not everybody has one you know." She squeezes my elbow and the pressure helps to ease my racing heart. Her comforting tone helps me to relax. We sit side-by-side during Mass, my legs straight with my feet on the floor. She sits with her right leg crossed at the knees, exposing part of her thigh. At some point she whispers into my ear. "I love the Coronation window, don't you?"

I turn my head slightly toward her and find our faces less than a foot apart. She smells of something exotic. "Yes," I say. She pats the top of my hand and faces forward again. I can't believe this is happening to me.

EVERYTHING IS MOVING so fast and I struggle to keep up with what it all means. Now as I sit in her bedroom two weeks into our relationship, I no longer plan to join the priesthood. I no longer have any plans at all. For the first time in my structured, isolated life, I'm flying by the seat of my pants, and Rose is the unpredictable copilot. The days pass so quickly now that I've made the decision to move from my childhood home. The memories of the fight of biblical proportions with my mother are still fresh in my mind—the broken kitchen dishes she'd thrown at me when I'd first told her of my intentions of moving in with Rose; the hole in the living room wall where I'd punctured it with my father's cello in an attempt to smash it; and my mother's sobbing on the floor, pounding her little fists against the rug and pleading to God, asking why the devil had taken away her son. *How dare I disgrace my father's memory*, she tells me? *Running off with a Catholic girl who dresses like a whore from Babylon.*

Rose lives in a Victorian house south of Central Park and she's convinced me to move in with her. Her home is now full of my father's instruments I'd managed to take from home, all but the piano. Rose loves when I play for her. She has convinced me to enter her bedroom. I shouldn't be doing this. We're not married, but I want her. I want her more than anything. I've been dreaming of touching her since the day I'd first watched her enter the church nearly a month ago. I'm lying almost naked on her four-post bed, with only my underwear and ratty black socks to shield my insecurities. I'm experiencing feelings never felt before. My skin is alive. My mind is swimming with images of my parents making love in their bedroom while I watch through the hole in my wall.

I'd never thought Rose could look more beautiful than what I'd seen on our secret dates through the park at night, strolling hand-in-hand under the moonlight and dancing along the wading pool to the sound of a distant violin. But now as she stands before me I'm amazed and speechless. She grips the straps of her yellow summer dress and lowers them down over her bare shoulders. Her breasts appear heavy behind the cups of her bra. I have no idea what to do next, so she leads me. It's been this way since she first kissed me.

I sit trembling on the bed. "I shouldn't be doing this," I say.

"Is that you or your mother speaking?"

"We aren't married, Rose."

She steps closer, the flat of her stomach inches from my face. She bends down and kisses my lips. "Maybe we should be." She kisses my forehead. "This isn't a sin."

Her newly bobbed hair shimmers in the light. The bed is surrounded with stuffed dolls. I feel guilty all over again. She bends down so that her face is near my knees. I quiver at the thought of what she's going to do and she surprises me yet again by rolling my left sock down and *sliding it off my foot. She looks me in the eyes as if asking for permission. I grant it with a reluctant nod. She looks to my right foot and carefully begins to lower the black sock. This is the first time she's seen my deformity—the twisted part of my lower calf, the arched thrust of my shin bone near the top of the foot, the thickness of flesh and bone and tightened ligaments and joints that resulted in one big skeletal mess, uncorrectable with a mere splint or brace. She slides the sock off and drops it to the floor. I force myself to watch as she runs her fingers down my deformed calf and across the top of my foot. She lowers her head and kisses my shin. She kisses the top of my foot, my ankle, my calf, the part of my foot just before the toes. A tear forms in my eyes, but I refuse to let it fall. No one has ever touched my foot that way, with such tenderness. Rose stands before me again. I'm more in love with her now than ever. I grip the waistline of her pink underwear.*

"Go ahead," she whispers. I pull her underwear down and feel the firm roundness of her buttocks giving the slightest resistance against the waistband. I pull them down the rest of the way and let go as they slide down to her bare ankles and fall into the folds of her yellow dress around her feet.

My heart thumps faster and faster. "Rose," I whisper.

She crawls on the bed with me, gently forces me down onto the mattress. This beautiful woman, this flapper, this stylish, brash and hedonistic young woman with short skirts and short hair . . . she loves me, she wants me . . . she's told me so every day. Is she saving me from the priesthood? Or is it the devil sending me one final test?

As much as Wolfgang wanted the dream to be real, as soon as he blinked the weariness from his eyes, the vision of Rose faded into a cruel trick of memory. By the time he and Susannah walked to the sanatorium he could barely remember what his mind's eye had rehashed during the night. He was in a hurry to see if Doctor Barker had removed the piano. It was still there. Wolfgang found McVain playing it as if nothing had occurred last night. Shortly after lunchtime Doctor Barker stopped Wolfgang in the second floor hallway, his face solemn, his voice surprisingly non-combative. "These are my rules, Father Pike, and you will obey them or it's all over, whether *God* allows it or not."

Wolfgang stood with his black bag of instruments and waited.

"You and the choir can meet three times a week," he said, "but for no longer than an hour and a half. Choir members must sit in chairs—I can't have them standing that long. And you're to finish before sundown. I can't have the children up late." He sighed. "And we shouldn't have the colored patients up here. It could anger some of the other patients."

Wolfgang wondered if he'd heard about the note stuck to the pig's head? "Have you heard specific threats?"

"He's not supposed to be up here."

"I would refuse to go on without Rufus."

His eyebrows furrowed. "Really?"

"No, I'll play no matter what, but it can only be complete with Rufus. The healing."

"With what's already gone on here, there's too much at risk."

Wolfgang tempted fate by opening his mouth. "I read that doctors made millions last year writing prescriptions for whiskey to patients."

"I can assure you that I'm not one of them."

"And neither am I."

"Don't allow the rehearsals to interfere with your work, or I *will* go over your head. I hear priests can be moved quite easily."

They followed Doctor Barker's rules and met three times a week to practice. McVain was allowed to play any time of the day because the piano was considered his at this point. Wolfgang sensed that Barker was afraid of McVain anyway. Rufus practiced from the colored hospital during rehearsals, and at various times of the day Wolfgang could hear Josef playing the violin from the second floor. Wolfgang could see their anxiousness to play but he'd warned them to not stray—at least for now. The chorus came along quickly and Wolfgang had almost everything he needed except a strong bass singer. Learning the words of the pieces was a challenge because so few were written in English, but they quickly adapted. The *Cantate Domino* was now part of their program. Wolfgang put together packets for all choir members. Many of the singers studied the music all day long and their hard work was evident in the improvements heard at every practice.

They'd been hit by a string of days that refused to climb above twenty degrees, canceling five rehearsals. Two weeks passed and the bodies continued to mount. Old patients were replaced with new. Lincoln declared that they were living and working atop a growing graveyard. Wolfgang held Mass alongside his assistant Jesse, who'd been fitted with altar boy garments. Wolfgang made his rounds. He heard confessions. He listened to their questions and gave them answers that would ease their passing. While doing so, he came up with another idea. He asked Susannah to gather the choir a few minutes early because he had an announcement to make. Even she didn't know what he had planned.

Wolfgang cleared his throat, stood by McVain at the piano, and faced the choir. "We've set a date."

Abel shouted from the front row. "For what?"

"A date for our first concert, Abel. One month from today."

Susannah half-raised her hand. "That's Valentine's Day."

"You have plans?" McVain asked.

"No."

"Well, now you do," Wolfgang said. "We'll throw a party better than New Year's and play for everyone here. From the rooftop."

McVain coughed. "What about Barker?"

Someone else coughed in the background and when Wolfgang turned he spotted Susannah covering her mouth. It was so cold. Her cheeks were pink.

"Doctor Barker doesn't know yet," Wolfgang said. "But I believe

I can convince him. If the temperature is decent and, God willing, it doesn't snow, we'll have lawn chairs out on the grounds for all the patients and we'll play from above."

Susannah raised her voice above the wind. "What will we perform?"

"A bit of everything. We'll decide in the coming days." Wolfgang pointed to the chorus. "With your input, of course."

Abel raised his hand. "We need a name." His comment drew snickers from the rest of the choir.

McVain rolled his eyes. "And what name shall that be?"

Abel shrugged. "I don't know. The Waverly Hills Orchestra."

"Sounds reasonable enough." Wolfgang surveyed the crowd. "Any objections?" There were none, not even from McVain, who appeared more tired than normal as he slumped lower against the piano. "Very well then. One month from tonight, the Waverly Hills Orchestra will present its debut performance."

WOLFGANG'S ENTHUSIASM OVER the concert made the night's work go by much more quickly. When his rounds were finished he searched every floor and solarium porch but couldn't find Susannah anywhere. He couldn't wait to pick her brain on the way back home and see first-hand what she thought of his surprise announcement. She'd appeared happy but there was something in her departure after the rehearsal that made Wolfgang think her mind was preoccupied with other business. Like she was hiding something, he thought.

He ran into Nurse Marlene on the third floor thirty minutes before midnight and questioned her without awkwardness, although his eyes now instinctively settled on her eyes. "Have you seen Susannah?"

"She left a few minutes ago," Nurse Marlene said. "She told me to tell you she'd see you in the morning."

Wolfgang sighed, perplexed, and walked over toward the screen window inside the solarium wall. It didn't make any sense. They always told the other when they'd be unable to walk the hillside at night. He quickly grew worried. He looked down the slope of the snow-dusted hill below but didn't see her walking toward their trail in the woods. He breathed in the frigid air and inched closer to the window, the cool screen clipping his nose. Down the hillside to the left, some movement caught his eye.

Nurse Susannah's white dress blew behind her as she carefully stepped over the frozen ruts in the muddy road near the sanatorium's entrance. Her left hand held her white cap pinned to her head while her right arm clutched something against her chest. He strained but couldn't tell what it was. She entered the line of trees on the far side of the road, navigated a sharp grassy downhill toward a narrow footpath and disappeared under a canopy of low-lying limbs.

Where was she going? He walked down the solarium, his face nearly brushing the screen window as he peered down into the woods. And then he saw the only cottage on that side of the hill about thirty yards deep in the trees. He knew where the footpath would take her. A light was on in Doctor Barker's cottage and he seemingly awaited her presence.

19

Wind blew snow against the solarium screens, scattering four pages of concert notes from Wolfgang's podium. The choir barely broke stride, pausing only for a second when their conductor squatted to grab the first sheet from the floor. Wolfgang continued to conduct with his free hand. It had taken him two days to finalize their program for the concert and he wasn't about to let the wind blow them away. So he squatted and grabbed the fleeing sheets, bouncing from one to the next, hopping and conducting like some deranged frog, all while keeping his chin up and his eyes on the choir. Their passion had increased since the announcement of the concert and Doctor Barker's reluctant approval of it, although Wolfgang had failed to mention the length of it. Nearly three hours with an intermission in the middle.

Wolfgang moved back to his podium, his face red from bending over, and his hair windblown and dotted with wet snowflakes. The inclement weather and the hardship it presented never once stopped his choir from singing or his musicians from performing, despite the numbness in their hands. Rufus must have heard them playing because after only a few minutes into their first piece he'd joined in, blowing his flute from down the hillside, practicing with them from afar.

Wolfgang conducted like an orator, his vision roaming the choir from side-to-side, leaving no one out. On each pass he did make sure Susannah was in view. For two days he'd wanted to ask her about her clandestine visit to Doctor Barker's house, but he feared upsetting her with such protective questions. He didn't want to seem a pest. He already sensed that she'd become annoyed at his insistence that she not attend to Herman alone on the rooftop. And other than leaving him to walk the hillside alone that night, she'd acted no different around Wolfgang. She'd knocked on Wolfgang's door the very next morning as usual—her eyes a bit heavier than normal—and apologized for leaving without him the night before, although he'd noticed that she'd conveniently not offered any explanation. It was none of his business. That was her attitude, and that was how he'd left it—an irksome mystery.

Halfway through the rehearsal Wolfgang spotted Doctor Barker standing in the shadows at the end of the solarium porch. Five minutes he stood there, listening, watching, spying. And then he was gone. Wolfgang watched him leave and then stopped rehearsal after completing a Haydn piece. Susannah stepped away from the choir, eyeing the spot where Doctor Barker had stood. "Did you see him watching?"

"I think he's up to something." Wolfgang watched Susannah carefully, wondering if she knew something more. His mind again went to her sneaking through the woods to Doctor Barker's cottage and then he forced it away.

Susannah folded her arms, her typical thinking pose. "He pulled the case files on all the musicians and choir members today."

"What for?"

"I don't know." Susannah looked upward as a voice soared over the weather.

"My cakes . . . My cakes . . ."

"How long has he been carrying on?" asked Wolfgang.

Nurse Cleary came running across the solarium, panting and calling for Susannah. She'd taken on Rita's hours in the mental ward and she'd been none-too-pleased about it. "It's Herman," she cried. "He's going mad. I can't take it anymore. Susannah's the only one he'll talk to."

Susannah brushed quickly beside Wolfgang. "You don't have to come."

"I don't trust him."

Susannah hurried to the stairwell, her feet pounding the steps in rapid motion, her hand gliding up the rail. Wolfgang had to hustle to keep up. When she reached the rooftop she held onto her hat and never broke stride as she lowered her shoulders into the wall of wind that threatened to push them back down the steps.

"Susannah," Herman shouted. "I want my cake! Bring me my fucking cake! Susannah!"

Wolfgang could have strangled him. Susannah opened the door to the nurses' station and stormed inside, fumbling for her keys. She quickly unlocked Room 502. "My Lord, Herman. What is wrong with you?"

Herman sat cross-legged on the floor beneath his window, yelling through the screen. He looked up when Susannah entered. He was fully clothed this time. Benson's bulk was concealed and moving ever so slightly beneath the covers on his bed. Wolfgang wondered how he could even breathe under there.

Herman unfolded his long legs, grunted and braced his hands on the wall to stand. He faced Susannah, his voice under control. "Nobody listens." Tears welled in his eyes. "Nobody hears me." He stepped closer to the doorway. "Nobody ever listens to me."

"Stay back," Wolfgang told him.

Susannah stepped in front. "He's not a criminal, Wolf."

Benson poked his head out from beneath the covers. "I can hear him. I can most certainly hear him. I ate my dog. They let him out but I ate him. Rita's feet . . . they dangled . . . " Benson ducked his head back beneath his turtle shell of blankets and stopped talking.

"I'm better than all of them," Herman said. "Don't you see?"

"Better at what?" Susannah asked.

Herman sat on his bed, defeated and tired. "I want my cake."

Susannah sat bravely beside him. "What is it, Herman?" She lifted his hand and looked into his dark eyes. "Better at what?" Herman stared past Susannah at Wolfgang and then whispered something into her left ear. Susannah's eyes widened and she spoke to Nurse Cleary, who stood behind Wolfgang in the doorway, panting. "Go to the kitchen and get me a cake. Any kind of cake."

"But—"

"Just do it," Susannah yelled. Nurse Cleary turned away and seconds later the door to the nurses' station flew open and slammed against the outside wall. Wolfgang closed it, but not before the wind had scattered the papers atop the desk in the center of the room. He left them where they landed and returned to Room 502, where Susannah continued to comfort Herman. Wolfgang couldn't believe how she'd tamed the monstrous, unpredictable man. Well . . . yes he did believe it. She had a way of controlling any man. He'd seen it for the past four years. And what had he whispered in her ear? How dare he get that close to her. And what was he talking about—no one listens? How could they not, as loud as he was?

"No one listens," Herman said softly.

Susannah touched his shoulder. "We'll listen, Herman." Wolfgang saw a look of determination in Susannah's eyes that wouldn't be squashed by his fear and distrust of Herman. She stood from the bed and tugged on Herman's elbow. Herman stood beside her, dwarfing her by at least a foot, the top of her head barely reaching his shoulders. She walked Herman out of Room 502 and into the body of the nurses' station. She left him standing in the middle of the room while she hustled around to the back of the desk for a folding chair.

"Susannah," Wolfgang said. "What on earth are you doing?" It was the same chair Rita had used to hang herself. Seeing it in her grip made him uneasy.

Susannah placed the chair behind Herman and told him to sit. He did, lowering his body slowly down to the small seat that moaned and creaked under his massive bulk. Susannah tied a towel around his neck. Not once did he ask what she was about to do to him, not even when she'd reached across the desk for a pair of scissors.

"Susannah?" Wolfgang said.

She gave him an annoyed look. "Relax, Wolf. I'm just going to cut his hair."

"Cut his hair?" Wolfgang stared at the top of Herman's head, where strands of hair stuck out at odd tangents like plant growth. "Such a project could take days."

Susannah rolled her eyes and worked like the barber she wasn't. "He's been ignored his entire life, I bet." She lifted a tangled patch of Herman's dirty brown-and-gray hair. Snip—the clump fell to the floor with a slight bounce. "But not anymore. Not tonight." Herman stared straight ahead into Room 502 as if they weren't discussing him right in front of him. Susannah clipped another patch of hair.

Lincoln opened the door to the nurses' station and stuck his head in. "Wolf, second floor. We're losing another patient."

Wolfgang looked at Susannah and then specifically to the scissors in her right hand. Herman was calm now but he didn't trust him. He'd bruised her before.

"Go, Wolf," said Susannah. "I'll be fine."

Wolfgang turned and left. He trusted her.

THE DYING PATIENT was a man in his twenties whom Wolfgang had seen only a handful of times. He'd arrived in a bad state two weeks ago and he had the disease everywhere—lungs, bones, eyes, skin—and it was progressing so far that bed rest and fresh air proved useless. His face was covered with sores. He coughed up blood and shivered violently in the cold. His skin was turning a shade of blue under the bedside lamp. His reddened eyes followed

Wolfgang as he read the man's chart and then sat beside him. He appeared scared to death, his condition far past the help of a doctor. He needed Wolfgang as a priest.

"Brent . . . can you hear me?"

Between coughs he choked out a few barely audible words. "So . . . hot . . . "

Wolfgang touched his arm and for a moment the man's frail body settled. Like so many before him, he feared his next destination. Wolfgang could see it in his eyes, the question marks. Wolfgang's voice calmed him. "You have nothing to fear." He touched the top of the man's head with his open right hand. "Lord Jesus Christ, King of Glory—"

"So . . . scared . . . " The man choked and gagged. "I . . . have . . . sinned."

Lincoln watched from the background, stone-faced.

Wolfgang knew he didn't have time to hear about the man's sins. He had to ease his fears. "Forgive, O Lord, the souls from all the chains of their sins and may they deserve to avoid judgment of revenge by your fostering grace, and enjoy the blessedness of everlasting light."

The man choked again, spewing blood. A drop of it hit Wolfgang's forehead.

Wolfgang comforted him by touching his forehead again, smoothing his hand over the man's brown hair. "You are forgiven . . . you are forgiven . . . you are forgiven . . . "

The man's torso lifted up from the bed and dropped. His lower jaw sagged. His eyes opened wide. His hands settled atop his blankets and his shoulders relaxed back to the mattress. A final breath pushed from his bloody, chapped lips, and a look of peace swept over his face. The hint of a smile formed on his lips.

Wolfgang closed his eyes and motioned the sign of the cross over the deceased. "Grant him eternal rest, O Lord. He shall be justified in everlasting memory . . . and shall not fear evil reports."

Lincoln stood silent. Wolfgang walked across the room to a small sink. He washed his hands and dried them on a towel. He touched the young man's head again, the flesh still warm with fever. What had he seen just before his final heartbeat, Wolfgang wondered? Had he seen anything at all? Did his soul really pass to Heaven? Or was it Wolfgang's words that had calmed him—the belief that there was more? Or had his brain conjured up a convincing but attainable image to ease his last moments? Was it all trickery?

Wolfgang tossed the wet towel to a basket in the corner of the room and considered himself lucky that he had yet to be infected by the dreaded disease. Was he immune or was God's hand keeping him safe because of his work—or for a worse fate?

Lincoln patted Wolfgang on the shoulder, reached up with a clean white towel and wiped the spots of blood from Wolfgang's forehead.

"Thank you."

"I'll clean up," Lincoln said.

Wolfgang left the room and just as soon as he'd stepped out to the solarium porch Nurse Cleary was upon him again. "Doctor, come quickly."

"What is it now?"

"Susannah, she—"

Wolfgang didn't even hear her finish. All he could think about was the scissors slicing Susannah's throat or the sharp blades piercing her chest. His heart raced so quickly he feared it would jump from his rib cage. He sprinted to the stairwell and took the steps two and three at a time, ignoring the pain that shot down his right leg with every awkward step of his deformed hoof, unable to block out the horrible visions that assaulted his mind. Would he make it in time? He could see her now, lying on the floor in a pool of blood, the scissors sticking from her slender neck. He hated himself for doubting her, and then leaving her alone with Herman.

He hit the rooftop with a wild burst of speed, lunging with his left foot while dragging his right. A pig snorted near the doorway to the nurses' station. Wolfgang gave it a glance and only a second to wonder why in the hell it was up on the rooftop before stepping around it. Wind rattled the door. Wolfgang flung it open.

"Susannah!"

"What is it, Wolf?" Susannah smiled at him. She stood with her arms folded, leaning against the front of the desk. Herman sat in a chair looking like a totally different man, twenty years younger at least, and handsome. The gray had been mostly cut from his strands. His hair was now short, trimmed around the ears and parted to the side. His beard had been shaved completely off. "Doesn't he look great?"

Wolfgang nodded like an idiot. Herman did look great. His face was long, his jaw sculpted, his cheekbones high beneath dark eyes that now showed life and promise. Wolfgang touched his own beard and wondered, given the choice and a razor, if Susannah would have shaved his as well? Herman looked at Wolfgang and grinned. In his right hand he tightly clutched a fork. Before him, resting on a small rounded table, was an entire chocolate cake Nurse Cleary must have retrieved from the kitchen. A good chunk of it had already been eaten. A tall glass of milk stood next to it. Herman took another bite of cake and washed it down with a loud gulp of milk.

Nurse Cleary stepped inside. "Well, what do you think?"

"I think you should have told me—"

"Relax," said Susannah.

"You ran before I had the chance," said Nurse Cleary.

Wolfgang stepped closer to Herman. "He looks like a new man."

"No, about the surprise," Nurse Cleary said.

Wolfgang looked at Susannah. "What surprise?"

Susannah laughed. "Herman. Show Father Pike what you're better at than the others."

Herman scooted his chair back from the table and stood, slowly, dramatically. It seemed to take forever for his long frame to unfold from the chair and straighten, but then he faced Wolfgang with a military alertness. He cleared his throat and began to sing an aria from Mozart's *Magic Flute*.

Wolfgang's knees buckled. Susannah hurried over to catch him. He couldn't believe his ears. From the giant lunatic Wolfgang was hearing one of the strongest and deepest bass voices he'd ever heard, the sound resonating from the unseen cavern inside the man's massive chest.

God had sent Wolfgang's choir the bass it had been missing.

WOLFGANG AND SUSANNAH wasted no time hurrying Herman down to the fourth floor, where McVain was in bed with his hands behind his head, eyes closed. Susannah giggled and skipped her way down the solarium, stopping at the piano with a playful hop. Herman waited patiently with a fork clutched in his right hand. Wolfgang struck one of the piano keys and McVain's eyes snapped open as if a fire alarm had sounded. He sat up in bed, staring at Herman's towering figure standing shyly beside Wolfgang and the piano. McVain's jaw dropped, first because of Herman's transformed appearance, and then when he began an aria from *Don Giovanni*. He easily had the best voice of the entire chorus—a professional voice that was seemingly barely hampered by the tuberculosis. McVain nearly broke into a grin upon hearing Herman's voice, as if, finally, he'd been given a voice equal to his own talents.

Susannah rubbed her hands together, her joy evident in the glow that infused her face. Herman stopped abruptly and stood stiff as a board, staring over McVain's piano toward the bed, fork in hand.

Wolfgang, too, looked to McVain for a verdict. They all did.

McVain craned his head for a better look. "What's with the fork?"

* * *

WOLFGANG WALKED SUSANNAH home that night, wondering
every step if she would veer off in the direction of his cottage and
decide to sleep on his couch again. Or would she venture up to
Doctor Barker's residence after he dropped her off? They continued
toward the nurses' station. As it should be, he thought, relieved
and annoyed at the same time.

"I knew there was something hiding inside of him," Susannah
said.

"And the fork?" Wolfgang asked.

"Herman spent ten years singing opera in Italy." Susannah was
in a playful mood, stepping carefully over twigs that had fallen
on the footpath, maneuvering in a way that reminded Wolfgang
of how he used to avoid the cracks on the sidewalk on his way
through Central Park as a kid. "After his girlfriend left him for a
baker, he stabbed the baker with a fork, half a dozen times, claiming . . . get this," she slapped Wolfgang on the shoulder, "claiming
that he'd stolen his cake."

Wolfgang raised his eyebrows. "So he is a little crazy." Wolfgang
pictured the fork in Herman's tight grip, the same fork he'd taken
with him back into Room 502. "Hopefully he doesn't use it on
Benson."

"If he wanted to hurt Benson he could have long ago," she said.

Wolfgang watched her hop on one foot over a fallen tree branch,
balance herself for a second and then hop to the other foot. It was
her childlike nature that he loved about her. "That was a beautiful
thing you did tonight. For Herman."

"It was long overdue," she said.

Wolfgang acted on impulse and did what he'd wanted to do for
a long time now. He reached down and gripped her right hand as
they walked. She looked at him with surprise in her eyes. Wolfgang averted his gaze and stared straight ahead, expecting her, at
any moment, to move her hand away from his grip, but she didn't.

She even swung her arm slightly, which was enough of a reaction to give Wolfgang the confidence to not let go and run into the woods from embarrassment. He'd already done it, driven as it was by a deeply rooted jealousy of her trip to Barker's cottage, and he couldn't undo it or pretend that he, a Catholic priest, hadn't just taken the hand of a pretty young woman on a stroll through the woods under the moonlight.

What am I doing, he thought? Before they knew it they stood outside Susannah's dormitory. She removed her hand from Wolfgang's slackening grip. It was an awkward moment that became very awkward when she stood on her toes and kissed his left cheek, her wet lips pressing just above the hair over his beard and on the cheekbone under his left eye. The wind made the wet sensation on his cheekbone even more prominent.

"Goodnight . . . Father Pike."

WOLFGANG LAY IN bed staring at the ceiling, excited about the concert, especially now that Susannah had discovered Herman's voice. He prayed for a crisp, clear night on Valentine's Day so the entire city could hear them perform. He blew out the candle beside his bed and hoped that sleep would come before his eyes adjusted to the dark.

It didn't. His mind began to wander. He faced the right side of his bed and thought of Rose. He pictured her here beside him, lying on her side, the fingers of her right hand spread out against the curve of her hip, looking into his eyes as she had on so many nights. And then he thought of Susannah. He could still feel the touch of her lips on his cheek. He felt childish and foolish but he couldn't help but relive the moment.

He rolled over to his back and faced the ceiling again. His eyes caught a glimpse of the crucifix hanging on the wall. He turned away from it and forced his eyes closed.

All night he felt Him watching.

20

SLEET AND SNOW turned the blades of grass to silvery daggers. Tendrils of ice hung from the tree branches and glistened under the clear night sky, where thousands of stars had come out to view what nature had brought down during the evening. Wolfgang squatted in the frosted grass behind his cottage, perusing the rose garden, where the precipitation had already melted under the warmth of Lincoln's heat lamps. Wolfgang thought of Herman as he searched for the right rose. Herman's addition to the choir had, at first, a negative effect on the rest of the singers. The children knew him only as the crazy cake man from the rooftop and it took them awhile to get used to his new, albeit more normal, appearance. He smiled more and talked less, and because of it the children, after several days of warming up, had started to become enamored with his talent and stature. The men and women were at first not jealous of his voice and immediate seniority, but a bit intimidated by him. They didn't sing as loud in his presence, as if they were afraid they'd be inferior, which they all knew they were. For days the rehearsals dragged on with Herman the only one fully invested, standing a good ten feet away from the rest of the choir with the fork in his right hand. Wolfgang would watch their eyes, and how they'd watch Herman sing, and he'd wonder if the addition was hurting morale. He seemed a loner, standing as he was apart from the group. In four days Herman had yet to utter a word to anyone except Susannah.

Just when Wolfgang began to get a bit down over the situation, Herman surprised them all. In the middle of a Vivaldi piece he held up his arms, waving them wildly, his fork nearly scraping the solarium's ceiling. Wolfgang halted the choir and musicians and they all stared at Herman, who had broken from his spot away from the group and stepped closer. He faced the choir with a huge smile on his shaved face. "You can do this," he said, his eyes darting from person to person as if tracking the flight of a gnat. "You can do this. I'm better than all of you . . . but you can do this. We can do this. We can make this the best concert. Sing with all your might." He ruffled Abel's hair and it sparked a grin from the rest of the kids. He ruffled the hair of all six children in the front row and then opened his arms to a young woman named Clarice in the front row. He held his arms out as if to hug her, the grin still dominating his face. She looked ready to turn and run from him, but he stepped closer and wrapped his arms around her slender figure, nearly squashing her with a bear hug. The children laughed, clearly not as unnerved by the situation as the adults in the choir.

"What the shit is this?" McVain said under his breath from the piano. Josef lowered his violin and watched as Herman moved to the next lady. He hugged her as well. "You can do this," he said with authority, clutching her by the shoulders.

Wolfgang, amused but surprisingly not worried, put his baton on the podium and watched Herman proceed to hug all thirty members of the choir, mostly one at a time, until he reached two of the men near the end and he took them both into his embrace. With each hug the choir's uneasiness seemed to lessen. Their insecurity became less with every embrace. By the end of his shenanigans the children were laughing, Susannah along with them. His strange emergence into the group had galvanized them as a choir. He'd given them confidence somehow. After his hugging spree he faced the choir again and said, "I'm better than all of you . . . It is true, but we can do this." He returned to his spot away from the choir and stood straight again, regripping the fork and ready to sing.

Wolfgang laughed out loud as he clipped a rose and held it up to the light coming from the heat lamps. It would be perfect. Footsteps drew Wolfgang's attention away from the rose garden and to the dark side of the cottage. "Who goes there?"

Lincoln stepped out of the shadows, breathing heavily, his cheeks red from running. "Wolf . . ."

"What is it?"

"McVain . . . he's missing."

"He's what?" Wolfgang placed the rose inside the birdbath. "What do you mean, he's missing?"

"He's gone." Lincoln stood with hands on hips. "Josef too. And I had Big 15 check for Rufus."

"Missing as well?"

Lincoln nodded. "I found their clothes out near the bottom of the body chute."

"They escaped." Wolfgang gripped a thin tree and pulled himself up to more level ground. "McVain said nothing to you?"

"About what?"

"Anything that sounded suspicious?"

Lincoln thought for a second. "I ate lunch with McVain today out by the piano. He asked me about the Seelbach Hotel. I told him a few stories about Capone. He said he used to play the piano there as a kid. They had one in the mezzanine."

"Oh, Lord."

"In high school he'd play for tips after school—in the Rathskeller."

"But why go there now?"

"Maybe they wanted a night out on the town before . . ."

"Before what?"

"Before they die."

* * *

Wolfgang, Big 15 and Lincoln took flashlights down the body chute, and the deeper they penetrated the seemingly endless tunnel the more claustrophobic Wolfgang became, to the point where, near the end of the chute, he was scaling the cold walls in fear of doubling over. The chute had never caused any panic before, but his heart was already racing from the panic of losing three of Waverly's patients and three pivotal members of his concert. When he hit the fresh air at the bottom he let out an enormous gush of breath, not realizing how long he'd been holding it in. His lungs ached. He felt as if he'd just had one of his nightmares, the ones where his mother would suffocate him with a pillow.

Big 15 placed his hand on Wolfgang's back. "You okay, Boss?"

"I'll be fine." Wolfgang stood straight in the grass, where train tracks crossed their path. Lincoln was right about the pile of clothes, three distinct piles in fact. Josef and McVain had tossed their attire in heaps while Rufus had folded his, neatly placing it next to the beginning of the chute. Three sets of footprints marked the icy grass along the railroad tracks. "What are they wearing now, I wonder?"

Lincoln and Big 15 shrugged.

They weren't supposed to be leaving the hillside, but if Doctor Barker found out that three of his highly infectious patients had escaped, he'd have an aneurysm. He'd cancel the concert. Wolfgang started up the slippery slope toward the tracks and then Lincoln led the way as they jogged toward Dixie Highway. To hell with the pain in Wolfgang's leg.

Lincoln looked over his shoulder as he ran. "My uncle's house is only two blocks away. He's the one I get the booze from. He's got a brand new Cadillac I'm sure he'll let us borrow."

To Wolfgang's amazement, Lincoln's Uncle Frank—a short, stocky man in an expensive three-piece suit, fancy brown shoes and a head of dark hair slicked back with what appeared to be an entire can of grease—didn't even hesitate when Lincoln asked to borrow the car.

"Be my guest." He patted Lincoln on the shoulder. "Have yourself a ball. You and your buddies." He suspiciously eyed Wolfgang's clerical collar and instead took a step toward Big 15 and offered his hand. "You're one big son of a bitch."

Big 15 shook his hand. "Reckon I am."

"I'm Uncle Frank." He lit a cigar and looked Big 15 up and down. "I could probably use you sometime. Would you like that? Little extra dough for the pockets, hey? Perhaps some women." He slipped a second cigar into Big 15's breast pocket, then turned quickly toward Lincoln. "Have the car back by morning. Got to drive to Cincinnati." He winked. "Important meeting."

Lincoln turned into a madman behind the wheel of his uncle's expensive car, speeding in and out of traffic despite the snowy roads, driving as if the price of the car wouldn't make a dent in Uncle Frank's pocket had they wrecked it. Big 15 laughed in the back seat. Wolfgang's beef-and-rice dinner was about to come back up and ruin the interior of Uncle Frank's fancy car. Lincoln glanced over toward him. "You okay?"

"Maybe you should slow down a bit." Wolfgang cracked the window about an inch and the cool air made him feel better. "You know where you're going?"

"Of course." Lincoln gripped the steering wheel harder as the car fishtailed slightly on a patch of ice. He regained control, eyes peeled. "Been to the Seelbach dozens of times with Uncle Frank."

"What exactly for?"

Lincoln shrugged. "Important stuff, you know. But mostly I'd wait in the car. He'd run in for about a half hour, then come back out." Lincoln bounded over a pothole and it sounded as if something had come off the right tire. Wolfgang raised up off his seat and his head nearly hit the ceiling. He braced his hands on the dashboard. Lincoln finally decreased his speed, not because of the pothole or ice on the road but because the lights of downtown loomed just over the horizon. The traffic grew thicker as they neared the famous hotel. Lincoln rolled down his window and a rush of freezing air filled the car. Lincoln honked the horn three times at three women standing alongside Fourth Street. "Hey, dolls!" Wolfgang hunkered down in his seat as the ladies waved.

Big 15 leaned enthusiastically forward from the back seat. "Never been here before."

Street lamps were aglow with yellow fires of light. Snow flurries danced wildly through the air. The clip-clop of a horse carriage echoed off the walls of the surrounding buildings and storefronts. The smell of horse dung wafted in with the wind. The road turned to cobblestone as they closed in and the ride suddenly became much bumpier, the shocks of the Cadillac not enough to counterbalance the patchwork of stone and ice that covered the crowded road. Lincoln pointed to an old car parked with one wheel on the curb. "Got us a petting party inside that flivver." Lincoln honked and whooped out the window. "Four of'em with kissers locked." Wolfgang glanced away. Lincoln focused on the road again, where the hotel loomed. "George Remus spent a lot of time at the Seelbach."

"Who's he?" Big 15 asked.

Wolfgang rolled his eyes. "Oh, Lord . . . here we go."

Lincoln's tone was serious. "Cincinnati mobster. Made a fortune running whiskey. That writer Fitzpatrick? He based the main character from *The Great Catspee* on Remus."

"Fitzgerald," said Wolfgang.

"What?"

"And it's Gatsby . . . not Catspee, you baboon."

Lincoln slowed the car and coasted past a brand new Oldsmobile with a fancily dressed couple inside. He tapped the steering wheel with his thumbs, looking for a place to park. The street was teeming with people, standing, walking, talking, most everyone wearing extravagant suits and pretty dresses as if heading to a party or ball.

Wolfgang's modest clerics would hardly fit in, but they weren't coming to socialize. If their runaways were there, they'd quickly snatch them, cause as little ruckus as possible doing so and be on their way. Wolfgang planted his palms against the dash again as Lincoln cut off a Desoto and dove into a parking spot vacated by a delivery truck.

"I'll wait in the car," Big 15 said.

"You sure?" Wolfgang asked.

Big 15 nodded. Lincoln tossed him the keys and he and Wolfgang hurried across the busy street. Lincoln's face lit up as he looked up at the hotel, which stood ten stories tall and dwarfed the buildings around it. "I heard there's a small alcove off The Oakroom where Capone plays blackjack and poker when he's in town. He had a big mirror brought down from Chicago so he could watch his back."

Wolfgang found himself stepping over the cracks in the sidewalk, limping noticeably. "And check out his opponents' cards, I bet." He folded his arms against the cold wind and moved beside a parked horse-drawn carriage. Long plumes of steam jetted from the horse's nose as it fidgeted in the freezing temperatures. They passed a brick building with a poster attached to the front door— *Keep Your Bedroom Windows Open: Prevent Tuberculosis.*

On the corner of Fourth and Walnut, the European style hotel, designed with the French Renaissance in mind, was brightly lit and alive with chatter. It was the first skyscraper in Louisville, one of the grandest hotels in the country, and Wolfgang had heard rumors of women fainting the day it opened. Portions of the facade reminded Wolfgang of the grandeur of Waverly. The Seelbach's exterior was made of stone and dark brick pieced together with charm and elegance. Charles Dickens had been ejected from the hotel for showing poor manners. Presidents Taft and Wilson had stayed in the hotel, apparently without suffering Dickens' fate. Already in its short existence, history seeped from every door and window and Wolfgang felt a rush of blood to his head as he stepped under the canopied entrance and moved up the stairs. The merry atmosphere was contagious. A glass of wine would have felt appropriate for the moment. He remembered Rose and the nights they'd celebrated much as these people did now, carefree and tipsy from alcohol. Wolfgang nodded to the young and handsomely dressed doorman. "Good evening, Father," he said.

"Thank you."

Wolfgang was first inside the lobby and he waited for a moment for Lincoln to take it all in. Evidently his Uncle Frank had rarely brought him inside on their visits to the hotel. The boy was awestruck—European marble everywhere, beautiful carpets, exquisitely carved wood, bronze railings, friezes and frescoes on the walls, fancy chandeliers and wall sconces, and a skylight above made of hundreds of panels of glass. A palace fit for royalty, but during Prohibition, gangsters would do.

Men in suits stood shoulder-to-shoulder smoking cigars or cigarettes, drinking and laughing, their faces flushed and happy. The women wore their hair bobbed like Rose's. They wore makeup and long cylindrical silhouette dresses, Basque dresses, or the popular one-hour dress that allowed more freedom for dancing. They wore silk, cotton, linen and wool with colors ranging from bright greens, reds and blues to pastels. Assertive colors. Aggressive colors. Free-spirited, smart and sexy. Women out on dates without chaperones. How times had changed. How dearly he missed Rose. He tore himself from his reverie. Amongst the chattering of the dozens of people crammed in the lobby, from the back corner to the right of the ornate set of stairs that led up to the mezzanine, Wolfgang heard music. "Oh, my Lord," he said. "Beethoven."

Wolfgang fought his way through the clouds of cigar smoke to where a larger crowd had gathered in the back corner, listening to a musical trio of piano, flute and violin. Lincoln tapped Wolfgang's shoulder. "I think we found them."

Wolfgang wormed his way through the crowd, close enough to smell the alcohol and perfume and see the intoxication in their reddened eyes. But they all seem fascinated with the musicians who had set up shop around the piano on the right side of the stairs—a black man on the flute, a violinist with a chalkboard on his chest and a piano player who dazzled despite missing three fingers on his left hand. Their music soared high off the tall lobby ceiling and filtered down to everyone. On the floor next to Josef's feet sat an upside-down bowler hat—the same one McVain had the day he arrived at Waverly. It wasn't large enough to hold the bills and coins that had been dropped at their feet. Where had they gotten the nice suits? How long had they planned this, Wolfgang wondered?

Despite the urgency to get them out of the hotel before they infected someone, it was a beautiful scene to watch. If only Susannah had been there with him. Maybe one night they'd have a harmless night out, away from the sanatorium, away from the patients, away from the hillside, and away from the death. There was a world moving on outside the woods in which they roamed daily, an exciting world that part of him wanted to re-enter. He imagined Susannah's hand in his grip again as he slithered through the crowd. He stopped abruptly. The row of men in front of him wouldn't budge. A tall man with a pencil neck and tiny ears told him to get lost, evidently not seeing Wolfgang's collar or not caring.

A woman in an orange silhouette dress and heavy makeup pointed toward the piano. "Darling . . . that man only has two fingers on his left hand."

"He's fantastic."

They deserved every bit of this, thought Wolfgang, but he had to get them out all the same. He thought of Mr. Weaver when a fat man with heavy jowls shouted over the crowd. "Play some jazz! Jazz!"

"Ragtime!" a woman yelled from the center of the crowd. Ragtime? Jazz? Wolfgang's trio didn't play ragtime or jazz. But during a short pause, McVain, Josef and Rufus huddled together. The crowd hushed.

McVain looked excited and utterly exhausted at the same time. Wolfgang feared for his health. His skin was so pale. Sweat beaded along his red hairline. "We'll wing it," said McVain, his throat raspy. "I once heard a man say it ain't jazz if you go into it knowing exactly what you're gonna play." They broke from their huddle and readied their instruments. Wolfgang couldn't help but laugh, and soon stopped. What these people didn't know could kill them.

Josef started playing some kind of jazzy sound and McVain chimed in. Rufus joined them a few seconds later to the delight of the crowd, many of whom began dancing right there in the packed lobby. Wolfgang felt his legs moving to the beat. Lincoln was having a ball—he'd found a girl to dance with him.

And then a tall, slender, conservative-looking man with jet-black hair and a finely trimmed mustache to match barged his way into the crowd with an exquisitely dressed woman on his arm. His aura of bloated self-importance made Wolfgang hate him before he even opened his mouth. "Those musicians!" he shouted with his right hand and index finger pumping up and down in the air. Everyone looked at him. "They're diseased!" The crowd hushed. "They all have TB! They escaped from Waverly Hills!"

Rufus dropped to his knees and stuffed money into the hat. Josef grabbed his coat. McVain stood quickly from the piano. They looked around for an escape route. Wolfgang and Lincoln used the moment of stunned silence to skitter past the crowd and join their musicians.

The arrogant man was still yelling. "They threatened me on the trolley tonight. They let the nigger sit with the decent folks!" The crowd quickly backed away from the trio, gasping. A woman fainted in a red heap to the floor.

The front doors were now blocked with people, some of them coming in to see the excitement and some fleeing in fear of catching tuberculosis. Their fear soon turned to anger.

"Up the stairs," Wolfgang said. Lincoln was the first onto the set of steps that curved left and right on the first landing. They went left, needing to get out before the crowd tore them apart.

Wolfgang hurried past McVain. McVain smiled. "Hey, Father."

"Come on." Wolfgang grabbed him by the elbow and urged him along. The element of the crowd whose anger was stronger than its fear gained ground, shouting and cursing. Wolfgang was afraid McVain would collapse behind him, but his adrenaline must have spurred him along. He matched Wolfgang step for hobbled step. Wolfgang spoke to McVain over the chaos. "I'm glad you're having so much fun. You'll probably be dead in the morning."

McVain laughed.

The mob had reason for fear and anger. Waverly was a popular place. Chances are that every one of the men and women chasing them had, at some point, known someone to enter Waverly without coming back out. They knew the danger and the crisis. Louisville had the highest tuberculosis death rate in the country. It was one of the largest cities in the country because of the bordering Ohio River, but the swampland around it was a breeding ground for bacteria.

From ahead, Lincoln waved them on. "This way!" He led them directly into The Oakroom, past elegant diners, plates of roasted duck and stunned waiters. The next thing Wolfgang knew was that he'd tripped over a man's foot and stumbled into a bullish bodyguard, who then lost his balance and toppled a table of shrimp and lobster. The mob was gaining. A door opened. The five of them rushed inside a small, cramped room swimming with cigar smoke. A spring-loaded door slammed behind them, locking them inside. Pistols cocked. Five gun barrels materialized through the haze and were pointed their way, one for each of them.

A man's clipped Chicago accent penetrated the smoke. "Don't move a fuckin' muscle."

Wolfgang gulped and stared across a poker table at Al Capone.

WOLFGANG NEARLY PISSED his pants. Five men in white button-downs and suspenders sat around a card table drinking bourbon and playing blackjack—or at least that's what they *had* been doing before their unfortunate arrival. Now they pointed pistols, probably contemplating how quickly to kill them. One of the men to the left of Capone held an automatic weapon so big it required two hands. His nose had been broken so many times it no longer resembled any nose Wolfgang had ever seen before.

Capone yanked the wet stub of his cigar from his mouth and blew smoke into the miasma that failed to conceal his deadly eyes. "Never killed a priest before."

Maybe this was why Wolfgang had joined the priesthood. For the exact moment in his life when he'd stumble upon the world's most notorious gangster and his life would be spared because of his clerical collar. "I hope you wouldn't start now," Wolfgang managed to say.

The mob outside the door was growing louder and began to pound on the walls. Lincoln stood beside Wolfgang, grinning like a fool. Wolfgang watched him from the corner of his eye. It didn't matter to Lincoln that any moment they could all be filled with lead.

"Wipe that smile off your face you fuckin' cake-eater." Capone chewed on his cigar. He locked eyes with Josef. "What's with the violin, paleface?"

"He's a musician," Wolfgang said. "We're all musicians."

"I didn't ask you, Father." Capone pointed his gun at Josef. "Can't you talk?"

Josef wrote on his chalkboard. **No.**

"He's got—" Lincoln started.

"Got what?"

"He's a mute, sir," Wolfgang said.

"This some kind of traveling circus?" Capone gave Rufus a good once-over. Then McVain next. "This clown's missing fingers. What instrument do you play, carrot top?"

McVain was sweating profusely and staggering. He straightened himself against the back wall. "Piano."

Capone laughed. On his front tooth rested a speck of brown from his cigar. "How'd you lose them fingers?"

"The war." McVain buffed the nails of his five right fingers against his lapel. "Not that it's any of your goddamn business."

Only Wolfgang's stifled groan broke the frozen silence.

"I say we skin'em, boss," said a thin man with greased hair and wicked burns across the tight red flesh of his forehead.

The sound they heard from outside saved them. "Police sirens," one of the men said, standing but remaining in a shooters stance.

"Fuckin' bulls," said another. They heard screaming outside the doors.

Something clanked and a whoosh of air sucked smoke from the room. Capone was gone in a flash. A wood-paneled door opened behind the table and he quickly disappeared down a dark staircase. One by one his men, each of them pointing their weapons at them one last time, followed him down the secret passageway until they were left alone in the smoky room staring at their reflection in the mirrored wall.

Lincoln nudged Wolfgang. "Told you."

McVain labored around the table toward the secret passage. "Shut the hell up, Lincoln. Let's get out of here."

"The mirror." Lincoln followed McVain. "Did you see the mirror?"

McVain pushed the secret doorway open. The door behind them nearly rattled off its hinges from the mob banging on it. "You guys gonna wait around for them?"

They funneled in behind McVain and the escape route. Rufus patted Wolfgang on the back. "You saved us, Father." Wolfgang didn't feel like a hero. His collar had only bought them time until the police arrived, which Wolfgang thought ironic—the police had most likely been called to detain his trio of TB-infected musicians and not Capone and his men. Wolfgang waited for Josef to pass and then took up the rear as they all headed into the secret passage, following in the footsteps of Al Capone. The scent of bourbon and cigars led them down the dark staircase and into an even darker kitchen, where McVain doubled over into a coughing fit. Rufus helped McVain along the darkened room.

Lincoln grabbed a biscuit from a food tray. "They went that way." He pointed with the biscuit to another set of downward stairs. At the foot of the stairs was a basement full of wooden crates, old furniture, broken sinks, brooms and mops, slop buckets and bottles of bourbon. "Bootleggers," Lincoln cried out to no one in particular. He entered a drainage tunnel that smelled of dirty water and mildew and cigar smoke. His voice echoed off the cold, curved walls. Moisture had collected on the ceiling and dripped to the floor from one central spot. Lincoln inhaled the dank, coppery air. "This is probably how they bootleg the bourbon." He put a finger to his lips. Up ahead, the boots of the final gangster climbed up an iron ladder attached to the grimy walls of the tunnel. They waited for a few minutes, then hurried to catch up, the manhole cover in the street still displaced and tossed aside. A faint line shone into the tunnel and snow flurries spit downward. Wolfgang was the last up the ladder, and just as he poked his head up into the fresh cool air of some unknown street, he heard the squealing of two getaway cars. Just like that, Capone and his cronies were gone. Wolfgang would live to tell about them.

McVain staggered out into the middle of the street. The lights from an oncoming car grew brighter. The car squealed and slid to a stop on the icy, rutted street and honked the horn at them.

McVain shielded his eyes from the glare and then collapsed right in the middle of the road.

THEY ALL CRAMMED in Uncle Frank's Cadillac and Lincoln drove straight to the sanatorium with McVain barely breathing in the back seat, his head resting on Big 15's lap. "Don't die on us . . . don't die on us," Big 15 said repeatedly, stroking McVain's red hair. As soon as Lincoln skidded to a halt on the packed ice and gravel before the entrance, Big 15 took it upon himself to pull McVain from the car. He lifted McVain's bulk, cradled him in his arms and ran into the sanatorium, while Wolfgang and Lincoln held the doors.

"Take him to the operating room," Wolfgang said.

"Should I get Doctor Barker?" asked Lincoln, his face near panic, his night of fun a distant memory.

Wolfgang hesitated briefly before saying, "Yes. Go get him." Doctor Barker was a better surgeon and he would find out about what had happened eventually. He couldn't risk McVain's life on an attempt to conceal the night's events. "Go. Hurry." Lincoln flung open the front doors and sprinted across the road while Wolfgang led the way to the operating room.

Doctor Barker was ready with his white coat and mask over his face within twenty minutes. He didn't ask any questions. He said nothing of them pulling him from his slumber in the middle of the night. There was a man's life to be saved, or at least prolonged. Wolfgang admired the professionalism. Doctor Barker opened McVain's chest with swift tugs of his scalpel and got immediately to work. His face was red with fury, but still he said nothing. There was no need to fight over the man's body in the middle of surgery. The fight would most assuredly come later. Wolfgang's eyes danced from McVain to Doctor Barker—one man barely alive while the other stewed with so much anger that his jaw never came un-clenched in nearly forty minutes of surgery. When Doctor Barker pulled his hands from the wall of McVain's open chest, his gloves and wrists covered with blood, he backed away from the table in silence, the shuffling of his feet palpable in the dim light. Wolfgang began to stitch McVain's chest while Doctor Barker washed his hands for what seemed like twenty minutes. Doctor Barker turned and left the operating room without a glance and without uttering a word.

21

Doctor Barker stopped Wolfgang outside the chapel first thing in the morning. He slapped a folded newspaper against his open palm to get Wolfgang's attention and then unfolded it to the front page when Wolfgang turned his way. The words he'd bottled up last night came out in torrents. "TB patients on the loose. Three patients have a night on the town. Real headlines, Father Pike!"

Wolfgang could hardly stand to look at it, but then again he knew it wasn't totally his fault. "Do you think I would encourage this, Doctor Barker?"

Doctor Barker forced the newspaper into Wolfgang's chest. Jesse Jacobs emerged from the chapel to see what the commotion was about. Wolfgang told him everything was okay and so he moved slowly down the hall and up the steps. Doctor Barker waited until it was clear to continue his tirade. "Bad press. Your fault. Your trio nearly started a riot."

"A night on the town."

"The city is already panicked. They didn't need this. Now they think we have no discipline," he said, eyeballs bulging. "They were highly contagious patients. You may not have known, but you've encouraged them by your actions. Careless actions."

"Are you more worried about the people or your reputation?"

Doctor Barker's nostrils flared. "How dare you."

Wolfgang backed off. "Thank you for last night. McVain's stabilized somewhat."

"What else was I to do . . . let him die because of the foolishness?"

Wolfgang had nothing to say.

Doctor Barker wasn't finished. "Rehearsals are cancelled until further notice."

Wolfgang started to disagree but stopped. It was a good idea. McVain would not be capable of playing for several weeks, if ever again. He needed rest. He didn't need a crowd around him. Wolfgang lowered his head and started down the hallway.

"And Father Pike."

Wolfgang turned toward Doctor Barker again. "Yes."

"I've written a letter to the archdiocese."

"Why?"

"I'm looking into having you transferred."

FOR THE REST of the day Wolfgang could think of nothing else. If he was transferred he couldn't continue the work with his musicians. He'd be taken away from Susannah, and Lincoln, and Big 15. He wouldn't let it happen. It was only a threat, he told himself. The archdiocese certainly wouldn't listen.

"Doctor?" Wolfgang looked down at the top of Miss Schultz's head as he wheeled her to her room. She continued to grow stronger every day, and after her new hairdo her face was full of life and color. "Something bothering you?"

"I'm fine. Thank you, Miss Schultz."

She looked up at him. "You were right. Your barber does nice work. I shouldn't have doubted you."

Wolfgang wheeled her across the solarium porch, eyeing several of the patients as he passed. So many of them were new. He wondered if his attackers had passed away as well. They hadn't heard from them in awhile.

"Where do you put all of them, Father?"

Wolfgang had gone from Doctor to Father within seconds and he now dreaded the conversation. He put on a fake smile to disguise his true thoughts of possibly having to leave Waverly. "They go straight to Heaven, Miss Schultz."

She waved her hand through the air as if swatting his platitudinous answer to the wind. "Always quick with your answers, sonny." She held up her crooked index finger. "But I figured it out."

"You have, have you?"

"You sneak them out somehow," she said. "So we don't see the hearse pulling up here twenty times a day. That would be bad for our morale, wouldn't it?"

"Far be it for me to contradict you, Miss Schultz."

She looked over her shoulder. "Don't give me that, Father. I know I'm right."

AFTER SUNDOWN THE temperature dropped drastically, the wind chill putting the mercury in single digits and in danger of plummeting more. Some patients would die of exposure. Wolfgang worked with his requiem on his lap, watching McVain sleep. He hoped the freeze would finally waken McVain from his surgery. It had been nearly twenty-four hours.

McVain's hand moved involuntarily against his bed sheets. Wolfgang scooted up in his chair, praying he would open his eyes, hoping he would live to play the piano again. Please God, don't let it end like this. They'd come so far. The concert was not far off. A neighboring patient down the solarium opened an envelope, pulled out a letter and smiled as she began to read. In all his weeks at Waverly, Wolfgang hadn't seen McVain receive one piece of mail from anyone. Not a wife, a sibling, or even a friend. Had he burned that many bridges? Was he really so alone?

McVain's eyelids fluttered. His hands moved again. Wolfgang scooted closer and felt McVain's forehead. It was warm. Perhaps the cold temperature would help to lower his fever. McVain's eyes opened, blinked and opened again. Wolfgang gripped his mangled left hand, no longer fearing his own health. He'd long passed that point of worry. McVain's green eyes moved left, right and then left again, before settling on Wolfgang. He smiled, which was rare. His voice was low.

"They loved us," McVain hissed.

Wolfgang nodded. "Yes, they did. Until they learned the truth."

McVain looked past Wolfgang toward Mr. Weaver's bed. It no longer housed Mr. Weaver. Now an older man with white hair called it home. "Where's Weaver?"

"He died this morning."

McVain stared at the man in Weaver's bed. "Then the jazz we played was for him." He made a move to sit up, but then winced deeply and settled back down. "I feel dizzy."

"Your temperature is nearly a hundred and four," Wolfgang said. "We performed surgery. Doctor Barker removed half of your left lung. I'm surprised you're even lucid."

McVain blinked slowly. "I don't have much longer do I?"

Wolfgang couldn't lie. He couldn't even sugarcoat it. McVain was one patient who could handle nothing less than the blunt truth. "We almost never have a turnaround when the disease has progressed this far." Wolfgang paused to let it sink in. "What you did last night was dangerous."

"Barker?"

"Rehearsals are cancelled for the foreseeable future," Wolfgang said. "But don't worry. He hasn't cancelled the concert. I think he's afraid to let the patients down."

McVain shook his head. His pale face showed little gratification at the news, as if his flesh wouldn't allow it. Consumption was another name for tuberculosis because it absolutely consumed its victims. McVain needed rest if he was ever going to make it to the concert.

"Lincoln said you used to play at the Rathskeller."

McVain nodded. "My father was . . . a bartender there. It was a beautiful place." He closed his eyes, as if focusing on the memories of playing the piano in the basement of the Seelbach Hotel, at the Rathskeller, which was mostly closed down because of Prohibition. In its day it was the premier watering hole, one of the first air-conditioned rooms ever built, and the only surviving Rockwood Pottery room in the world, with ornate columns and terra cotta ceiling. Its medieval-style walls depicted cities in the Rhenish region of Germany, where the Seelbach's founders had been born. McVain's eyes fluttered open again. "I wanted . . . to go back there . . . one more time before . . . "

"We'll have none of that," Wolfgang said. He couldn't blame McVain for wanting to go back. He was showing signs of opening up though. His secrets were his demons. Wolfgang could see the truth festering behind those stark green Irish eyes. "Tell me about your father, McVain."

"Like yours . . . mine wanted me to be a famous . . . musician."

"But you became one."

McVain readjusted his bed sheets and pulled them up higher, wincing noticeably. "He died when I was in Europe. Heard I lost my fingers. Went crazy . . . shot himself."

McVain's anger probably turned further inward after his father's suicide, thought Wolfgang. Tragedy in layers. Hopefully they were beginning to unravel. "Barker sometimes reminds me of my father," Wolfgang said. "Which is why I have a natural inclination to disobey him."

A brief smile from McVain again.

"You guys were responsible for a riot."

"They loved us. They tossed money. Did Rufus get it all?"

"He still has it." Wolfgang couldn't be mad at them. They'd bonded. They'd simply taken a much-needed night of freedom, albeit a dangerous one for everyone. "Who was the stiff with the mustache who ratted you guys out?"

McVain tried to laugh. "We took a trolley downtown. That flat tire and his wife were sitting . . . near the front when . . . we came in." McVain closed his eyes and took a few painful breaths. "We sat down and the guy . . . he said no niggers were allowed up front."

"Poor Rufus."

"I threatened to . . . bump him off, you know." McVain licked his lips, and even that task seemed difficult. He swallowed, wincing. "Niggers, I said to him . . . how dare you call . . . Rufus a name like that . . . " McVain sniffed. His eyes grew heavy. "The wife went hysterical. Then Josef started . . . writing on that . . . damn chalkboard." McVain wheezed another laugh and tears pooled in his eyes from the pain.

Wolfgang touched McVain's shoulder. "What did he write?"

"We all have TB." McVain coughed so violently his reddened eyes bulged. "I waved my left hand . . . in the man's face. He cringed back so hard he fell . . . off his seat."

Wolfgang wanted to be stern but he was enjoying it too much.

"They jumped up . . . ran to the back of the trolley . . . so fast it nearly . . . tipped over." McVain's eyes wandered toward the piano at the foot of the bed. "How'd I get back?"

"Big 15 carried you. Lincoln drove like mad."

"And Capone? Was that neat or what?"

Wolfgang tried his hardest not to crack a smile. Capone had frightened the life out of him. McVain, Rufus and Josef had all lived the horrors of war and were now dying of an incurable disease, but for Wolfgang and his deformed foot, staring into the eyes of a drunk gangster and his gun barrel was the most danger he'd ever experienced. He still felt the lingering invigoration of the adrenaline. It was as if he was going against his mother's wishes all over again.

McVain grinned. "He nearly shot us all . . . but he didn't count on you. You and your buddies." He pointed his left pinkie heavenward. They both burst out laughing.

WOLFGANG PACED THE length of the small center aisle in Waverly's chapel. It was the second night Susannah had left early in the past week and a half and he didn't have to wonder about where she was going. He paced in the dark, his footfalls clicking against the floor. In his hand was a wine bottle. He tipped it to his mouth, drank for a solid four seconds and then wiped the warm taste from his lips. He envisioned Susannah and Doctor Barker having some kind of deranged, torrid affair. His hands touching her bare flesh. Wolfgang tilted the bottle back again, swallowed two gulps and then raised the bottle in the air. "Sacramental wine, Doctor Barker." Doctor Barker was twenty years older than Susannah. There was just no way, he thought, remembering several weeks ago when Susannah had asked, *How am I supposed to find anyone to marry on this hillside?* And Doctor Barker was having problems with his marriage. Supposedly Anne was not sleeping with him anymore because she was afraid of becoming infected— at least that was the rumor. Had Susannah filled the void?

Wolfgang breathed deeply, starting to feel the alcohol. He'd consumed so much so fast the drunkenness hit him like a tsunami wave. It was wrong of him to spy on Susannah and to feel these serious pangs of jealousy, but he had to know. He placed the open wine on the altar, cracking the bottle with the force of the movement. His head was beginning to swim. The top of the altar had been a foot higher than his depth perception had thought. Glass sprinkled to the floor of the chapel and the remaining fourth of wine dripped down atop the glass like blood. He left it to pool and spread.

WEARING ONLY A thin lab coat over his clerics, the single digit temperature invaded every open slit of his clothing and turned his

skin to ice. His feet felt numb by the time he'd entered the woods
and found the footpath on the far side of the main road, which
was covered with frozen patches of snow that the temperature
never allowed to thaw even in the afternoon sunlight. It was now
eleven o'clock at night and the wind chill had dropped it to near
zero. He buried his hands in the folds of his coat, hunkered down
and plowed his way over fallen limbs and ice-smothered leaves. He
ducked under low-hanging boughs and spiraling vines and pushed
out crystallized bursts of air from his nose and mouth. His nose
was beginning to run. The hair inside his nostrils felt like daggers. Only the remnants of the wine kept him warm. Up ahead was
Doctor Barker's cottage. Smoke puffed up from a stone chimney.
He dragged his numb right leg down the footpath and spotted the
glow of a light coming from the side window of Barker's one-floor
cottage, which, unlike Wolfgang's, had a narrow veranda with
posts that wrapped around three walls of the structure.

Wolfgang didn't hesitate up the side steps. He knelt down on
the wood-planked porch, wetting the knees of his pants, and peered
into a frost-smeared window. A fire burned across the room. Beside
the hearth rested an iron prod and shovel and a black bucket of
ashes. In the center of the room was a yellow couch. Behind it was
a desk with a lamp. Susannah sat at the desk with two stacks of
papers in front of her and Doctor Barker stood behind her with
a glass of something in his hand. Something golden brown on ice,
like whiskey? A hint of relief poured over Wolfgang's frozen body.
Perhaps they were only working on her book? He'd overheard
him tell Susannah that he could maybe help her get it published.
Wolfgang still didn't trust him.

When Doctor Barker placed his right hand on Susannah's left
shoulder the uneasy feeling stormed back. What was he doing?
Susannah looked up at Doctor Barker, but Wolfgang couldn't tell
if she was smiling or unnerved by her boss' touch. Wolfgang lowered his head just below the window, where he felt and heard a soft

whistling of air in the minuscule cracks between wall and window-sill. He heard Doctor Barker's voice.

"Can I get you anything?" he asked.

"No, thank you," said Susannah.

"Are you sure? Not a drink? I've got bourbon."

There was a hesitation before Susannah answered. "I need to be getting home anyway."

Wolfgang agreed. She needed to be getting home. His vision swirled slightly from the wine. His ears were so numb they hurt. He felt foolish sitting on Doctor Barker's deck, eavesdropping on a dear friend, but the way he had his body hunkered down and his arms draped around his bent knees, he'd begun to gather some warmth. He didn't want to venture back out into the cold, where the wind could get to him again. He wondered if he was drunk. His head was already starting to throb. He needed more wine. He craned his neck and peered in through the window again. Doctor Barker stood by a closet next to the desk.

"Let me show you something." Doctor Barker waved her over toward the couch. "Come, sit for a moment."

Susannah piled her papers into one stack and clutched her manuscript against her chest. She walked with reluctance to the couch and sat on the edge of the center cushion. Wolfgang could tell by her body language that Doctor Barker's cottage made her a bit uncomfortable. He knew he should get up and leave them now that his worries had been sated. But then Doctor Barker returned to the closet beside the desk and opened the door. What he pulled, rather clumsily, from the depths of the dark closet shocked Wolfgang so intensely that he nearly fell over and rolled down the steps. In Doctor Barker's hands was a massive musical instrument, a double bass that nearly stretched his own height. He carried it over to the couch and sat beside Susannah. Her eyes grew as large as saucers on sight of the double bass in Doctor Barker's hands. The fingers of her right hand touched her chest in surprise.

"Doctor Barker . . . "

He plucked a few strings and grabbed a bow from beside the couch. He ran the bow over the strings and a low hum resonated throughout the cottage and seeped through the windows. "I can play music too, Susannah." He gave the strings another strike. "I've played for most of my life."

"I don't understand," said Susannah.

Doctor Barker put the double bass aside and scooted closer to her. "We work long days here. Nonstop work, death . . . and misery. We all need release." He put his left hand on her knee. She didn't move it away or stand up to get away from his claw.

Wolfgang flinched and raised a bit, to the point where his head from the nose up would have been visible had they both turned around to look out the window. He'd be careful to not make any noise.

Susannah clutched the manuscript against her chest, holding it with both arms folded. "Doctor Barker . . . you're married."

"Call me Evan," he said, the sound of his name hovering on the apparent awkwardness. "Anne won't touch me anymore, Susannah. She fears it."

Susannah's voice was laced with fear. "We all do."

Doctor Barker gave her knee a soft squeeze. "Do you not feel something between us, Susannah?" He leaned in and kissed her neck.

Wolfgang wanted to come through the window but he waited to see Susannah's reaction. If he felt she needed to be protected he'd barge through the door without a care for their curiosity of him being there. He'd answer her questions later. He was proud and relieved to see Susannah jump up from her seat on the couch.

"How dare you, Doctor Barker." She held her manuscript tighter. "You didn't care about my book at all . . . you pig."

"You're making a fool of yourself." Doctor Barker stood, red-faced and seething. He pointed to the door. "You're in love with a man you can't have."

Susannah appeared to be crying. Her shoulders trembled. She paused and then hurried to the door. Wolfgang didn't have time to leave now or he'd be seen. He stayed in his spot on the side porch of the cottage as Susannah burst out the front door and down the main steps. The side of the house concealed his position under the window. He watched Susannah hurry toward the footpath. She stopped as if she had forgotten something, but then she looked up into the dark sky. Wolfgang looked up as well. Past the main sanatorium, thick, heavy clouds of billowing smoke hovered over the horizon. It hung over where the colored hospital rested down the hillside.

Susannah turned toward Doctor Barker's cottage, her feelings of him set aside, and shouted. "Doctor Barker!"

A few seconds later Doctor Barker stood on the front porch, hands on the railing, his eyes focused on the same smoke Susannah had seen. "Jesus."

"I think the colored hospital is on fire."

Susannah and Doctor Barker took off into the woods.

WOLFGANG GAVE THEM a few seconds head start before heading off in the same direction. He couldn't move at their running pace and quickly fell behind, so he didn't need to worry about them seeing him in their wake. He would tell them he was in the sanatorium and saw the smoke himself. He limped quickly over the main road and hurried across the frozen mud and grass and sloping grounds. He saw Abel standing next to the entrance portico on the south side of the sanatorium, dazed, unblinking.

"Abel, what are you doing up?"

Abel didn't answer. He stared into the woods, shivering in the cold. Wolfgang hugged the young, frightened boy, pulling him to his chest. He rubbed the kid's back to warm him. "You need to go inside right now. Do you hear me, Abel? Go inside and warm yourself."

Abel nodded. Wolfgang released him and waited until the boy was inside before turning down the hillside again. Wolfgang focused on the footpath before him, a downhill track that was dangerous at the unbalanced pace he was moving. The wind ripped into his face and moved brittle tree branches in a rickety, ominous song. After another twenty yards Wolfgang heard footsteps coming from another direction. Branches moved and cracked. Lincoln emerged from another cluster of trees, huffing his way down the hill toward the wisps of smoke below. The further they descended the more noticeable the smell of smoke became until they finally burst into the clearing around the colored hospital.

The wind blew a thick haze of smoke into Wolfgang's face. Lincoln stormed ahead. Susannah was bent over in the grass, coughing. Wolfgang helped her up.

She looked at him with a bundle of emotions teetering on the precipice. "I stopped by your cottage."

"I was still at the sanatorium." Wolfgang crouched and shielded his eyes. Smoke swirled low as they stood on a slope overlooking the hospital. Nearly a hundred patients huddled in groups along the tree line as three men from the maintenance staff shot water from hoses toward the front of the hospital. The flames had been put out. Thick, dark, billowing smoke stretched up past the tips of the trees. The fire hadn't been as bad as the smoke had made it appear. It had been contained to only the front entrance of the hospital. A flood, Wolfgang thought, and now a fire. Patients in a run-down building with smoke in their TB-infected lungs. What would be next? He searched the crowd for Smokey and found him sitting on the ground next to the tree line, his baseball bat resting on his thighs. He coughed into his hands and stared at the smoke.

Doctor Barker stood about ten yards from the building, ushering an old black woman up the hill toward the others. Susannah watched with tears in her eyes. Soot and smoke darkened her wet cheeks. She coughed again into her hand, still clutching the manuscript to her chest. Wolfgang saw it and didn't need to question her about holding it. He felt horrible about spying on her, but a part of him felt calmed by it—the same part that fueled his addiction of watching those who didn't know they were being watched.

She started to offer an explanation of why she'd run through the woods with her prized book, but she lowered her head and said nothing. Her chest rose and fell with deep gasps. The air was not healthy to breathe.

Wolfgang touched her shoulder. "Susannah, go back up the hill. Check the sanatorium. Every bed. Every room. If anyone's missing we'll know the reason why." She nodded and without hesitation ran into the woods. "Start with the fourth floor," Wolfgang shouted, watching her as she disappeared into the darkness. Wolfgang navigated the slope made slippery by errant water from the fire hoses and caught up with Lincoln, who was consoling a young boy who couldn't find his mother. Only then did he realize that he'd just sent Susannah into the woods alone. He started to run after her but Rufus' voice stopped him.

"Wolfgang?"

Wolfgang faced Rufus, who hobbled up the incline, his boots crunching over quickly freezing pockets of slushy water and ice. "Rufus, was anyone hurt?"

"No." His breathing was labored. "We were lucky." He held his flute tightly in his left hand. "The fire wasn't so big. But it got our attention." The damage to the charred front of the building was extensive. Water dripped from the eaves. The wooden posts had splinted and snapped in half. The roof had separated from the main building and drooped toward the ground. It would all have to be repaired quickly. It appeared the fire hadn't spread to the rooms or the sleeping porch. Rufus coughed and then spat a hunk of phlegm to the wet grass. "Doctor Barker was down here in a flash."

Wolfgang watched Doctor Barker work with an intensity he

hadn't seen from him before. Hints of anger showed in his quick movements, but underneath he could see a deeply rooted passion to protect everyone on the hillside regardless of color and no matter what the obstacles.

It hit Wolfgang suddenly. "Where's Big 15?"

Rufus surveyed the surrounding woods. "Haven't seen him."

Lincoln approached with the same thing on his mind. "Where's Big 15, Wolf? He would have been down here."

"Yes, I know." Wolfgang turned toward the woods up the hillside. "He would have . . ."

"What?" Lincoln asked.

Wolfgang's eyes lit up. "I think the fire was a diversion."

Wolfgang hurried up the hillside, fueled by adrenaline alone—otherwise hypothermia would have set in. The alcohol had worn off—the circumstances had demanded it. Wolfgang moved in fits and starts around the trees, unsure where to go but following Susannah's general direction. A pungent odor emanated from somewhere in the woods, a nauseating but familiar stench. "You smell that, Lincoln?"

Lincoln wiggled his nose. "Smoke."

"No . . . something more." They continued on. They checked Big 15's dormitory but found it empty, everyone apparently down with the fire. Wolfgang moved further up the hill, his mind starting to panic with thoughts of Susannah injured, Big 15 missing and even Abel too frightened to utter a single word. He and Lincoln just kept bouncing from tree to tree, ducking here, stepping there, calling Big 15's name and hearing nothing but the wind and crunching deadfall. Wolfgang sniffed, the sweet smell becoming more noticeable. "Ether. Lincoln, it's ether."

"I can smell it now . . . a whole truck load of it. And gasoline." Lincoln grabbed Wolfgang's arm and shushed him. They stopped and listened. Someone was crying. Wolfgang followed the sound. It was a child.

Lincoln found him first, sitting with his back against a tree trunk, and called out to him. "Abel?" Abel's face was muddy. Tears streaked the grime on his cheeks. His teeth chattered.

Wolfgang knelt beside the terrified boy and clutched his small shoulders. "What happened? Abel . . . what are you doing out here?"

Abel pointed to his left.

"Holy shit," Lincoln said, darting off toward the trees to their right. "Oh, my God."

Big 15's massive bulk hung naked from the limb of a tall white oak. Fingers of light bled down from the moon above, spotlighting his body and giving them a glimpse of light and shadow, darkness and blood. The smell of ether permeated Big 15's entire body as it rotated slightly from the tree limb. Fear, terror and pain cried out from his red, bulging eyes as he twisted on the thick rope. His wet body trembled beneath the noose. The smell of gasoline mixed with the ether. Lincoln coughed and Wolfgang felt nauseous. A towel soaked with what Wolfgang assumed to be ether stolen from the sanatorium rested on the grass next to the base of the tree. Knocking him out was the only way to move Big 15's body to such a position. But still, the strength it must have taken to get him up into the tree. How many?

Lincoln ran to Big 15, grabbed his swaying right foot and tried to support his weight so he wouldn't strangle any more. Big 15's legs were limp. Lincoln attempted to grab Big 15's left foot as well but couldn't reach it. Abel leapt from Wolfgang's arms, ran to Big 15, jumped up and caught the swaying left foot. The tree limb cracked, sagged, then broke. As Lincoln and Abel scrambled to get out of the way, Big 15 collapsed in a heap to the frozen forest floor. The huge tree limb landed beside him with a thud and bounced before settling. It reminded Wolfgang of cutting down Rita weeks ago, except this was no suicide. Wolfgang squatted beside Big 15's body, which reeked of ether, gasoline and urine, and felt for a pulse—and found one! He moved very little. His neck was a bloody mess from where the rope had rubbed against it and Wolfgang feared it was broken as well. Big 15's wadded socks had been stuffed inside his mouth. Wolfgang pulled them out and a big gush of air escaped. Wolfgang took off his lab coat and draped it over Big 15's waist. Big 15 moaned and struggled to keep his eyes open and focused. His breathing was shallow.

Lincoln knelt beside them, his words laced with venom. "The bastards poured gasoline on him. They pissed on him. He never hurt anyone!"

Wolfgang remembered Big 15 carrying McVain's lifeless body into the sanatorium the other night. Had that been the final straw? Was that his crime? Wolfgang wondered if he'd put Big 15 in harm's way. He gripped Big 15's gasoline-soaked hand and stared into his eyes, which moved every which way, as if he couldn't see. "Who did this to you? Big 15 . . . who did this to you?"

Big 15's eyes focused on Father Wolfgang Pike. Or maybe it was only his voice that he'd centered on. "Boss?"

Wolfgang smiled despite his fury. "Yes, it's me. Boss."

Big 15 smiled with big white teeth. His face and chest had been lacerated with cuts and slashes as if by whips or chains. How long had they tortured him? A calculated surprise attack on a man who risked his life every day to save others. Attacked because of the color of his skin.

Wolfgang pounded a fist against the hard ground. "Don't die on me." He pleaded to both Big 15 and to God. "I was the one who was supposed to be the victim. I was the one they should have been after."

"Boss . . ."

Wolfgang gripped both of his hands now. "Don't talk. Lincoln, run for a stretcher and a couple of men—four men—to carry it." Lincoln ran off.

Just then Susannah emerged from the trees. Abel ran to her and hugged her. Susannah saw Big 15's abused body and dropped to the ground, crying and sobbing.

Wolfgang checked Big 15's pulse again but felt almost nothing. He'd stopped fighting, stopped moving. His eyelids blinked once, reptilian-like, before opening. "My . . . my papa called *me* boss . . . I . . . I respected my papa . . . " He choked, his chest rose from the frozen ground, and then his body settled. His eyes no longer moved.

Big 15 was dead.

Wolfgang closed Big 15's eyes and prayed over his slain body. He stood, weak-kneed and stiff, and hobbled over toward Susannah and Abel. His right foot was numb. He embraced Susannah and Abel. Susannah sobbed into his chest, but it wasn't enough to muffle the sound of her anguish.

22

EVERYTHING HAPPENS FOR *a reason ...*

It's God's will, Wolfgang. *The words my mother had uttered weeks after my father had "died in his sleep." She'd uttered those same words when, as a confused child, I'd asked her about a father I remembered less every day—a father I'd come to love more and more only because he was dead.* It was his time to go.

So now it was Rose's time? Was it that simple? She looks up at me trustingly as I slowly rake my fingers through her hair, holding them there in the growth, never wanting to let go. Rose is under my protection now, inside a tuberculosis hospital that badly needs to expand. It's my job to make her feel safe, much as it had been her job to do the same when she'd first embraced me inside her bedroom.

I am her doctor and I refuse to let the tuberculosis take her.

This is not God's will. This is God's cruel punishment. My mother would believe the same thing. Rose was sent to me on the church steps as a test. A devilish vixen. A temptress luring me away from the church and into her arms and I'd taken the plunge with little thought. I refuse to believe it . . . not this sweet, innocent, beautiful woman.

My Rose.

We'd yet to start that family we'd always talked about, although it was not for a lack of trying. He'll send us children when the time is *right, Wolfgang. That was what she'd always told me. She cups her hand to my cheek and smiles. When the time is right . . .*

Rose reaches up and touches my cheek. "Tell me your thoughts."

Coughing all around me. It's so overcrowded. I have no hope for her but I can't tell her this. "I think only of your recovery," I tell her. "I won't let this disease take you." But in my mind I speak to God and demand that He listen. *If Rose's death is my punishment, then so be it. But I will not regret my decision to be with her—the best years of my life. The memories will never fade like those of my father. I am a better man because of her. Free her from this dreaded disease and I will follow You always.*

Rose grips my hand and squeezes it. I feel her strength returning. I see it in her eyes, which sparkle of life. I can hear it in her voice. "I'll wait for you in Heaven, Wolfgang."

"Don't say that, Rose."

She laughs, although I'm not sure why. "I'll answer your questions if there's a way." She squeezes my hand again and coughs. "I'll speak to you from the other side. You'll know I'm there. You'll never be alone."

To be alone . . . my greatest fear.

WOLFGANG STOOD AT the private cemetery at the bottom of the hillside, where a dozen headstones stuck up from the ground, chipped and cracked, protruding like uneven teeth from the grassy gums of the earth. The sunlight shone brightly for Big 15's funeral. The wind eased and the temperature was a comfortable thirty degrees. He would not go down Lincoln's Death Tunnel. He would be allowed to sleep in peace with the people he took care of daily. As far as they knew, Big 15 had no family, but every ambulatory patient from the colored hospital attended, as did most of the staff and a few white patients from the top of the hill. Big 15 would outlast them all now. His bones would still be there when tuberculosis was long gone and the sanatorium was cold and abandoned but for the traces of the souls that had passed through.

Wolfgang said a prayer over his grave while Susannah cried behind him. She knelt down and placed a handful of flowers over the grave, then stood up and slid her hand inside the bend of Wolfgang's arm. "He was a good man," she said. "He didn't deserve my cold shoulder." Wolfgang patted the top of her hand. Susannah sniffled, wiped a tear from her right eye. "My mother was robbed on the streets by a black man when I was seven."

Wolfgang watched her stare at Big 15's grave, crying quietly. She'd put the robber's face on every black man she'd ever met, he thought. He held her close, knowing that Doctor Barker stood watching them in the crowd.

"We will remember Big 15 wheeling his supply cart up and down the hillside three times a day, in the heat . . . in the cold . . . in the snow. We will remember his kind smile. His generosity. His big feet for which he was so appropriately named." This drew laughter from the crowd. "Yet he had an even bigger heart." Nodding from the onlookers. "His last moments will not be what we remember of him. Instead it will be replaced by the memory of him running down Fourth Street toward Uncle Frank's new Cadillac with Tad McVain draped over his shoulder."

More laughter. Susannah squeezed his hand much like Rose had done during his dream. They all stood silent for a full minute and then Wolfgang started the procession back up the hillside. Wolfgang thought of Abel. He'd asked the boy if he'd seen anyone in the woods last night, anyone wearing white robes and hoods. Nothing, he'd said, the petrified look still in his eyes.

Susannah had no luck searching the sanatorium for missing patients. Because of the smoke and the noise down the hillside, most of the patients had been out of their beds gawking from the solarium porches. So either the murderers had been fast to get back or Wolfgang's theory was shaky. They'd found no white Klan robes, no whips or chains. No guilty faces. The police came briefly to investigate the fire and Big 15's death, and they questioned just enough people to give them the appearance that they cared. They left the grounds less than an hour after they arrived. Upon Wolfgang's insistence, in deference to the cassock Wolfgang had donned for that very purpose, they'd left a man behind to stand guard. But they didn't buy his theory. "No dying patient could have done this," they'd said.

"Not everyone here is dying," Wolfgang had told them.

"Even so," said the lead cop—a burly red-haired man with a bushy red mustache and a toothpick who couldn't stop glancing at the sanatorium's creepy facade the entire time he spoke. "Even so."

"If you stay long enough to hear what some of our *dying* patients could do with their voices and instruments, maybe you wouldn't dismiss the idea so easily."

They'd turned to leave, but Wolfgang wasn't finished with them. "Go if you must," said Wolfgang, tempting fate. "If Big 15 had been white, would you have tried harder?"

The red-headed cop turned and stuck up a finger in warning. "Don't push us, Father."

Wolfgang held up his hands, palms toward the police. "I apologize. Go on. I know it frightens you to death to be around us. The way you look at the sanatorium, it's as if you're afraid our wind, the very wind that's ruffling your bangs and entering your nostrils there at this moment, carries with it thousands of tubercular germs, spewed from the diseased mouths of the hundreds of our *dying* patients."

The man touched his hair, protected his nose from the wind by covering it with his fat hand and turned away at a quicker pace, his men following right behind.

"Cowards!"

WOLFGANG WALKED BACK up the hillside, kicking various twigs from the footpath, cursing under his breath. The grass in the clearing was wet from melted snow and it soaked his black shoes.

Grass stuck to the bottoms of them as he trudged along the side of the sanatorium, passing the bushes and shrubbery that would be sprouting tiny green leaves in a month. He moved with his head lowered, wishing for spring, his motivation for the concert heightened by Big 15's horrendous death.

He opened the sanatorium's front doors and looked up finally when he entered the Grand Lobby, which was busy with nurses pushing new patients to and from in wheelchairs, visitors talking . . . a middle-aged woman in a long beige coat with red hair standing with her hands clutching a blue purse. She watched Wolfgang with interest.

"Wolfgang."

Wolfgang took a few more steps. His pace slowed as he remembered her voice.

"Wolfgang . . . wait."

He stopped, turned and forced himself to look into her eyes. She took a step forward, and then another, as if waiting for him to repel, step away and run. He didn't. He stood frozen as the hustle and bustle continued around him. The woman took yet another step closer, reached out and grabbed his right hand.

"Wolfgang . . . It's good to see you."

Wolfgang slid his hand from her grip. "Mother . . . what are you doing here?"

"Is there somewhere we can talk?"

He studied her hands. They'd aged slightly in the ten years, the knuckles beneath the skin more prominent. Her red hair was longer, more curly and streaked with gray. Her eyes were marked with crow's feet. The skin around her cheeks had become touched with the tiniest of wrinkles. She was still a pretty woman. Part of him wanted to embrace her. Hug her as tightly as he could and cry on her shoulder. Instead he motioned toward the front doors. "There's a bench outside . . . in the sunshine where it's warm."

They walked side-by-side but several feet apart toward the main road, where a black Model T was parked, engine idling with a dark-haired man in the driver's seat. The man waved to Wolfgang, but Wolfgang ignored him. He assumed he'd come with his mother. Her driver? Her lover? He didn't want to know. Any thoughts of embracing her had left him as soon as he'd seen her male companion. He walked away from the road to a wooden bench near the tree line. It was big enough for three. Wolfgang sat on the end. His mother sat on the other end with two feet of space between them. She squinted, unbuttoned a few of her coat buttons. "The sun feels nice."

Wolfgang nodded.

"You look good, Wolfgang." He watched her from the corner of his eye but didn't face her when she spoke. "I like the beard. Last time we spoke you were just growing it. It's very becoming."

"What do you want, mother?"

She folded her hands on her lap. "You used to call me mom."

"You used to be my mom." He shot her a glance and then faced the sanatorium again. Thirty feet away her idling car puffed clouds of smoke from an annoyingly loud muffler. The sun glistened off the windshield, smearing her man's face in a prism of blinding light. "Rose died four years ago."

"I know, Wolfgang . . ."

"You didn't come to the funeral."

"I . . ." She sighed, flicked the handle of her purse with her thumbs and turned toward Wolfgang on the bench. "Why did you turn against me, Wolfgang? I needed you after your father passed away."

Wolfgang finally looked at her. His eyes were moist. "How can you say that? I know what you did."

Doris Pike's face sagged. Her wrinkles became more pronounced.

"Are you going to deny it, mother." Wolfgang wiped his eyes. The wind magnified the wetness. "Are you going to deny smothering him with that pillow? Are you going to say it never happened? You told me natural causes. It was his time to go. I saw you enter your bedroom and lock the door. I saw his feet, mother. I saw him struggling for breath. You stood on your tiptoes for more leverage."

Doris wiped tears from her eyes and reached her hand toward Wolfgang. Oh, how he wanted to grab it and clutch it in his own. He hadn't even seen her for ten years. He hated her. He loved her. He didn't make a move to hold her hand.

"I used to watch your bedroom," said Wolfgang. "There was a hole in the wall. I'd watch him beat you."

"He used to beat you too, Wolfgang."

"Don't turn him bad again, mother. He gave me music. Don't turn him bad to me." He looked at her again. "Is that why you did it, because he beat you? Tell me it is. At least that would somewhat justify it. Tell me it was some kind of revenge . . . that you would murder your own husband when he was too weak to defend himself."

"If you only knew . . ." Doris folded her arms, bit her lip.

"What?"

"I didn't murder your father."

"I saw you."

Doris scooted closer on the bench. Wolfgang had nowhere to go to get away from her except for standing up. He remained still. "How could you wait twenty years to bring this up, Wolfgang? You saw what you saw but you don't know the facts. We could have stayed together."

"I've had nightmares ever since that night. You come to my bed and smother me with a pillow."

Doris' hand covered her mouth.

"Every night I lay in bed, unable to move because of the polio. I waited for my bedroom door to open and for you to come in . . . with a pillow in your hands and finish me off just as you finished dad off. There was always something secretive about you, mother. You were loving, yet distant. You always washed my cuts in the tub and kissed my bruises, yet you never protected me."

"He asked me to kill him, Wolfgang." Her hands trembled. The gold bracelets around her wrists clanked together like wind chimes. She clutched her purse to keep her hands from shaking. "He asked me to do it." Wolfgang stared at her, shocked, wanting more, and she gave it. "He had cancer. It started in his stomach and ended up in his liver. He was in so much pain. You saw him. You heard how much pain he was in. When it got to the point where it was too painful to even hold a pen and write his fugues . . . he didn't want to live anymore. He couldn't take the pain, Wolfgang. He begged me for days to kill him. To smother him with that pillow. He didn't want you to see him like that. He wanted you to remember him as a strong man. I got myself drunk enough to do it and I did it."

Wolfgang remembered her tears as she pressed the pillow over his father's head, not tears of rage or anger but of pain and anguish. As if she never wanted to do it. It made sense. She'd euthanised Charles Pike. The good death. Several patients had asked Wolfgang to do the same to them over the years but he'd refused.

Wolfgang placed his hand overtop his mother's hand in between them on the bench but didn't look at her. He looked at the idling black car. The sun had moved ever so slightly on the windshield and the man's face was visible again. "Why are you here? Why today?" He moved his hand back to his lap.

Doris reeled her hand back in. "I'm moving to Minnesota, Wolfgang. Today. I'm married to Bruce over there. He's a minister." Bruce waved again from the car. Wolfgang nodded this time. "We're going to Minnesota to start a church. That's where he's from. Would you like to meet him?"

"No," Wolfgang said. "I don't think so." He looked at her again. "You came to tell me you were leaving . . . that's it?"

"I came for Charles' violin," she said. "You took all of his instruments. I'd like to have one to keep."

"Which one?"

"You know the one."

Wolfgang nodded. He braced his hands on his knees and stood. "Wait here." He walked a few paces and stopped to face his mother again. "I'm almost thirty years old now. What did you guys do at the factory?"

Doris sighed heavily, as if contemplating another lie. "There was no factory, Wolfgang."

"Were you a whore?"

She shook her head, apparently not offended by the accusation. "No, I wasn't a whore."

"Where would you go at night? And where would he go during the day?"

She bit her lip again. "We were thieves, Wolfgang." She looked to the ground, staring at her shoes and petite feet.

"Look in my eyes."

She looked up. "Yes, we were thieves. That was our work, Wolfgang. I was a pickpocket. Your father, this man you elevated to greatness after his death, he was a professional thief. Diamonds, jewels, rubies . . ."

"Devoted Christians, I see."

"Don't judge us," she said. "I gave it all up years ago. They were hard times, Wolfgang. Your father . . . he just wanted to get enough money to move to Vienna. He wanted—"

"I know what he wanted." Wolfgang glanced at her new husband in the idling car. "That was why the curtains were always closed. He was constantly checking out our curtains at night. He rarely let me go outside. He was afraid someone would come for what you guys stole."

"He was paranoid all the time." She sniffled, wiped her eyes again. "He'd hide the jewels and money inside his instruments." She paused long enough to let it sink in. "Inside the violins, the violas, the cellos, the bass . . ."

"I see."

Wolfgang limped past the Model T but didn't so much as glance at Bruce, his mother's preacher husband. He moved as quickly as he could down the footpath to his cottage. He entered and left the door open. Across the room seven of his father's violins rested against the wall—the eighth being used by Josef. He grabbed the *P* violin, ran his fingers over the small *f holes* and decided there was no way his fingers could fit inside that way. He slid his fingers beneath the strings. He shook the violin and heard nothing rattle inside. He turned it over and saw a circular groove about the size of a baseball in the back of the violin. And a tiny metal latch. Out of curiosity he'd opened it before, seeing nothing. But he'd never felt inside. He unlatched it, removed the round wooden plate and felt around until his long middle finger brushed up against something hard and angled and secured against the inside lining. He flattened his hand as far as he could, reached inside until the skin between his thumb and index finger felt as if it would split against the carefully carved opening in the wood. He flicked at the object until it started to become loose. After a few minutes of rocking it back and forth it came loose in his fingers. When he pulled his hand out, a huge diamond sat in between his middle and index finger. It sparkled in silver and blue. His front door blew slightly open. Wind rustled leaves across his porch. His mother was still out there, up the hill, waiting. So that was why she'd come . . . for the diamond? She could have it. He felt like throwing it into the woods. It felt like poison in his hand. He fixed the back of the violin and carried it by the neck out the door.

Doris Pike waited patiently on the bench. She stood when Wolfgang approached. Wolfgang handed her the diamond, which was about half the size of a golf ball, but held onto his father's favorite violin. "You can go now."

"Wolfgang . . ." Doris grabbed Wolfgang's hand, placed the diamond inside of it and closed his fingers over it. "I want the violin."

He looked at his closed right fist and then lowered it to his side. He extended his left hand and offered her the violin. He hadn't seen her smile so big in twenty years. A look of warmth and relief showered over her face, a cleansing smile that made her instantly look young again. He'd taken every one of his father's instruments ten years ago without a thought that he'd be taking one of the only parts of his father that Doris cherished most—his music. He'd left her nothing.

Doris took the violin from him and clutched it to her chest. "Thank you." She kissed his cheek and he didn't pull away. "Do something good with the money."

"What money?"

Doris grinned as she walked around the hood of her husband's Model T and stopped before opening the passenger's side door. "Good bye, Wolfgang."

"There's a concert." Wolfgang stepped closer to the car. "Valentine's Day. On the rooftop. You can come."

Doris didn't give him an answer. She lowered her head into the car and closed the door. She did wave as Bruce pulled away, leaving Wolfgang standing in a pocket of car fumes and rock dust holding a diamond that would have made even Al Capone weak in the knees.

WOLFGANG SAID NOTHING to anyone about the content of their conversation on the bench. Susannah and Lincoln had both seen him out there sitting in the sunshine with his mother, but they didn't pry. He would tell them eventually. He lacked emotion the rest of the afternoon, drained as they were from Big 15's funeral and the shocking arrival of his mother. He moved slowly from patient to patient, gave a homily at Mass that lacked passion, and started the night's rehearsal with an uncharacteristic flatness to the way he conducted his choir and trio of musicians.

Snow flickered against the screens. The cold wind whistled. Winter was back, having only left for the afternoon hours before returning with the downing of the sun. McVain watched from his bed, unable to muster the strength to even get out of bed, let alone play the piano. Five minutes into rehearsal, which had quickly taken the flat, emotionless mood of their leader, Doctor Barker arrived with a flurry of loud footsteps. "Wolfgang . . . shut it down."

Wolfgang's shoulders dropped. "We just started."

"A man has died for Christ's sake!" Doctor Barker shouted. "All of you, back to your rooms . . . please." He shot Susannah an angry glance and she looked away.

How dare he take it out on her for rejecting him, thought Wolfgang? His fighting spirit was rekindled. "The concert is almost here, Doctor Barker."

"There will be no concert!" He stormed off. "It's finished."

Herman stared at Doctor Barker with hate and rage in his eyes. Susannah took him by the arm and walked him up to the rooftop.

Wolfgang stood alone as the choir departed. Doctor Barker blamed him for what had happened to Big 15. He could tell by the implacable look in his hawkish eyes. The music had driven the trio to escape the other night and now McVain was on death's door and knocking with both fists. He was responsible for mixing the races and the fire at the colored hospital. Was he responsible? So why did he still feel the urge to push on?

WOLFGANG DROPPED SUSANNAH off at the dormitory and the moment was decidedly uneventful. They both mulled over the secrets that rendered them quiet. There was no handholding and no kiss on the cheek. He watched her until the door was closed and then finished the walk home, craving his sacramental wine.

He removed his collar and dropped it to the floor next to the bed. He took a bottle of wine from the kitchen and had the top off within seconds. He tilted the bottle back as he walked into the main room. In his pocket was the diamond. He took it out and placed it on the stone hearth of the fireplace. He lit a fire and sat with his back against the warmth, drinking and staring at the violins against the wall.

Do something good with the money . . .

He grabbed one of the violins and turned it over. It too had a secret compartment on the back. He opened it and stuck his hand inside. After some fiddling his hand came out with a stack of bills. Two hundred dollars. He dropped the violin on the floor without a care of damaging it and reached for another one. In it he found a ruby the size of a walnut. He drank more wine, wiped his mouth and reached for another violin. Another wad of cash—three hundred dollars worth. This violin he hammered to the ground, snapping the instrument at the neck and sending tiny slivers of wood across the floor. He chuckled and drank from the bottle again. He checked the violins one by one and after he'd finished he'd compiled a stack of cash worth two thousand dollars, along with two diamonds, an emerald and two rubies.

He asked me to do it . . . He asked me to kill him, Wolfgang . . .

He stood with a grunt from the fireplace and hobbled across the room. He opened the closet and pulled out his father's cello, viola and bass. Two thousand more dollars and six more diamonds. The bass he'd thrown against the wall and kicked until it was in a half dozen pieces and the strings jutted out like live wire. He pictured Doctor Barker playing the bass the other night and trying to impress Susannah with his skills. How dare he? Wolfgang gave the fragments of the bass one last kick and nudged it aside. He left the cello and viola intact for no other reason than being too tired and drunk.

"Thieves," he hissed. "Raised by damn thieves."

He turned the bottle up again and staggered toward the bed, where he sat on Rose's side with a plop of groaning springs. The empty wine bottle dropped from his slack grip and rolled across the floor. Visions of Susannah swam through his dizziness. He pictured her standing naked in the middle of his floor with shower water streaming down from the middle of his ceiling, soaking her hair and body. He got up too fast and nearly fell back over. Before he knew it he was outside and bundled in his heavy winter coat. He stumbled up the hillside, bracing himself on every tree in his path, hugging and touching, bouncing and limping, giggling like a child—a grown man who'd had no childhood all because he'd seen something he'd never understood until now. He wanted it back. He wanted Rose back. He wanted Susannah.

He stumbled until he reached the nurses' dormitory, his body warm from his thick coat and the alcohol coursing through his veins. For every two trees he saw twenty and he bumped into half of them. He was forced to walk with his arms out in front like a blind man feeling for walls. He limped and stumbled right past the front porch, put his back against the side wall and sidestepped along like some sneak thief. His parents' son. How proud they would be of him. A voyeuristic priest, drunk from an entire bottle of wine and searching desperately for a hole. He turned the back corner of the brick building and began to study the wall where Lincoln promised there was a hole to spy through. He'd chiseled it himself. You could see right into the showers, he'd told him. Just don't look when Nurse Cleary was in there. Wolfgang gulped and fought back the urge to vomit. His excitement helped to clear his vision momentarily, just long enough to spot the log in the grass about ten feet away. Lincoln's log. Wolfgang chuckled his way over to it and lifted it up with both hands. He walked hunchbacked with the weight of the log swaying between his legs, and dropped it to the ground next to the building's concrete foundation. He looked up to the hole. It would be about the right height. Lincoln was only a few inches taller. Perhaps he'd have to tiptoe. Susannah had to tiptoe to reach his cheek when she'd kissed him. Wolfgang stepped up onto the two-foot-high log and balanced himself on the sawed shelf. He closed his left eye and peered through the tiny tunnel with his right, the bricks cold against his nose and cheek. He waited. No water running. He questioned his sanity and blamed it on drunkenness.

"Sacramental wine," he whispered, resting his forehead on the cold bricks, wanting to see Susannah and not wanting to see Susannah simultaneously. He couldn't believe he was up there, looking through Lincoln's hole. He heard the shower door open inside. He shifted on the log and lost his balance. He fell to the grass and the log toppled and rolled against his right leg. He started to get up but couldn't. He was too dizzy. He rested his head against the frozen ground and stared up at the stars and moving tree limbs. Inside he heard shower water running and splashing against floor tiles. He buried his hands inside his coat and hugged himself. He closed his eyes and blacked out.

THE TEMPERATURE IS *warm for February and the downtown streets are full of the hustle and bustle of a rapidly growing city. A young boy in a flimsy brown hat sells newspapers on the street corner. And a block down a man gives a hot dog to a little girl in a green dress. A horse pulls a black carriage over the cobbles of Fourth Street while the Seelbach Hotel looms in the sun-drenched distance. White clouds hover across a clear blue sky. I wait happily tapping my foot against the curb as my wife emerges from a clothing store, two pink bags in her grasp, one in each hand.*

Rose. She squints against the glare of sunlight that reflects off the storefront window and smiles as she catches my eye. I wait for her in the street—the clothing concealed in the bags a surprise for that night. I remember back to the morning and her reaction to the warm weather after she'd opened the front door to test it with an extension of her bare left leg and foot. She'd decided right then and there to wear her yellow dress with a white shawl over the shoulders. I was so glad to have her back. God had answered all of our prayers. She was healthy again, free of the tuberculosis.

Her dress moves in flowery ripples as she bounds down the sidewalk to my extended hand. A rose rests in her curled hair. A rose for a Rose, I'd told her in the morning. No tears this time as she'd kissed me, grabbed the stem and carefully tucked the rose in the hair above her right ear. I take one of her bags and we walk hand-in-hand down the sidewalk to the sound of puttering cars and horse hooves. And then all the commotion starts. People scream behind us. We turn to see what is happening.

I never saw the bullet ricochet off the lamppost, but I heard the pinging sound mixed with the screams. Rose's eyes grow wide and an audible push of air comes from her open mouth. I look down from her eyes to her chest, where a circle of red has formed. The bullet has already penetrated the cotton of her dress and burrowed its way into the flesh below her left breast. She spins into my arms and we drop down to the cobblestone street. Another gunshot sounds, echoing off the buildings. A woman screams hysterically.

I squeeze Rose tightly, hunker down over her and survey the downtown area. Dozens of men and women run frantically from a nearby bank. A man in a brown fedora and long black coat stares at us from two blocks away, much of his figure lost in the sunlight. He ducks into an alley and disappears. The mob follows.

A horse-drawn carriage comes to a skidding halt several yards away. The carriage driver's hat blows away in the wind as he runs toward us, but my outstretched hand keeps him at a distance. Fear leaves me paralyzed, my skills as a doctor weighted down by the beautiful woman in my arms, who only moments ago hurried excitedly from the clothing store with a bag in each arm, smiling with her newly bobbed hair and flapper dress. Now one of the bags rests against the curb, the handle dangling in a rivulet of rainwater and horse piss that drains down the street, draining much like the blood from Rose's chest.

Rose is pale, so frightfully pale. Tears pool in her eyes. I wipe them away with my blood-soaked fingers and bite my lip when she smiles—only Rose would smile.

"Wolfgang . . . "

"Shhhh." I touch my right index finger to her lips. "Don't speak." I straighten the rose above her ear and kiss her forehead, leaving my lips pressed against her skin until I'm certain that my senses will never forget the scent of her. I rock her in my arms as my mother had done with me as a child, smoothing my hand across her back and over her hair, before futilely attempting to plug the hole in her chest with my shaking fingers. But the blood only pumps faster, coming out in gushing waves, pulsing with the lingering beats of her heart.

A crowd has gathered, blanketing us in shadows. Rose stares up through the sunlight, her eyes focused directly on me. "Where do we go when we die?"

"To a good place," I tell her. But my voice carries with it a note of fear and doubt that I simply couldn't disguise. My tears begin to flow. The blood spreads through the cloth of her yellow dress, forming stained rose petals around the wound. I look away, trying so hard to squash the hate that is quickly overwhelming me. The hate, the anger and the confusion.

I gaze skyward as a cluster of clouds cover the sun. "Damn you!" I hiss. I couldn't help but to blame God. He'd healed her from the tuberculosis and now He's taking her away from me. I grip her hands and stroke her face as her last breath oozes from her lips. I lean down and kiss them one last time.

"Rose . . . "

Wolfgang's eyes peeled open to find a raccoon sniffing his left boot and something crawling across his forehead. He jerked his legs, disoriented. The quick movement frightened the raccoon into the surrounding woods. He wiped at his face, smacking himself as if clearing cobwebs. His ears were frozen, his nose like ice. How long had he been out? The stars were still out. An owl hooted. His head ached from the wine. He felt sick to his stomach. He took a few deep breaths to settle himself. Drool had frozen on the hair on his chin. It flaked away like crumbs when he wiped it with his hand. He managed to prop himself up to a sitting position. His head swirled with dizziness. He couldn't believe he'd actually blacked out. He couldn't remember ever drinking so much so quickly. His legs felt stiff. He massaged them with his hands and slowly worked the kinks out. A minute later he was up on his feet and leaning against the brick wall. He was ashamed of himself for being behind the nurses' dormitory this late. He closed his coat together and hopped up and down a few times to get the blood flowing. His right foot was numb.

Rose was on his mind. He felt he needed to work on the requiem, but it was up on the fourth floor beside McVain's bed. Regardless, he would have to go and get it. Pain be damned, he marched up the hillside to the sanatorium, hoping his exposed body parts would thaw by the time he got there.

Wolfgang blew into his hands repeatedly on his way down to the solarium. His head throbbed, but at least he no longer felt like he was going to vomit. A long hot bath would be nice, he thought. But upon spotting the piano he felt the urge to play and write. He walked quietly beside McVain's bed and started to remove the requiem from the box underneath. McVain's voice startled him.

"I'm freezing." McVain's breath came out in clouds.

Wolfgang held out his hands. "My fingers are numb."

"You look like shit," said McVain, eyeing Wolfgang's clothing—his coat matted with frozen leaves and sticky burrs. "Fall asleep in the woods?"

"Yes."

McVain watched him suspiciously.

Wolfgang handed McVain an extra blanket. "How are you feeling?"

"I think that bastard Barker stitched me up with barbed wire."

"I stitched you."

"Well I feel like I'm dying."

Wolfgang knew he was serious, which left him only humor as an answer. "Not until the concert."

"My curtain call, huh?"

"Or the great awakening."

"You think he'll come around on the concert?" McVain asked.

"He has to."

"I'll figure out something." McVain's two left fingers gripped the blanket Wolfgang had just given him. "How did Rose die?"

Wolfgang sat stunned for a moment. He looked away, but only momentarily. "I liked you better when you didn't speak."

McVain's head settled on his frozen pillow and waited.

Wolfgang closed his eyes to allow a surge of pain to pass through his brain and then he opened them again. "We were married for almost four years. I was set to go to the priesthood. I believed that was my calling."

"And you met her?"

Wolfgang smiled as he remembered Rose. Truth be told he was glad McVain had asked about her. He needed to talk. He never talked about her, which was why he still saw her in so many dreams. Instead he bottled his emotions until they began to make his decisions for him. "On the steps of the Cathedral. She had beautiful eyes and dark hair."

"You were a sheltered mama's boy," said McVain.

"I was a nervous kid, especially around girls," Wolfgang said. "That was partly my reason to enter the priesthood, so I wouldn't have to worry about meeting them." He folded his hands and leaned closer to the bed. "I waited for dozens of people to enter the church just so I could hold the door for her. An innocent gesture, right?"

"Sounds like a man who knows what he wants."

"She was a weekly churchgoer. But I soon learned her other side as well."

"Was she trouble?"

"No . . . she was stylish and brash and unpredictable. Just what

I needed. She was a walking example of what I'd never had in my life."

"A flapper, huh?"

"I was drawn to her like a magnet," Wolfgang said. "Short skirts, makeup, everything. I began to live the moment I saw her. And I trusted her. I knew my parents wouldn't have approved, but that was part of the allure."

"She saw a naïve, shy stick-in-the-mud looking for a way out."

Wolfgang laughed, beginning to warm. But the laughter hurt his head. He rubbed his eyes and blinked the pain away.

"Are you drunk, Father?"

"Possibly," Wolfgang said. "The ladies of the church used to question my decision to join the priesthood. You're too handsome . . ."

"Please."

"You should get married, they'd say. No matter how badly I wanted to get close to a woman, in the end I'd always turn tail and run."

McVain shifted his weight beneath the covers. "But not with Rose?"

"She made me feel safe. Normal—no, alive. I knew the moment I saw her that the priesthood wasn't for me."

"And now it is?"

"Things have changed."

"Have they?"

Wolfgang didn't answer him, although his questions had begun to unravel answers thought long buried. He fidgeted with the zipper on his coat and spotted the rose and vase atop the piano. "We had a rose garden. I would pick one for her every day. A rose for a Rose, I'd say." He took a deep breath. "One morning during our third year of marriage I approached her in the kitchen with a rose. A rose for a Rose. She turned toward me with tears in her eyes. I hated to see her cry. She took the rose from me as always, and then she kissed me on the cheek. Not on the lips, you see."

"What did she say?"

"Wolfgang, I think I have TB." Tears welled in his eyes from the memory. "My heart sank."

"That's when you moved here?"

Wolfgang nodded. "I became a doctor here. She was a patient here just before this building was built. The sanatorium was much smaller then." He pulled McVain's blanket back up where it had fallen from his arm. "I took care of her every day. Rose was strong. Our love was strong. She was the only person in the world that understood me. She just couldn't die."

"But TB took her anyway."

"No." Wolfgang shook his head slowly, his drunken smile returning. His moist eyes blinked out a sole tear that he quickly cleared with his hand. "She was one of the few whom our rest and fresh air cured."

McVain furrowed his brow. "I don't get it."

"You said the other day . . . you asked how God could give something such as your piano talent and then take it away?" Wolfgang wiped his mouth and sat straight. "She left this place free of the disease eleven months after we'd arrived. She'd lost a lot of weight . . . but she was in the clear. A week later we were shopping downtown. It was Valentine's Day. She wore a rose in her hair. A rose I'd given her."

McVain's face became tense as he listened.

Wolfgang went on. "There was a bank robbery. A shootout with a cop inside. A stray bullet from the robber's gun ricocheted off a lamppost and struck Rose in the heart."

McVain looked shocked and stayed silent for a while. "Oh, God. I'm sorry. I'm . . . that's horrible."

"I held her in my arms until she died."

McVain wiped his unshaven jaw. "This concert . . . on Valentine's Day . . ."

Wolfgang nodded. "It was for her."

23

God continued to deliver. A new patient, a fifty-year-old man named Cecil, arrived three days after Big 15's death. He'd played the clarinet for forty years and agreed to join the ensemble if and when Doctor Barker reinstated the concert and allowed the rehearsals to go on. Two days later a new nurse arrived at Waverly. Beverly was a twenty-five-year-old brunette with a deep southern drawl and a budding violin hobby, and was spotted taking tips from Josef after hours on her first night on the job. Four new patients volunteered for the chorus, three men and a woman—not professionals but willing and eager to sing—and their ranges included two tenors, one contralto and one soprano.

Wolfgang stopped Doctor Barker in the hall one afternoon. "God is sending us musicians to replace the dead. I truly believe we all have a purpose here." To which Doctor Barker moved on without comment. Wolfgang also believed there would be a price to pay later for God's dealings. For him there were always repercussions.

The new arrivals fueled Wolfgang's spirit and advanced his cause of music therapy. He continued to work with the choir members individually and in small groups, by their bedsides, as often as he could. He encouraged them to not give up hope, leaving the door open for Barker to have a change of heart. Valentine's Day was rapidly approaching and Wolfgang, for many reasons, couldn't get the date from his head. Despite the spotty security in the woods, or maybe because of it, Wolfgang continued to walk Susannah home every night, but instead of going home he returned to the piano and the fourth floor solarium to work on the requiem. It was progressing quite well. He was three-fourths of the way through and moving quickly, even more so now that rehearsal had been cancelled. But underfoot he was beginning to feel the quagmire of doubts and uncertainties that had bogged him down before McVain's arrival. He was still in need of the perfect ending.

AT NIGHT HERMAN'S voice carried to the point where, Wolfgang assumed, it reached the ears of those outside the hillside. Rumors had started that Waverly was turning into a lunatic asylum. Because of such rumors and the fact that they'd learned through experience that Herman would not stop his ranting from Room 502 until checked upon, Wolfgang wasted no time in retrieving Doctor Barker when Herman called out for him. He'd started at sundown, shouting Doctor Barker's name from the rooftop, as loud as his tubercular lungs would allow. Wolfgang endured the craziness for no more than five minutes before slamming his pen down on his requiem, standing from the piano—his creative spark shot for the moment—and marching down to his boss' office, where he found Doctor Barker at his desk with his fingers massaging his temples.

"What does that lunatic want?" Doctor Barker asked Wolfgang.

"I don't know." Wolfgang leaned against the doorway. "What I do know is he won't stop until you pay him a visit."

Doctor Barker slammed *his* pen down and stood so fast from his desk that his chair toppled over.

When they reached the nurses' station on the rooftop they found Susannah standing at the door to Room 502. Apparently Herman wouldn't even allow her inside. She knocked on the door patiently. Herman probably couldn't hear her over his continuous chanting,

"Doctor Barker . . . Doctor Barker . . . Doctor Barker . . ." Herman's voice seemed magnified because of their close proximity.

Wolfgang placed his hands over his ears and stood next to Susannah, who had backed away from the door upon their arrival. Doctor Barker stormed over to Room 502 without shooting Susannah a glance. Wolfgang could feel the tension between the two and told himself to be careful not to say anything that would incriminate him or lead them to ask questions about his spying on their dispute the other night.

Doctor Barker hammered on the door to Room 502. "Herman . . . open up, it's me. Stop screaming . . . HERMAN!"

Maverly Simms showed herself in the doorway to her darkened room. "Maverly at Waverly . . . Maverly at Waverly . . ."

Doctor Barker turned toward Wolfgang and Susannah and hissed. "Shut her up."

Maverly shut up before Wolfgang had taken his second step toward her room. They could all see the anger in Doctor Barker's eyes and Maverly started to whimper like a pained mutt. Doctor Barker pounded on Herman's door again and finally Herman stopped screaming. The door opened a crack and Herman's face was visible, his wandering eyes looking Doctor Barker up and down.

"What is it, Herman?" asked Doctor Barker.

The door opened wide and Herman took up most of the space in the doorway. "You stopped the concert."

Doctor Barker closed his eyes and sighed, as if trying with every fiber of his being not to strangle Herman for bringing it up and most assuredly for calling him up to the rooftop for it.

Herman stepped closer. "You stopped my concert." He raised his fork in his right hand. Wolfgang saw the overhead light glisten off the polished tines but couldn't get out his warning in time. He didn't know exactly what Herman was doing until the deed had been done. Herman brought the fork down with amazing force, arching it down toward Doctor Barker's left shoulder. The tines of the fork stuck in the meat of Doctor Barker's shoulder.

Susannah screamed and ran toward Herman. Before Herman could pull the fork back out and attempt a second plunge, Doctor Barker rocked back in shock, moaning in disbelief, staring at the fork protruding and wiggling from his shoulder and lab coat.

"Doctor Barker!" Wolfgang ran to his teetering boss and caught him before he hit the floor unabated. He lowered him to the ground and watched the blood drain from his face and begin to leak from the puncture wound.

"Herman . . . what have you done?" Susannah ran for Room 502 and slammed the door on Herman's face. She stood with her back to the door, panting, her chest heaving. She placed her right hand to her chest and stared down to the floor where Doctor Barker rested in Wolfgang's lap, grimacing. Doctor Barker bit his lip and pulled the fork out himself. He looked to Susannah and then to Wolfgang. He rolled from Wolfgang's arms and stood, wobbling, with his right hand pressed to his shoulder. Bright red blood stained his white coat and fingers. "Get away from me . . . both of you." He staggered, backed his way out of the station with crazed, paranoid eyes and took off running across the rooftop as the wind battered the door against the side of the building.

Wolfgang and Susannah stared at each other, speechless.

WOLFGANG AND SUSANNAH left work at the same time that night and stopped in the middle of the Grand Lobby when they heard footsteps approaching quickly behind them. Doctor Barker was leaving for the night as well. He walked with a brisk pace, his footfalls heavy and echoing off the tall ceiling, his gait long and awkwardly rushed, trying to pass them without a word, as if the faster he passed them the less likely they'd be to ask him about his shoulder. Wolfgang was also aware that Doctor Barker could have waited thirty seconds and they would have been out the door. The coast would have been clear for him to depart without notice. But he assumed Barker wanted to be seen. He wanted his heavy footfalls heard. He wanted them to see the fury in his stilted, clumsy gait. He was throwing a walking tantrum, Wolfgang thought, and nearly verbalized to Susannah when the sanatorium's front doors opened and a cluster of leaves flew inside and across the floor, skittering across like mice in an attic.

It seemed the pain was just beginning for Doctor Barker, who was the first to stop upon sight of the after-hours visitor. Doctor Barker stood stiff with his briefcase at his right side and his left shoulder bandaged. His posture softened when Anne, his wife of twenty-five years, walked into the lobby with a gray satchel in each hand. She stood in her black shoes and ivory coat, staring at her husband. Her hair was brown but beginning to gray beneath a rounded ivory hat. Wolfgang had always thought her smile was pretty, her lips small but distinct, but tonight she didn't smile. Her green eyes were tired and focused on her husband, the surprise on her aged face as apparent as the shock that must have masked Doctor Barker's had Wolfgang been able to get a look at it. Susannah and Wolfgang stood ten paces behind their boss, the three of them facing Anne Barker, waiting for someone to break the silence. Anne lowered the satchel in her left hand to the floor and coughed into her fist.

Doctor Barker's head lowered. The newest patient had arrived at Waverly.

CHARLES PIKE STANDS in the center of a floorless room, hovering, rapidly striking the strings of his violin, not with a bow but a bottle of wine as the walls around him are aglow with thundering flames. Pieces of glass fly with every stroke and wine pours over his hands . . . yet he plays on despite Big 15's body dropping from the ceiling and dangling from a noose made of diamonds and rubies, and Doctor Barker stands facing the corner and stabbing the wall with a fork while Susannah and Rose and Jesus Christ attempt to strangle each other on the far side of the room, or maybe they're dancing to the violent and macabre motions of Charles Pike's violin playing as McVain sits across the room on a piano bench jamming the nubs of his three missing fingers into his mouth and saying, do you really want to know what happened to 'em, do you really wanna know when Doris walks in with a pillow clutched in both hands and she's coming closer and closer and closer and the sky is turning black around the edges . . .

"Rose . . ." Wolfgang awoke sweating and breathing heavily in the middle of the night. The smothering pillow had just blanketed him in darkness and his mother's laughter still whipped through his mind.

He asked me to kill him, Wolfgang . . .

He rested his head back inside the dent of his warm pillow and shook the image of Rose and Susannah from his mind. Had they been strangling each other? And Jesus? He wondered for the millionth time if Rose was listening. Could she hear his thoughts? Could God?

Nothing. Always nothing.

Maybe that's where we go when we die, thought Wolfgang. Everyone fades into the same nothingness as before conception, floating around in a dark abyss with no identity or mind, waiting for someone to open a door and create. He knew that Rose wouldn't deceive him on purpose. Perhaps she couldn't make contact. He constantly asked her questions but she never answered back. Maybe God was answering him, not with words but with actions of others, arrivals of musicians, the untimely coincidence of stray bullets. He answers with riddles and puzzles that seemingly have no answers. Maybe McVain was right all along. Heaven was invented to keep people honest, to keep the world from defeating itself.

He thought of Susannah on his couch, snoring, or holding her hand, feeling the wet kiss of her lips on his cheek. One thing about Susannah . . . Wolfgang knew she was real. He could touch her. He could speak to her. And she always answered back.

THE FOLLOWING DAY Wolfgang walked down the third floor solarium and spotted Anne Barker in bed with her covers up to her shoulders and her head propped on two pillows. Beside the bed sat Doctor Barker, and upon first glance Wolfgang thought they were in the middle of a conversation, but the closer he got to her bed the more he realized what was going on. Doctor Barker sat in contemplation, hands formed in a triangle and propped under his chin, watching his wife sleep. Wolfgang asked him if they needed anything and Doctor Barker shook his head no. Wolfgang placed his hand on Doctor Barker's shoulder. "Rose fought the disease and won, sir."

Doctor Barker nodded. Wolfgang moved on.

THE NEXT DAY Doctor Barker surprised Wolfgang with an appearance in the chapel near the end of mass, where seven choir members had volunteered to sing. Wolfgang's slight choir viewed him cautiously from afar, never slowing their song as he leaned against the column in the back of the chapel and waited for Mass to finish. After everyone cleared out, he accosted Wolfgang in the center aisle. "Are you behind this?"

"Behind what?" Wolfgang asked.

"The choir members. And others. A hundred others. They're refusing to take any medication. They're refusing to eat. They're refusing treatment unless—"

"I knew nothing about this," said Wolfgang.

Doctor Barker's mouth closed. He held up his index finger. "Have your damn concert. But only by my rules. We're being reckless as it is. Rehearsals are limited to thirty minutes. I've seen your program . . . the concert itself must be shortened." He stopped before the last row of chairs. "And any work with Rufus will be done down the hillside."

"Is that all?"

"And no more secret practices after I leave at night." He smirked. "Did you think I couldn't hear you?"

"What if I need to work at the piano at night?"

"I have no problem with that." He pointed to his ear. "But give me some credit. I can tell the difference between you and McVain on the piano."

"How?"

"I know the difference between a genius and a dabbler."

WOLFGANG COULDN'T FLEX his fingers enough. No matter how much he moved them and blew his warm sticky breath into them they still remained numb. Tiny white cracks in the skin scarred his knuckles and the webbing between his fingers. He stared at the rose atop the piano. The stem shifted ever so slightly in the vase as a dark red petal dropped to the piano top. The rose needed to be changed. The cold wind killed them much too quickly. The moon was nearly full and jaundiced, hovering in the starlit sky like a medallion. McVain coughed behind him on the bed. Wolfgang turned around on the piano bench and faced McVain. "How are you feeling?"

McVain cleared his throat. "Hollow."

"It must be torture to watch us practice and be bedridden."

"What's torture is listening to you play," he said, smiling but sincere. He winked. "Concert back on? Told you I'd think of something."

"Blackmail? Cute. He would have reinstated the concert anyway."

McVain's eyes found Wolfgang's wedding band on his right hand. "Ever think of marrying again?"

"I'm a priest, in case you haven't noticed." Wolfgang folded his arms, hiding his right hand. "Anyway, before Rose died, I told her I'd see her in Heaven."

McVain chuckled. "One day, Father, maybe you will, but not now." His tone was condescending. Wolfgang started to get up but McVain's voice stopped him. "Are you afraid that if you married again you'd have two wives in Heaven?" Wolfgang tried to laugh but it came out as a guilty gasp. "That's it, isn't it?" McVain said. "I know how you think. Wow, two wives in Heaven. Eternal bliss or eternal torture?" McVain chuckled. "Good thing the priesthood makes it easier for you."

"Tell me about your wife, McVain."

"I'm divorced." Wolfgang waited while McVain picked at a scab on the top of his right hand, his left pinkie prodding like an alien tentacle. "We were happy before the war. I came back a different man."

"How long has it been since you've spoken with her."

"Not as long as you went without seeing your mother," McVain said. "Six years if you need to know." He looked away from his scab, winced as he shifted more to his left side and switched the line of questioning. "Are your answers any clearer now that the pope tells you how to dress?" He folded his hands on his chest. "This is why it's easier not to believe in God."

"What happened during the war?" Wolfgang asked.

McVain sniffled, wiped his runny nose. "I wasn't a violent man. I'd never fired a gun in my life. How was I supposed to kill? But I did. I was scared to death."

Wolfgang leaned forward, begging for more. "I can't imagine the horror. Tell me about it, McVain."

"Don't act like my psychologist, Father."

"Go on . . ."

"Trench warfare." McVain's eyes looked at the piano, but his real vision was probably somewhere much darker. "Mud and rain. Bombs everywhere. Mustard gas. I started smoking to calm my nerves. Couldn't sleep."

"Do the dreams still haunt you?"

McVain looked at Wolfgang sharply, as if he'd touched a nerve. "I was an animal. I chased a Kraut out of a trench one time. He got stuck in the barbed wire without a gun. I couldn't understand what he was yelling at me, but with his tone I could tell he was pleading for his life. I shot him. I shot him in the face. Then I shot him in the heart. I wanted to believe I'd shot him so he didn't suffer in the wire, but I'm not so sure. By that time I'd become so numb I could hardly control why or when I fired." He wiped his eyes. "Like I was standing there outside myself, watching from a different person . . . a different place."

"I've heard similar stories from other soldiers." Wolfgang touched McVain's covered foot, which was buried under layers of blankets. "Like they lost control. You're not alone."

McVain coughed heavily, leaned to his side and let a bloody chunk of sputum fall from his lips and into a bucket. He straightened himself on the bed and watched Wolfgang again. "I believed in God before the war."

Wolfgang looked to the three missing fingers and couldn't help seeing McVain ramming the nubs into his mouth during the nightmare he'd had. "Tell me what happened."

McVain sighed. "I'm tired. Another night."

Wolfgang touched the mound of his concealed foot again and stood.

"You said you believe in fate, Wolfgang?" McVain stared blankly up toward the ceiling. "A man makes a choice to avoid danger, only to walk right into it. Choice A or B. I made a choice at Chateau-

Thierry. My decision determined my fate." He wiggled the nubs on his mangled hand. "I chose B."

"Everything happens for a reason, McVain. Perhaps A would have killed you."

"Might have been better." He found Wolfgang's gaze. "For all of us."

24

A SNOWSTORM BLEW in unexpectedly from the southeast, dumping seven inches of pristine white fluff atop the hillside overnight. The morning walk up the hillside was a painting of beauty. The air seemed fresher than normal, untainted by the buried stench of wet leaves. A trio of deer watched from thirty yards away, half of their skinny legs hidden under the accumulation. Susannah stepped on a patch of snow-covered bramble and her foot sunk to the knee. Instead of helping her up, Wolfgang made a tightly packed snowball and hurled it toward Susannah, hitting her on the rump. She freed herself and chased Wolfgang up the slippery hillside. The noise sent the deer scattering through the dips and hollows of the woods. The topography of the hill had changed. Snowdrifts that virtually buried some of the tree trunks left the bases of others seemingly untouched. Squirrels danced overtop the snow, sprinting to avoid sinking. The escaped pig pushed through the snow, nose digging in like a shovel and snorting and sniffing for buried acorns. By the time they'd reached the sanatorium Susannah had managed to make contact with one of her several throws, hitting Wolfgang with an explosion of white fluff right in the center of his back. They walked into work, laughing and slightly soaked, but their mood soon changed. Tuberculosis didn't take snow days off.

By noon Lincoln had begun to use the freezer room as temporary storage for the dead, placing three bodies respectfully, side-by-side, next to the canned goods. By mid-afternoon Wolfgang's pants were almost dry, but his legs were numb from the wind that wreaked havoc on the solarium screens, for the snow hadn't stopped the nurses from keeping the patients out on the solarium porches. They'd slept outside all night, most of them watching the snowfall and some cheering. But now miniature drifts frosted the foots of patients' beds, their blankets and some of the bedside tables. Patients too close to the end of the solarium's screen windows had been rolled closer to the middle to avoid direct contact with the snow. Someone had thrown a blue tarp over McVain's piano. When Wolfgang had asked who'd covered it McVain shrugged, claiming he'd first seen it when he'd opened his eyes in the morning.

Ten patients died overnight, three from exposure and the rest because it was simply their time to go. Ten new patients arrived from the waiting list to the picture-book scene of snow and death. They were welcomed as guests and would be treated as such.

Wolfgang hoped they liked music. He wheeled one of them up to the third floor, a young woman with yellow hair, a slender face and fear in her eyes. She shivered terribly—a mixture of cold and nerves. "Father, I'm freezing."

Wolfgang touched her forehead. She was burning with fever. "We'll take care of you." She leaned back. Her shivering calmed somewhat. His collar gave her solace. Her eyes followed a patient's bed as Wolfgang rolled her along—the bed was half-covered with a layer of snow. It wasn't torture, Wolfgang wanted to tell her, although at times it felt like it, especially during some of the experiments and surgeries. But they were performed in search of answers. "Tons of air circulates through the hospital to carry away the germs when the patients sneeze and exhale," Wolfgang told her. "The fresh air replenishes the bad with good."

"More blankets," a patient cried out.

Wolfgang had heard that electric blankets were being developed for places like Waverly. If only they had them now. The day seemed incredibly long.

WOLFGANG SAT BESIDE Anne Barker's bed and played a song on his piccolo for her. She'd requested his music and he'd reluctantly obliged. But he'd played nervously, stopping after several miscues before continuing, afraid at any moment that Doctor Barker would show up and hound him for disturbing his wife. He lowered the piccolo and Anne thanked him with her magnetic smile. Doctor Barker did see Wolfgang sitting there, which, Wolfgang had known, was inevitable because he'd been checking on her at least two times every hour since she'd been admitted to the sanatorium. Upon sight of his boss, Wolfgang stood from Anne's bedside as if to leave.

"It isn't the music that he dislikes, Wolfgang." Anne's smile had faded to an emotionless shell. "Give him time."

"I'll play for you any time, Mrs. Barker."

"He isn't a bad man," she said. "He's just confused."

"Aren't we all." Wolfgang nodded and left her alone.

WOLFGANG OPENED THE door to the small chapel freezer and removed a bag of frozen communion bread, hoping that it would not be as hard as Jesse's last batch, which had caused most of the crowd to chew for several minutes after they'd returned to their seats. He carried it to the altar to thaw and spotted Susannah and Abel entering the chapel. Abel appeared a little distraught, his face blotchy. Wolfgang knelt down and touched Abel's skinny shoulders, showing him even more love since the child's ordeal the night of Big 15's murder. "You've been crying."

Abel stood stiff with his hands to his sides. Susannah squatted beside Abel and put her right arm around his back. "He didn't sleep all night."

"I have a confession, Father Pike," Abel said. "I'm a liar."

Wolfgang gave him a warm smile. "How so?"

"I did see somebody the other night." Abel looked up toward Susannah, who kissed his forehead and nodded encouragement. "The night we found Big 15 in the tree."

"Who did you see, Abel?"

He wiped his nose with a fist. "Two men. Dressed in white. With hoods. I ran into one of them when I was going through the woods."

"Then what happened?" asked Susannah.

"One of 'em knocked me down in the mud. Said he'd kill me if I told anybody I saw 'em."

"You poor child." Wolfgang sighed heavily. "I can see why you can't sleep. Did you recognize either of them?"

"No, but I seen 'em coming out of the maintenance shed."

"The shed?"

He nodded. "One of 'em was watching me last night."

"Watching you?"

"From the woods." Abel became more courageous with each word spoken. "I was in bed on my porch. He watched from the woods, staring at me with his white hood on. Like a ghost. He put his finger to his face like this." Abel put his right index finger to his lips as if shushing someone.

Susannah squeezed Abel's shoulders. "They're trying to scare him, Wolf."

"You're sure it wasn't just the snow and shadows?"

Abel shook his head adamantly. "No, he was there to remind me . . . not to tell."

Wolfgang pulled Abel forward and embraced him.

That night Doctor Barker demanded that the police bring in more security to stand guard at the children's pavilion. Susannah wanted Abel to stay with her but he'd insisted on sleeping with the other children. He was their leader of sorts. He claimed it was his job to keep *them* calm. Two white robes with hoods had been found behind an old tractor in the back of the maintenance shed, concealed under a wooden crate that still carried the smell of ether. The maintenance staff had been questioned thoroughly, but none of the three men seemed strong enough to pull Big 15 up into a tree, and their answers had all checked out. They'd been too busy fighting the fire at the colored hospital to hunt down Big 15 in the woods and hang him.

After Wolfgang and Susannah dropped Abel off and met with the three new police officers, Susannah felt more comforted. The men were dressed warmly for the entire night shift and they seemed to take their jobs seriously. They all had children at home. Wolfgang believed Abel and the children would be safe.

Susannah followed Wolfgang home and they lit a fire. They shared a bottle of wine and Wolfgang told her about his talk with his mother, about how she'd euthanized his father and how it hadn't been murder at all. He told her about his parents being thieves, his mother remarrying and moving to start a new Protestant church in Minnesota. In the silence that ensued, Susannah stood from the couch and lifted one of the violins on the floor— the wine gripping her slight figure with ease. She laughed as she tried to play and then nearly fell over. Wolfgang caught her and led her back to the couch, where the heat of the fire had warmed the cushions. He eased her down so that her head rested against the arm of the couch. She giggled, gripped Wolfgang's shirt and pulled him close, so close he could smell the sweet wine on her breath. "I feel safe right now," she whispered. He knew he should pull away but he didn't. He found room on the cushion beside her, enough to sit awkwardly, half on and half off the couch, while she continued to grip his shirt and gaze into his eyes.

"Oh, Wolf . . ."

He so badly wanted her to finish the sentence. It was snowing outside again. The doors were locked. The fire snapped beside them. Shadows caressed the angles of her cheekbones, the curve of her lips, the rounded turn of her chin . . . and no one was watching. Wolfgang bent down, closed his eyes and softly pressed his lips against her mouth. He felt as if a bolt of electricity had struck him. Her mouth eased open.

She ran her fingers across the back of his head and through his wavy hair. And then suddenly she pushed him away. Wolfgang dropped to his knees beside the couch, staring at her, mortified. How could he have done it? A priest? A servant of the Lord? He'd sworn an oath of celibacy. Why was she looking at him like that? With wet eyes full of sorrow and remorse? Why?

"I'm sorry," he whispered.

She kept her head still on the arm of the couch, her eyes on his. "Don't be. I can't . . . I just can't. I'm sorry." She turned away and closed her eyes.

Wolfgang's insecurities came flooding back with a vengeance. Had he been reading her wrong? Did she have feelings for Doctor Barker? Wolfgang was being totally unfair to her. If she did have feelings for him, what he'd done had been a tease, a selfish tease. He stood up, hobbled because his right food had gone numb, and backed away. He blew out all the candles. He couldn't get the cottage dark enough, not with the fire licking the stones of the fireplace. He wanted to crawl in a deep, dark hole and never come out. He shuffled to the bed and rested his head on the pillow, full of regret as he eyed the crucifix on the wall. Would she be gone in the morning? Had he wrecked their friendship by kissing her? That was his worst fear. He'd acted on impulse and he'd been helpless to stop it. He hated himself.

Eventually he drifted off to sleep, but not until he heard her snoring.

WOLFGANG NEVER REACHED a deep sleep, and the few questionable hours he did manage to get were interrupted by the sound of footsteps. Susannah remained asleep on the couch. The fire had gone out, leaving only the smell of burned wood to fester inside the stone cave. The porch steps creaked under the weight of an intruder. The clock on the wall read four in the morning. A loud thump sounded against the door. Wolfgang shot up and his first instinct was to protect Susannah. She shifted on the couch but her eyes remained closed. Wolfgang moved around the foot of his bed, grabbed the iron poker from beside the fireplace and walked quietly past Susannah and toward the front door. The knob rattled. Something slid against it on the outside, and then another snow-muffled thump followed. Someone spoke to Wolfgang from outside, his voice dampened by the wind and flakes of snowing beating against the window.

"Father . . . " It was more of a groan than a threat.

Wolfgang kept the poker in his hand but felt better about opening the door. A male patient knelt on the porch, shivering. Blood dripped down his chin. Wolfgang recognized the thin young man from the east wing of the fourth floor, Ray Lot, and he couldn't have been far from death. What was he doing here? How did he know where to find me, Wolfgang wondered?

"Father . . . I have a confession."

Wolfgang knelt before Ray. Snowflakes stuck to his blood-crusted lips. His eyelids fluttered like butterfly wings. He coughed blood onto Wolfgang's hands and Wolfgang didn't even hesitate to wipe them off before putting his hands on the man's shoulders. "What is it, my son?"

Tears welled in his darkened eyes. Wolfgang glanced over his shoulder; Susannah still slept. He returned his attention on Ray. "What have you done?"

"I was with him . . . when he tossed the brick." Ray unfolded his legs and rested back on the porch, his head in a pile of hardened snow. He sneezed and left his yellow snot to freeze on his crusted upper lip. "I helped attack you in the woods."

Ray's hands shook violently. Wolfgang grabbed them and it seemed to calm him somewhat. "Go on," said Wolfgang, studying the young man before him, a young man who had attended many of his Catholic Masses over the duration of his stay at Waverly.

Tears dripped from Ray's eyes, the wetness forming smooth lines down the roughness of his pale, dirty cheeks. "I didn't want to hang that nigger. I only wanted to . . . to . . . to scare him. I promise." His teeth chattered. "It was always *his* idea. I don't want to go to Hell."

"Who?" Wolfgang leaned over Ray's body, reliving the moment when he'd first seen Big 15's body hanging from the thick branch of the oak tree. "Tell me, Ray. Who?"

"We hid our Klan robes in the shed." His eyes widened. "He scared that boy last night. I didn't want to go. He won't hurt that kid, Father."

"Who did this?"

"This is a confession, Father." Ray gulped and breathed heavily. Loose fluid gargled in his weak lungs. "Just between you and me, right?" Wolfgang nodded. "Promise me you won't go after him, Father." Ray coughed up blood and nearly choked on it. "Promise me you'll just let him die like me."

Wolfgang gritted his teeth and lifted Ray's head from the porch. "I promise. Tell me and the good Lord shall judge you."

"Will I go to Heaven? I . . . have to know. I ain't a Catholic, Father . . . but you're all . . . I got now."

"If it's God's will."

Ray stared for a second. "It was Jesse."

The air deflated from Wolfgang's lungs, a huge ball of it resting in his throat and primed to come out as rage. Jesse was Ray's roommate. Wolfgang had taken Jesse under his wings. The young man had claimed to be interested in the priesthood but it had all been a cover for his evil.

"Jesse killed that nigger," Ray said. "We got the ether from the hospital . . . to knock him out. The rope from the shed. It was Jesse's idea . . . "

Wolfgang fought back the urge to strike the dying young man on his porch. "Thank you, son," he said softly.

"Our secret." Ray closed his eyes. "Our secret, Father." His words lowered to a delirious whisper. "Our secret. You . . . promised . . . "

Wolfgang waited until Ray was silent before checking his pulse. Finding none, Wolfgang stood, backed away and retreated inside to wash the infected blood from his hands.

25

THE NEXT MORNING the sun came out and the snow began to melt. The ice thawed quickly and dripped from the solariums. Water sluiced through the gutters, clanked through the down-spouts and poured out to portions of the grass that had started to turn back to mud. Wolfgang stood at the foot of Jesse's bed on the fourth floor solarium and watched the doughy farm boy stare at Ray's vacant bed. "He died on my doorstep," Wolfgang told him.

Jesse's eyebrows furrowed but gave no hint of nerves. "He was a good kid, Father. I prayed for him last night."

Wolfgang clenched his teeth. If a dying man couldn't trust the words of a priest, then whom could he trust? Big 15's killer rested only a few feet away. He'd disguised himself as a devoted Catholic so Wolfgang wouldn't suspect him, despite his hulking size. He's mocking me, thought Wolfgang. Inwardly he laughs at me. What did he owe this man, this coward? What did Wolfgang owe the man who had died last night on his porch? A man who, by the time they'd carted him back up the hill in the morning, had been nearly frozen. A man who had caused him harm. A man who had allowed fear to fester and boil on the hillside when there should have been nothing but peace, tranquility and resting. What did he owe this man? But he'd given him his word in confession.

Wolfgang cleared a divot of snow from the footboard of Jesse's bed with his fingers and flicked it to the floor. Wolfgang stood only a few feet from the man who'd killed a dear friend. How badly he wanted him gone from the sanatorium. An eye for an eye—was that wrong? Wolfgang hoped Jesse's tuberculosis spread painfully and quickly. Unfortunately, Jesse appeared stronger than the day he'd arrived. The fresh air was helping the criminal . . . the racist. Wolfgang walked away wondering if there really was a Hell.

WOLFGANG CONTINUED TO monitor Jesse daily, both inside the chapel and out in the sanatorium, and he had yet to see him leave the building. To take his mind from it all he turned his focus back to the music. The snow had melted and the temperature had settled on a pleasant forty-five degrees under clear skies. Birds chirped from the woods. The grass, having shed the weight of precipitation, had turned greener and more upright. Wolfgang was determined to take advantage of the weather and catch up on the time they'd missed. All the musicians had bonded, not only the original trio, but also Beverly on the violin and Cecil on the clarinet. Their sense of ensemble was nearly perfect. The quality of the choir had increased tenfold just by the addition of Herman's booming voice, which gave the rest the confidence to sing even louder. Herman was allowed out of his room for the first time in several days and he stood in his typical spot away from the rest of the choir, without the security of his fork.

"Herman, why do you insist on standing away from the group?" Wolfgang asked him before rehearsal had started.

"I don't want to catch their TB," Herman said.

Wolfgang stared up at him, wondering if he'd crack a smile but he never did. Herman was seriously afraid of catching a disease that he already had.

Anne Barker arrived ten minutes into rehearsal after hearing them play and sing from her floor directly below.

"Room for another?" Anne asked.

"Of course." Wolfgang walked her over toward the women's section and she stood beside Susannah. Anne Barker apparently knew her music. Her voice was soft and overshadowed by the rest of the women but she knew most of the pieces. Her smile was a pleasant addition to the chorus, and her arrival at Waverly had made her husband less belligerent. He was by her bedside more every day, and often Wolfgang had seen them laughing.

They were barely over their allotted time when the choir stopped singing and stared past Wolfgang. Doctor Barker stood behind him. Wolfgang turned, his arms still conducting a choir that had already stopped making music.

Doctor Barker spotted his wife in the crowd and then faced Wolfgang. "Shut it down for the night, Father."

"But—"

"Shut it down." His voice was somber, his eyes sad. For once Wolfgang didn't argue. Doctor Barker held out an envelope. "This came today from the archdiocese."

Wolfgang took the envelope and waited until everyone had left before opening it. The archdiocese was transferring him to a church in Lexington. He had only three more months on the hillside.

WOLFGANG'S PRESSURE TO finish the requiem was now magnified by his impending departure. He would write all night if that was what it took to finish while McVain was still alive. Every so often Wolfgang would glance over his shoulder at McVain, who appeared asleep most of the time. Occasionally his eyes would be open, watching Wolfgang or staring out toward the woods. No one slept soundly.

Wolfgang's couch had remained empty ever since the kiss, and Susannah had only spoken to him in fits and starts, the content mostly about work—nothing meaningful. He contemplated telling her about the letter but dreaded the actual conversation. He'd decided to wait to tell anyone, just in case he found a way out of it. How could Barker do this to him? A fellow doctor?

Wolfgang's hands eased from the piano keys. He started to write but McVain startled him by calling out from his bed.

"Where is she?"

Wolfgang touched the pen to the paper. "Who?"

"Who do you think? Susannah."

"She went home early. She felt tired." Wolfgang returned to his work. He began to play again, stopping every so often to jot down notes. Ten minutes later, when he looked over his shoulder, McVain sat with his knees propped up below the sheets as if hiding something in his lap. Wolfgang quietly lifted off the piano bench and hurried to McVain's bedside. McVain was slow in shoving an envelope under the sheets.

"What do you have there?"

McVain scowled. "Nothing."

"Looks like a letter."

"Speaking of letters, what did yours say?"

"*Church* business, McVain, which means it's none of yours."

McVain grunted, and for a moment Wolfgang feared he would lapse back into muteness, but then he spoke. "So what if it's a letter. Big deal."

Wolfgang sat down on the chair beside the bed. "You've been here for how many months without getting one piece of mail? Who's it from?"

McVain pulled the letter out from under the sheets. The envelope looked as if it had been through Hell getting into his hands. The penmanship on the front was curvy and elegant. "Choice A or B?"

"Excuse me?"

McVain held up his left hand, showing Wolfgang the nubs. "You wanted to know how I lost my fingers? Why I turned my back on God?"

"It has something to do with that letter?"

"Long story."

"I've got all night."

McVain shifted in the bed, looked at the letter and began. "It was May, 1918. The Germans were closing in on Paris. They broke the French line to pieces." His head settled deep into the pillow and he stared blankly up toward the ceiling. "I was in the Third American Division. We were sent to Chateau-Thierry to fight. Under French command. We were to defend the Marne."

Wolfgang nodded. "I've read about the Marne bloodbath."

"Chateau-Thierry was about thirty-five miles northeast of Paris." McVain coughed into his right fist, careful not to drop the letter. He closed his eyes in obvious discomfort and then opened them a few seconds later. "It was a nice river town. Forty-one days of continuous fighting. Most of the citizens had fled." He breathed for a moment as if to regroup his lungs. "I lost my mind after only a few days of it. I didn't want to fight anymore."

"I don't blame you."

The letter shook slightly in his grip.

"You were a musician, McVain, not a soldier."

"I never slept at night. I was afraid a Kraut would sneak up and slit my throat. I prayed to God every day . . . keep my hands safe. Keep my hands safe. Every day I was cautious when the rest of the men were brave. The Germans threatened our position. My Division was called to make a stand. On the West Bridge." He sighed and exhaled from his nostrils. Loose phlegm rattled inside his lungs. "I didn't go with them. I ran away. My friends were coming back with limbs blown off, massive head injuries, some of them dead. I ran like a coward."

"I would have done the same thing," Wolfgang said.

"Like I said, a coward."

"Touché."

"I hid in the town," McVain said. "Most of the homes were abandoned. One night I ducked into a small stone house and fell asleep in a back bedroom. I could hear the fighting in the distance. Bombs and shells. Light flashing against the walls. My fellow men. Brave men. Somehow I fell asleep—with my gun on my chest." McVain coughed again, tilted to the side and spat another bloody gob of phlegm to the bucket, missing. "I woke up in the middle of the night when the fighting died down. Sounded like distant thunder. Standing right there in the bedroom was a woman holding a candle. A French woman with short black hair, about thirty years old and sexy. She wore a dirty blue dress and no shoes. She was trembling . . . scared out of her mind."

"She never evacuated?"

"My first reaction was to point my gun at her. And when I did . . . tears rolled down her cheeks. She didn't make a sound though . . . as if she'd had practice whimpering and crying in such a way that if anyone heard her she'd be killed. I could see her pretty face in the candlelight. I lowered my gun and waved her closer. She ran to me on the bed and buried her head in my chest. I held her, rubbed her back. She was so scared. We both were." McVain stopped to prepare for a cough but none came. "Maybe she'd lost her husband. Or her parents. She fell asleep in my arms while I stroked her back."

McVain winced and held his chest. "Damn stitches." He adjusted his position and went on. "That night I cheated on my wife. Being close to that French girl was the only thing that made sense. The next morning, I found her naked under the sheets. She hurried from the room. I heard her rattling around downstairs, then she came back with a bottle of wine and a block of moldy cheese." McVain wiped his mouth and took another breath. Wolfgang could tell the talking was wearing him down but he had to hear it to the finish. "We ate like we were starved."

"Did you speak any French?"

"We communicated with our eyes. And our hands. Her body was . . ." McVain looked at Wolfgang and stopped the description.

"We hid there the entire day, making love to block out the sounds of warfare."

Wolfgang couldn't help thinking of Rose when he pictured the French woman.

McVain exhaled, his throat raspy. "The second night . . . she led me out of the house. Just grabbed my hand and pulled me across the street into a small stone church. Heavy wood doors. It smelled like incense and candles. Our whispers echoed, and we laughed. Still couldn't speak to each other." McVain winced, bit his lip.

"You okay?"

McVain nodded. "She took me to the back of the church. Lit a candle. There in the shadows was a piano. She sat on the bench and played for me."

"Unbelievable," said Wolfgang.

"She wasn't very good, but I could tell it helped her fight her fears. I never knew why she stayed in town. I knew nothing about her, yet I knew enough. I knew every inch of her body. She had a small birthmark under her left breast that looked like an apple . . ." McVain glanced at Wolfgang. "I'm sorry."

"Go on."

"She made room for me on the bench. I thought God had answered my prayers." McVain sniffled and wiped his nose. "I played that piano like I'd never played before, my eyes lit with passion. She was shocked. Completely shocked. She looked at me like I was some God. She looked up to the ceiling and motioned the sign of the cross." McVain stopped for a moment and smiled. "We took breaks only to make love on the floor of the church as mice watched us from the corners. That dusty old church. We drank more wine. I played all night for her." He closed his eyes again, as if resting.

"McVain . . ."

McVain's eyes slowly opened.

"Do you need to stop?" Wolfgang asked. "We can finish tomorrow."

McVain shook his head. "The next morning the sun came in through a broken stained-glass window. I woke up on the floor. She was at the piano, half-dressed, dabbling. I didn't hear any bombs in the distance. Right away I sensed trouble. I heard footsteps outside the church and then the doors creaked open. An American soldier came in. Crazy son of a bitch named Cotton Meeks. From Mississippi. He walked up the center aisle, staring at her. I watched from the floor, still groggy and hung over."

"He didn't see you?"

"Not yet." McVain wiped his mouth and licked his chapped lips. The movement of his tongue made a dry clicking sound. "My Division. They'd been successful in holding the bridge . . . without me. Meeks returned to check out the town. Must have heard the piano. It was stupid, I know. Meeks said in his southern drawl, 'So, what do we have here? Some French cunny?' She jumped off the piano and ran to me on the floor. I had no clue where my gun was. I didn't even have my pants on. Just my undershorts. Meeks pointed his machine gun right at me. 'Well, if it ain't the piano man. Missed ya at the bridge, traitor.'"

McVain's hands shook. He gripped the letter to help calm them. "Meeks was crazy enough to kill me. I'd gone AWOL. I raised my hands. Tried to talk him down. He gave me a smile. Pointed his gun at my left hand. Pulled the fucking trigger."

"Jesus."

"Thought I'd lost my hand. It exploded in a cloud of mist and bone. I landed back on the floor. Against the wall. Blood everywhere. The girl was hiding in the corner of the church, screaming. Meeks was laughing. He knelt down beside me." McVain shook his head. "Meeks always made fun of me. I liked music better than bullets."

"What did he say?"

"He had the smell of tobacco and alcohol on his breath. 'Piano man,' he said. 'Losing that many fingers'll get you sent back home.

I think you owe me some thanks.' Then he looked at the girl. I threw myself at him. Meeks grabbed me by the throat. I spat in his face. He smacked my head with the butt of his gun. Knocked me out."

McVain wiped his eyes, massaging them with the two fingers on his left hand while still clutching the letter with his right. "I woke up and saw him. He'd bent the girl over the altar, pounding away at her with his pants around his ankles." McVain pursed his lips, tightened his jaw. "Found my gun on the floor. My left hand was a mass of clotted blood and bone. I approached Meeks from behind. Pulled the trigger. Blew his brains out his right eyeball." McVain stopped abruptly. He remained silent for a few moments, fighting with his emotions, fingering the bed sheets. Wolfgang touched his shoulder as if to say, enough.

"Meeks was right," McVain said. "I was sent home. We hid Meeks' body in an alley behind the church. Left him for the rabid dogs. I got a medal for being wounded." He held up his left hand. "The battle at Chateau-Thierry."

"What happened to the girl?"

McVain wiped his nose. "Never saw her again."

Wolfgang eyed the letter in McVain's right hand. "That's from her, isn't it?"

McVain slowly opened the envelope and pulled out a folded letter, his hands unsteady. "She's been looking for me for years. But she didn't even know my name. And I didn't know hers." He unfolded the letter to reveal a picture. "Amelie. She learned English."

"Where is she now?"

"Here. In Louisville. She hunted me down. Wants to visit me." McVain handed Wolfgang the picture. "It's a few years old."

Wolfgang took the black and white picture from McVain and stared at the dark-haired woman named Amelie. She was pretty. With her hair and sympathetic eyes she did resemble Rose. Standing in a light dress that ended at the knees, her eyes dark, her face friendly, her stance one of shyness and insecurity. In the background was a small house, and behind it was a winding river spotted with trees and edged with farmland. Beside Amelie was a little boy, probably seven or eight years old. Wolfgang focused on the eyes. He wondered if his hair was red. He looked like a young McVain in the face.

McVain took the picture back and looked at it. "She thinks he's mine."

Or Meeks? No, thought Wolfgang, the resemblance was too uncanny. The boy had to be McVain's. "Will you see her?" Wolfgang asked.

"If she comes. I don't think I have many days left."

Wolfgang stood slowly from the chair, his knees stiff.

"I made a choice at Chateau-Thierry," McVain said. "I ran from the violence to avoid injuring my hands. If I'd gone to defend that bridge—"

"You could have been killed."

"Or come back whole." McVain studied Wolfgang. "Try living with that. Was that fate or coincidence, Father? Or was it a result of my actions? A punishment?"

"God doesn't work that way."

"You don't really believe that, do you?"

Wolfgang looked down. "What do *you* believe?"

"At first I believed it was a punishment."

But now?"

"Now that I've ended up here—and met you—maybe I believe in fate."

Wolfgang didn't understand what McVain could have meant. But McVain closed his eyes and kept them closed. A few minutes later he was snoring. He had more to tell. But not tonight.

ON WOLFGANG'S WAY out he stopped by Jesse's bed, where he snored annoyingly loud in the cool air. After McVain's story,

Wolfgang felt like strangling Jesse and ending his dilemma. He grabbed a spare pillow from a chair beside the bed and took a few steps toward where Jesse slept. Wolfgang looked over his shoulder to see if anyone was watching. It would be too risky. They were asleep now but if someone were to wake up amidst the struggles and see their priest forcing a pillow over the face of a patient . . . He squeezed the pillow with both hands, squeezing and releasing repeatedly. Was this what his mother had felt before she'd killed her husband?

Just let him die, like me, Ray had said.

It wouldn't take long to smother him. No one would suspect a thing as long as he wasn't seen. Jesse's lungs were diseased. They die one per hour at Waverly. Death was as common and predictable as the hours ticking away on a clock. But something stopped him. He stopped with the pillow a few feet from Jesse's face, close enough to feel Jesse's breath on his knuckles. He held it there for a moment while his rationality took back over. He stepped away from the bed, dropped the pillow back on the chair and walked on. He wanted Jesse dead. He wanted him to pay for what he'd done to Big 15, but he would not be the one to do it. He would not play God as his mother had done.

"Let God play God," he muttered on his way down the solarium.

INSIDE HIS COTTAGE, Wolfgang lit a fire and tossed his letter from the archdiocese into the flames, where the edges quickly curled in the heat. He watched until the paper had darkened. In his head he worked on the requiem but he was too unfocused to think straight—not after McVain's story. He wished Susannah would come and knock on his door, but she didn't come. He needed to share McVain's story with her. He feared the kiss had driven a wedge in their relationship and he hated himself for it. He knelt beside his bed as a penitent and folded his hands to Heaven. "Bless me Lord, for I, your humble servant and unworthy priest, have sinned."

26

WOLFGANG WOKE UP shivering, and no matter how far he buried himself under the blankets he couldn't find warmth. His pillow was cold, his nose even colder, and his ears felt like ice against the draft that had seemingly risen from the floor to envelop his bed like a frozen cocoon. The windowpanes had frosted over during the night. Tiny motes of dry ash lifted and spun inside the fireplace before settling as the wind reached down the chimney in search of warmth. Not going to find it in here, Wolfgang thought, staring at the wall clock. He didn't need to be up yet. He was tired but too cold to attempt going back to sleep. Susannah would not arrive for over an hour, and the thought of walking across the cold wooden planks to the bathroom sent his knees into a fetal position. He tucked his folded hands between his thighs and found a little warmth there, but it wouldn't last. Soon the frigid air slivered beneath the sheets and found his toes. He flung the covers off the bed and swung his feet to the floor, where he tested the wood with his toes before moving on around the foot of the bed. He blew into his hands and spotted the brown leather sack he'd left beneath the window. In it was all the cash, rubies and diamonds he'd found inside his father's instruments—the stolen money his mother had so valiantly given to him. He knew exactly what he was going to do with the money. He cleared a swath of frost from the window and stood witness to a gray slated day. He hurried across the floor to the kitchen, where a throw rug offered protection against the cold floor. He fixed coffee and gripped the mug with both hands, inhaling the aroma as it thawed his face. He was eager for another walk up the hillside with Susannah. He hoped her attitude toward him had improved. The concert was only a few days away and he needed her support. He wanted her to be happy, so he'd decided to not tell her about his transfer.

He opened the taps on the bathtub and cold water splashed and swirled around the drain. He waited with his hand under the downpour but the water never became hot. He'd forgo the bath and settle for washing his face. It was too cold to be naked. He dressed quickly, put on his lab coat, grabbed his black bag of instruments, sat on his couch like a statue and waited for Susannah to come knocking.

Forty minutes later he paced back and forth across the floor, the arch in his right foot throbbing and more stiff than normal, which made his limp more pronounced. He checked his pocket watch to make sure his wall clock had not stopped during the night. It was after seven. Susannah was never late. He sighed, stood with his hands on his hips and facing the closed door, and then forced himself to sit back on the couch.

After another twenty minutes he started pacing again, hop clopping like a man on one stilt, fuming and convinced that she hated him. He understood that he'd made a mistake in kissing her, but to be so upset . . . he grabbed his black bag, opened the front door and hurried up the hill alone, his shoulders tucked into the headwind.

Ten minutes later Wolfgang knocked on the door to the nurses' dormitory and waited impatiently for about four seconds before rapping again on the wood until his knuckles hurt. Finally, the door opened and Nurse Marlene greeted him with a kind smile. "No hot water either, Father?"

Wolfgang noticed she was looking at his hair. He touched the top of his head with his hand and found several strands of hair sticking up. Without thinking of the vulgarity of it or not caring in his present mood he licked his fingers and rubbed it down with three haphazard strokes of his numb hand. "Is Susannah in, Marlene?"

Nurse Marlene shook her head. "She left in the middle of the night."

"Where did she go?"

"I assumed she went to . . . "

"Where?"

Marlene blushed. "Your house, Father."

Wolfgang covered his embarrassment with anger. "Don't be ridiculous."

"Maybe she was working."

Wolfgang left Nurse Marlene standing in the open doorway as he turned, fuming, toward the woods and up the hill to the sanatorium. Susannah never worked in the middle of the night. Perhaps she'd gone to visit Doctor Barker again? What if she'd spent the night on his couch? Or even worse . . . ? He refused to believe she would share her boss' bed when his wife was sick with the very disease they were supposed to be stopping. Wolfgang opened the door to the lobby and dashed inside.

Doctor Barker stood there, as if waiting for his arrival, and then grabbed his arm. "Slow down."

Wolfgang wrestled his arm free from Doctor Barker's surprisingly strong grip. "Susannah . . . Where is she?"

Doctor Barker put the fingertips of his right hand to his forehead, as if lost for words. "I'm sorry, Father."

"About what? Where is she?"

"Second floor," Doctor Barker said. "Room two-oh-seven. I admitted her in the middle of the night."

Wolfgang's face went slack. It couldn't be. He sprinted up the stairwell, nearly knocking over several nurses and a new young doctor he'd yet to meet. He kept a hand on the brick wall to brace himself, hurdling the steps two and three at a time. Admitted last night? Patients he passed spoke out to him but he didn't stop to listen. None of them mattered now. Outside Room 207 was one bed. The woman on it was middle-aged with short blonde hair and curious eyes.

"Father?" she said.

Wolfgang stepped past her bed and into Room 207, and there she was, resting beneath a thin sheet, on her back, her fingers laced together on her stomach, staring at the ceiling in the shadows of a sunless room. Susannah heard him and leaned up from her pillow. "Wolf?"

Wolfgang hurried to her bedside, collapsed onto a wooden chair and gripped her right hand. She didn't look sick like the others. She looked tired, but no more than usual.

Her smile said she wasn't frightened. "You had to have seen it coming."

Wolfgang squeezed her hand. "Your hand felt warm the other night. Your loss of appetite. You've lost weight. I should have seen it. This isn't fair."

"It isn't fair for any of us. We know the risks working here."

"I should be in the bed instead of you," said Wolfgang. "Why not me?"

"Don't say such things."

"I'll find a cure if it kills me."

"I'll still sing with the choir." Susannah moved her hand from his grip. Her fingers slithered away, weightless, like tethered ribbons. "I've been coughing now for weeks. My temperature comes and goes. I've been achy lately."

"We've caught it early then."

"Much earlier than with the rest of my family." She spoke confidently, much like she would to another patient. And then Wolfgang remembered her family. Tuberculosis had taken every one of them.

Only she had been spared. She'd thought herself immune because of it. She'd nearly completed her book. He'd been so consumed with finishing Rose's requiem that he'd failed to understand how important her work was to her. She'd been so persistent on finding a cure. "Barker met me here last night, Wolf. We ran tests. Both lungs are infected." She stared at him for a moment, her eyes unwavering. "Abel doesn't know." Wolfgang sighed deeply. It would crush the kid. Susannah was like a mother to him. "Can you bring him here?" she asked. "I'd like to tell him myself."

"Of course." Wolfgang patted her hand. "Fresh air and rest. That's what we prescribe." He pushed her bed out onto the solarium porch and parked her as close to the screen as possible, beside the blonde he'd ignored on his way in. The patients were turning over too quickly. He couldn't keep up. "How's this?"

"Perfect." The longer he stared at her the more frustrated he became.

"Wolf . . . remember that Rose was cured."

"And look what happened." Wolf looked away and started to walk off.

"The other night." Susannah spoke softly so that no one could hear.

Wolfgang froze, his back to Susannah.

"You kissed me," she said. "It was wonderful. I pushed you away because I knew I was sick. That was the *only* reason, Wolf. I didn't want to infect you."

He believed her. She loves me, he thought. He stormed away because he couldn't love her back.

WOLFGANG FOUND a spot on the porch where shadow and wind kept patients away and no one could see his tears. He was in no mood to see patients. They deserved more than what he could have given them in his current frame of mind. Nor did they want to speak to a priest who was beginning to believe that after death they did nothing but fertilize the earth for future generations. He cleared his eyes and walked up the stairs to the fourth floor solarium, determined to confront Jesse Jacobs and demand a confession of truth. He would pay for what he'd done. To Wolfgang's surprise and dismay, Lincoln stood next to Jesse's bed with a gurney.

Lincoln looked over his shoulder at Wolfgang with a sad look in his eyes. "I'm sorry, Wolf. I heard about Susannah."

Wolfgang ignored him. Jesse's face was pale, his lips parted but unmoving. His eyes were closed. His meaty right arm lay lifelessly off the table. Lincoln heaved Jesse onto the gurney. "He's dead?" Wolfgang asked.

"Doctor Barker noticed him early this morning. Must have passed during the night."

"How?"

Lincoln gave a slight chuckle and then masked it. "Wolf . . . he had tuberculosis."

"He wasn't that sick." Wolfgang paced beside the gurney, focusing on Jesse's bloodless face. "Of all the people on this hillside, he showed signs of improvement."

Lincoln started to push the gurney away.

"There'll be an autopsy?"

"Not unless you do it," Lincoln said. "No time . . . too many bodies, and we know how they died." He eyed Wolfgang suspiciously. "I know you got to know him pretty well, Wolf, but what's going on?"

Wolfgang pointed at Jesse's body. "He killed Big 15."

Lincoln's mouth opened in a gasp. "How do you know?"

"I also know he wasn't deathly ill last night."

"Swift justice then." Lincoln pushed the gurney past Wolfgang. "The Lord works in mysterious ways, right?"

Wolfgang stepped aside and let him go. Was this God's doing? Had he hastened the disease to make Jesse pay for his sins? But He wasn't a vindictive God, was He?

* * *

Wolfgang stood in the darkened, quiet chapel lit only by the small candles that lined the walls. He knelt before the altar and stared at the crucifix on the wall—the stake pinning Christ's feet to the wood, the stakes at his wrists and at the crown of thorns upon his head. He spoke softly but his words were laced with viciousness. "Last night I prayed for Jesse's passing . . . and now he's gone. My wish granted." The candle flames flickered. The chapel remained quiet. "Something is granted . . . and then something is taken away. Is that how it works, Lord? Susannah is sick now."

Nonsense, his mind cried. Mere coincidence. Just like when Rose was cured and then struck down by a stray bullet a week after leaving Waverly. Fate? Was this some kind of punishment?

Footsteps pulled him from his reverie yet he didn't turn around to confront the visitor. He could tell by the footfalls that it wasn't a woman. The nurses' shoes had a different sound. These were hard shoes. Doctor Barker's. He couldn't turn to face him now in fear of taking out his anger on him.

As Wolfgang focused straight ahead toward Christ and the cross, Doctor Barker sat on the first chair in the first row about ten feet behind Wolfgang. It was silent for a moment before Doctor Barker spoke in a hushed tone. "Father . . . will you hear my confession?"

Wolfgang's eyes grew large. He still didn't turn around. "Yes."

He could hear Doctor's Barker's nerves—the trembling in his voice. The rubbing of his dry hands sounded like sandpaper. "Jealousy has blackened my heart, Father."

Wolfgang took a deep breath. His posture straightened as he continued to kneel. "Go on."

More rubbing of the hands. A sniffle and a large exhale. "For months now . . . I've had improper thoughts . . . about another woman." Doctor Barker exhaled again. "I love my wife."

Wolfgang's jaw quivered. He nodded, still gazing with a bundle of emotions—fear, rage, betrayal and confusion—at the crucifix on the wall. "You're forgiven. Go and sin no more, Doctor."

Doctor Barker stood, took a few steps and then stopped. "The music has brightened Anne's spirits . . . "

Wolfgang nodded but didn't turn around until he heard Doctor Barker's footsteps fade from the chapel. He clenched his hands into fists and stood from the steps before the altar. It was easier to believe nothing. Maybe McVain was right. God didn't dictate how their lives would turn. He didn't punish us for our actions, nor did he reward us for doing good. "Our lives are Heaven and Hell." He backed away. "We're born, we live and we die." He bowed toward the crucifix. "And no more."

The harsh reality of it sent him reeling down the steps of the sanatorium and he didn't stop until he hit the woods, panting and weeping, bouncing from trunk to trunk, weaving like the drunk he couldn't wait to become, tripping over twigs and vines. He couldn't wait to lock himself inside his cottage and sit with the lights off. He wanted to be alone. He needed to be alone. Totally alone.

He hurried inside, frantically fumbled with the lock, finally clicked the bolt and leaned against the closed door. He slithered down to the floor, crying with his head in his hands, whispering, "No one is listening. No one is listening." He looked up toward the ceiling with drool dabbing the corners of his mouth and wetting his beard. "No one has ever been listening!"

He'd been lied to his entire life and he'd spent the last several years infecting others with the same lies. Faith . . . what was faith? His faith was lying in a hospital bed a few hundred yards away, dying because she insisted on helping others to live. Wolfgang crawled across the wooden floor to where his piano had been. Dust covered the baseboard. A cold draft pushed over his hands. He sat with his back against the wall, his head close enough to the window to feel the air seeping in through the cracks. Daylight lit the floor, a rectangle striped with the grid of the window frame. He wanted the night to come. He wanted the darkness. Against the wall was a bottle of wine left from . . . he couldn't remember when. He popped the cork with his thumb, closed an eye to check inside and figured there was just under half left. He tilted the bottle, opened his throat and swallowed three gulps.

He'd finished the bottle within ten minutes. He stood and tossed it into the fireplace, where it shattered against the stones and glistened in the dark ash. He made his way over to the closet and opened the doors. He yanked his vestments from their hangers and threw them to the floor. He kicked his Edison phonograph off the table and sent his cylinder records spinning and rolling across the floor like giant bubbles of quicksilver. Most of them ended up near the front door, where the floor slanted noticeably. He pulled the white collar from his shirt and threw it against the wall so hard he lost his balance and toppled over. He landed a few feet from the couch—Susannah's couch. His head was swimming and craving more alcohol. He smelled the charred ash in the fireplace and made it to his feet again.

In the kitchen he grabbed another bottle of wine. His sacramental wine. Contraband wine. He didn't care. Tears streamed down his face. In the main room he tilted his head back and chugged from the new bottle. He lifted the small crucifix from the wall and dropped it to the floor, where Christ lay facedown on the planks. He kicked the closet door against the wall and stepped closer to the darkness inside. He wondered if he could fit in there. Go to sleep in the closet and never come out. He squatted down, took another swig and ignored the red slosh that dripped from his beard. He reached inside the dark closet and pulled out a framed picture, a canvas painting that had hung over the fireplace in his home with Rose. It stood about three feet tall and two feet wide and it was enclosed with a nicely carved wooden frame. He remembered how Rose had approached the artist to strike up a friendship. He'd asked to paint her and she'd agreed. In the painting Rose wore a yellow dress, the same one she'd had on the day she was killed. In her black hair above her left ear was a rose. The background was a different shade of darkness than her hair. He'd had her sit in a way that accentuated her long eyelashes, small nose, the curve of her full lips and the slenderness of her neck—her profile with her head turned slightly to the left, facing the artist, curious and dignified. Her dark hair hung down on the left side, covering part of her cheekbone and caressing the hard line of her angled jaw. He loved the painting. He'd been addicted to looking at it. It was so real . . . so like Rose. He ran his fingers over the grooves of dry oil on the canvas. He touched her lips, her eyes, and then ran his index finger down the shimmer of her hair. She stared at him, her eyes dark and mischievous. He leaned the painting against the wall beside the closet and backed away. He sat beside the bed, on the floor, his back against the edge of the mattress, his head lolling back on the covers he'd kept so neat for Rose. He'd never see her again. She was dead just like Jesse was dead. He slumped down on the floor and closed his eyes.

He wanted to die, too.

WOLFGANG AWOKE SOMETIME during the night to light a fire and grab another bottle of wine to help quell the nausea that he felt rising from his gut. He moved Rose's portrait next to the fireplace. His head hurt. He was starving. He opened the bottle for more wine. He stepped over his strewn clothing, sat back down on the floor and stared at the growing flames.

MORNING CAME WITH passing sunlight. His eyelids fluttered. He moaned and turned back over. The floor was freezing cold. The fire had gone out. Through the slits of his eyes he spotted a white shirt. He reeled it in, used it as a pillow and closed his eyes.

*　*　*

THE ROOM GREW dark and much colder. His pants were soaked and the smell of urine permeated the air. He took his pants off, then his underwear. Six bottles of wine sat against the hearth. He reached out the toes of his deformed foot and kicked them over. He watched them roll across the floor, one of them making it as far as his cylinders by the front door. Another stopped against the crucifix and dripped red wine that Wolfgang thought was blood. He pulled a blanket from the couch, curled his legs up and covered his naked waist.

WIND BLEW AGAINST the windows and walls and climbed down the chimney. Ash puffed from the fireplace and landed on his face. He blew it away without opening his eyes. He couldn't. It was too painful even to blink. He smelled vomit and urine.

A mouse scurried across the floor, sniffed his exposed right foot and went on.

27

ROSE SEES HIM *first. He sits alone in the back pew of the Cathedral. She nudges me with her elbow and nods in his direction. At first glance he appears to be just a regular teenage boy, probably fifteen or sixteen years old. I look back to the pulpit as Father reads from the gospel. I admit I can't recall which gospel. When I sit in church holding Rose's hand I often lose focus. I hear but don't listen. Especially now, only days after she'd left Waverly cured of her TB. I stare at her constantly. She's very thin now but healthy.*

She nudges me again. "Wolfgang . . . look at him."

"I did," I whisper.

"No, look at him . . . "

I look left again. He's a dark-haired boy with curls that cover his ears and neck, a full head of hair that now appears too large for his body— as if grown only to conceal his noticeably narrow chin. He has the face of a young man but the jaw of a boy, disproportionate to his eyes and cheekbones. He appears to be at least six-foot-six in height. He's so thin, his wrists tiny, his forearms nearly nonexistent and partly con- cealed by a long shirt that reaches past his elbows. He lacks confidence. I can tell by the way he slouches and keeps his chin tilted downward, like he's avoiding eye contact with everyone. I know and understand the look. His knees rise high; folded in the pew, he's so tall. His feet, so abnormally long and narrow, rest on the kneeler. He wears sandals, not by choice, I muse, but because he probably can't find shoes to fit his feet—long toes and no arch.

"Look at his fingers," Rose whispers. A woman in front of us turns and gives us a sneer. We shouldn't be talking. Rose knows as much, but I know when she's latched onto something or someone she won't let go. She was drawn to my limping walk and deformed foot. She was drawn to this boy's extreme height, awkwardness and long fingers. I looked at his fingers. They were the longest fingers I had ever seen, seemingly twice as long as my own, although I had never been known to have large hands. I feel guilty staring at them. This poor boy probably has children staring at him all the time. He doesn't need adults doing the same.

We watch the boy return from communion and he limps like I do, although not as badly. He limps as if his feet hurt. His lanky arms sway at his sides, his fingertips reaching past his knees. He sits again and folds his knees up. Only then do I notice his fingertips, as Rose had. His index fingers have abnormally long nails and they're pointed at the tips, like daggers. The rest of his nails appear clipped and filed. His fingertips are stained with color—red, blue, yellow, white, black, green—some fingers marked by one distinct color and others smudged with a mixture of all.

Rose wastes no time in confronting him after church.

"Excuse me," she says. "Excuse me . . . "

Finally he turns toward her voice, his eyes focused on the ground, his insecurity oozing from every pore. He hates this, I can tell.

"I think you're beautiful," Rose says.

He lifts his chin slightly and stares down into her eyes. Rose has that gift of making everyone feel special. The boy instantly feels comfortable with her. His eyes have a twinkle that was not there all through church.

She lifts his hands and holds them in her own. He allows this. She looks at his large knuckles, the lines in his palms, the long fingernails on the index fingers. "What is your name?"

"Jonah," he says. His voice is low and distorted, I realize, probably an impediment caused by the deformation of the palate.

It doesn't stop Rose. "What do you do with these hands?"

He smiles. "I paint." He's self-conscious about his voice. "With my fingers."

Rose looks up at him in amazement. She touches the long nail on his right index finger. "And these?"

"F-F-For deth . . . detail." Jonah looks at me as if for permission. He then curls his index finger, as if sheathing the dagger at the tip of it, and lifts Rose's chin with his knuckle. He grins, reaches for Rose's right hand and then turns it over so that her palm faces upward. With his right index finger he begins to trace letters onto the surface of her palm, softly and delicately despite the point of his nail. This is how he must communicate. I'm too shocked to follow what he's tracing onto Rose's open palm, so when she turns to me almost blushing, I ask, "What did he say?"

She touches her left cheek, grinning. "He says I have a portrait face. And that he'd give anything to paint it."

SOMEONE KNOCKED ON the front door and they wouldn't stop. Wolfgang lifted his head from the floor and a string of drool stretched from his lips. Visions of light and dark rattled his brain. Inside his mind he was still inside the loft of Jonah's garage. The boy's long fingers dipped into the paint and touched the canvas with a technique like he'd never seen before, while Rose sat patiently and with ease on a stool, her face partially bathed in the sunlight that bleeds into the muggy loft. Jonah works in a brown cloak and sandals. His fingers maneuver so quickly and effortlessly. He was so particular in the way Rose sat on the stool, even at his age. He'd lift her chin one way, tuck the rose in her hair that way and turn her face ever so slightly away from the light. He slouched, he knelt, he squinted and he stepped back and viewed from his wooden chair where he would sit loosely with one leg tucked beneath the seat and the other stretched out in front in the style of Caesar. He paced periodically with a Louisville Slugger baseball bat—a Babe Ruth bat he'd given Wolfgang along with the painting when they'd left. He carved detail and grooves in the paint with his fingernails, scraping and lining like a sculptor, a master. Wolfgang would never forget watching him work, and how fulfilled Rose appeared posing for him. Such a unique and special talent— a boy stricken with the worst Marfan syndrome Wolfgang had ever seen. He watched him paint with his fingers and was convinced that God touched all in some way.

The knocking continued. Wolfgang's head throbbed. The door crashed open with a bang and colder air entered the cottage. Wind sent the cylinder records spinning back across the floor and into the scattered clothing. He opened his eyes, but the mere movement caused a rush of pain into his head. How long had he been down? He'd neglected his job. He'd neglected Susannah. And McVain? McVain was an atheist who feared nothing. Was he even still alive?

Wolfgang fought through the pain, made it to a sitting position and squinted as a bright ray of light bathed his face. His head felt like he'd been struck by Jonah's Babe Ruth baseball bat. His shirt was damp with wine and urine and freezing against his stomach. The blanket around his waist failed to cover his limp penis. Lincoln, silhouetted by the sunlight, knelt beside Wolfgang and lifted his left arm. Wolfgang turned away and vomited on the floor. A gush of putrid filth and nasty bile splattered across the wood and spread as if his head had exploded.

"His father worked at the bat factory," Wolfgang whispered, his throat raw.

Lincoln helped him up to a sitting position again. "What are you talking about?"

"Jonah." Wolfgang pointed toward Rose's portrait. He turned and vomited again, this time inside a bundle of clothes.

Lincoln covered his mouth with his coat.

Wolfgang panted like a dog on his hands and knees as strings of vomit stretched from his mouth to the floor. Lincoln covered Wolfgang's bare buttocks with a blanket. "We thought you'd died, Wolf." Wolfgang sat back on his heels, tucked the blanket to conceal his privates and wiped his face with his shirtsleeve.

"How long have I been here?"

"Almost two days," Lincoln said. "Valentine's Day is tomorrow."

"Our concert."

Lincoln helped Wolfgang to his feet and walked him over to the couch. He returned a few minutes later with a glass of water and a wet rag. "McVain has been asking for you. He said to do whatever it took to get you."

Wolfgang looked over toward the busted knob on his door.

"I'll get it fixed," Lincoln said.

"McVain . . . how's his health?"

"Near the end," Lincoln said. "He said he has a confession to make."

WOLFGANG TOOK A bath, shaved his neck and trimmed his beard while the aroma of coffee wafted in from the kitchen. By the time he came out dressed thirty minutes later, Lincoln had already cleaned out the wine bottles, wiped up the vomit and bundled the clothes on the porch to be washed. The busted front door moved in the breeze, allowing the sun glimpses of the cottage floor. Lincoln had gone back to the sanatorium, his job done.

Wolfgang hurried up the hillside alone. It wasn't the same without Susannah. Before it had been a time of joy in an otherwise depressing day. Now it meant nothing. Instead, shame dominated. He'd neglected her. He'd abandoned the musicians and choir he'd put together. He spent the day making it up to them. Although the white-tabbed collar around his neck felt like a lurid badge of deceit, he still heard confessions, calmed their fears and listened to their stories. He played songs for several patients, still a bit numb from what had happened in the past three days, but determined now to somehow move on.

He ate lunch alone and kept himself busy during the afternoon. In his mind he rehearsed tomorrow night's performance. He ran through the pieces they would play and worked out how best to use the choir. Herman would surely have to have a solo at some point, as would each of the instrumental musicians. He met briefly with Doctor Barker, and without going into the confession itself, he was able to convince him that the KKK threat was over and the culprits had been escorted by Lincoln down the Death Tunnel. It would be safe for Rufus to return up the hillside for the concert.

Thoughts of the program fueled him through the day. At every sneeze and cough he thought of the performance. When a patient spat on the floor or screamed of a high fever, he thought of Herman's voice or Josef's violin. Every hour when he glanced at his pocket watch, he blocked out the fact that another person had probably passed away. Instead he selfishly thought of how far the music would carry from the rooftop. It was the only way to get his mind off of Susannah resting on the solarium porch with the other patients, a floor he'd managed to avoid all day long.

Shortly after dinner, he finally made an obligatory visit. From the east end of the solarium, he spotted her bed several rooms down. He stood in the shadows so that if she happened to turn her head she wouldn't spot him. He would have felt much more comfortable behind a wall and peeking through a hole, but it wasn't an option. Abel sat in a chair beside Susannah's bed reading a book. They seemed to be happy together. He badly wanted to join them, but he didn't. He couldn't. Of all things, he was mad at her. Mad at her for leading him on. Mad at her because she'd enticed an emotion out of him that he'd thought dead. Because he was in love with her. And he was mad at her because, under the laws and oaths that he'd sworn to upon entering the priesthood, he simply could not have her.

Maybe being sent away to another church *was* the best solution. He would distance himself from her as much as possible, and right now being mad at her made it much easier and a whole lot less complicated than loving her. After ten minutes of spying and pretending that he was caring for other patients, he ducked back into the stairwell and sought out McVain.

THE DAYS WERE getting progressively longer, the sun hovering for a few extra minutes at dusk than the previous day. The sunset bled orange over the treetops. Tiny buds of green dotted many of the branches. Wolfgang wondered if spring had arrived during his drunken hibernation. McVain seemed not to see Wolfgang until he was right next to his bed. "You're smiling."

McVain looked up. "That a crime?"

Three members of the choir had arrived early for evening rehearsal.

"I wrote back," McVain said. "To Amelie. Told her about the concert."

"Think she'll come?"

He shrugged, then looked out toward the trees. "I'm sorry about Susannah."

"Thank you."

"Thought you might have killed yourself."

"Nearly did." Wolfgang leaned closer to McVain. Despite the grin, his skin looked paler and sicklier than ever. His eyes were swimming in dark pockets. "Lincoln said you had a confession."

More choir members arrived with copies of the music in their grips. McVain watched them cluster together and stand in rows. "Tonight. When we're alone."

Wolfgang touched his shoulder and started toward the piano. McVain caught Wolfgang's sleeve. "Still believe in Heaven?"

"I believe there is a God, and for now that's enough."

"Do you have to be a believer to repent?"

"Not on my hillside," said Wolfgang. "Just a conscience and a heart."

"Will you listen to my sin so that I can die?"

Wolfgang patted his arm. "No, McVain. I'll listen to your sin so that you can live."

SEVERAL TIMES DURING rehearsal Wolfgang caught Susannah watching him. His eyes would quickly move on and he'd continue as if nothing had bothered him. She appeared tired and broken down. He felt guilty for keeping a secret from her. He couldn't stop his eyes from straying from the choir to McVain's bed, where he was still beneath the covers, his eyelids fighting sleep, or worse. He had to make it through tomorrow night. He'd be too sick to play the piano, but Wolfgang wanted him alive to witness it. Wolfgang would play the piano and conduct from the bench somehow. He'd work it out. They were ready. He hoped the weather the next evening would be as pleasant as tonight—mid-fifties and clear. A local church had donated five hundred chairs for the front lawn. It was all coming together. Wolfgang dismissed rehearsal, his confidence brewing beneath the surface. He slapped several choir members on the back as they said goodnight and returned to their floors. He watched them go and pretended not to see Susannah several feet away, waiting with her arms folded.

"Wolfgang?"

Wolfgang spun toward her, acting surprised. "Oh . . . yes?"

"Why are you ignoring me?"

Wolfgang stood silent, heart racing.

"Is it because of the disease?"

"You know that's not it."

"Then why don't you talk to me?"

Wolfgang looked down. "I don't know." He looked back up only when he heard her departing footsteps and the faint sound of crying. "Sometimes I hate myself," he said softly.

McVain's voice called to him. "You know we'll have to move it up there."

"What?"

"The piano," McVain said. "How are we going to get it to the rooftop without Big 15?"

Wolfgang turned toward McVain. "Lincoln and a few others are on their way now. One more floor shouldn't kill us." And it didn't, not with the six helpers Lincoln had gathered—three cooks and three guys from the maintenance staff—knowing from experience they'd need them. Wolfgang spent an hour positioning the chairs for the choir along the rooftop, close enough to the edge to be seen when they stood but not so close as to be in danger of falling over the wall. Beside them they arranged the piano and chairs for the instrumentalists. After the help had gone back to their duties, Wolfgang stood alone for a few moments, taking in the cool air, welcoming the stiff wind on his face. Eventually he made his way back to the fourth floor solarium, where his chair awaited beside McVain's bed. The requiem rested in his lap.

"Put that away, McVain." Wolfgang lifted the requiem from McVain's grip and slid it under the bed. "You need rest."

McVain stared everywhere but at Wolfgang before speaking. "I'll know soon enough."

"Know what?"

"Where we go when we die," McVain said. "Isn't that what you've always wanted to know?"

Wolfgang gave him a warm smile. "We've got more music to play."

McVain wiped his runny nose on the back of his hand. "I'm a murderer."

"War," Wolfgang told him. "Kill or be killed. It's not the same as murder."

McVain's chin quivered, his tone suddenly serious and grave. "Are you going to hear my confession or not?"

"Sorry. Of course. Tell me."

"Fate." McVain played with the sheets while he spoke. "I told you I didn't believe in fate until I met you."

"Fate brought *all* of us together," Wolfgang said.

"More than the music."

"What then?"

"The day you told me how your wife died." McVain took in a deep breath and then let it out slowly. "How Rose was cured of TB, and then . . . "

Wolfgang leaned closer, McVain's tone of urgency and the mentioning of Rose's name completely drawing him in. His gut began to feel uneasy.

McVain's eyes locked on Wolfgang's. "I believed in fate the instant you told me that story. Or maybe it was karma." He stopped fumbling with the bed sheets. "I've seen your Rose before."

"When?" Wolfgang forced it out, his mind reliving the day the rain had come in torrents—the day of McVain's arrival, the day he'd pushed him into the mud. "When?"

"Wearing a yellow dress . . . " Tears formed in McVain's strained eyes. "I came back from the war a changed man. Full of hate. I had no family. I ran around with the worst people I could find. I lost all my money betting on bangtails at Churchill Downs."

Wolfgang felt a growing lump in his throat.

McVain wiped his cheeks with his left hand. "Valentine's Day, nineteen twenty-five. Me and two other bindlestiffs—"

"No."

"We robbed a bank downtown."

"No."

"A cop was inside the bank. We didn't know. He shot at us. I fired back blindly outside. One of my bullets ricocheted off a lamppost and hit an innocent woman . . . in a yellow dress." He swallowed. "She had a rose in her hair." More tears. "She was with a man."

Wolfgang thought he was suffocating. His mother's pillow had finally come down and stopped his breathing.

"She dropped to the cobblestones . . . "

"Stop it!"

"You knelt beside her, Wolf. I ran."

"Stop talking, damn it."

"I didn't want to do a bit in the big house."

Wolfgang's next breath came out as a moan, and then a whimper. Fate *had* brought him to Waverly. The rain on the day of McVain's arrival *had* been a sign, a warning.

"I'm so sorry." McVain reached for Wolfgang's hand, but Wolfgang quickly pulled it away. "I killed Rose. I didn't know until you told me the other day. I didn't mean to . . . I'm a murderer."

Wolfgang stood from the chair, mumbling. "No, no, no, it can't be . . . it . . . "

Never in his life had he performed an act of violence but he couldn't control himself. Wolfgang clenched his fingers into a fist and slammed it into McVain's face as hard as he could. McVain didn't try to dodge the first blow because it had come so unexpected by both of them. Wolfgang pulled his fist back to hit him again. McVain moaned and raised his hands to shield his face. Wolfgang wanted to strangle him . . . to smother him. He wanted to wrap his arms around him and tell him it was okay.

Patients along the solarium porch began to notice. Several screamed for help. Wolfgang's head was spinning, not from wine but from rage and an incomprehensible pang of disbelief. He felt out of himself. He gripped the folds of McVain's shirt with both hands, lifted him from his pillow and shook him. McVain's face was red. With his tear-filled eyes he begged for forgiveness. Wolfgang let go. Sparks of light shot across his vision. His hands shook uncontrollably. An orderly grabbed Wolfgang around the waist and pulled him away. McVain panted and coughed on his bed. Three nurses and a fellow doctor pulled Wolfgang away and leaned him against the solarium wall, where the cool breeze only heightened his delirium. He didn't fight the nurses. He didn't want to hurt them. But he didn't want to hurt McVain either. He wanted him to pay for what he had done to Rose. Wolfgang wouldn't forgive him. He slumped to the concrete floor of the solarium.

"Doctor?" Nurse Beverly knelt beside him and three other blurred figures stood behind her. "Are you okay? What happened?"

A male voice. "Did he hurt you?"

Wolfgang simply stared.

One of the nurses hurried over to check on McVain. Wolfgang watched through a blur of tears. For four years he'd hated a man with no face. It had been easier that way. Now the face belonged to his friend.

28

SLEEP DIDN'T COME that night. Memories of Rose lying dead in the street haunted him every time his eyelids flirted with closing. Susannah was probably dying. Abel was on his way to being alone. Wolfgang sat on the floor by the fireplace, the warmth of the flames against his back. Firelight cast shadows across the room while he dabbled with maudlin tunes on a violin. Shadowy figures danced along the far wall, wavering, floating, ducking in and out of the light, figures that would cease to exist once the flames began to die out. He sipped sacramental wine from a glass. The concert was less than twenty-four hours away. He couldn't go through with it. He couldn't get McVain out of his head.

Maybe God would forgive him?

He looked at Rose's portrait and fought back tears. How someone's fingers had captured her beauty to such perfection he would never understand. She looked so real. He braced his hands against the stone hearth and stood, weak-kneed and weary. He finished off his wine with a gulp and dropped the glass to the floor. No more. It was the middle of the night but he felt an urge to visit McVain again. He grabbed his coat, closed the door and made his way up the hillside, needing to see McVain's face but unable to conjure up any notion of what to say. The woods were quiet except for his footsteps and rapid breathing, but by the time he'd entered the sanatorium he'd composed himself. His fury returned by the time he reached the fourth floor solarium, but so was the feeling that all of them, including McVain, were just caught up in events they could do little about and whose cause was beyond their comprehension. Wolfgang was shocked to find McVain's bed empty.

"Doctor?" It was a woman's voice. Nurse Cleary approached. "He's gone."

Wolfgang pointed toward the empty bed. His punch must have snuffed out the little spark that was left. Was he a murderer too? "Is he in the morgue?"

"Not dead," Nurse Cleary said. "Gone. Disappeared."

"How—"

"I've been searching the floor for him."

"Father?" A man's voice.

Wolfgang ignored it. "How can a dying man just—"

"Father?"

Wolfgang's eyes moved from the empty bed to the man. He didn't know him. He was a new patient, brought in sometime during the night. He had brown hair and a short beard. "The man that was in that bed—"

"McVain," Wolfgang said. "His name is McVain."

"He got up in the middle of the night . . . and never came back."

Wolfgang's heart jumped. "Where did he go?"

"He couldn't walk," the man said. "He had something in his arms. He crawled on his hands and knees across the porch. I offered to help him but he told me to get lost." The man pointed across the solarium to the stairwell. "Went up them stairs."

Wolfgang sprinted to the stairwell. Spots of blood trailed up the steps. Wolfgang rubbed a spot with the tip of his boot and the blood spot smeared. It was fresh. Had he driven him to jump to his death? Wolfgang rushed up to the rooftop and saw nothing in the pre-dawn darkness but the chairs they'd set up earlier. He checked over the wall but could see nothing in the shadows below.

He turned around. From his angle, the piano's silhouette looked awkward. He moved closer and saw McVain slumped across the keyboard. His green eyes stared at Wolfgang, unmoving.

"No."

And then McVain blinked. Wolfgang let loose a long breath. Nurse Cleary rushed over. McVain lifted his head slightly from the keys. He clutched at some sheets of music on the piano's rack. "Father . . ."

Wolfgang pursed his lips. "He's sulking." He turned to Nurse Cleary. "Put him back to bed."

EVERY TIME IS *the same. Her blood runs through my fingers and onto the cobblestones but I'm helpless to stop it. I rock her in my arms, trying to plug the hole in her chest but the blood continues to flow. Everything on the street has turned to chaos. Down the block a man in a gray suit and gray bowler hat ducks between two brick buildings. The man who shot Rose is getting away. Every time is the same.*

And I am helpless to stop him . . .

WOLFGANG AWOKE WITH a jerk and found himself panting for breath inside a cold room that felt like a dungeon. It took him a moment to remember how he'd gotten there. After leaving McVain on the rooftop and retreating back down the hillside to his cottage, he'd locked himself in and watched out the windows as the sun rose above the trees. A feeling of paranoia had swept over him. He felt like his father's son, staring out the window and waiting . . . for what? For them to come. He knew they would come after him when he didn't show for work, and then for the concert, but he couldn't do it. He still felt numb from McVain's revelation. He didn't feel safe inside his cottage. When he didn't show for work, Lincoln was the first to come hunting.

He knocked on the door for several minutes. "Wolf, the church volunteers are here." Lincoln looked through his kitchen window while Wolfgang watched from behind a tree. "The chairs have arrived," he shouted through the walls. "They're beginning to set up." Lincoln walked to the side of the cottage and looked in through the window next to the bed, cupping his hands around his eyes to keep out the glare. He tried the rose garden and ended up on the other side of the cottage, perplexed enough to knock on the front door again before giving up to search the woods.

Nurse Marlene had come calling next. Wolfgang waited until she passed before making his way through the woods to the maintenance shed. In the back of his mind he knew his conduct verged on madness, but he still couldn't bring himself to go to the concert he'd created. The maintenance shed was a one thousand square-foot wooden building with a shingled roof in bad need of repair. At least a dozen birds had made nests in the rafters. A tall ladder was propped against a hayloft. Sunlight bled through the cracks of the roof where shingles had been blown away. It smelled of mechanical farm equipment and manure. Wolfgang sidled beside a dusty red tractor and sat on a layer of loose hay next to the wall. A crow sat on the tractor's seat, digging into the cushion as if searching for worms. It eyed Wolfgang and didn't fly away. Wolfgang was the one trespassing. The crow pulled brown, soggy stuffing from the seat with its beak and flew to a nearby windowsill. Wolfgang felt at home in the dark corner of the shed. He'd found the divide between two warped planks in the wall. He leaned until his nose touched the splintered wood, and peered through the crack. It was a familiar smell—the wood smell, the hole in the wall smell, although slightly different from the dry wooden wall of his childhood home. This one smelled wet and molded. He could see the front lawn perfectly though. He wished he'd brought something to eat, or drink.

Outside, Lincoln directed Nurse Marlene and Nurse Beverly as the threesome set up the hundreds of chairs in rows just as Wolfgang had planned. Lincoln had been paying attention. Doctor

Barker made an appearance, spoke to Lincoln in depth about something and then helped set up a few dozen chairs before returning inside.

By that time Wolfgang had been up most of the night. He felt comfortable watching through the wall, comfortable enough to rest on the loose hay and close his eyes for a bit. It turned into an hour. He awoke with hay in his hair and dust in his nose and a line of ants marching across the sole of his left boot. He wiped them away and knelt again. Through the hole in the wall he noticed that they'd finished setting up the chairs. Lincoln had gone inside. Wolfgang knew where to hide—a place where no one would find him. From the shed he crept to the entrance of the body chute, Lincoln's Death Tunnel, and slipped inside the sanatorium through the back. His clothes were covered with dirt, burrs and hay. His shirt had come untucked from his pants. His hair was disheveled. At the north wing corridor he opened a white door. Dark stairs led him down to the basement, where he hurried past a service elevator and hunkered down under a chase of pipes. A crawlspace ran under the corridor and opened up into another passageway tall enough for him to stand. His clothes were wet from the floor of the cramped crawlspace. The air was cold, dank and musty. He was directly under the Grand Lobby. He limped over to the concrete wall, curled up in a ball and closed his eyes.

It was Valentine's Day, the fourth anniversary of Rose's death. He was alone, hiding in the dark corners of a basement, shivering.

Hours later the feeling of paranoia returned. He strained his eyes to get a glimpse of his pocket watch. Outside the sun would be beginning to set, although he was far from seeing it, buried as he was under the building. Were they still looking for him? Surely they'd cancelled the show, with McVain out and the conductor missing. Wolfgang hugged his knees close to his chest, trying to stay warm. He coughed once, twice, and then went into an all out coughing fit that stopped only when he'd begun to gag. But there was nothing to vomit. His stomach was empty. He was starving. He realized that he hadn't eaten a meal in nearly three days. His head ached. He felt weak. His tongue craved the warmth of his wine.

What was he doing down here? Alone and in the dark?

He coughed again. Only the dust, he told himself. Nothing more. He was immune to the disease, he'd convinced himself.

And then he heard something . . . the sound of a piano. It traveled from the rooftop, carried by the wind. It slivered through the floors and reverberated off the walls. And then it stopped. Moments later he heard a violin tuning up. And then the clarinet. They were warming up. They were going on without him. He couldn't burrow deep enough under the building. The music would find him. It would seep like water through the cracked foundation until it found him.

He covered his ears but he could still hear them playing. The choir started running through its warm-up. Wolfgang pictured twilight on the hillside. His plan. The hundred or so colored patients walking up the hillside, holding lit candles, a meandering line of people on their way to join the white patients, all of them sitting together on the lawn.

Then he heard Herman . . . then silence. The warm-up was over.

In his wretched exile, Wolfgang suddenly felt another emotion. No one in the world could see him or even know where he was, yet he was impaled by acute pangs of stage fright. Would the concert go well, or would they fail miserably? He was the only one who knew how to coax the chorus to sing out with exultation. He closed his eyes and dreaded the worst, wondering how it had come to this, how he was alone in a dark, leaky basement with nothing but a stack of dry-rotted wood and a line of red ants marching alongside the wall to keep him company. Had he gone crazy? The more years that passed after his father died, the more he grew to love the man that had beaten him regularly. He'd grown to admire the man who'd taught him the joy of music, albeit with an iron fist and a bitter tongue. He'd come to realize, too, that his father had been somewhat of an eccentric and borderline crazy. Was he turning into him?

Wolfgang opened his eyes only after he heard total silence from above. If indeed they were going to start the show without him, any minute the piano would start playing Mozart, the first piece on the list. But it wasn't Mozart that he heard. Nor a piano. At first he might have mistaken it for the rumble of plumbing or even the bowels of the earth opening up to take him by the ankles and pull him into Hell through the cracks of the basement in which he'd selfishly, or crazily, sought shelter from the world. But it was the sound of a double bass. The deep droning of a bow pulled across tight strings shook his bones through the concrete walls and floor. Who was it? Could it be Doctor Barker? What were they playing?

It sounded so familiar . . . Wolfgang's mouth opened. His ears perked. It was the opening measures of *The Requiem Rose*. They were playing his requiem. But it wasn't finished yet! He sat straight against the basement wall. It was just as he had imagined it sounding, but better. He could picture Rose's coffin being lowered into the ground, the fog rising around his feet, the grass wet with so much dew, the air thick with moisture but beginning to invite the sun through the clouds. It was the music she so deserved.

And then the violin sounded, ever so softly, followed by the clarinet. In his mind he turned the page of music to the next, following along, his body swaying to the rhythm, his arms beginning to move as if conducting. And then he heard Susannah's voice. She was singing the introit, risking her lungs for him, for Rose. Her voice, infused with the Latin words, hovered with the wind and trickled below like a pleasant summer rainfall—soporific in its descent. Wolfgang's arms rose involuntarily in front of him, holding an imaginary baton. He closed his eyes and hummed along. She sang beautifully, and with passion. And then her voice led into the sound of Rufus' flute. And Josef's violin. He turned another imaginary page. They were playing his requiem. But it wasn't complete.

And then it hit him. That was what McVain had been doing last night on the rooftop. He'd crawled on his hands and knees up the stairs and across the terra cotta to finish Wolfgang's requiem. That's what he'd held in his hands.

Wolfgang brushed dirt, grime, splinters of hay and a few ants from his clothing and stood trance-like in the middle of the damp, dripping room. He followed the sound of the music. His music. He crawled back under the chase of pipes, oblivious to the puddles of water that wet his hands and knees and elbows. He followed his music. The service elevator took him to the second floor. He tapped his foot to the tempo and tucked his shirt inside his pants while he waited for the elevator to stop clanking upward. The doors opened and as soon as he stepped out into the hallway he was given a glimpse of the evening's weather, warm for mid-February. A crescent moon hung like a glowing cat's eye in the middle of the darkness. The sky was black and full of stars. The music would carry for miles.

Wolfgang was no longer cold, despite how his clothing clung to the wetness at his knees and elbows. His adrenaline had warmed him. His limp had thawed. He took the stairs two at a time, never slowing until his feet hit the surface of the rooftop. He steadied himself on the concrete caps along the rooftop and peered down toward the lawn. It was just as he'd imagined. The lawn was packed with people, twenty rows of patients, and ten chairs across on either side of a wide center aisle that cut down the knoll like a grassy road that would be trampled and worn by the end of the night. All the patients healthy enough sat outside for the performance. The rest were most assuredly listening from their beds on the solarium porches. Everyone in the crowd had been given a candle to hold. The woods glowed with their presence.

Sitting ten feet away from him were a woman and a young boy. She was young, with dark hair, piercing brown eyes and healthy skin. She wore a long red coat, a red bonnet and black shoes. Beside her, in a suit and tie, a boy with fiery red hair turned to look at Wolfgang with eyes as green and ornery as McVain's.

For the first time Wolfgang faced the musicians. They had gathered about thirty feet away, just as he had imagined them. The men were dressed in suits and ties and the women wore pink dresses. He didn't know where the clothing had come from, only that they all looked stunning. He spotted Susannah in the middle of the choir, her solo completed. Now she was singing with the others. She looked beautiful in her pink dress with white lace. Her curly hair was pulled and gathered behind in a flowing plait.

The musicians never broke stride as Wolfgang approached the podium. It would be vacant no longer. He picked up the baton that was waiting for him beside his requiem's score. McVain sat slumped over the piano keys, barely clinging to life. He didn't look at Wolfgang as he took his position at the podium in front of the choir. Rufus winked at Wolfgang. Josef nodded as he played. And the double bass? Wolfgang nearly dropped his baton. Doctor Barker stood behind Josef and Beverly with the weight of a double bass leaning against him. He drew his bow across the strings and a sound emerged from the instrument so deep that Wolfgang's heart vibrated. Anne Barker stood with the choir, singing proudly.

Wolfgang straightened his posture as if his father had been standing behind him and knocking his knees with the bow from his favorite violin. He flipped through the score to catch up, clutched his baton and began conducting them through the music of his orchestral mass. In his mind he could see Rose's coffin again, settled in the wispy fog. His heart was filled with joy and satisfaction. Herman's voice boomed over the softly flowing violins. Herman stood ramrod straight, sweating, his hands clenched into fists although without the security of his fork.

Near the end of the requiem, Wolfgang turned the page with a snap. It was time. This was the end. The perfect ending. It began with a short passage of solo piano. McVain played it with passion and soul, pouring out his heart while his body, so recently put back together with stitches, continued to slouch lower and lower toward the keys. His forehead nearly rested on the music rack above the keys. Four hundred patients listened below. Tiny candle flames lit their rapt, eager faces. The music alone would lift their spirits, fueling optimism and hopes to fight harder to stay alive. Whites and blacks all sat together. Each held a candle, unified as fighters of the disease that had brought them together to die. Tonight they were all one.

The music felt so right. So complete. As Wolfgang's arms moved to the flow he drifted back to the day of Rose's burial again. He'd been crushed with thoughts of doom. Rose was dead. And so was he. But not any longer.

The requiem would set them both free.

He checked the score on the podium and nodded toward Josef. Josef drew his bow over the violin strings with a touch so delicate Wolfgang thought the sky would crack, and then he held onto one high note for eternity, it seemed, before Rufus joined in with the flute. Moments later, Doctor Barker lifted his bow to the double bass for a long passage that moved the earth with its deep, rumbling tone. McVain reclaimed the lead next with a piano interlude. Then the choir—the children and women first, followed by the deeper voices of the men, and finally Herman. Their voices carried far over the trees, hovering on unseen wings of music.

And then the ending—a duo by McVain and Josef that left Wolfgang's cheeks wet with tears by the time the final cadence sounded. Wolfgang held onto that final chord, not wanting it to end but knowing that it had to, his hands shaking by the time the requiem melted into silence. The crowd hushed. Wind rippled their clothing. McVain eased his hands from the piano keys, slowly reeling them in like a lazy tide at the seashore. He was panting. He looked at Wolfgang with his tired eyes.

Wolfgang nodded.

McVain nodded back.

The crowd rose as one in a standing ovation. Wolfgang took a bow, panning the patients below, taking in the smiles, the warmth, the healing as tears dripped from his eyes and onto the final pages of the score in his grip. A vision of Rose sitting on Jonah's stool in the sunlight of his dusty loft, posing for her portrait, stuck in his mind. He would always remember her that way—a woman who would exclude no one for being different. A woman who would go out of her way to make someone feel wanted and special. She'd saved his life on the steps of the Cathedral and he'd never forget her for it.

Wolfgang gripped the final pages so tightly he nearly ripped them. The requiem was complete. The final ten pages, the ten pages Wolfgang had never been able to finish—he knew the writing. It *had* been McVain.

"Perfect," Wolfgang whispered. It *was* perfect. Wolfgang looked at the last page. At the bottom, McVain had written:

For Rose.

Wolfgang gathered all the pages in a stack and stared at the cover page before clutching it like a jewel against his chest.

The Requiem Rose.

Rufus stepped forward and patted Wolfgang's shoulder. "Welcome back, Maestro."

The musicians and choir all appeared eager to move on, to tackle the concert they'd planned to give. The work they had just performed was personal, deeply personal. The rest would be for the patients. The Waverly Hills Orchestra played and sang like the night would be their last upon the earth. Perfect harmony, perfect melody and perfect music, performed by the dying for the dying.

The crowd below listened, mesmerized by the music, and after each piece their applause would invigorate the musicians and choir even more. McVain sweated profusely. His skin looked waxy and a pale shade of green in the moonlight. But he refused to stop playing. After Tchaikovsky they played Mozart, Beethoven and the final movement of Vivaldi's *Four Seasons*. They took a brief intermission, where Wolfgang panned the crowd again in search of his mother, and after not finding her through several passes, they continued on with the concert with selections by Bach, Haydn and Brahms.

The patients loved them. They cheered and looked up to them, holding their candles high in the air. Like thousands of hovering fireflies. The concert Wolfgang had run away from. The music made them feel alive. It lifted them from their dark places, if only for one night. But the memories would last forever. As he conducted he imagined his father looking down on him, watching him conduct such a powerful musical force, watching him lead as he had dreamt of leading.

The patients weren't the only members of the audience. Doctor Barker had, without their knowledge and within the past three days, advertised the performance across the city, gathering volunteers to pass out thousands of pamphlets explaining the program. Word spread quickly. The weather cooperated. Valentine dates showed up in droves. Down Dixie Highway, thousands of candles seemed to run for miles—an avenue of fire leading to their music. The applause grew after every piece, silenced only by a new burst of music at the start of the next piece.

In the finale, Herman enthralled. The crowd watched and listened, breathless. They gasped at the beginning of his solo, "Ol' Man River" from *Show Boat*. Their resident madman was a king tonight. As Wolfgang had told Doctor Barker weeks before, everybody could be special, everybody had a story. Apparently Barker did as well, leaning comfortably against his double bass and listening to Herman sing while stealing flirty glances at his wife in the choir. Under his suit coat a bandage probably still covered the fork wound in his shoulder, yet it hadn't kept him from joining the concert and allowing Herman the thrill of staying involved and engaged.

At the very end, the ensemble and chorus joined together as one force, and had the harmony not been so perfect, Wolfgang's eardrums might have burst from the sheer volume of sound. He raised his arms high and slowly brought them together just above his head and then stopped abruptly. Just like that, the concert was over. The singers were silent. The music stopped on Wolfgang's cue. The applause then came with a roar and finished no sooner than ten minutes later, long after the musicians and choir had taken their bows. The entire city cheered them.

Wolfgang's eyes had long dried, the moisture replaced by a clean feeling of purity and solace. He looked at Rufus and Josef, who wore smiles nearly as wide as their faces. And then he saw McVain. McVain looked at Wolfgang and then stared over toward Amelie and his son. "He plays the piano," McVain hissed.

"He looks just like you." Wolfgang knelt beside the piano bench and lifted McVain's chin. "Does he know?"

McVain braced his right hand on Wolfgang's shoulder. "She didn't tell him who I was." Wolfgang understood. He thought of Abel. How would that little boy feel, meeting his father for the first time, only to have him die? "His name is Ryan." McVain's shoulders slumped. "From the Irish name meaning Red."

Wolfgang nodded. "His Irish eyes are smiling now, Tad."

McVain coughed up blood on his lips. "Get 'em out of here."

Wolfgang stood slightly under McVain's bulk and waved Amelie down the steps. She didn't hesitate in taking her son's hand and turning him away from the piano.

McVain coughed again. Something snapped inside his chest. Phlegm and blood rocketed up and onto his chin. He collapsed on the piano bench, then rolled to the rooftop floor with a thud.

McVain was dead. For a minute they all gathered around, just staring as the wind ruffled his red hair. Wolfgang knelt down and closed McVain's eyes. At least Amelie had led his son down the stairs before McVain had collapsed. One day Wolfgang hoped to meet her and tell her more about the man who had taken his wife's life and then helped to restore his. Susannah cried in the background. Wolfgang stood and draped his arm around her shoulders, hugging her from the side. He kissed the side of her head. She rested her head on his shoulder.

Josef's chalkboard propped against the leg of the chair he'd sat in during the concert forced a sudden laugh from Wolfgang's tight lips. "Fuck off, McVain."

They all looked at Father Wolfgang Pike—and although McVain himself would probably have considered it a fitting farewell—most of them appeared shocked at Wolfgang's choice of parting words. Not Josef though. He attempted to shield his laughter with a closed fist, and then Rufus joined in.

Wolfgang looked at the chalkboard again and grinned. "Were those your final words to him, Josef?"

Josef nodded, glancing at his chalkboard.

"Before we started playing," Rufus said, "McVain asked Josef to give us a pep talk. Except he said to *write* us a pep talk."

The chalkboard faced them all: **Fuck off, McVain.**

God would forgive McVain and so had Wolfgang.

"What should we do with him?" Susannah asked.

"Bury him," Wolfgang said.

"Where?" Doctor Barker asked.

"In the woods."

"Next to Big 15," Susannah said.

McVain would not be stored in the freezer room. He would not be stacked in the morgue. He would not be sent down Lincoln's Death Tunnel. He deserved a spot on the hillside for eternity, a spot where his only son could visit him one day. And so they buried him that same night. They all said a few words and then filled the grave with soil. Until they could do better, they marked the plot with a chunk of limestone upon which they'd written McVain's name and dates with black paint.

Perhaps one day Wolfgang would be buried next to him.

Afterwards, Wolfgang sought out Doctor Barker. He was in his office, still dressed in his suit and tie.

"Thank you," Wolfgang said. "For pulling the concert together without me, and for playing." Doctor Barker nodded once. Wolfgang turned to go.

"I spoke with the archdiocese," Doctor Barker said.

"You must be good friends with them by now."

Doctor Barker let out a push of air, his final combative breath. "I made a mistake sending them the letter, Wolfgang. I never thought they'd act on it." He scratched his gray hair and straightened his glasses. "I convinced them that I need you here. As a doctor *and* a priest. What you've done here is remarkable." He touched the lapels of his coat. "Do you like it? A clothing store downtown donated them."

"How's your shoulder?"

"I'll live."

"You promoted my concert. You insisted we have it after I'd all but killed it. Why?"

"I never hated the music, Wolfgang. I . . . " He sighed. "I wanted to be a musician. My father insisted on a respectable profession."

Wolfgang laughed. "Respectable, huh? How long have you played the bass?"

"Twenty-five years. My father never found out. I kept it at my grandmother's house and practiced there."

"What different lives we'd have led if we'd traded fathers," Wolfgang said.

Doctor Barker's face grew serious again. "The exact moment I bought into it all, Wolfgang? You stood in my office weeks ago and told me that we lose one patient an hour here. I knew the statistic, but only then did I do the math. Twenty-four per day on average. One hundred and sixty-eight per week. I checked the case files on the musicians and chorus. In the length of time you've had this choir, the sanatorium should have had a complete turnover in patients. Yet not one—" He held up a finger. "Not one patient from our choir has died. McVain was the first."

Wolfgang felt numb. A different kind of numbness. He was right.

"It's not a cure, but I believe your music is helping to keep them alive," Doctor Barker said with a smirk that made Wolfgang wonder who he'd been talking to about him. "That is not fate or coincidence, Father Pike. That is you touching someone's soul."

They looked at one another for a moment before Doctor Barker tidied his desk. "Time to go home. Perhaps tonight I'll have a glass of wine myself. Medicinal, of course." They shook hands. "Goodnight, Wolfgang."

"Goodnight, Evan."

29

THE CONCERT HAD seemingly flipped the switch on the weather, ushering in the spring in royal fashion, awakening the birds and the bees and the flowers and the trees. After a full night's sleep, Wolfgang awoke with a clear head. He walked up the hillside feeling something akin to optimism. Patients in droves thanked him for the performance. No one even alluded to his late arrival at the podium or his disheveled appearance. For a moment he felt like a celebrity, like Babe Ruth walking through a crowd of fans—not a response he had hoped for but thrilling nevertheless.

Doctor Barker stopped him outside the chapel after Mass. "Wolfgang, can I have a minute?"

"Sure."

"I found a leather bag on my porch this morning," Doctor Barker said. "It had thousands of dollars in it, and ten times that in rubies and diamonds."

"Really?"

"Anonymous donor, it said. You know anything about it?"

Wolfgang shook his head. "Can't say that I do."

"The note said to use it to renovate the colored hospital."

Wolfgang nodded, pursed his lips. "I think that would be a grand idea for it." And then he turned away in time to conceal his pleasure. Halfway down the hall Doctor Barker's voice called out to him.

"You know, Father. Is concealing the truth a sin?"

"No . . . I believe not. Not when one chooses to remain anonymous."

Doctor Barker smiled. "I'll see that the money is used as suggested. And Waverly thanks you."

"For what?"

They left it at that and both carried on with their days. Wolfgang gathered the courage to pay Susannah a visit between rounds. Her bed had already been pulled out onto the second floor solarium. Portions of her book rested on her lap above the bed sheets. Abel tossed a tennis ball in the air beside the bed. Wolfgang spent an hour with them, talking, laughing and watching Abel treat Susannah as if she were the only mother he'd ever known.

Wolfgang thought of McVain and the son he'd never known.

"Wolfgang, catch."

Wolfgang raised his right arm to catch the ball and nearly fell out of his seat, which elicited a brief chuckle from Susannah and an all out guffawing from Abel. Wolfgang picked up the ball and tossed it underhanded to Abel, who caught it with ease. Susannah smiled at him, and then at Wolfgang. Wolfgang didn't look away. Instead he smiled back and squeezed her hand. He knew what he had to do. He let go of her hand and stood abruptly.

"Back to work?" she asked.

"Something like that." Wolfgang hurried away. He would need Lincoln's help.

WOLFGANG HURRIED HOME that evening and bathed, trimmed his beard and changed his clothes, which he then covered up with his lab coat. Periodic pulses of trembling surged through his body as if chilled, but he knew better—he was nervous. In his rose garden he clipped a dozen red roses and bundled them with a length of twine. He hurried back up the hillside, watching the sunset with flowers in hand, a pleasant breeze in his face and sweaty palms. Inside the lobby of the sanatorium he ran into Miss Schultz, who was wearing a pretty blue dress and carrying a suitcase.

"Miss Schultz." Wolfgang spread his arms out wide. "You will be missed." He gave her a hug and then hid the flowers behind his back. Miss Schultz was on her way out of Waverly as a cured woman.

"You really shouldn't have, Father."

"What?"

"I saw the roses," she said.

Wolfgang hesitated before showing the bundle of roses. "What, these?"

She held her hand out and he handed them to her. She had not been the intended recipient but he had no qualms about giving them to her. She was a nice woman who never failed to tax him with difficult questions. Before stepping outside she stopped and looked over her shoulder toward Wolfgang. "Now you can tell me where the bodies go."

Wolfgang grinned. "Never."

Wolfgang headed for the stairs with his right hand in his pants pocket and felt his surprise between his fingers. Miss Schultz could have the flowers. It made him proud to send her off with roses from his garden. Lincoln had come through for him. Wolfgang found Susannah asleep on the second floor solarium. She opened her eyes after Wolfgang pushed her bed a few feet toward the very end of the porch, as close to the screened window as possible.

"Wolf . . . what are you doing?"

"Privacy." Wolfgang parked her bed a good twenty feet from the other patients. Spring was right around the corner. Wolfgang could smell it. He could feel the change in the wind. He ran his hand through her hair and cleared her bangs from her forehead.

He rested his palm there to feel for a temperature. She felt cool, certainly not feverish. "How are you feeling?"

"What are you up to, Wolfgang Pike? You ignore me for days, and then—"

Wolfgang put a finger to her lips. "I miss walking up the hillside with you every morning."

"I—"

"Shh, let me finish." Wolfgang knelt beside the bed. "The best part of my day, every day, was that moment when your knuckles touched my front door. Because in that instant of time, I knew you were safe. The anticipation of opening my door and seeing your face made the sun rise for me. I'm a very ordinary man, Susannah Figgens, but I do love you."

Susannah wiped a tear from her eye, but otherwise stared as if comatose. Wolfgang took her hand. "The church doesn't believe a priest can love a woman and be fully committed to serving God." He rubbed his left hand over his mouth and then returned it to her hands. His mouth felt dry. "Your childhood dream was to get married. You doubted you'd ever find anyone on the hillside."

"I didn't."

Wolfgang gazed into her eyes. "Marry me."

"You're a priest."

"A priest who's fallen in love with an incredible woman." Wolfgang reached into his pocket and pulled out a ring. The diamond in it sparkled under the florescent porch light. "The church will have to share me with you. I'll worry about the repercussions later. I was a doctor first, remember? Go down the aisle with me, Susannah."

She wiped her eyes again. "I want to more than anything, but you can't have both, can you?"

"If I go to Hell because of this, so be it." He scooted closer, squeezed her hand in both of his. "If loving you keeps me out of Heaven, if there is such a place, then I'll gladly exclude myself. I will love you for the rest of my life."

"In sickness and in health?"

"Especially in sickness."

"And Rose?"

"If Rose taught me anything, it was to not conform to every rule and to go with my gut." Wolfgang slid the ring onto her left ring finger. It was a little big, but it stayed on. "You and Rose would have been best of friends, I assure you."

Susannah stared at her ring finger, moving her fingers and rotating her wrist as if it was the first time she'd ever seen a diamond. "Where did you get this?"

"I have my sources."

"Lincoln's Uncle?"

"Lincoln helped me with the ring, Susannah." Wolfgang touched the diamond, gently pinching it between his thumb and index finger. "The diamond was a gift from my mother."

"Your mother, huh?"

Wolfgang nodded, opting not to elaborate. His mother had told him to do something good with the money and jewels. He couldn't think of anything better.

Susannah took her eyes off the ring, but only for a second. "I heard a rumor you were leaving Waverly. I wondered when you would tell me."

"I'm not going anywhere." He leaned down and kissed her closed lips. "Meet me on the rooftop in an hour."

"Why?"

Wolfgang unbuttoned his lab coat to reveal his tuxedo. "So I can give you the wedding you've always dreamed of."

Her eyes lit up. "Tonight?" She leaned up in bed. "I have no makeup. I'm pale. Diseased. I've been—"

"I don't care." Wolfgang ran his hand across her cheek. "If you stayed as you are right now I'd be the happiest man in the world."

"I have nothing to wear."

"Yes . . . you do," he said. "Lying on the piano upstairs is a white wedding dress."

BUTTERFLIES SWIRLED IN Wolfgang's stomach. It was a windy evening, one spotlighted by a clear moon and thousands of stars and no cloud cover. He paced along the edge of the rooftop, trying not to doubt what he was about to do. He placed his hands on the concrete capped wall and stared out toward the trees. It wasn't orthodox to perform the marriage himself, but at Waverly, where death ruled over life, he'd learned to throw out the rules that didn't help. He turned and leaned against the wall, sitting on the edge, his back open to the weather. Across the rooftop, Nurse Cleary and Nurse Marlene fiddled with Susannah's dress and veil. He no longer felt embarrassed around Marlene and he assumed the feeling was mutual. She'd obviously felt comfortable enough when she'd asked him a few minutes ago, before attending to Susannah, if he didn't want one more look before he took the plunge. It had taken him a few seconds to get her reference, but then they'd shared a quiet laugh and she'd moved on. Susannah was beautiful. Her hair was long and curled around her slender neck that rose from her shoulders like a swan. He could see her collarbones above the dress line, and just below he couldn't help but notice the swell of her breasts. The dress conformed to the shapely figure he'd been visualizing for weeks now.

Wolfgang no longer felt guilty. He wiped his sweaty hands on his pants for the eleventh time and began pacing again. He wiped sweat from his brow and felt the wetness dripping from his armpits.

"Relax, Wolf." Lincoln clapped him on the shoulder and straightened his jacket.

"How do I look?"

"Like a Catholic priest about ready to marry a tuberculosis patient."

Rufus and Josef walked toward them, smiling. Josef held up his chalkboard.

You ready?

"Guess so." Wolfgang turned toward the piano. "I only wish McVain was here with us."

"Oh, he is," Rufus said. "I saw the piano keys moving earlier and there wasn't anybody sitting by it."

Josef wrote. **Just the wind.**

Rufus looked at him. "Don't you believe in ghosts?"

Lincoln smacked Wolfgang's chest with the back of his hand. "Here she comes, Father."

"Lincoln, under the circumstances let's hold off referring to me as Father."

"Here she comes, Father."

Abel walked before her, dropping rose petals down their imaginary center aisle. Wolfgang sat at the piano and played a quick bridal processional. Josef and Rufus accompanied with their instruments. It was a small crowd: Susannah, Abel, Nurse Cleary and Nurse Marlene, and the four men. Doctor Barker knew nothing about it and they'd waited until he'd gone home for the ceremony to begin.

Wolfgang stopped playing when Susannah took her position beside the piano. His knees shook as he stood from the bench. He stared into her eyes and took both of her hands. Wolfgang married the two of them right there on the rooftop with Herman singing in the background from Room 502 and Maverly chanting from Waverly. The small group of friends formed a protective circle around them. They all knew what they were doing went against Wolfgang's vows to the church. They said nothing to stop him. Deep down they knew it was right. Perhaps the vows were wrong.

It was March 2, 1929.

A bell chimed when Wolfgang kissed her. They both glanced

at the looming bell tower. Maybe McVain *was* close by and watching.

WOLFGANG RETURNED TO Waverly in the middle of the night when most of the patients were asleep. He had to see his new bride. He tiptoed past her neighbors on the second floor solarium and knelt beside her bed. He tapped her arm.

Susannah opened her eyes and rolled her head toward him. "Wolf? What . . ."

Wolfgang silenced her by placing his hand over her mouth. Beneath her sheets she still wore the wedding dress. He slid his arms under her slight weight and lifted her from the bed. It would not be the first time for him to take a patient from Waverly. He carried her to the closest stairwell with a smooth rhythm to his limp and they laughed like high school kids until Susannah insisted that she walk down the stairs on her own. No one saw them leave the sanatorium. They hurried hand-in-hand down the hillside to his cottage, where he scooped her up in his arms and carried her over the threshold. He kicked the door closed and set her on her feet again. His cottage was lit with candles. A fire crackled in the fireplace. Rose petals had been scattered over the floor. Comforting shadows danced, shifting and sliding with the movement of the flames. He gripped Susannah's hand and walked her to the bed.

"Wolfgang," she whispered. "What are you doing?"

Wolfgang reached out and pulled back the covers that had enshrined Rose's memory for so long.

"Wolf?"

He gently lifted her onto the bed. She leaned back and rested her head on the pillow. He knelt above her, his knees locked against her slender waist. "You're beautiful, Susannah."

She stifled a laugh. Her cheeks turned red. She reached up and traced her fingers across his beard, his chin and then down the side of his face. She loosened his tie and unbuttoned his shirt. He leaned down and kissed her forehead. She was breathing heavily. "We can't," she whispered. "I want to so badly, but we can't."

"We can." Wolfgang kissed her neck on the left side, and then the right. She quivered. Her neckline became flushed. Her breasts heaved against the lining of her dress, as if begging to be uncaged. She planted her hands on the side of his head and pulled his face to hers. She kissed his cheek. Their mouths opened instinctively. Wolfgang pressed his lips against hers but she pulled away and kissed his cheek, carefully avoiding his parted lips. Her lips touched his nose, his neck and danced around his mouth. She kissed every part of his face *but* the lips, as if afraid to infect him. They paused, panting, petting, stroking each other's hair and face, and then Susannah ripped Wolfgang's shirt free of the buttons that held it together. Buttons flew across the bed. She giggled and bit her lip. She ran her fingers across his chest and then gripped him around the neck again. Awkward, passionate kissing ensued and she never touched her mouth directly to his, but he felt her warm breath against his cheeks, his neck, his ears and his eyes. He pulled her dress down, revealing the strings, laces and frills of her corset.

"We can't," she whispered, but it had no life to it.

Wolfgang kissed her bare stomach and then looked up into her eyes.

"We shouldn't," she said. "I'm sick. I might be dying."

Wolfgang kissed her open lips. "Then so will I."

30

SUSANNAH WAS BACK in her bed when Doctor Barker came by for his morning rounds. He'd noticed her smile. She'd told him she was feeling stronger. He never questioned Wolfgang's extended visits with her. He knew they were friends. He just didn't know how close they had become, and they were able to keep it that way. Wolfgang was a priest after all—for now—so why would Doctor Barker suspect anything? Wolfgang had the piano moved down to the second floor, where he played for her every evening and held her hand until she fell asleep every night.

Not once had he showed any signs of developing tuberculosis, despite the numerous times he'd put himself in harm's way simply by touching her and being around her constantly. Perhaps it wasn't meant to be, or maybe he was immune for some inexplicable reason. They'd only made love that one night, their wedding night, before he'd sneaked her back into the sanatorium just before sunrise.

Wolfgang's mind hadn't been so peaceful since before Rose was killed. Susannah understood him in the same way Rose had. No, not in the same way, he thought one morning, but in her own unique way, yet just as deeply. They listened to the radio a lot to pass the time. Herbert Hoover was inaugurated as the thirty-first President of the United States, succeeding Calvin Coolidge. Susannah and Wolfgang were optimistic about their future. She continued to work on her book and Wolfgang helped her by typing and writing when she was too tired to do so. The relationship reminded him of McVain, although he was far from the expert on tuberculosis that McVain was with music.

On the night of their rooftop performance, Al Capone elevated the nation's fear of organized crime a notch higher with the Valentine's Day Massacre. His men gunned down seven people in hopes of killing Bugsy Moran, who was the leader of another Chicago gang. Moran was not in the group that night; like Wolfgang, so far he'd beaten the odds. The incident heightened the nation's need to find and capture Capone. Lincoln kept them updated.

ONE MORNING ON his way to the sanatorium, Wolfgang took a different route. He walked by the livestock and stumbled across Abel and a couple of his friends, who didn't realize him watching among the trees. Abel lifted the gate to the pigpen and lured three pigs out with a handful of acorns. The boys laughed and ducked into the woods. That evening Wolfgang had taken Abel up to see Susannah. She surprised him by wrinkling up her nose and snorting like a pig. They'd all laughed over it. His game was up. Susannah made him apologize to Jakes the next morning.

PATIENTS CONTINUED TO arrive and patients continued to die, and as the months moved on, Susannah's health declined. The infection had spread from her lungs to her bones. Wolfgang tried to remain optimistic. He had to be. He refused to cut on her like they'd operated on McVain.

Josef spent more time with them on the second floor. He continued to grow stronger until he no longer had to use the chalkboard to talk. His wife Steffi often brought cookies and told stories of Josef's days in Germany. He and Rufus would meet several times a week to play music together. Wolfgang was no McVain and he never pretended to be, but sometimes the three of them would play for Susannah. Rufus was a regular in the main sanatorium and renovations that included a new roof and a new entrance had begun at the colored sanatorium.

Spring came, along with the thunderstorms and rain showers, but the downpours had been nothing like the rain when McVain had arrived. Susannah seemed to have a constant fever. Anything below 102 degrees was a blessing. She improved briefly during the beginning of the summer—just about the same time that Anne Barker checked out of Waverly, cured, with her husband happily escorting her to their idling car.

Susannah's energy level rose, her complexion improved and her appetite grew. Wolfgang had begun to flirt with notions of officially leaving the priesthood and finding a house for the two of them, but he never allowed himself to become too engaged with the future. In late August they laughed together to the new "Amos and Andy" radio show. They couldn't wait for it to come on each week. He loved the way Susannah's nose pinched when she laughed.

ON OCTOBER 24TH, 1929, 12.9 million shares were traded on Wall Street. The market was crashing. The floor of the New York Stock Exchange was in a panic. By noon that day, eleven prominent investors had committed suicide. Black Thursday, they called it.

Over the weekend, the newspapers spread fear across the states. It led to Black Monday. Nervous investors cashed in from the market and the slide continued. On Black Tuesday, complete panic overtook the market, with 16.4 million shares traded. Despite help from Durant and Rockefeller, the market continued to plummet. Millions lost their savings. Businesses lost their credit lines and were forced to close across the country. Massive unemployment ensued.

A patient on the fourth floor, a banker with a wife and six kids to support, tried jumping off the Waverly rooftop. Wolfgang and Lincoln stopped him. He died three weeks later from TB. It was better that way.

IN NOVEMBER, SUSANNAH took a turn for the worse. She began coughing a lot, and after a while she began to spit up blood. Not enough fresh air. Not enough rest. For the first time Wolfgang began to truly fear for her life. His optimism had all but left. On the surface he still urged her to fight. With no foreseeable cure, Wolfgang felt helpless against her continuous decline. By the end of October she'd aged ten years. She lost weight. Flecks of gray began to show in her hair. Tuberculosis had stolen her youth.

ON NOVEMBER 24TH, Al Capone was sentenced to eleven years in federal prison. Wolfgang failed to mirror the excitement on Lincoln's face when he'd told them. His Uncle Frank was being investigated as well, he'd said. Wolfgang didn't ask why.

Wolfgang rarely played his instruments for the patients. His original choir had all but vanished—some dead, a handful of them on the way and several others gone from Waverly Hills the right way, cured from the tuberculosis that had brought them there.

They celebrated Christmas on the second floor solarium—Susannah, Abel and Wolfgang. Susannah was too weak to see the Christmas tree that Wolfgang had set up at his cottage, so he'd arranged to have it brought to her. Abel had helped decorate it. They opened presents and drank hot chocolate.

The New Year brought with it eight inches of snow. Wolfgang held Susannah's hand all night as she shivered her way into the new decade. Wolfgang wiped snow from her cheeks and covered her with blankets. Her fever would not stop. After midnight, when the party in the cafeteria had died down and most of the patients had gone to sleep, Wolfgang crawled into bed with Susannah. He covered them both with a blanket, scooted behind her like a spoon in a drawer and draped his left arm over her. He held her tight, as if his closeness could reduce the heat that was making her half delirious.

"I would take your pain in an instant if I could." He kissed the back of her neck and smelled her hair.

"Why are you crying?" she whispered.

He sniffled. "I miss you."

She coughed. Wolfgang could hear the disease rattling loose inside her frail body. She sighed. "Take care of Abel."

"I will."

Susannah lay still for a moment. "Bless me, Father, for I have sinned."

Wolfgang held her close. "What is your sin, Susannah?"

"I'm a murderer."

His hands immediately tensed up. McVain had said the same thing about himself before he'd died, but he couldn't fathom the idea coming from Susannah.

She spoke in a whisper as he stared at the back of her head. "The night I was admitted here, before I met Doctor Barker to get tested. I stopped by Jesse Jacob's bed." She coughed into her fist and then slid her open hand beneath her cheek and pillow. Wolfgang stroked her hair. She sniffled and went on. "He'd threatened Abel, Wolf. I poisoned him in his sleep."

So he *had* been murdered, Wolfgang thought. But Susannah? How had she known? He'd told no one of Jesse's part in Big 15's murder—and then it all made sense. The night Ray stumbled upon Wolfgang's doorstep, Susannah had been asleep on his couch—or so he'd thought. She must have listened to Ray's confession. It hadn't been God's Hand after all.

"Why don't you say anything?" she asked.

Wolfgang squeezed her tight, hugging her with both arms.

His prayer of absolution was to hold her. "Jesse would have died anyway. I absolve you from your sin, Susannah. In the name of the Father, and of the Son, and—"

"He threatened Abel."

"—of the Holy Spirit." Wolfgang smiled because of her courage and her willingness to defend those she loved. He gathered her in a warm embrace. His left hand rested on her left breast and there was nothing sexual in his touch. He wanted to feel her heartbeat, which was growing weak. "There's a hole in the wall . . . in your shower room."

Susannah giggled. "I know. I used to imagine you watching me when I'd shower." She squeezed his hand. "I think Heaven, Wolf, is now." She coughed. "Or maybe in Heaven we return to the place in our lives where we were most happy . . . and comfortable . . . and safe."

Wolfgang kissed her neck. "And where would that be for you?"

"Here, at Waverly," Susannah said. "Right now. With you."

31

Wolfgang opened his eyes in the morning to the caress of Susannah's hair against his nose and cheek. Wind moved the tiny strands but nothing else. He nudged her and got no reaction. He gripped her hand and found it freezing cold. He felt for a pulse and found nothing. He blinked tears from his eyes and left them to gather in the whiskers of his beard. He swung his legs from beneath the covers, stood and hobbled around to her side of the bed, where her left hand dangled from the mattress, her index finger pointing as if showing him the way to whatever she'd seen before her heart stopped beating during the night. Her diamond ring glistened in the morning sun. She'd never taken it off. She'd wanted to be buried with it. Her eyebrows had collected a few scant snowflakes that her vanished body heat had been unable to melt away. Her eyes were open and staring off toward the woods. He closed them with a slow swipe of his hand. A look of peace marked her face with a slight upturn at the lips—a grin that could have easily been viewed as a smirk.

How long had she been dead? Minutes? Hours? Snow covered the solarium porch. Tiny daggers of ice hung from the top of the piano. Heavy coughing sounded up and down the solarium. Wolfgang gripped Susannah's cold, stiff hand. Her flesh was a pale shade of blue. Her lips were purple. Not caring who would see him,

Wolfgang knelt down beside her face and kissed her lips. Wherever she was, he hoped she was in a better place. Unlike with Rose's death, Wolfgang wasn't burdened with the mysteries of who or what had killed Susannah. Tuberculosis, consumption, the white death had killed her. Her bravery and compassion had killed her.

In the coming weeks, Wolfgang turned his sorrow into motivation. He focused on the patients again. They needed him. They needed the music. They needed him to hear their confessions. He decided to remain a priest until his time at Waverly was finished, or until another priest or minister came along to rescue him from his duties of faith.

The memories of Rose and Susannah fueled him each day. He enjoyed helping others and listening to their problems. He'd come to realize that there were two women in the entire world for him, and he'd been fortunate enough to meet and love them both.

God never struck him down for the vows he'd broken. Wolfgang moved on.

In November of 1930 Josef was given a clean bill of health. He left Waverly a cured man, arm-in-arm with his wife. Wolfgang's original ensemble quickly dwindled. But others replaced them. Three weeks later Rufus was released, cured, free to play his music wherever and whenever he wanted.

One day a little boy asked Wolfgang the very question Rose had often teased him about—the afterlife. Without hesitation he told the boy about Heaven and clouds and angels and God. His answers calmed the child, however mundane they had been. Yet afterward the question got him thinking about Rose and Susannah. Were they together somewhere? Could they hear his thoughts? One day before Wolfgang was set to open his door and venture up the hillside to the sanatorium, he heard a knocking on the front door. He opened it to find no one there. Just a few rustling leaves.

A year had passed since Susannah's death. He talked to them both every night. So far they never answered back.

Wolfgang began to write again, a new requiem mass for Susannah. In his head he could see it all clearly, even the ending. He'd gotten the pleasure of getting to know the mother of McVain's child and he'd become friends with Amelie and Ryan. He played piano alongside the boy and he showed glimpses of his father's talents. Wolfgang told him stories and made sure the kid knew his father.

Abel was cured of TB with nowhere to go, and Wolfgang didn't want to keep him at Waverly and risk re-infection. Amelie offered to take him in. Abel and Ryan became fast friends.

Wolfgang still played for the patients even though his choir and cluster of musicians hadn't regained the glory it had attained with McVain, Josef, Rufus, Herman—who was probably at Waverly for eternity—and Susannah. Wolfgang didn't give up hope. He often walked along the rooftop for inspiration. He carried a picture with him at all times, one taken a week before the big concert, of McVain, Josef, Rufus, Susannah and Lincoln. He often looked at it and laughed. Whether it had been fate or coincidence or God's doing that brought them all together during the winter of 1929, nothing could change the fact that it had indeed happened. Stories of McVain circulated through the staff and patients until his name became legend. The seven-fingered pianist.

One day at lunch Wolfgang laughed with Doctor Barker about McVain and their run-in with Capone at the Seelbach Hotel. He and Barker had become friends, if not close ones. They both grew silent as a new patient, a young sandy-haired man named Hilton Banks, approached their table. "Doctors." He nodded. "Father."

"What can we do for you, Mr. Banks?"

He cleared his throat. "I heard you have a choir here. I play the piano."

Historical Note

The Requiem Rose is a fictional story about a very real place. In 1900, Louisville had the worst tuberculosis rate in the country. Waverly Hills Tuberculosis Sanatorium, built on one of the highest hills in Jefferson County, was considered the most advanced tuberculosis hospital in the country. But antibiotics hadn't yet been developed, treatment was primitive at best, and most came simply to die. According to legend, at the height of the epidemic, patients were dying at Waverly at the rate of one per hour.

Because the sight of the hearses pulling up to the sanatorium so often would have broken the morale of the patients, the supply tunnel was used to slide the dead bodies down the hillside to the railroad tracks. It became known as the body chute, and later as the Death Tunnel.

There was a separate hospital down the hillside for the African American patients. Although there were accounts and stories of poor conditions in this hospital in the early days, the conditions as described in the book were embellished for the purpose of drama and fiction. There was an African American man in the 1920s who walked the hillside three times a day, carting food and supplies between the two hospitals. They named him Big 14 because of his 14-inch feet and his enormous hands.

The patients spent most of their time on the solarium porches so they could breathe fresh air. Even in the winter, patients were kept outside in their beds, and because the solarium windows only had screens, it was not uncommon for snow to accumulate.

Doctors and nurses risked their lives to care for patients and try to find a cure for tuberculosis. Many contracted the disease and died with their patients. But because of the experiments performed at Waverly and hospitals like it, tuberculosis began to decline near the end of the 1930s. It wasn't until the discovery of streptomycin in 1943 that doctors had the first real medicine to fight the disease. By the 1950s tuberculosis had been mostly eradicated.

In 1939, Jonah, the teenage boy with Marfan disease who painted Rose's portrait with his fingers, died at Waverly. Rumors of his ghost still remain. The painting on the back cover of this book is one of his earliest. It was found in an undisclosed place along with Jonah's life story, which will soon follow this story in some capacity.

In 1961, Waverly Hills Sanatorium was closed. The building was reopened in 1962 as the Woodhaven Geriatrics Sanitarium. The doors were closed for good in 1982 due to horrible conditions, budget cuts and evidence of patient abuse. From that point, the building went the way of decay and rumor. Tales of unusual experiments, electroshock therapy and patient mistreatment began to surface. Some have been proven false, but not all. Rumors that it was once an insane asylum came forth. Vagrants moved in. Vandals defaced every inch of the place. Stories were told of satanic rituals held within the walls. It was a place of death and disease, a place of legend, a place where, many believe, the haunted still roam the halls. According to legend, well over 60,000 patients died inside Waverly Hills. Some say the number is much less, some believe it could be more.

Waverly Hills has become known as one of the most haunted places in the world, spotlighted on "Fox's Scariest Places on Earth" and dubbed the world's mecca of paranormal activity. One of the most popular legends revolves around Room 502, which was rumored to house mentally ill patients. Folklore says that two nurses committed suicide in this room. One hung herself and another jumped five stories to her death.

The current owners have begun a restoration project and hope to turn Waverly Hills into a five-star hotel. Tours can be arranged and all proceeds go to renovating the building. I took a tour of the abandoned building several years ago, before any restoration. I've been inside the body chute and Room 502. Of the rolls of film I shot inside the building, all but four pictures came out clearly. Those four blurry pictures were all taken inside Room 502, as if something didn't want the pictures to be seen. In many of the pictures, mysterious orbs are visible, none more prominent than those inside the Death Tunnel, or body chute, where we seemed surrounded by them.

Although it was the intrigue of hauntings that brought me to Waverly, I soon realized that the most riveting stories could come from its former flesh-and-blood inhabitants. So I looked down the length of the massive fourth floor solarium porch and imagined the patients lying in their beds. I imagined the sound of a violin hovering over the swaying trees. I imagined a piano and a choir and Wolfgang Pike standing and conducting at a podium with his deformed leg, and *The Requiem Rose* came to life.

Over two million people still die from tuberculosis every year, mostly in developing countries. Someone in the world still dies of TB every 18 seconds. The tragedy is that most of the deaths could be prevented with money and existing treatments.

Acknowledgments

I'd like to thank everyone at Butler Books for their hard work on this book, especially Carol Butler, Eric Butler and Elizabeth Sawyer. I was convinced from the start that Butler Books was the perfect home for this book. And to Bill Butler, who inspired me to keep writing—thank you for our conversations over the past year, conversations that encouraged me to dive deeper into the Waverly lore and come back out with the legend of Jonah. To Franklin Foshee for your timely editorial work. Many thanks. To my dad, C. Robert Markert, for his behind-the-scenes work. You truly are a genius at what you do. And to my mother, Patricia Markert . . . best parents in the world. Thanks to Peter Gelfan at The Editorial Department for your early work on *The Requiem Rose*. Right as always! Thanks to my sister, Michelle—all those countless hours of practicing the piano . . . I was listening. The sound of you playing classical music has always stuck with me and helped inspire me to write this story. Unfortunately, my piano playing skills never got past *Mary Had a Little Lamb*, a song, I have to admit, I can still play successfully when cornered. Thank you, Mickey and Roger Keys, for your perusal of the manuscript early on. Roger—of Carnegie Hall Fame—your help with all things musical in the book was brilliant. Any mistakes are most certainly mine. Jamie Buckner, your advice, especially with the old beginning to the novel, proved very useful in the final rewrite. To my cousin, John Markert, for allowing me to bounce my initial ideas of *The Requiem Rose* off of him, and for reading through that very first draft of the screenplay. Your advice is always helpful. To my brothers, David and Joseph, your friendship has always provided me with the encouragement to be creative. Thanks for reading everything I write and for being honest about it. *Leif Ericson Day Day* was the beginning, not the end. To Craig Kremer . . . it's always fun talking about Waverly with you . . . one of these days we'll stay there. To William Akers, your advice on the screenplay made it a much better story. Thanks to everyone at Louisville Tennis Club for your support over the years. And to my southern Indiana families, you make it very easy to go to work every day. And for everyone who played a part in the process over the past few years, from reading various drafts to listening, and in no particular order (if you did read this novel before publication and I left you out, please email me and complain ferociously and I'll gladly acknowledge you in the next one): Dan, Erika, and Tammy, D'Ann, Bobby Hofmann, Tim Burke, Todd Blankenship, Jenny Branson, for your advice on music therapy, Fr. Joe Graffis, Gretchen Holm and the entire Holm family, Debbie Rieger, Margaret Duncan, Stephanie Cooper, Sue Kline, "Doc" Rhodes, . . . "The Four Horseman". Special thanks to Madeline Abramson, Jason Weinberger, and David Domine for your time and kind words. Most importantly, I'd like to thank my wife, Tracy, for allowing me the time and the freedom to write and for never letting me give up on a dream. You've given me the best gifts imaginable in our two beautiful children. I want for nothing because I believe I already have it all.

James Markert
2010

JAMES MARKERT is the author of two other novels. He has a history degree from the University of Louisville and is a USPTA certified tennis pro at the Louisville Tennis Club. He lives in Louisville with his wife and two children. While visiting Waverly Hills to research *The Requiem Rose*, he encountered a ghost named Jonah on the fourth floor solarium and was given the key to Jonah's vault, which includes hundreds of lost manuscripts and paintings. To learn more about the Legend of Jonah and the forthcoming novel, *The Book of Jonah*, visit www.jamesmarkertbooks.com and www.thewaverlyhillsnovels.com.